THE WATERS UNDER THE EARTH

BY THE SAME AUTHOR

THE WATERS

UNDER THE EARTH

by John Moore

J. B. LIPPINCOTT COMPANY

PHILADELPHIA & NEW YORK

To my old friend, Paul Humphreys

CONTENTS

PART ONE

The Day of the Last Red Squirrel

¶ 1

'*SAW RED SQUIRREL*,' wrote Janet Seldon in her extraordinary diary, sitting at her dressing-table before she began to change for dinner, '*Rare as dodo now!*' The date was July the 31st 1950. Over her shoulder she said to Ferdo, who stood before the looking-glass tying his black tie:

"When did we see the last one? Can you remember?"

"The last red squirrel? Must be months ago. Maybe a year. They've been steadily getting fewer ever since those grey bastards came."

The alien grey squirrels had arrived at Doddington during the late Thirties, just before the war which seemed in retrospect like a sort of curtain, cutting one's life in two. Janet associated them with the recurring autumnal crises, headlines prophesying war, and pictures of Neville Chamberlain, who seen in profile with his lips parted, the teeth showing under the grizzled moustache, wore much the same expression as the little rodents did.

Some misguided rich man had introduced them into England, from North Carolina of all places; and they had spread by fits and starts all over the country, ousting the accustomed red squirrels from the woods where they belonged. Until then the red ones had been as common as magpies or jays. They thrived among the oak-trees which Ferdo's ancestors had planted hundreds of years ago; and they sat up primly on the family coat-of-arms, which incorporated "A Squirrel sejant cracking a Nut." Ever since the days of the first Ferdinando, who acquired that coat-of-arms and who built Doddington Manor in the Fifteen-eighties, the Seldons had regarded them as creatures under their special protection and patronage; and because of this, or because the two words went well together, there were all sorts of countrified sayings which bound up the fortunes of the squirrels with those of the squires. They were mostly in rhyme, which only the old men remembered and perhaps remembered wrong; but the idea seemed to be that so long as there were

Doddington squirrels and Doddington squires

all would be well with the land; but woe betide

Should squirrels be gone and oak-trees fall,
Then down go Seldons and down goes all.

So you were always pleased, in those days before the war, when the red squirrels came into the garden, and you forgave them when they stole the walnuts off the big walnut-tree, from which they would sometimes peer cheekily in through the bedroom-windows of Doddington Manor. You would see them in the Park whenever you took a walk there: seized by the fear of open spaces which seems to cause sudden panic in squirrels, they would scurry like mad for the shelter of the solitary trees! You could be sure of finding one any day in the capacious cover of the great oak called Ferdinando's. But their special haunt was a southward-sloping clearing where Janet and Ferdo used to take Susan for picnics when she was a child. She would pick the spotted orchids which smelt of tomcat, and chase the skipper butterflies and the frail wood-whites which blew about like pear-petals upon the least breeze. Then when she'd washed the orchid-smell off her hands in the trickle that went between the bracken, the three of them would collect wild strawberries and squash them with caster sugar on their bread and butter for tea. They would lie in the sun after tea, and with the great trees to shelter and enclose them it was like bathing in a warm pale-sherry-coloured pool. Now and then they'd catch a glimpse of the squirrels moving among the trees, and have the agreeable feeling that they were being watched by the bright-eyed creatures, tails up, ears pricked, attentively sejant.

ON SUSAN'S SIXTH BIRTHDAY, September the 30th 1938, they took a wireless-set with them to listen to the news, and basking in the last of the sun they heard how the Prime Minister had come crowing back from Munich with his umbrella and his precious piece of paper which, he said, meant "Peace in our time." Janet turned to Ferdo at that point, raising her eyebrows, and Ferdo just shook his head. The sun sank behind the treetops and there was a queer chill in the air, all the golden-green luminous trees put out their lights and turned sepia suddenly, and sable shadows crept out from them across the darkening green.

WALKING HOME under the woodside, walking in the chilly shadow, they debated whether they should send Susan to America for safety when—not if—the war started. So much for "Peace in our time." They decided against America because, characteristically, they thought she might with reason feel resentful afterwards, if she had been kept out of danger while the country fought for its life. They arranged that she should go to an aunt's house near Oxford instead. Janet next day applied to join the Fannies: and while playboys in London celebrated Munich with champagne, and the Members of the House of Commons behaved very like the Bandarlog, Ferdo tried on his old naval uniform to see if it would fit and began to pack into a bulging suitcase some things which he fancied might come in handy during the course of a world catastrophe:

Fishing line and hooks
Two spare pairs of braces
Two tins of curry powder
French and German dictionaries
Pate de Foie Gras from Fortnums
Mittens
Some soft expensive toilet paper
Sloe gin
Bible

Catapult
Two bottles of Lea and Perrins' Worchestershire Sauce
Prayer Book
Cherry brandy
A device for rolling cigarettes
Bottle opener
Two corkscrews
The Wrong Box, by R. L. Stevenson and Lloyd
    Osborne [his favourite novel]
Gentleman's Relish
A book on sea-birds
The six-inch-to-the-mile Ordnance Sheets of
    Doddington with all the field-names written
    in by hand
Two large jars of Cooper's Oxford Marmalade.

Ferdo knew what he was doing when he compiled this peculiar
list; he chose his minor impedimenta with a view to saving up a
few scraps of comfort and crumbs of civilisation against the time
when such trifles might constitute a feast. He'd had four years at
sea, from 1914 to 1918. He knew a bit about war; and he could
smell this one coming.

AFTER MUNICH you went on doing the same kind of things
you always did though you were well aware of their irrelevance.
Janet bought a new hunter and Ferdo put down some pheasants
and Old Northover, his gamekeeper, conducted a campaign
against the newly-arrived grey squirrels. He killed the first pair
which came to Doddington, in accordance with his practice of
promptly shooting anything unusual or strange. But next week
the invaders were all over the place, and Old Northover, driven
frantic by xenophonobia, was after them morning, noon and
night. Soon he had a whole row hanging by their tails from the
gallows in front of his cottage. But however many he killed, there
were others to take their places. Furtive, hardy, proliferous; in-
trusive and persistent as the doubts and uncertainties which during those Nineteen-thirties had been gradually creeping into
many an English mind, the upstart rodents remained, nested,
brought forth. Ferdo and Northover between them just about
held them in check, until September 1939. On the first morning

of that month, Ferdo and Janet listened to the Eight O'clock News and heard without surprise that the war had started. Janet said: "We ought to put off the guns, oughtn't we?" but it sounded so silly, in the context of events, that they both laughed. There had always been a shoot at Doddington on the First of September; but it would have seemed somehow unfitting to be shooting partridges when Hitler was shooting Poles.

The postman rat-tat-tatting just after the News brought the expected summons: the Lords Commissioners of the Admiralty enjoined Commander Sir Ferdinando Seldon Bt., D.S.O., R.N. (Retd), in much the same terms as they had once used to Nelson, to "repair to his duties forthwith"; and off he went to what he was already calling his Second German War. The family flag, which by a small affectation of the Seldons always flew from the roof of Doddington Manor when the Squire was in residence, was solemnly hauled down by the old butler. Susan was delivered over to the aunt, Janet joined the Fannies at their headquarters in London; the hunters were sold to the Army (which strangely enough still had a Remount Depôt somewhere), Young North-over the groom was set to dig for victory in the vegetable garden, Old Northover carried on for a little longer his private war against the grey squirrels which seemed to him a more real and immediate foe than the Germans across the Channel . . .

Before long, however, Doddington was taken over by the Army. Old Northover, who believed all soldiers to be poachers, got up against the authorities and was barred from the woods which he'd walked ever since his childhood. The tree-rats multiplied; and by the time Ferdo got home (long after the war ended, because the bureaucrats were reluctant to hand Doddington back) they were so plentiful that he gave up the fight altogether, it would have been a waste of cartridges to go on. Relentlessly they colonised Doddington, spinney by spinney and copse by copse, and simultaneously the red squirrels declined, until they were apparitions surprising as woodcocks, you were apt to give a shout whenever you saw one.

SO JANET IN HER DIARY underlined *'Rare as dodo!'* and added two more exclamation marks.

"I wonder where he's got to now." She was looking out at the acres of treetops like green foam, tumbling down the long slope towards the river two miles away. Beyond the river she could see the great Norman Tower of the Abbey standing foursquare over Elmbury, burning-bright as it took fire from the westering sun.

Ferdo tugging at his tie said, "Yes, I wonder where the little chap hides himself."

They couldn't know that it was the last red squirrel they would ever see at Doddington: the very last; and that they would remember this day on account of it, July the 31st 1950. For other reasons too they would remember the Day of the Last Red Squirrel as long as they lived. Looking back upon it out of the bewilderment of the years which followed, they would discover warnings, omens, auguries—unnoticed, unheeded at the time, but only too significant in retrospect; and they would come to see this day as the source and starting-point of all the winds of change which blew so chilly into their lives. Janet would thumb her way back through that old diary, a proceeding which was like a journey through a thick forest, for every page was crammed with exhortations addressed to herself, underlined, strangely abbreviated, or in capital letters. Some personal things were recorded in French. Frenetic question-marks posed unanswered and often unanswerable questions. Addenda, for which there was never enough room, were scribbled on top of, and at right angles to, what Janet had written before. Everywhere exclamation-marks in triplicate exploded like hand-grenades. Decoding, translating, guessing, half-remembering, Janet would eventually light upon this day, July 31st, which she had put a ring round because it was the twenty-first anniversary of her marriage to Ferdo; and reading what she had written, she would say to herself: There, and *there*, and *there*, was a cloud the size of a man's hand—

OUR ANNIE!! *1st at home since 1939!!! Kedgeree F's best crumpets T. Bsmith to shoe Trumpeter a.m.* catch him SUSAN COMES BACK FROM SCHOOL *meet 11:45 Elmbury (her last term!! goodness soon 18!!!)* TONY *to stay see his bed aired the Upper Swells (!) to dine saddle lamb mint sce red currant jell. pick raspberries order cream from Honeysett.* FENTON *(new gdner) and* FAMILY *(!!) arrive (feel we're taking a risk—on dit bolshie type but nous verrons)* Make sure cott. ready *Ferdo fix E. light bulbs Rosemary to scrub Does loo work? Pull! How many kids? Sex? Ages???*

That filled the space allotted to July the 31st; so Janet had turned the diary sideways and written on top of the self-exhortations:

> *Susan marvellous grown up suddenly long legs tall as me Tony charming as ever What a couple they would make!!?? Korea news still bad T. says might be serious Mysterious* FLOOD *in cellar F. says 2 ins deep rising? underground stream.* FENTONS *installed brats all ages spiky little Mrs. Still suspect he's Red but time will tell Saw red squirrel Rare as dodo now!!!*

Into a tiny remaining space Janet somehow squeezed the words:

> *Good omen on our Annie?? Hope so!*

¶ 2

THE ANNIVERSARY hadn't begun very well: Ferdo's Bank Sheets came with the post. He opened the envelope at once, over his kedgeree which Janet always gave him on their anniversary because it was his favourite thing for breakfast, and he had to put on his glasses to read the figures. The glasses suddenly aged him. Without them he looked much younger than fifty-seven: looked a sailor still, with his round red face and sea-blue eyes screwed up at the corners,—you could still imagine him on the bridge in his duffle-coat and muffler and his old grease-stained sea-stained cap worn jauntily at an angle. But now with his glasses on he looked like—oh dear, thought Janet, an elderly country postman puzzling with bowed head over the address on a letter! As he sat opposite her and pored over the Bank Sheets she could see how bald he was getting, could see through the thinning hair the long scar on his scalp, which used to be hidden by the hair. If the German rifleman had used a shade less foresight, at Zeebrugge in 1918, Ferdo wouldn't have been sitting there today. The after-effects of the wound included a slight stammer and occasional blinding headaches; though in his own view the bullet had 'stirred up his brains a bit,' which he regarded as beneficial.

He suddenly realised that Janet was watching him, and in clumsy deceit shuffled his pile of mail like an inept conjurer trying to do an unaccustomed card-trick; he continued to stare at the Bank Sheets, but had half-hidden them behind a wine-merchant's catalogue.

" 'Forty-nine seems to have been a wonderful year for Burgundy," he observed unconvincingly. And Janet knew that he wasn't going to tell her about his overdraft, in case it should worry her on their anniversary.

THE FIGURES HAD LEAPT forth at him as soon as he put on his glasses, in red of course, £1066. He'd been prepared for about £950; but four figures were disproportionately more shocking than three. The Bank Manager wouldn't be worrying; he held ample security: but it seemed an enormous overdraft all the same, and the mnemonic 1066, jogging at Ferdo's mind, quite spoiled his breakfast. And all that, he kept thinking. He remembered his wine-merchant's bill, and his tailor's, and the Surtax, and the Lord-only-knew-how-much he owed to the builders, who seemed to have settled down at Doddington for good. Looking out of the window now he could see their ladders and scaffolding. The house being four hundred years old, it was hardly surprising that there were recurrent leaks in the roof and damp patches on the wall, that a chimney should be leaning like the Tower of Pisa. When the builders finished one job they passed on to another. Only this morning the tenant of Honeysett Farm, bringing the milk, had left a message: Could Squire please see him when convenient on an important matter? That would be more roof-trouble, Ferdo thought, or a cowshed falling down, or something wrong with the drains. The builders would move on to Honeysett, and by the time they'd done what was necessary there they'd be wanted back at the Manor. They had become part of Ferdo's establishment. It was like having a little private army, feudal retainers. He knew them all by their Christian names; they addressed him jovially as Gaffer. At set intervals every day they trooped into the kitchen to make tea, and one of them, twelve months ago, had courted and carried away the girl who came in to help with the washing up, marrying into the estate as it were. Recently this man had asked Janet to be godmother to the baby. In about sixteen years' time, Ferdo had commented gloomily, she would probably have her godson working up on the roof, as a new generation of builders, bred up on the place, took over the never-ending task of preventing the house from actually falling down.

At the thought of what he must owe the builders, superadded to all the other bills and that historic overdraft, Ferdo had one of those twinges of unreasonable panic to which he was subject nowadays. They were associated with what he called his dinosaur moods, when he felt himself outdated, outmoded, imperceptive and puzzled, defensive and ill-at-ease, in a world which he seemed to know less about each day as he grew older. The panic didn't last long this morning, and it wasn't really justified by his situation; he was still pretty well-breeched, as the Bank Manager would cheerfully and a shade enviously put it. But it frightened him, just for a moment; it was like a brief cold wind out of season, blowing suddenly into his mind.

AFTER BREAKFAST HE LEFT Janet reading her paper and, to cheer himself up, went down to the cellar to choose the wine for dinner. The wedding anniversary, and Susan coming home from school, and young Cousin Tony coming to stay, surely added up to a good excuse for the Château Lafite or the Château Latour, or the Vieux Château Certan 1937 which at the moment was Ferdo's favourite claret. He enjoyed thinking about wine as well as drinking it, and it was one of his minor pleasures nowadays to potter about in his cellar, looking at the labels on the bottles and choosing the right vintage to match an occasion, a guest or a mood. For tonight's guests Janet had asked Colonel Daglingworth, and his missus, Heaven knew why; and Daglingworth, thought Ferdo with distaste, was a rough, coarse, vulgar Châteauneuf-du-Pape of a man. On the other hand there would be Tony, whose father had brought him up to understand and appreciate decent claret. That kind of good taste was rare in Tony's generation. Ferdo, who often wished he'd had a son, thought it would be fun to teach Susan about wine. Then when the young men began to take her out to dinner she would be able to choose something she would enjoy at a price they could afford, and so save them the awful embarrassment of staring helplessly at a wine-list which they didn't understand, terrified of the waiter, petrified by the prices . . . Silly young asses, Ferdo thought unrea-

sonably, discovering in himself, and examining with some surprise, a mild resentment against the young men who would take
Susan out to dinner. He'd better get used to the idea—there
would be plenty of 'em before long! Janet, of course, cherished a
romantic hope that one day she would marry her second cousin
once removed, or whatever he was, young Tony, whom she had
worshipped ever since she was about six; and that Tony's sizeable
fortune would save the estate from the ruin which, because of
taxation and death duties, loomed grimly ahead. But that was a
novelettish notion, Ferdo thought; he didn't believe things would
work out like that at all; and to tell the truth—much as he liked
Tony—he wouldn't have been very happy for Susan to marry
him, though if Janet cross-examined him on the matter he'd be
hard put to it to say why.

AT THE BOTTOM OF THE CELLAR STEPS he stopped and
stared. Upon the stone floor there was a long slimy smear which
glistened under the electric-light as if a whole army of slugs had
been marching about there. In the middle of the floor this trail
widened into a large patch of wet, with puddles forming among
the well-worn flagstones. There was a clammy chill and a sort of
miasmic smell which Ferdo had never before known in the cellar;
within his memory it had stayed bone-dry even in the wettest
seasons. His shoes squelched as he prowled round in search of the
source of the water. He had the idea of floating a match-stick in a
puddle to see if there was a current; also he traced the tide-line
with a pencil on an uneven bit of floor. The match-stick definitely moved, though at a snail's pace, circumnavigating the
puddle; and even as Ferdo watched, the tide-line became submerged. The little flood was rising, then. He couldn't imagine
where the water was coming from, and was puzzled, fascinated,
and a trifle disturbed by it. He chose the wine without much
thought—a Château Mouton-Rothschild, too good for that oaf
Daglingworth, but Tony would appreciate it—and went back
into the breakfast-room to tell Janet about the flood. But unexplained natural phenomena, which excite the curious minds of
men, are hateful to practical women. Janet always shut her
thoughts tight against inexplicable things.

"Well, down in the cellar it can't do much harm." She turned back to her *Express* propped up against the coffee-pot. "Ferdo, it looks bad in Korea. Oh, I hope Tony doesn't have to go!"

It had looked bad in Ferdo's *Times* too. The South Koreans were still retreating on Pusan; and that was the vital supply-port through which the American help was coming.

"It always happens to our side at the beginning," Ferdo said, "because after all we never begin the flaming war. The characters who do so naturally have the first advantage."

Even as he spoke that sentence, he remembered when he had said it before. Janet's expression told him that she remembered too—that morning of the First of September when she had switched on the wireless by the bed.

"This is it, then?" she'd said.

"This is it."

They had got up then, and Janet had drawn back the curtains from the open window. A morning coo of wood-pigeons filled the room. Ferdo went and stood beside her, though he could hardly bear to look out of the window this morning at the fields and woods which he loved so much. The Park lay shining in a pool of light, the Jersey cows were like little deer, pale-tawny, almost spectral, where they grazed against the charcoal-black of the wood. A long-legged chestnut foal was twinned to its ungainly shadow. Mushroom-mists here and there were stretched like theatrical gauzes over the grass, and the dew in the sun lay white as hoar-frost; the great solitary trees spattered down on it their black blotches like ink-bottles upset. So sharp was the contrast of light and shade that the whole scene looked like a wood-engraving, it put Ferdo in mind of something by Thomas Bewick —a tailpiece, he thought, marking the end of a chapter?

Janet said suddenly, as if she echoed his thoughts:

"Nothing is going to be the same again, ever," and turned away.

¶ 3

NOTHING IS GOING to be the same again, ever.

Ferdo remembered Janet's words uncomfortably, as he glanced over her shoulder at those big black headlines about yet another new war. She, of course, had long forgotten her prophetic moment; and was quite determined that whatever went on elsewhere, everything was going to be just the same again at Doddington. She had bought two new hunters, which meant that Jack Northover, who'd been turned into a gardener, was needed in the stables again. To replace him in the garden Ferdo had taken on the new man called Fenton. Two unoccupied cottages, Huntsman's and Keeper's, just outside the courtyard gates, had been knocked into one and made ready for him and his large family; so Janet and Ferdo now walked across there to inspect the cottage and make sure that everything was shipshape. "I have a feeling," said Janet, who was ruffled by little catspaws of apprehension whenever she thought about the Fentons, "that they are the kind of people who would make difficulties over *anything*. One must leave them no loopholes." In particular she wanted Ferdo to see if the electrics all worked: bulbs and fuses and so on. She herself, who was afraid of hardly anything under the sun (and had won a dozen Ladies' Races at the local Point to Points), was scared stiff of electricity; she flatly refused to have anything to do with it. She was frightened of thunder too, though with marvellous inconsistency she had got a thrill out of the London air raids, much the same as she had from a fast run out hunting. She used to go up on the roof and watch the fireworks, the shellbursts like November the Fifth sparklers in the sky, brightness falling from the air as the flares floated down, the flicker of the gun-flashes on the eastern horizon, the balloons orange-bellied like salamanders as they reflected the fires down below. But one day, instead of the usual air raid, there was a sharp and noisy thunderstorm. Janet was terrified. She sat in a corner as far as she could get from the windows, listening to the pitter-patter of her heart while she counted the seconds between the lightning-flash and the crack of thunder. Reminded of this, as he fixed up the lights for her, Ferdo began to tease her about it; soon they'd forgotten his overdraft, and their worry over the builders, and that far-away war in Korea, and they were easy-minded under the blue sky as they leaned on the garden-gate of Huntsman's Cottage, taking advantage of a shaft of sunshine that slanted down between the trees. Within the cottage the little maid Rosemary was doing a last-minute clean-up, and they could hear her humming to herself as she scrubbed a floor. The garden in front of the cottage badly needed a clean-up too. The weedy borders displayed only some pale mauve worn-out Michaelmas daisies and some lank spindly hollyhocks going to seed, with small green Catherine wheels all the way up their stems. Nothing grew very well there because the cottage stood right at the edge of the oak-woods, the octopus roots of the trees stole the goodness from the soil, and the boughs making a sort of thicket in the air shut out most of the light. Little drops of sunshine, seeping through the foliage, fell upon the Seldons like a warm and luminous rain. Small green caterpillars also descended from the trees on silken threads which swung and tickled.

"They ought to be happy here," said Janet rather defensively. "Anybody ought."

She bent down to straighten a horseshoe somewhat askew on the gate.

"That'll stop the luck from running out of it."

"I doubt if they're the sort of people who b-bother much about horseshoes," Ferdo said.

"We've never had anybody *bolshie* on the estate before. . . . Old Northover would turn in his grave!"

Ferdo had inherited the gamekeeper along with Doddington, soon after the First War. He had seemed as old as the hills even then: backbent as a crab-tree, grey as its lichen, red-faced as the crabs and sometimes as sour, he was single-minded in his devotion to the Seldons and in his hatred of their foes. Into that category fell all creatures furred or feathered, two-legged or four-legged, brute or human, that might steal or slay or cast covetous eyes upon the game which God had given to the Seldons and had called on Northover to preserve. He belonged in spirit to the pole-trap and man-trap age. Bedridden in 1944, seventy-five years old, his wits gone woolgathering, he'd lain in his cottage and listened to the rifle-shots of the soldiers practising in the Park; and he had supposed them to be a huge gang of poachers, in pursuit of the Seldons' pheasants. "We must be up and arter them, boy Jack," he had said to his son standing at his bedside; and raising himself on his elbows had died.

Old Northover's gallows used to be right opposite the cottage windows; perhaps he enjoyed gloating over the culprits he hung there. Strung along a low bough you would be sure to see at least a score of maggoty corpses, crows, jays, jackdaws, hawks as beaky and proud as assassinated Caesars, a barn-owl perhaps with a face like that of an old pinch-cheeked judge, rats in a row hung by their tails, harmless hedgehogs slain because Old Northover chose to believe they sucked pheasants' eggs, magpies still jaunty in decay, russet ranks of attenuated stoats and weasels; all stinking or skeletal, and swinging like medieval malefactors in the least breath of wind.

Remembering this gallows-tree, Ferdo's glance strayed to the low-dipping oak-bough. The leaves were thick about it, and suddenly among them he thought something stirred. It gave him a start; it was almost as if the ghost of one of Old Northover's weasels walked! Then the brown bright creature came fully into view, Ferdo seized Janet's hand and whispered:

"Look! Quick! Over there!"

But the squirrel was wary. It had seen a movement or sensed a presence. It hesitated, then jumped on to a higher branch, where the foliage hid it. Ferdo meanwhile had drawn Janet into a deeper shadow. She watched him now, with amused affection, making himself invisible against the bole of an oak, which he matched perfectly in his old lichen-coloured suit. It was a sort of vanishing-trick of the Seldons—Janet remembered that Ferdo's father and brother had practised it too. In their rough tweeds, generally greenish or brownish or some deadleaf colour in between, they seemed to melt into their background as animals in their natural habitats do.

It always surprised her that Ferdo, who was rather clumsy as a rule, should be capable at moments like this of staying so still. He'd settled himself easily against the tree-trunk, gazing up into the boughs, his head cocked sideways with that slightly puzzled air which was characteristic of him and which seemed to express his attitude to the whole world. If need be he would stand motionless like this for a quarter of an hour. In the presence of wild creatures, and even domestic animals such as horses or cows, he was always quiet and careful to avoid any action or gesture which might cause them alarm; regarding them with a kind of diffident courtesy, as if apologising for his intrusion or for his appearance, which to them must surely seem alarming and odd.

"Shshsh," he breathed suddenly. The squirrel was there again. Its little mask, framed by the leaves, was right overhead. Fearful but inquisitive, while Ferdo and Janet stared up into the tree on the chance of getting another glimpse of it, the audacious beast much have crept along the overhanging bough in order to take a daring peep at *them;* and now it was scarcely a dozen feet away. They could see its twitching muzzle and tremulous whiskers, its bootbutton eyes looking straight into theirs, its tail tidily arranged along its back so that the tip lay exactly between its tufted ears, its forepaws folded together like the hands of a Victorian miss holding her muff. Then panic took hold of it. With a frisk and a flurry it turned about, rippled along the bough, poured itself like molten squirrel through the tangled twigs on to the ground, streaked across the sunlit clearing and up a broad tree-trunk in a shaft of sunlight which sharpened its shadow and gave it twin tails. Up, up into the jungly treetops; whence if it were so minded it could make its acrobat way from oak to oak, along the drive skirting the village green, then high above Doddington Lane, all the way to the very last tree of all, from which it could gaze across the river at Elmbury town!

FERDO FELT HIS HEART PITTERING, as the squirrel's probably was. Seeing this wild thing at such close quarters he was aware of a moment's intense curiosity, a kind of wondering tenderness which he associated with boyhood; then it had sometimes made him cry. It became less intense as he grew older, so many things got in the way of it, the indifference of middle-age, the nagging headaches from his old wound, all that claret and port! But now and then he experienced it still, the sense of pity and wonder unaccountably fused together—occasioned it might be by the swallows' departure in autumn, the tiny chiffchaff's coming in the spring; by a spider spinning, on a morning of dew; by the foxcubs playing at dusk outside their earth at the edge of the wood; and now by this brief encounter with the timid beautiful creature to which he and Janet must look as fearsome as giants, as monstrous as Martians!

He tried to say "How marvellous!" but when he was excited his tiresome stammer, which stemmed from that First War head-wound, generally got the better of him; so he helplessly mum-mum-mummed, as he squeezed Janet's hand and grinned at her like a schoolboy.

¶ 4

BECAUSE OF THE SQUIRREL Ferdo clean forgot about meeting Susan. At least the squirrel was his excuse; but he was always forgetting things nowadays. It was a quarter to twelve already; so her train should just be coming in. Never mind, Ferdo said, the trains were always half an hour late at Elmbury; and he'd still be there in time if he took a short cut and drove the Land Rover across the Park. So he left Janet waiting for the Fentons, who were due to arrive at mid-day, got the Land Rover out of the garage, and went bumping and bouncing down the slope towards Ferdinando's Oak which stood in solitary state in the very centre of Doddington Park. It was a landmark of enormous grandeur; its girth was twenty-four feet at six feet from the ground, and it cast so generous a shade that it could keep a whole herd of cattle bone-dry in a thunderstorm. Some badgers had their sett among its gnarled roots, bats flew out of the hollow part of it in the evening, and it possessed its own private owl which hooted from it so regularly that he was known as Ferdinando's Owl. The tree was as old as the parish church, old as the thatched cottages round Doddington village green, old as the Manor,—getting on for four centuries old. Maybe the first Ferdinando had planted it with his own hands; at any rate it had been called after him for as long as anyone could remember.

FERDO WAS VERY PROUD of this progenitor, who had fought against the Armada but was also a bit of a pirate, and coming by his fortune not altogether honestly, nevertheless had the large altruism to plant a thousand oak-trees so that his descendants might delight in them.

As a commerce-raiding privateer, he had been lucky enough to capture a Spanish carrack from the East Indies that had her holds full of nutmegs, cinnamon, green-ginger, frankincense, camphor, taffetas, damask, calico, carpets, pearls, ebony, ambergris, elephants' teeth and coconuts: a marvellous mixed bag, which he sold off at Plymouth in a hell of a hurry in order to cheat his "very loving Sovereign" the Queen, who was a partner in his privateering and would certainly have demanded a lioness's share of the prize. As it was he managed to get away with about £50,000, which enabled him to lay out the Park and plant the woodlands, and to make his Manor at Doddington one of the grandest houses in all his native shire.

Nobody knew where he got his 'Ferdinando' from, for he was as English as they make 'em and as Gloucestershire as Justice Shallow. But the swashbuckling name had tickled the fancy of succeeding Seldons, who had passed it down from father to son. The first Baronet was Sir Ferdinando—he lost his sword-arm in the Battle of Worcester, and got the Baronetcy in return for it when the King came into his own. He celebrated the occasion (being like-minded with his ancestor) by planting in the Park clumps of young oaks which he had piously grown during the dismal Commonwealth from acorns fetched all the way from Shropshire, that were sworn on the Bible to come from the very tree at Boscobel in which King Charles had hid.

Subsequent Squires of Doddington had seized upon every excuse provided by Coronations, Jubilees and victories by sea and land to plant still more commemorative trees, so that soon the Park was 'umbrageous as a tropick scene,' according to a peripatetic author who wrote about it during the Seventeen-nineties. His book was fulsome concerning what he called on its title-page

THE PICTURESQUE SEATS
OF THE
NOBILITY AND GENTRY

but it was clear all the same that Doddington had occasioned him some dismay. He mildly disapproved of its general boskiness; but he must have been quite shocked by a spectacle which met his eyes when he cast them up into the boughs overhead:

> *Some half-dozen or more of the younger Progeny of the much-respected Baronet (Young Gentlemen and Ladies alike) clambering among the upper branches as if they were Marmosetts; whence peering forth they might have put the surpris'd Visitor in mind of Hamadryads, or Fauns of the Woodland, but for their Human Mischief in showering*

down Acorns and Chestnuts upon the Head of an unwitting
Tradesman who made his way along the Avenue to purvey
his Goods to Doddington Manor.

Perhaps not all those Marmosetts and Hamadryads were legitimate Progeny; for the much-respected Baronet of those days exercised a kind of unofficial and benevolent *droit de seigneur,* popu-
lating the neighbourhood with his recognisable by-blows. When
at last he reformed, and married a wealthy Quakeress, he lost no
time in getting a lawful quiverful of boys and girls cast in much
the same mould as those who played outside the doors of his
labourers' cottages or scampered about on the village green. A
family portrait in which Ferdo took particular pleasure showed
him with some of his brood. Ageing a little but rubicund still,
this most luxurious of the Doddington Squires leaned back and
regarded with a smile, as it were of happy reminiscence, the
cluster of charming children gathered about his chair. (The
Quakeress was missing from the picture; she had died young,
worn out with bearing so many.) They were a good-looking lot,
especially the girls, and clearly they were trying hard to keep
straight faces for the artist's benefit; nevertheless one got a delightful impression as of the sun about to break through the
clouds—at any moment, out of that broad-browed gravity, the
Human Mischief might burst forth! It was easy to imagine them
high up in the oak-tree, parting the branches to gaze down at the
solemn and surpris'd Visitor, the boys grinning like little monkeys, the long-haired girls delicate as Dryads, their April faces
framed by the green leaves.

SOON AFTER THE DEATH of this philoprogenitive fellow,
the family had fallen upon bad times. Horses were much more
ruinous than women, in the early Eighteen Hundreds. Your crack
four-in-hand set you back seven hundred guineas; each of your
five hunters cost about four hundred, if you were as determined
as the Seldons to be in at the kill. It took only a couple of young
bucks, who both died in their thirties, to squander two-thirds of
the Quaker fortune; and it became a close-run thing whether the
moneylenders got hold of Doddington and the timber-merchants
moved into the precious oak-woods, or whether the third in suc-

cession of those crazy Corinthians broke his neck first. A tall thick blackthorn-hedge with a ditch on the far side of it, a slippery take-off and a winded horse, settled the issue; and this particular Ferdo went home on a hurdle, escorted by his boon-companions carrying their tophats in their hands.

THE PROFLIGATES WERE SUCCEEDED by respectable Victorians, who restored the Seldons' finances, added a hideous wing to the Manor, took the portrait of the wicked squire down from the wall, and spoke of his doings in whispers if they ever spoke of them at all. But that story was never quite forgotten, and people still talked about the old squire's bastards in Doddington cottages and Elmbury pubs. They believed, or pretended to believe, that the ancient mischief persisted at Doddington, like mushroom-spawn which lies dormant in the soil for a decade, then throws up an unexpected crop some September when the climate's just right for it. So whenever handsome bad lads grew up in the village, or pretty girls ran wild there, it was the old squire's hot blood coming out in 'em, people said. The butcher, the baker, the grocer from Elmbury, driving their vans along that winding road between the trees, would remember the lustful legend and wish they'd been Squire Seldon when George the Whatsit was King! Once in a way perhaps, as they did their rounds in these parts, they'd set eyes on some village girl who looked 'different' or walked 'different,' as they fondly imagined: brown eyes going with blonde hair, a broad forehead, a long stride, a gay toss of the head; and they'd say to themselves, delighted, There you are, see, there's *quality* for you, there's a sprig of the old squire sprouting again after all these years!

DODDINGTON DEEP IN ITS GREENWOOD always seemed a back-of-beyond to Elmbury. Anything might go on there, any old-fashioned thing! The distance was less than three miles, as the rooks and the clacking jackdaws flew, from Elmbury Abbey Tower to the crooked chimneys of Doddington Manor; but the tradesmen in their vans couldn't fly across the river, they had to go up to the bridge at the far end of the straggling town and then take the roundabout route by leafy lanes which meandered for six miles or so as if they had been designed for connoisseurs of oaks and of squirrels. If, however, you went to Doddington on foot or on a bicycle there was another way, curiously melodramatic. Going down Ferry Lane, on the outskirts of the town, you came to the river bank, where there was a rusty bell hanging from a white post. On a hook beside the bell you found an iron bar, with which you smote it hard, producing a horrible clangour. If you beat loud and long enough—it often took a quarter of an hour—an old man called Jakey would come forth from his cottage on the opposite bank and hobble down to a punt as old as he was. Standing crooked in the stern, he'd paddle with long sweeping strokes rather like the wing-flaps of some slow black bird, aiming the bows well upstream to allow for the current. When he reached your bank he held out his hand without speaking, as Charon might, and you put threepence into it. He motioned to you where to sit so as to avoid the stickiest patches of tar, and in silence began to paddle again with that strange flapping action which made you think of a cormorant.

There used to be a proper ferry, a floating platform that creaked and cranked as it was wound across the river by means of chains. It would bear a horse and cart, or even a couple of small cars; and it had its hour of glory on a winter's day in the late Thirties, when it carried over the half-flooded river a pack of hounds, four horses, three Hunt Servants, the terrier man and his bicycle, and General Bouverie, M.F.H., swearing like mad, all in pursuit of a fox which had made the passage in a less complicated way, by swimming. But soon after that the capacious craft began to show its age, the blacksmith was called more often to attend to its pulleys and worn-out chains, all fell into disrepair. The war came, the Squire of Doddington as usual went off to the war, the petrol rationing started, nobody had occasion to drive to Doddington any more. The old man, who was heartily sick of winding the ever-stiffening handles, took to his punt instead. The ferry-boat, half sunk, was used as a landing-stage, from which you climbed up the bank into the dark leaf-mouldy deep-cut lane between the woods, which led to Doddington.

IT WAS 'OVER THE RIVER and into the trees': the woods began less than fifty yards from the river. The oak-boughs meeting overhead turned the lane into a green arcade all the summer, and however hot the day it was as cool as a church there: as you went in out of the sunshine you felt 'someone walking over your grave.' You stayed in this dim religious light until you got to Doddington village, which stood in a patch of brightness about its green. Here it always seemed to the folk of Elmbury as if they had stepped right back into the past. There was old Hipkins' smithy on the edge of the green, with a stamping and sizzling going on inside it, sparks flying, a burnt-hoof smell, and often two or three horses waiting their turn outside. Close by was the cobbler's-cum-saddler's owned by Mr. Turberville, who always sat outside his little shop on fine days, leather-aproned, with his mouth full of sprigs. Three generations of Turbervilles had shod the Seldons, while three generations of blacksmith Hipkins had shod their horses. Then there was the village store which still displayed the advertisements it had enterprisingly shown fifty years ago: 'Homocea touches the spot,' 'That schoolgirl complexion' and 'Always welcome, always handy, Grant's Morella cherry brandy.' There was a village pub called The Green Man, with an old-fashioned gamekeeper painted on its inn-sign. There were the cottage-gardens with old-fashioned flowers, gillies and cherry-pie and stocks and sweet-williams, and hollyhocks standing against the cottage walls. There were the old men you saw outside their cottages, who wore their corduroys hitched up with straps below their knees, who touched their hats even to strangers, and gave you a slow-spoken "Maarnin'" or "Aartenüne." There were the crooked chimneys of the Manor, just visible above the tops of the trees.

The Park entrance, through elegant if rusty drive-gates, was at the top of the green, just past the old rambling rectory and the church. Beyond these gates a long avenue swept grandly up the slope towards the big house, which was built of rose-red old bricks and pitch-black timbers, and looked as if it were falling down, but had probably looked so for a couple of centuries. Elmbury people never spoke of Doddington Manor; they called it the House in the Trees, and wondered why Squire Seldon didn't have a few felled here and there, to let in the sun. For round about it, seven tall oaks stood in a ring; so close to the Manor on one side that their twigs tapped bedroom-windows with a let-me-in rhythm whenever there was a wild wind. It would give you the willies, said the tradesmen from Elmbury, to spend all your days in that green shade, like tropical fishes in an aquarium!

BUT FERDO NEVER FELT SO MUCH AT HOME as when he was in the woods; the Seldons belonged there. Now on his way to meet Susan he came out of the brightness of the sun-drenched Park into the leafy coolness of what was called the Elmbury Back Lane and was among his beloved trees again. Some of these great ones, which overlooked the lane, might have been saplings when Shakespeare was but a little tiny boy, thirty miles away at Stratford-upon-Avon. Ferdo as he drove between them recognised them as he would recognise people, by their shapes, their attitudes, their character: all of them different, each one unique. During the war, when he was a Commodore of convoys going between Greenock and Halifax, he used to think about Elmbury Back Lane in moments of weary homesickness on the bridge, and shutting his eyes he would play a little game with himself, pretending that he was hacking along on his old horse between the oaks and hazels and trying to remember the individual trees in their proper order as he passed them by. Thus in imagination he would make his way from Doddington to Elmbury, while the white horses tossed their manes all round him, and the steep Atlantic, dark-green yet semi-transparent as his woods at twilight, reared up over the foredeck and hung there for a pregnant moment before the wave crashed down.

THE TREES THINNED OUT towards Elmbury, where the Back Lane joined the main road. Here in the early spring primroses were like spilt milk splashed all over the banks, and later on it was the bluebells which tempted the children from Elmbury's new housing estate just across the river. This part of the woods had never been 'preserved,' even in Old Northover's day; anybody could walk here who pleased. But now the old market-town was changing its character. It had acquired a factory or two, and a depôt for repairing military vehicles, and it proliferated ugly little suburbs sprawling out into the green fields. The 'new people' from these suburbs invaded the woods in hordes, but they no longer picked primroses, they lay down two by two and made love among the primroses, while the boys and girls who weren't old enough for love-making swung on the oak-boughs and broke down any saplings that weren't too strong for them to break.

Ferdo last spring (his first at home since the war) had watched these goings-on in astonishment and alarm. But he hadn't done anything about it, because Elmbury people traditionally had the freedom of this part of his land and it would have seemed mean and hateful to fence it off from them. In any case, he was always meeting strangers in his woods nowadays: hikers and rambling-clubs and botanists and butterfly-collectors and riding-schools, to say nothing of bird's-nesters and courting-couples. He generally let them be, unless they looked like setting the woods on fire.

This morning, just at the junction of the Back Lane with the main road, he saw two young men who were doing something new and surprising. One of them, half-way up the bank where the primroses grew in April, held up a striped pole; the other, standing by the side of the road, bent down over his instrument, a level or theodolite, and aimed it at the pole. It struck Ferdo as odd that they should be surveying his land without a by-your-leave; but then he thought they were probably students putting in some practice or articled pupils from the local auctioneers', getting ready for their exams. Again, they might be working for the Ordnance Survey, bringing the maps up to date.

He'd crossed the bridge over the river, and was turning into Elmbury's long main street, when it occurred to him that it might have been a good idea to stop and ask the young men why they were surveying in a private woodland. But Susan, he thought, would be waiting at the station; he wouldn't turn back now, perhaps he'd stop on the way home and ask them politely what they were up to.

Of course he would have been told of any plans or propositions affecting Doddington. . . . All the same, in retrospect, there seemed something rather sinister about that striped pole; and for the second time this morning Ferdo was aware of a kind of cloud-shadow crossing his mind, whose passage brought a chilly moment of bewilderment and dismay.

⊄ 5

MEANWHILE JANET who never wasted a moment if she could help it weeded the little garden in front of Huntsman's, pulling up armfuls of groundsel and chickweed and sanspurge and Good King Henry, and dumping them among the foxgloves under the oak-trees across the drive.

At last she heard the sound of a lorry, and the Fentons came into view, in a ramshackle vehicle piled high with furniture and with children perched on top of the furniture. The lorry stopped right opposite Huntsman's Cottage, and only then did Janet realise that the topmost of all those children clinging on to the bedsteads and washstands and chests-of-drawers was her own child Susan, waving and shouting and looking about a year older —well, a year more grown-up—than she had done when she left home at the beginning of term last May.

Fenton and his wife got out of the cab of the lorry and came up to Janet. She shook their hands perfunctorily, vaguely dismayed by them but hardly noticing because she was so bewildered at the fashion of Susan's arrival. What seemed like hordes of Fenton children had scrambled down (monkeyish, Janet thought, not absolutely human), leaving her sitting on top of the furniture. Perhaps the idea was that they should give her a hand down—indeed one of the boys was offering to do so. But no, Susan insisted she could manage. She'd slide down on a mattress to the side of the lorry, then she'd jump. She pushed her school hat jauntily on to the back of her head, yelled, *"Hallelujah, here I come!"* and slid. But she slipped off the mattress; her skirt, which she seemed to have grown out of anyhow, caught on a table-leg, and there she hung, displaying marvellous long legs, suspenders, pants (luckily her sedate school ones), everything. There was an appreciative murmur among the children below, which made Janet furious. One of them giggled, and one of the boys actually started a cheer. Then Susan wriggled herself free and jumped down and ran laughing to give Janet a kiss. Breathlessly excited: "Nobody at the station I guessed Daddy had forgotten he always does; so I left my luggage and walked. I whanged the bell for Jakey I always love doing that and he ferried me over and I sat on the tar, look." Almost everybody who took passage in Jakey's punt got tar on their bottom sooner or later. "Never mind," Susan said, "I shan't be wearing that old uniform again ever ever ever. Put it on a scarecrow. Hurray hurray we're leaving school today we sang before breakfast. Mr. Fenton overtook me in the lane I didn't know he was coming here of course but I said Hi and he gave me a lift. *Piles* of luggage still at the station."

Then Susan dashed off to ring up the station-master and ask him to look out for the Land Rover and tell Ferdo to bring the luggage home. The Fentons meanwhile had gone to the other side of the lorry to untie the ropes which secured the furniture, and Janet had time to observe the Fenton children, who seemed to be of all shapes and sizes; indeed their bewildering diversity gave her an alarming first impression of more children than there actually were. (Later she counted them and was surprised that there were only six). She noticed a peaky carroty girl with a very pale skin, freckles, glasses and warts. There was a shambling, scowling, dark-faced youth of about sixteen (he was the one who had dared to shout Hurray at the sight of Susan's pants) and there was a cheeky, bouncy, overdeveloped girl aged four-teen or so, the sort, Janet thought, whose misfortunes at puberty you read about in *The News of the World*. (She was the one who had giggled.) There were two snotty-nosed destructive-looking small ones; and there was a tall good-looking serious boy with a thin sallow face, the one who had offered to help Susan down off the lorry. His skin was stretched taut over high cheek-bones, and he had grey eyes, which when Janet spoke to him looked straight into hers with a cool calm gaze as he said, "How do you do, my lady?" in a tone so grave and grown up that Janet wondered, for a disturbing second, whether he was making fun of her. He was obviously the senior of the assorted brood; and he supervised the unloading from the lorry of three or four large packing-cases of books, while the scowling youth, inside the cottage, was already hammering away, putting up shelves to accommodate them. Janet's better nature, seeing this enthusiasm for books as a good sign, fought a losing battle against a despicable instinct which warned her that it was odd, unnatural and ominous for a gar-dener's children to possess so many. While they unpacked the books they kept peering over their shoulders—she had gone into the cottage to show the Fentons round—and studied her with wary curiosity, as if they had never seen anybody quite like her before. This made her nervous, so that when she tried to talk to them she found herself saying the wrong things, asking questions which they didn't or couldn't answer, using expressions which they didn't understand. She tried to put them at ease by explaining that they could wander about anywhere on the estate, play in the woods, no restrictions; but she found herself by accident using an absurd family expression which her mother had been addicted to, "Nobody minds what you do so long as you don't frighten the horses!" In other words, behave yourselves how you like so long as you don't do anything outrageous which causes public offence. But of course the Fentons didn't understand that. They thought she meant real horses. All the heads turned and all the mouths seemed to gape at her. She felt a fool, especially as this happened in front of Mrs. Fenton, who according to the arrangement Ferdo had made was going to 'give a hand now and then in the house.' She turned out to be one of these angular, waspish, red-haired, hygienic, purposive women with spectacles who look intellectual even if they aren't. Janet, who distrusted intellectuality anywhere but especially in the kitchen, somehow couldn't imagine her helping to wash up. She thought too, with unhappy prescience: She'll know all about Committees and be a bloody nuisance at the Women's Institute.

Fenton himself was tall, stooping, simian, long-armed, with huge hands and feet, a sardonic expression, and a voice like the croak of a raven: 'definitely sinister.' Yet it was not he, nor even his unpleasing wife, who stayed in Janet's thoughts and vaguely troubled them, all through her Anniversary: a tiny grub of apprehension gnawing at the heart of the day. It was the children, and especially that tall, withdrawn, defensive or defiant one, whom she kept thinking of with an odd, unaccountable, premonitory disquiet.

⁋ 6

"IS IT FIVE OR SIX Fenton kids?" she said to Ferdo now, as she closed her diary and put it away in her bag. "I wish I could remember what sex and ages. We don't want to be accused of

encouraging incest, do we? They just seemed a horde. Even with the two cottages thrown into one there's sure to be a bit of a squash. And if he's by way of being a Communist he's bound to be extra fussy and tiresome, I suppose?"

"I've told you before," said Ferdo, "we've no real reason to imagine he's a Communist or anything of the kind."

But Janet perfectly remembered the reference which Colonel Daglingworth had written concerning Fenton: 'I parted with him because he was obstinate and opinionated. I make every allowance for his having been a P.O.W. of the Japs during the war; but he strikes me as a bit of a sea-lawyer, and I suspect his politics.' As it happened, Daglingworth could hardly have written anything more likely to appeal to Ferdo's liberal principles, which Janet respected but did not often share. Ex-Petty-Officer, Royal Navy—had a pretty tough war—victimized, unjustly sacked, chucked out of his cottage, on account of political opinions honestly held and courageously expressed: monstrous! Not even Fenton's formidable appearance had prevented Ferdo from engaging him at once. It was true that his liberal principles were reinforced in this case by a lively disapproval of Daglingworth's calling himself a Colonel, when in fact he had only held a war-time commission in some mechanical Corps. Subsequently he had made a good deal of money out of quarries and gravel-pits which disfigured the countryside, and had bought himself a 300-acre farm on the north side of Doddington. Ferdo, who had heard him speak at a Conservative meeting, thought he had the outlook of a pre-war Blimp, but Janet had agreed with every word he said about the Russians, and being, as Ferdo put it, 'quite swep' away by the fellow's gift of the gab,' had then and there invited the Daglingworths to dinner. After all, they were new neighbours, having only recently come down into the valley off the Cotswolds, where they had lived near a village called Upper Swell. Janet, who could never resist giving nicknames, had called them after it, because of their obvious social ambitions.

"Anyhow, Colonel D. hinted this Fenton was——"

She was about to say 'an awkward cuss,' but just then Rosemary knocked at the door and came in with the dress which she'd been ironing; so Janet made a quick amendment:

"—*un peu difficile.*"

She had an uncomfortable way of using French in front of the servants if she did not want them to know what she was saying. It was an Edwardian thing which she had caught from her mother, who was an Earl's daughter, but it seemed awful bad manners to Ferdo, however high-born her mama might be. In any case for all he knew Rosemary might have learned much better French at school; they were taught all kinds of things nowadays. We must seem very odd to her, Ferdo thought, while Janet in her Winston Churchill accent went on about *le nouveau jardinier,* and he in his embarrassment fingered the billygoat tuft of cotton-wool which was stuck to his chin where he'd scraped it with his razor-blade. However, if Rosemary noticed any oddity she was too well-trained to show it. As she laid Janet's dress on the bed she included them both in her quick diffident smile. She was Old Northover's grand-daughter; her father was Jack the groom. He was a small nutty wholesome man, with crows-feet etched deep at the corners of his grey eyes, and lips which seemed to have become permanently pursed through hissing to horses: pleasantly old-fashioned in all his ways, and his child took after him, Janet thought, approving her nice manners and demure good looks. She gave her a quick glance-over, since the girl was about to wait at table for the first time at a party: not too much make-up, no nail varnish thank goodness, clean shoes, neat hair. How pretty they always looked in black and white,—it made one think of old times, when there were lots of them!

"I do hope I'll manage," Rosemary said.

"Of course you will. Oh, tell your mother I didn't ask Mrs. Fenton to give a hand in the kitchen tonight, hardly fair before she's properly settled in. So many of them—they'll have to sort themselves out somehow! . . . I hope they'll like it there," added Janet, suddenly rippled by another catspaw of disquiet.

"The cottage looks lovely," said Rosemary unexpectedly. Even Janet would hardly have called it that. But Rosemary, of course, had known it in her grandfather's day. She would remember the smoky oil-lamps, the blackened ceiling, the pump with the squeaky handle over the well by the back-door, the nauseous whiff from Old Northover's gallows blowing in through the front windows on a hot day, the extraordinary companionable privy at the bottom of the garden, where two people could sit side by side! A picture of Old Northover and his wife, suddenly conjured up in her mind, captivated Janet. It was queer how he kept hobbling backbent into her thoughts today.

"—Now just run along and see if Miss Susan wants any help," Janet said. "You'll probably have to zip her into that new dress!"

Rosemary paused at the door as she went out. "I nearly forgot, Mummy and Daddy both said to wish you many happy returns." She gave them another of those quick endearing smiles, which made Ferdo and Janet suddenly turn to each other and smile too, both thinking the same thing: that she seemed to belong to their past rather than to their present, to Old Northover's vanished England, to the times when the red squirrels flourished, to what Janet thought of as the palmy days.

¶ 7

SUSAN IN HER PETTICOAT, puzzled by her own face in the glass which looked so different when she put up her hair, didn't hear Rosemary's knock. She turned round when the door opened and there was an awkward little silence, Rosemary standing there uncomfortably, Susan still holding on to the switch of hair which she'd wound on to the top of her head, and both of them blushing, because of what had happened this afternoon.

At last Rosemary said:

"Miss Susan: you won't tell her ladyship, will you?"

"Of course not," said Susan shortly. She was cross not with Rosemary but with herself, for blushing and for feeling such a fool. She went on fiddling with her hair because she didn't know what to say.

They hadn't seen each other since the afternoon. Susan on the first day of the holidays always tore round looking at all the things and revisiting all the places which she had missed or had remembered affectionately during the term; it was an exciting secret ritual which she'd practised ever since she was a child coming home after the first miserable term at boarding-school. Today it was all the more exciting because for one thing the holidays were going to last for ever, for another Tony was coming to stay.

He was her second cousin, ten years older than she was, and she'd been in love with him ever since she had first thought about love. Long before that he'd been her childhood hero: he was back from Dunkirk, he'd got an M.C., he was fighting the Japs in Burma, he'd been wounded and brought home, he was back with his regiment, he'd landed in Normandy, he was across the Rhine! After the war he had stayed on in the Gloucesters, which for generations had been the 'family regiment' of those of the Seldons who didn't, like Ferdo, choose to go to sea.

Now he had three weeks' leave, and he was going to spend it all at Doddington! Susan couldn't keep her feet still; she grandly persuaded herself that she felt like that King in Yeats's poem who *filled his marriage-day With banneret and pennon, Trumpet and kettledrum, And the outrageous cannon, To bundle time away Till the night come!* She went to see the horses and talked to Northover and climbed up to the hayloft for no special reason except that it used to be one of her hiding-places; she played with Ophelia the Siamese cat, and went into the dark Priest Hole under the stairs, and then she unpacked some of her things, and took *The Oxford Book of English Verse* into Tony's bedroom and laid it on the table beside the bed, then had second thoughts and replaced it with *The Shooting-Man's Week-End Book,* then changed her mind again, fetched her own copy of Shakespeare's *Sonnets* and put all three books on the table together, but with the shooting one on top. To bundle time away, she hurried across the Park to Ferdinando's Oak where she used to wish special wishes; and then she went down through the garden to her favourite place of all, which was called the Lily Pond, though it began as an otter-pond really, back in Mummy's palmy days when she could afford to build a pool for a pet otter. Susan could just remember her mother's extraordinary appearance when she was, for a season or two, an M.O.H., Master of Otterhounds: red woollen stockings, blue coat and skirt, a peculiar blue beret with a silver-mounted otterpaw pinned on to it, and a long pole with notches representing her tally of dead otters. She had found nothing incompatible with her Mastership in loving this pet otter, which she had rescued from the hounds when it was a small cub; and she had spent a hundred pounds or so on making a pool for it to play in and a little summerhouse where she could watch it play. Susan remembered vividly—it was

the thing she remembered best about the beginning of the war—
the letting-loose of the otter, which had been necessary because
everybody was going away and there would be no one to look
after it. They had set it free by moonlight, in the little stream
that ran through the wood; it had gone swiftly between the
bracken like a trickle of quicksilver, and Susan heard her mother
give a series of sniffs and snorts which at last she identified with
dismay as grown-up crying.

T H E R E W E R E P I N K W A T E R - L I L I E S in the pool, as well as
the ordinary white ones; they were the colour, Susan imagined, of
pink champagne, which she had never drunk but was confident
that on some glorious romantic occasion she would drink in time
to come. The flowers planted round the pool were rather exciting
too: there were some brown irises with dewlaps like blood-
hounds, and pink flowering rushes, and lots of yellow mimulus,
and there was a thing called gunnera which looked like a jungle
rhubarb, with vast umbrella leaves, and a buddleia bush that
blossomed with butterflies, four or five to a stem. At the far end
of the pool stood a beautiful bronze statue of a naked boy, which
Susan's great-great-grandfather had brought home from Italy,
after a tour. Something had gone wrong with his little private
fountain, and he no longer pee'd all day as he had done, to the
great delight of Susan, in the days of Bella the Otter.

But the best thing of all was the very tall, thick, black cypress-
hedge planted round the pool on three sides and hiding it from
view, so that you could, if you wanted, take a dip. A splendid
orange-red climber ran up the cypress-hedge and fanned out like
a bonfire's blaze against the black. This was the thing which
Susan always saw in her mind's eye when she thought about the
lily-pool; and this afternoon it was just as gorgeous as it had been
in her recollection. She sat on the seat for a minute or two,
admiring it.

There was no wind between the cypress-hedges, and it was so
hot that Susan thought she'd undress and go in. No need for a
bathing-dress, but there used to be some towels kept in the summerhouse. She wondered if they were still there, and she went
and opened the summerhouse door.

She hadn't, until then, heard a sound; and finding Rosemary
and the man there she was so taken by surprise that she squeaked

or squealed, she didn't know which, and got an absurdly wrong impression of what was going on. She thought, in a confused way, that the man was somehow *attacking* Rosemary; and this mistake was understandable because he had his hands on her, pressing her against the wall, and his face, as he turned it towards Susan, had a sort of wild wolfish look, quite alarming; though she realised later that it was probably a combination of breathlessness and fright which gave him that snarl. At any rate, in her silly bewilderment, Susan had cried out: "Let her go!"; and she'd probably added, "You brute!" or something like that—she couldn't exactly remember. Then, as obediently and rather surprisingly he did let go of Rosemary, Susan had suddenly realised that Rosemary's dress was open in front and pulled down over her shoulder, leaving one breast quite bare, and much too late she had understood that he hadn't been attacking her. She'd heard herself saying, "Oh . . . sorry," in a foolish flat voice, then she had banged the summerhouse door on them and fled. Running up the path through the garden she had heard the scrape of Tony's tyres on the drive, Tony cheerfully hooting his horn.

SHE'D BEEN TERRIFIED of meeting Rosemary ever since; and she'd decided that when she did meet her she wouldn't say anything about the summerhouse, she would simply behave as if nothing had happened. But now Rosemary had gone to the window and was studiously looking out of it, and Susan felt she had to say something, so in the most grown-up and casual voice she could manage she said:

"Oh, Rosemary, what's your boyfriend's name?"

"Goff," said Rosemary, without looking round.

"Goff?"

"It's short for Godfrey, Miss Susan."

Susan puzzled over this, then without really thinking what she was saying blurted out:

"Oh, I see. You couldn't call him God, could you?"

"No, Miss Susan," said Rosemary in a small voice, serious and, Susan thought, a bit shocked.

A sense of agreeable absurdity, like a fresh wind, began to blow Susan's embarrassment away.

"I'd better get going or I'll be late for dinner." She put in the last hairpins, tied a scarf over her head to keep her hair in place and began to pull on her dress. It was a tight fit. "Headless woman," she said, wriggling her way into it. She heard Rosemary giggle, and they were both at ease suddenly; Rosemary gave the dress a last tug and zipped up the back. Susan took off the scarf and looked at herself in the glass.

The dress was flame-coloured satin, almost the same shade as that creeper by the pool. There didn't seem to be much of it, now she'd got it on. She felt fine and free and a bit adventurous in it. She wore it specially for Tony, she told herself. It was an unexpected present from her mother, to celebrate her leaving school perhaps, the first taste of grown-up delights.

"You look lovely, Miss Susan," Rosemary said.

Susan turned round to her, studied her for a moment and exclaimed, "So do you!" realising this for the first time.

"I like your hair up," Rosemary said. "It makes you look much older though."

"Try yours!"

"Mine?"

"Try putting yours up, and see! I'll help. Sit there in front of the glass. Look, you catch it up like this——"

Susan scooped the hair up from the nape of Rosemary's neck and pinned it on top as she had done her own.

"Hey presto! D'you like it?"

"I'm not sure . . . Yes, I think so."

"Let it stay, then. It looks fine."

"Won't her ladyship mind?"

"Why ever should she? She'll think you've grown up suddenly. I say, how old *are* you, Rosemary?"

"Seventeen and a bit."

Goodness, and I'm nearly eighteen, Susan thought, astonished afresh about the summerhouse; still dismayed, but also awed by it. The wolfish young man, it now occurred to her, certainly didn't belong to Doddington.

"Where does your boyfriend come from?" she said.

"Elmbury. He's got a motor-bike. He takes me out on it sometimes. We're walking out, you see . . . It'll do a ton—a hundred," Rosemary amended quickly.

"A hundred!"

Susan could see the grandeur of that: man and girl and bike fused together into a streamlined missile hurtling along, the roar in your ears, the prickling in your eyes, the surge under your bottom, the rough wind trying to undress you! Walking out at a hundred miles an hour!

"Well, you tell him he'd better be careful," she said; and Rosemary gave her a sly little glance, wondering about a double meaning, not quite daring to grin.

The old grandfather clock on the landing began to strike.

"Help! The guests will be here!" cried Susan.

"Mr. Anthony's down already. He was in the sitting-room when I took in the drink tray——"

"He's *down?* Why didn't you tell me? Oh, I must *dash*——"

At the door, as Rosemary opened it for Susan, the two girls for a second stood face to face: surprised, by the hair-do or by something else, they gazed at each other and a kind of excitement flickered between them. It went like wildfire from one to other, kindling their spirits, so that Susan began to laugh, then Rosemary, as they ran down the stairs together, trying to race the old clock with the whirring innards, still laboriously striking eight.

⊄ 8

THAT STRANGE EXCITEMENT, staying with Susan all through dinner, sharpened her perceptions, gave her extra eyes, ears, understandings. For example, she was swopping a quick glance and a little grin with Tony across the candles, yet at the very same time she was noticing that her father was drinking too much because of his boredom with Mrs. Daglingworth. She was observing how very odd her mother looked in evening dress, weatherbeaten on top, all white and scraggly below, and she was seeing Colonel Daglingworth, who sat on her left, pouring a most inordinate quantity of mint sauce over his saddle of lamb, over the potatoes and the peas and the cauliflower, and even aiming a special dollop to fall accurately upon his dab of red currant jelly. And still at the very same time, Susan was hearing, across the table, Mrs. Daglingworth remarking to her father, rather disloyally it seemed:

"I never take it. It's death to me. But *he* adores it. We're opposites, like Jack Spratt and his wife, I suppose. He has it with everything: chicken, salmon, dover sole."

And if he were a Roman emperor, Susan thought, peeping at Colonel Daglingworth out of the corner of her eye, he'd pour it over his nightingales' tongues. When you come to think of it he looks a bit like a Roman emperor. He has a large, powerful, handsome, jowly face, and a complexion that goes coppery in the candlelight; he has rather nasty, large pores in the fleshy part of his nose, if you look at it closely, which of course you would only do by accident; he has big eyes to stare at you and large podgy hands to paw with. He had, in fact, touched her once, high up on her arm, and although she gave him the benefit of the doubt and assumed he hadn't meant to she had had a slight gooseflesh feeling.

In between mouthfuls of mint sauce, he admired the family portraits, which peered out of the shadows beyond the pool of candlelight: the original Ferdinando, the cunning old sea-dog, looking every inch a pirate; the cavalier, the acorn-planter, with bright bay ringlets and the stump of his right arm proudly displayed; the two Regency bucks with foxy faces peeking wild-eyed out of high collars up to their ears, who had nearly brought Doddington to ruin; the hell-for-leather foxhunter who had broken his neck; and the soldiers and sailors in their uniforms, 'the serviceable Seldons,' as some high-up in the Army or Navy had once described them, who'd fought by land or sea in most of England's wars for two and a half centuries.

"A patriotic lot," Daglingworth said.

"Don't you believe it," said Janet. "Parochial. They may *think* they go to war for England; but what they mean by England is just home, Doddington, this old house, the church, the trees, the village people, the fields, streams, cows, pheasants, squirrels."

She began to tell him about the red squirrel they'd seen that morning.

Meanwhile Mrs. Daglingworth, who looked a bit fish-like with her petulant mouth and round cheeks which suddenly became pendulous when she made surprised faces, had stopped talking about her husband's gastronomic peculiarities and was discoursing on the iniquities of the gardener, Fenton,—

"You didn't rarly engage him after what my husband had told you!"

Susan saw Ferdo take another long swig at his wine, understood his embarrassment, and admired the gentle good manners with which, even if he *was* getting a bit tight, he tried to prevent the woman talking loudly about Fenton while Rosemary was in the room. He was leaning across to her confidentially, bending his head so low that Susan could see the long furrow of the war-wound which had given his hair a second parting. It always went a bit red when he'd been drinking a lot. Mrs. Daglingworth, dropping her voice at last to a stage whisper, was saying:

"He's a rabid Socialist, for one thing," pronouncing 'rabid' with a long A as in 'gravy.' It struck Susan that nobody ever spoke of rabid Conservatives. She saw her father make the smallest possible protesting gesture with his left hand, and Mrs. Daglingworth stopped talking as Rosemary came round with the raspberries and cream.

THE FAVOURITE FAMILY PORTRAIT, of course, was the one which showed the philoprogenitive Seldon of the Seventeen-eighties smiling at his recollection of joys long past, as he leaned back easefully in his big chair and contemplated the legitimate moiety of his offspring. It hung at the end of the room, behind Ferdo, who was so proud of it that he'd recently had it cleaned and properly lit. Towards this picture, continuing his researches into the Seldons' ancestry, Colonel Daglingworth now craned his thick neck.

"So he was the bad boy, was he?" said the Colonel, who'd been getting snippets of old scandal from Janet; and since he spoke, as always, in a rather loud and hectoring voice, everybody at the table dutifully turned their heads towards the portrait of the black sheep,—everybody except Susan, that is, who was preoccupied with three things at once. She was trying to help herself to the raspberries which Rosemary, not very expertly, was offering her; she was being aware of a mysterious kind of closeness with Rosemary, because of the summerhouse secret and their talk in her bedroom; and she was concerned with a suspicion that Colonel Daglingworth might be using his interest in the picture as a cloak for certain alarming manoeuvres which had brought his thigh into contact with hers. Also, she was being addressed across Ferdo by the plump garrulous Mrs. Daglingworth, who was saying:

"You must meet my Sandra when she comes home next week. You and Sandra will get on like a house on fire. She's mad on horses too. We've bought her a new show-jumper. But don't you have to pay an awful lot for them? This one cost Father a cool——"

Suddenly Mrs. Daglingworth stopped, with her mouth half open, and stared at Susan, in difficulties over the raspberries, and at Rosemary, trying to make it easier for Susan to reach them. Their intent faces were close together, their blonde heads almost touching; and they looked exactly alike!

It was Mrs. Daglingworth's breaking-off in the middle of a sentence that drew the others' attention to the likeness. From the picture of Ferdo's ancestor they turned their eyes towards her, to see what was up; and then following her glance they found themselves staring at the unknowing Susan and Rosemary. Only Colonel Daglingworth, whose view was blocked by Rosemary's shoulder, remained unaware of the revelation by candlelight. Ferdo, puzzled at first, then suddenly understanding, reacted with the cheerfullest grin imaginable. He cupped his chin in his hand and gazed at the two girls, frankly delighting in their prettiness and similarity. He was feeling immoderately proud of the ancestor behind his head, the fruit of whose loins persisted still.

Janet was thinking: Like as peas in a pod! Why on earth haven't I noticed it before? Rosemary must have put her hair up *after* she came into my room. I wonder why she did that—rather pert of the child, to copy Susan. It's the hair up that shows how alike they are, that broad Seldon brow . . . Extraordinary manners the Upper Swells have, Mrs. D. staring at them as if to say "Well, I never!" . . .

TONY WAS THE LAST to notice the sudden silence and the turning of heads. Left to himself while his neighbours chatted away, he'd been amusedly watching Mrs. Daglingworth boring the pants off Cousin Ferdo, while Ferdo in desperate self-defence swigged a whole glass of the Mouton-Rothschild '47 in one go. The claret was first-rate, as it always was at Doddington. Poor old

Ferdo, the way he was going, would probably drink himself to death on it in the end; in which case he, Tony, would wake up one morning and find himself a blessed Baronet. Well, he supposed that would be rather fun; but because he was very fond of Cousin Ferdo and Cousin Janet, he hoped it wouldn't happen for a long time yet Meanwhile almost everything seemed rather fun to Tony. He happily sipped his wine and contemplated a long vista of pleasurable diversions stretching out before him as far as his mind's eye could see. Three weeks' leave; staying at Doddington, which he loved; the chance that he might be picked to keep wicket for the Army, and get a game at Lord's; then back to the Regimental Depôt, a bit dull, but there was some decent trout-fishing not far away, and he'd taken a share in a shooting syndicate, he'd got a couple of hunters, and he was toying with the idea of keeping a steeplechaser in training, which he could well afford to do since his father had left him nearly £50,000. He'd have time for a bit of racing this winter, unless that schemozzle in Korea turned out to be something serious. And even if it did, there would be compensations: some real soldiering again, commanding his own company instead of training recruits, new countries to look at, new cities to have fun in, Tokyo, Hong Kong. He reflected that he had never been to bed with a Chinese girl, and his comprehensive category of fun made room for the possibility of his doing so, along with the cricket and cubbing, the pheasants, the fishing, the fighting and all.

His thoughts now turned lightly to girls. How amusing it was to see that long-legged Sue suddenly growing up! It always surprised you, when you had known them as kids . . . Tony, who was feeling very gay because of the gin he'd drunk with Ferdo before dinner and the claret he'd put on top of it since, allowed a sort of caliph's-eye view of the world to float before his eyes: he saw it momentarily as a kind of girl-garden, in which they continually sprouted, charmingly budded, opened their skin-soft petals, blossomed into young womanhood, and were plucked. This agreeable prospect of *jeunes filles en fleur,* growing in a horticultural succession of every enchanting shape and colour and size, tickled his simple fancy; he lifted his eyes from the wine-glass to look across the candles at Susan, and at Rosemary standing beside her with the raspberries on the tray.

The two girls might have been twins! Amazed, enchanted, and

enormously appreciative of what he recognised at once as one of Nature's better jokes, he glanced at the family portrait behind Ferdo, which of course he knew well—he'd been spending his holidays at Doddington ever since he was a schoolboy. His eyes went back to Susan and Rosemary, then to the portrait again, —and there they were, to the life, standing beside Papa's arm-chair! The young girls in the picture wore Sunday-solemn expressions put on specially for the occasion, they were concentrating hard. So were Susan and Rosemary, in difficulties over the raspberries; and in all four faces just the same intent seriousness. It was altogether fascinating, and even as Tony watched them Susan, carefully hunching herself to avoid any contact with Daglingworth, managed to scoop up the last spoonful of raspberries and glanced round at Rosemary with a small thank-goodness smile; Rosemary smiled back, and Tony suddenly got a glimpse of the mischief beneath the gravity, of what that pompous old traveller had seen peering at him out of the oak-boughs overhead!

SUSAN, FOR THE FIRST TIME, became aware of all the eyes on her; and since she hadn't the faintest idea of what it was all about, she panicked. Some sinister action of Colonel Daglingworth's, she immediately assumed, must be the cause of everybody's stare; he must be *obviously* leaning her way, edging himself towards her; his frightful ambition to paw and to smoodge must be manifest to all! She felt a blush like warm rising sap surging up her neck, her cheeks, her forehead. In utter embarrassment she tried to make herself smaller, to take up less room on her chair, and wriggling to do so she jogged Rosemary's tray. At once an appalling thing happened. The tray being knocked up, two or three raspberries dislodged from the dish rolled off the edge of it and fell into her lap. In a fraction of a second—you wouldn't think a fat man could move so fast—the terrible Colonel pounced; with one great lingering paw he rescued the raspberries, with the other he quite unnecessarily patted her arm in a gesture of Nothing-to-worry-about-might-have-been-worse-no-damage-done-my-dear or something of the kind. It was quite deliberate this time; she hadn't a shadow of doubt about it; and though it was over so quickly she felt sure that everybody must have seen it, must have known it was deliberate, must have watched her being pawed. She bent down over her plate, while the silly blushes came and went like waves; and to make matters worse, Colonel Daglingworth insisted on talking to her,—she was so confused she didn't know what he was saying, she was only aware of the jocular tone. She didn't dare look up to answer the old toad, anyway; for her face, she was convinced, was as red as the raspberries, which she fiercely bashed up with sugar and cream.

¶ 9

AFTER DINNER, WHILE HER MOTHER and Mrs. Daglingworth drank their coffee in the sitting-room, Susan pretended she wanted to go to the loo; but instead she tiptoed past the dining-room where the men were talking over their port, and went out by the front-door. She was still feeling ruffled, and she longed to be by herself. The night was black and velvety and cool. The tiniest drops of rain tickled her shoulders and arms like cobwebs. Big moths circling round the bright light above the door made the shadows dance in the courtyard, where she could see Daglingworth's enormous Bentley with an unnatural quantity of badges on its bonnet and a swanky silver naked lady (as you might jolly well expect, Susan thought) preparing to do a high-dive off the radiator-cap. Although she realised how gauche and silly she had been, her sense of outrage persisted; partly because he was so awfully old, forty-five at least, which was more or less Methuselah, and partly because this absurd, embarrassing thing had happened when Tony was watching. Everybody had been watching, for that matter; she still didn't know why. And what *ought* she to have done about it, she wondered? Supposing she'd smiled sweetly at him when he picked up the raspberries and said: "How clever of you, Colonel Daglingworth, to save my new dress!" at the same time hacking his shin hard with the heel of her shoe, unseen by anybody, just to show him? Or, of course, she could have pretended he was just being paternal; but then he would have done it again. Or she could have taken it in her stride as just one of those things a girl's got to expect as she goes through life, and what the hell? *Never mind, dear, said her mother, One man's very like another,* ran a naughty little rhyme which she and the other girls had been giggling over late last night. It was odd how grownup she had felt, that last-time-ever in the dormitory, talking to the other leavers after they'd all had dinner with the Headmistress. This Farewell Dinner was a little ceremony, rather civilised in its way, designed to mark your hatching-forth as it were out of the chrysalis of schoolgirlhood. There was fried scampi and chicken vol-au-vent, beautifully cooked and served to show you that it wasn't just another school meal. The English mistress, who was one of the guests, assumed in the course of conversation that you had read various books which she would officially have deplored your reading only yesterday. Your amontillado before dinner, and then the pale-pink Anjou rosé that looked so pretty in your glass, were tacit admissions on the part of authority that you were no longer subject to its prohibitions. You were only given one glass of the *vin rosé*, but nevertheless it seemed to induce a sort of pseudo-tightness, which fortunately didn't manifest itself until everybody had said their formal goodbyes to the Headmistress and had emerged into the cool fresh air. All the girls then became marvellously uninhibited. Back in the dormitory they sat in a row on Susan's bed and talked about sex, and used some of the words as airily as they could, pretending hard that they weren't saying them aloud for the very first time. Susan, who was beginning to feel sleepy, contrived to combine her own hair-raising contribution with a plausible yawn. Someone noticed it was past midnight, and invented a rhyme: *Hoobloodyray, we're leaving school today!* They sang this refrain, emphasising the bloody, and felt that they knew almost everything about almost everything already.

But growing-up wasn't accomplished as easily as all that, Susan thought now, sighing.

THE COLD AIR WAS LOVELY, it washed that creepy-crawly touch out of her skin. A bat came out of the blackness of the trees and hawked at the moths round the light above the door. The shadows jigged crazily, and as they did so Susan caught the briefest glimpse of something or someone moving, *crawling*, she thought, close to the rear wheels of the Bentley. Immediately her senses sharpened; and standing stock-still she heard a peculiar noise, a faint slow hissing, such as Northover made to the horses, but continuous. How extraordinary. She could no longer see any movement beside the car, but by now she was quite sure that something was going on there. At the moment she was frightened of nothing in the world except Colonel Daglingworth, and making a fool of herself in front of people, so it was with pleasurable excitement that she gathered herself together and sprinted to the car. Twenty long strides; the stiff taffeta petticoat under her full skirt swung with a swish as she stopped. Not a sound except the hissing, which was very close; and now she understood what was causing it. She dashed round to the back of the car and saw legs on the ground: two pairs. She said:

"Come out."

They began to wriggle out, backwards. Her eyes growing accustomed to the dark, she now saw a third figure crouching close to one of the rear wheels.

"Who are you, and what on earth do you think you are doing?"

But by now she had guessed who they were. The one by the wheel said at last, in a whisper:

"Fentons. Fair cop."

She moved round to get a better view of them, and the three heads turned towards the light. She recognised the soft-spoken tall boy, the oldest of the Fenton children, who had sat beside her on top of the furniture in the lorry, and the shaggy-looking, dark, hairy one whom she hadn't liked: his thatch of thick hair and black eyebrows showed up in the glimmer of light. The third was a young podgy girl in jeans.

"You're letting the air out of the tyre," Susan said.

"Yes," said the tall one, still sitting by the wheel, where the leaking valve sizzled away. His thin, pale, interesting face looked a bit like a sad clown's in the gleam that came from above the door.

"Why?" Susan said.

"We hate his guts, if you want to know."

"Why?"

"Our Dad worked there."

"Yes?"

The younger boy spoke for the first time. He had more of an

accent, something half-way between Cockney and country; and he was much more aggressive. He said:

"We thought we'd got away from him, see. Then we see this B——"

"Bentley," Susan said, and because of the 'B' in it, coming after that little pause, the round girl gave the first squeak of a giggle, and the black-browed boy growled: "Gloria, shut your trap."

Susan crouched down beside the other one, who was intently staring at the wheel. She saw that he had jammed a match-stick in the valve; it hissed like an angry snake. The tyre was about three-quarters flat.

"Can you stop it?" she said.

"Of course." He took out the match-stick and it stopped.

"Otherwise, you see," Susan explained, "*we'll* have to pump the tyre when he goes. He's our guest, after all. If you leave it as it is, with luck he won't notice it till he's half-way down the drive, and then *he'll* have to do the pumping."

The three faces solemnly turned to gape at her. The podge, Gloria, at last gave an appreciative nod. The sullen boy with thunderous brows continued to stare at her in bewildered hostility.

The pale-faced one at her side said in a whisper:

"Whose side are you on, then?"

"Never you mind."

He turned his eyes quickly and began to hunt for the valve-cap on the ground. As he scrabbled about in the gravel, his arm brushed hers, and in quick alarm (how unlike Daglingworth!) he jerked it away. Supersensitive about physical contacts tonight, she noticed his careful avoidance of her, his wary edging-away made her conscious of her bare shoulders, and the little secret antennae in her mind were aware not only of a breathless shyness but of something mixed up with it, a perturbation, a quickening.

"What's your name?" she asked.

"Ben," he said.

"And the others'?"

"Gloria. William. Willum we call him."

She glanced at the blackavized one, still glowering at her, and felt that Willum was apt.

"How many are there of you, for goodness' sake?" Sue said.
"Three more at home."

"Six altogether? What fun," she whispered, remembering the
long loneliness of being a single child.

"How many of *you?*" For some reason he was whispering too.

"Only me. Susan Seldon."

"Miss Susan," he said, she thought ironically. Embarrassed, she
jumped up.

"I must go in. I won't tell. But go, quick, before you're
caught!"

She ran across the courtyard and opened the front-door very
quietly, lest anybody should hear her come in. She looked over
her shoulder and saw the three figures still crouching by the car.
Upon an impulse she waved her hand, but only the one called
Ben waved back. Going in, she got a glimpse through a chink in
the dining-room curtains of the men still sitting at the table.
Colonel Daglingworth was holding forth to her father. Dirty
stories she wouldn't be surprised.

❡ 10

"*THAT CHAP, WHAT'S-'IS-NAME,*—used to be a Commie
but saw the light," Daglingworth was saying, "—you know, Or-
well, *Animal Farm,*—'All pigs are equal but some are more equal
than others.' Damned funny, I thought. Well, this Trottie of ours
was a hell of an equal pig. Because as long as the petrol rationing
lasted, wherever we went—pheasant-shooting, cocktail-parties,
what have you—Trottie came too. In the trailer. Then if any
inquisitive bobby asked questions, *Farm business,* we'd say, *Look
in the trailer, you poor sap!*—And Bob's your uncle."

Ferdo was scarcely listening. The long story was about Daglingworth's cleverness in justifying his journeys during that
winter two years ago when there was a financial crisis and a
petrol shortage. What they called the basic ration had been
stopped; and you only got coupons for your specified business
needs. Daglingworth took round a small pig in a trailer to pretend he was on a business journey even if, in fact, he was going to
the races. It didn't seem to Ferdo a thing one would want to

boast about. But while Daglingworth had been talking he had scarcely heard one word in three. He'd been thrown into a panic by what Daglingworth had told him five minutes ago. It had frightened him so much that he could hear the pulses thudding like dull hammers in the side of his head. Daglingworth had said, apropos of the place he'd bought recently, Doublegates Farm on the north side of Doddington:

"God knows whether we'll want to go on living there when the new road's finished; but after all, that may not be for years."

Ferdo's reactions were slow tonight; it was Tony who asked, in surprise:

"What new road?" Doddington was such a backwater, there wouldn't be much point in making a new road to it, surely.

"The motor-road, of course. One of those new ones, M-something or other. Hadn't you heard?"

Ferdo, still bewildered, shook his head.

"Well I'm jiggered," Daglingworth said. 'I thought you'd know everything that went on in the County, being a J.P. and a what-d'you-call-it, Deputy Lieutenant, and all that." Watching him across the table, Tony could see that he was geniunely astonished. He had really believed that people in Ferdo's position had mysterious privileges; were told things in advance but kept mum about them for their own profitable purposes, manipulated M.P.'s with whom they'd been at Eton, exercised secret powers. Whereas in fact, Tony said to himself, it's always Daglingworth's lot who know which way the wind's blowing. They hobnob with Mayors and Councillors and Town Clerks. They meet the chaps who dish out the contracts. They're in on all the fiddles. Bet he bought that farm of his for some reason other than farming!

"—Nobody tells *me* anything." Daglingworth smiled, deliberately inviting their disbelief. "But I certainly understand that it's planned to bring this road down from Brum, and to join it up with the main Bristol road just beyond Elmbury. It would cross the river somewhere near the Ferry; which by my reckoning takes it bang across my farm, and slap through Doddington."

"D–D–Doddington?" Suddenly Ferdo remembered the two young men with the theodolite and the striped pole. He'd looked for them on the way back from Elmbury, meaning to ask them what they were doing; but they had gone.

"Shortest way, my dear chap."

"But from any part of your farm to the Ferry, that—that means it would have to go through the oak-woods?"

"Yes."

It was then that those pulses began hammering in Ferdo's temples. He poured out another glass of port, and knew he was getting fuddled, but he didn't care.

"But they couldn't come through *Doddington?*" he said.

"Couldn't? Those buggers, our lords and masters now, can do what they b. well like, and don't we know it? It's a fat lot of use us trying to stand up against 'em, like old oaks in a gale! You've got to be flexible. If the road comes here," said Daglingworth with a grin, "cash in on it, say I. Brum within an hour. It'll send land values rocketing. Elmbury's been ripe for development for years: a sleepy old place like that, with a great city only forty miles away! It's crying out for expansion, isn't it? You take my tip, and if the road does come to Doddington, get out! With what your land would fetch,—plus a fortune I daresay for the standing timber—you could buy your own private island in the Bahamas, a place in Scotland *and* an estate in the South of France!"

He beamed at Ferdo, beamed at Tony, waved his fat hand towards the window and the black night outside.

"Oak," he said, "is fetching three bob a cubic foot. At that price some of those big fellows out there would cut up for damn near a hundred quid apiece. Now's the time, my boy, if you're thinking of cashing in."

There was such a long silence that even Tony became embarrassed. He was desperately sorry for Ferdo, and he was thinking that Daglingworth must be even more pachydermatous a beast than he looked, not to realise what an appalling thing he was saying. 'A fortune I daresay for the standing timber'! The oaf, thought Tony, the great clumsy galumphing rhinoceros-hided mint-sauce–swilling oaf! He remembered that precious map of the Doddington estate which hung on Ferdo's study-wall: two six-inch-to-the-mile Ordnance sheets joined together and lovingly decorated with thumbnail sketches, of a snipe for instance in the field where there were always snipe, of two buzzards where once a pair had nested, of the rarest flowers in the places where they grew, of all the greatest trees. Every petty place-name was devoutly recorded: Parson's Patch, Cuckoo Pen, the Long Furlong, Kidnapper's Lane, Cold Elm Corner, Sexton's Spinney, Seven Men's Tump . . . Ferdo had told him how he had taken the map with him to the war, and how he'd pinned it up on the wall of his cabin when he was convoying ships across the Atlantic. The dog-eared Ordnance sheets had been stained by sea water when a great wave had broken over the bridge and half-flooded the Commodore's cabin beneath. All round the margin there were rough amateurish sketches of Ferdinando's Oak. Over the port one evening Ferdo had confessed to Tony that he'd been trying to remember the exact shape of the tree, trying to see it in his mind's eye, one day when the convoy was hove-to in thick fog off the Greenland Banks.

When the silence had lasted for several seconds Tony tried to explain to Daglingworth:

"You see, Sir, the Seldons have been here for nearly four hundred years. I don't think they'd contemplate living anywhere else, it just isn't on the cards."

"Ah well, not to worry," said Daglingworth breezily. "It may never happen." He turned to Ferdo. "We'll keep in touch; and if I hear anything I'll let you know. If it comes to a fight, of course, I'm with you."

Ferdo clutched at this straw; perhaps the fellow wasn't so bad after all, perhaps it was just his horrible manner. "That's neighbourly," he said. "After all, we march together, it concerns us both." He meant of course that they had a common boundary; but Daglingworth didn't know the landowners' phrase, and muttered something about marching together against the bureaucrats. Tony caught Ferdo's eye across the table and raised his eyebrows as if to say 'Haven't we had enough of him, don't you think?'; and Ferdo was beginning to push back his chair, was just about to say "Shall we join the ladies?" when Daglingworth launched forth on his story about the pig.

"'SHE'LL BE ALLOWED to die a natural death," he was saying now, "which I should think is a pretty rare privilege in the pig-world. She's quite a family pet; and we owe her a pleasant retirement, after all the little fiddles she's managed on our behalf! But there *was* a bit of trouble about her in the end. It didn't come to anything because we'd got a decent bobby. He dropped me a hint that someone had been talking. Wouldn't tell me who; but a wink's as good as a nod between friends. Do you know who I think was the nigger in the woodpile?"

Ferdo had been hearing in his mind the long banshee shriek of trees coming down; the last screaming protest of sound timber tearing apart, the long roar and the crackle dying away. He stammered:

"I—I'm sorry I didn't c-catch——"

"If you ask me, the tittle-tattle came from my own gardener's cottage! Not the man, perhaps, though I wouldn't trust him farther than I could see him; but most likely his wife. She's the vicious one: a waspish little red-haired piece, agin everything. And a prig; if there's one thing I can't abide it's a female prig! Well, I couldn't do anything about it at the time; but I bore it in mind. I mean, if you can't trust your own people,—there is such a thing as common loyalty, isn't there?"

"Yes," said Ferdo at last.

"And only a couple of days ago I found out something else. You'd already engaged the chap then, in spite of what I'd said about him. It was our bobby who told me. Seems he found out that this chap Fenton has had a conviction for *theft*. Didn't go to jug, bound over for a first offence or something; I don't know the details. Anyhow I thought I'd better tell you. One doesn't like to feel one's got a thief about the place, does one? But that's up to you. It's your funeral, old man," said Daglingworth cheerfully.

¶ 11

IN THE FRONT GARDEN OF Huntsman's Cottage the children waited for the Bentley to go by.

The drive, like much else at Doddington, had fallen into decay. It had been designed with an eye to vistas, and it swept grandly between the trees, but it was also pock-marked and rutted, and rough with loose clinkers; the potholes made a chain of little lakes along it after rain. Ben reckoned that the Bentley, gaining speed as it came out of the courtyard, would hit the first of the potholes just opposite the garden-gate. Daglingworth would realise he'd got a soft tyre, and would stop to investigate it: then with any luck he'd decide he had to pump it up or change the wheel before he could go any farther.

The children looked forward to the simple pleasure of watching him do so.

"Give him a pain in the belly, give him the wind," growled Willum. "Serve him right arter all he's bin eating."

"How d'you know what they've been eating?" asked the pale, grave, bespectacled girl Carolyn, who had come out of the cottage to join the three who had let down the tyre. "Suppose you was sniffing round like Bisto kids outside the window."

"To that lot," said Gloria, "anything less than eight courses is just a snack, like, I daresay."

Carolyn declared solemnly:

"More people die of overeating than undernourishment: Mum read it in a book."

"Then perhaps when he pumps up the tyre he'll seize up sudden," said Gloria. She had a breathless way of speaking, the words tumbled out of her mouth in a bright stream: Ben always said it was like pulling the plug. "Perhaps he'll go like that old hen of Dad's that ate a needle of Mum's which got into the fowl-bowl by accident and we found it in the gizzard afterwards: that flapped its wings and spun round and round like you do when you've bowed to the new moon, and said Rrrrrrrrr and died."

THEY'D BEEN WAITING in the garden for more than half an hour. Every five minutes or so an owl which sounded crazy hooted out of the blackness. It made Carolyn jump, who herself looked owlish in the little light which spilled out from the front-room window across the so-called lawn. Mum always sat up reading half the night, it was the only time she got to read. She read enormously long books like Wells's *Outline of History* and Shaw's *Intelligent Woman's Guide to Socialism and Capitalism*. Dad, at the back of his cottage, was hammering and sawing: beginning to fix up a loft for his racing pigeons, the first thing he did when he arrived at a new place, always. The rain had stopped, though it still furred the scrawny plants in the herbaceous border. A warm wind began to blow and shook the hollyhocks; Gloria squeaked as the cold drops showered down on her. " 'Eavily 'angs the 'olly'ock," she recited in exaggerated Cockney.

Then she imitated Janet Seldon: "They seem to have rather *gorn* to seed: but you've got the woods *acrorse* the lane to play in, and I'm shuah your father is so clever at growin' things he'll soon have the garden lookin' simply ravishin'." The loony owl blew its top again, right overhead. All at once the night quickened, and the town-bred children got a sense of adventure from the rustlings and whisperings and the sea-surge sound in the great dark trees.

"I like it here," Gloria said.

"Then you better make the best of it," said Willum.

"Why?"

"Use your loaf. That ess aitch'll *tell things* about our Dad. And he'll get the sack again, most likely."

"You wouldn't think this lot would cotton on to his lot," said Ben with percipience. He was a boy who didn't talk much and he spoke as slowly as Gloria spoke fast.

"All the same old gang," said Willum.

Then they saw the Bentley's lights, cutting a scythe-swath out of the darkness as the car swung on to the drive.

SO FEW THINGS WENT QUITE RIGHT with the Fentons, so little had ever been predictable in their disrupted lives or had worked out tidily according to plan, that it seemed almost miraculous to the children when the Bentley came to a stop not ten yards away from the garden-gate. They listened, awestricken, to the dull bump and rumble; held their breaths, lay so flat that they felt cold ground against their bellies, kept their heads down, peering between the stalks. Heavily hung the hollyhock, dripping onto their necks. Out of the car got Daglingworth, black and white like a giant panda, or, as Gloria thought, a pregnant magpie, in his tight dinner jacket. He stumped round to the back of the car, hit his shin against the bumper, used a four-letter word, routed in the boot. He couldn't lay hands on the jack; and where the bloody hell was the wheel-brace? He petulantly threw things about, blamed Mrs. D. for the 'rubbish' she'd put in the boot, while she sounded plaintive inside the car. He grumbled about the drive and the blasted Baronet who expected his neighbours to risk breaking their springs every time they paid him a visit. Then he found the jack but apparently didn't know how it worked. In the end he threw it back into the boot and decided to try the pump instead. He bent down, grunting, to screw the nozzle into the valve, and began to work the pump-handle, jerking up and down like a marionette but getting slower, slower, so that Gloria kidded herself the fatal seizure was on its way; but that was wishful thinking, it never came. His breath and the pump's wheezed in time together, but when at last he stopped pumping his gulping gasps continued solo, while he went round picking up the cushions and rugs and things which he'd thrown on to the drive. He shut the boot with a bang, flopped into his seat, voices were raised briefly in some new argument, the Bentley went purring away. The children relaxed happily, scratched tickling noses and midge-bitten ears. Willum still marvelling cried out to Ben:

"It worked. You was right. It worked just as you said!"

"*She* was right." Ben corrected him. "If I'd let the tyre quite flat, as I meant to, it wouldn't have been any good."

"Who's she?" said Carolyn, sharply inquisitive.

"Susan Seldon. She came out and caught us," said Ben.

"But she didn't tell," said Gloria. "We dunno why, she didn't like old D. either. Even though she copped us she didn't let on."

"She was all dolled up for the party," said Willum. "Scent and all. And she squats down on the drive by Ben, half naked, nothing on top."

"Shut up," said Ben in an unfamiliar tone.

"So what?" said Willum sitting up on the lawn, surprised, defiant, ready to tease. "That's how she was anyway. When she bent down, you could see her titties, you could see the lot."

All at once Ben leapt at him. He didn't fight often, and when he did it was mostly in fun; his unexpected fury took Willum by surprise. Light and lithe as a wolf he sprang, seized Willum by the shoulders, pushed him backwards, knelt on his chest and, still on his knees, bounced up and down there. *"Shut your mouth, shut your bloody mouth."* Then he suddenly let go, and ran into the house without another word.

PART TWO

Set Her Alight

¶ 1

JANET FOLLOWING HER CUSTOM consulted her diary over breakfast on the morning after the Annie, and read the self-exhortations as usual:

> *Tell Northover to start Fenton in gdn (make sure he knows which are weeds!!) See if Susan will be Sec. Young Conservatives (falln into sad decline!) Talk to Rector re Church Fete Northover to run bowling for pig me white elephant F. bottle stall ca va sans dire!! Hint to Rosemary re her hair-do— not copy Susan. Order Christening mug for Godson (brick layer's) whatsisname?*

Then she came upon the reminder 'STOW!!!' Amid the excitement of yesterday she'd forgotten about Stow Horse Fair; but it deserved three exclamation-marks, it was a day out which you never missed if you could possibly help it, so Mrs. Northover was set to work cutting sandwiches in a hurry, cold lamb and lettuce from last night's leftovers, Janet changed into the right sort of old clothes and drove off with Tony and Susan in the Land Rover, towing the horse-box just in case she might be tempted to buy. Ferdo wouldn't come. He had one of his headaches, and he told them he just wanted to potter. Bumping along the drive they caught a glimpse of him, in moss-green tweeds, standing at the corner of Jubilee Wood. A couple of seconds later they looked again, he'd done the Seldon vanishing-trick, he wasn't to be seen!

BEYOND ELMBURY THE ROAD began to climb towards the hills. Signposts pointed to places with names which were lordlier, lovelier or stranger than those which belonged to the vale: Temple Guiting and Guiting Power, Condicote and Evenlode, Turkdean and Cutsdean, Upper and Lower Slaughter, Upper and Lower Swell . . . "Getting into the Daglingworth country," laughed Janet; and over the next rise they came in sight of Stow-on-the-Wold, 'where the Devil caught cold,' standing on the summit of its sheep-bitten down. The Devil wouldn't have caught cold there today: out of a sky as empty as the wold the sun blazed down upon the surging, murmurous, whinneying conglomerate of men and horses, on the slope beneath the old stone town.

Stow Fair was an Occasion; nothing remotely like it happened within hundreds of miles. You stepped back centuries when you followed the multitudinous hoof marks down to that field full of folk. Only the horses were contemporary: the humans all seemed to belong to some other day than ours. There were huge Hogarthian farmers, rolling as they walked, landlubbers who had caught a sailor's gait from their undulating downs. There were shepherds lean as their collies, Landseer-subjects with Landseer-dogs at heel. There were immemorial gipsies bitterly bargaining as they sold each other piebald ponies; the Romany version of taking in each other's washing. There were impoverished gentry, starveling by comparison with those tun-bellied yeomen who'd grown fat out of their flocks—the kind of faded, shrunken, mildly eccentric, threadbare but unmistakeable gentry who lived on the crumbs of dividends deriving from the minutest holdings of War Loan, in dilapidated draughty cottages situated at Dead Ends; who kept, perhaps, in a tumbledown orchard a single, sacred, elderly, beloved brood mare, and brought her annual foals to be sold at Stow. (And when she grew old and barren, Tony fantasticated to Susan, the family would stint themselves to buy her oats and good hay, they would make her linseed mashes every Saturday until she died, when they would dig a deep grave among the broken barren apple-trees and bury her with their own hands rather than handle the abhorred knacker's four-pounds-ten!)

Then there were the sharp-nosed, narrow-eyed horse-dealers, with tiny fishlike mouths, so that everything they said seemed to be top secret. Fellows like them had hung about the heels of John Mytton, and sold the thoroughbreds which they coarsely called cattle to such breakneck young bucks as Susan's ancestors, back in the Eighteen Hundreds. Today they stood in the crowd turning wary eyes this way and that, picking out the hunting folk, who indeed were as colourful a lot as you'd find in the pages of Jorrocks, ranging from a hermaphrodite Squarson (half a parson, half a squire) to the fiery General Bouverie who swore most terribly out hunting and whose rich repertory of oaths included such curiosities as "Fishcakes and Haemorrhoids!"

Lastly there was the usual rout of ragtag-and-bobtail hangers-on who inhabit the fringe of the horse-world always, the very spit and image of those you meet with in faded sporting prints of the inferior kind, hung in the snugs and back-bars of old-fashioned countrified hotels: old brokendown grooms, vagabonds from Ireland, warned-off jockeys, bowlegged ex-huntsmen and whips, ex-farmers ruined by racing and booze, who in their cups remembered, as if it were another life, the Point to Points they'd won in the Nineteen-thirties. Crippled by long horsemanship, these stable riffraff hobbled to and fro between the two beer-tents, leaning on sticks, cursing the arthritis in hip and knee; yet if they could live their lives over again they'd ride just as hard and recklessly, swig their Dutch courage out of the same-shaped bottles, take the same tosses, and break the same bones!

AND THERE WERE THE CHILDREN, wild as those broken ones had once been, wilder than the Cotswold hares.

The children galloped everywhere. In whatever direction you looked there was a bit of a rodeo going on. Tony and Susan watched two boys holding a long pole between them while a pretty little blonde aged fourteen or so, trying out a new pony, jumped it backwards and forwards, bareback, with only a halter rope to hold on by. Each time she jumped, the boys lifted the pole higher. Soon she fell off, the tough little boys yelled with delight, and the pony tore away riderless, scattering the crowd, barging into the slow ones and causing the nervous ones to barge into their neighbours, followed by shouts, guffaws, oaths and cheers wherever it galloped.

Tony protectively took Susan's arm after that, and she, filled with indescribable bliss, squeezed his to her side, greatly surprising him. He remembered her last night, suddenly grown up in that scanty flame-coloured dress, and he let the speculations play idly in his mind. Susan, knowing nothing about them, tossed her head like the young horses, and thought she would have liked to buck and plunge too in accord with their high spirits. Janet stopped to pass the time of day with someone who long ago had sold her a horse or bought one from her, while Tony and Susan wandered on together among the eighteenth-century crowd. In one ring an auctioneer with a voice like a corncrake was selling the hunters. In another an auctioneer who roared like the Bull of Basham was selling second-hand farm-machinery. In yet a third a young clerk with a chirp as penetrating and persistent as a chiff-chaff's was selling harness and stable sundries,—Here's a job lot for you, ladies and gents, halter and two headropes, martingale, haynet, lungeing-rein, canvas stable bucket, old horse-rug had the moth in it but still serviceable, one pound fifteen shillings, thank you sir, two pounds I'm bid, going at forty shillings. . . .

Horses everywhere, browns, bays, chestnuts, dapples, duns, palominos, skewbalds, strawberry roans, fleabitten greys, one albino with vacant pale china blue eyes, 17-hand hunters, chunky cobs, broken-down hacks, children's ponies podgy from grass, argybargy young colts, fat mares with spindle-legged foals, screamed, neighed, whinneyed, said Ha! ha!, stamped, kicked, bit, reared. All round there was bustle and bargaining, chipping, cheating, cozening, shouting, swearing; rough fun, broad comedy, grotesquerie, sheer savagery. The cruelties made Susan wince. A man who wasn't a gipsy but looked gipsyish pointlessly slashed with a heavy whip a Shetland pony no bigger than a dog. An oaf with a suffused and bloated face, running along with a young horse to show his paces to a possible buyer, gave him a cunning backhanded flip with a cane under his belly, deliberately aimed at his genitals, with the idea of making him step out. Susan *became horse* for a horrible second, writhed in *her* belly, felt the cut between *her* legs. She cried out and tugged at Tony's arm. She wanted him to perform some large dramatic act of chivalry: stride nobly forward, knock the brute down . . . But Tony, if he noticed it at all, accepted the incident as part of the pattern, something inherent in the rough tough scene, which was rather like a Breughel canvas—sometimes you saw it whole, a teeming microcosm of life, at others some trifling detail held your eye and you found yourself dwelling on it willy-nilly. Into his vision now came galumphing a tubby roan mare whose owner had no doubt represented her as being faster and more spirited— even perhaps more dangerous to life and limb—than she had ever been in her long-lost youth. But the moment of truth had now arrived, the owner had been challenged by the prospective buyer to get up on her back, and however hard he dug his heels into her well-covered ribs she loped along leisurely, pursued by mocking cries:

"*Light her up for me, then, set her alight!*"

The phrase made a kind of poetry in Tony's ears, and as he turned with a grin to Susan she nodded in quick appreciation, he didn't have to explain why that '*Set her alight!*' had stirred his spirit. Suddenly they were as close as they'd been when they went birdnesting and climbing together in the woods at Doddington.

JANET REJOINED THEM, and they looked for a quiet spot where they might eat their sandwiches without the risk of being trampled to death. Tony thought he saw an open space against the railings, at the far corner of the field; so they made their way towards it.

"Oh, look!" cried Susan suddenly; and they all three stopped and stared.

The ribby, rakish, dangerous-looking mare had four white fet-locks, perfectly matching. For the rest she was jet-black all over from nose to tail. Probably the open space which Tony had noticed was one she had cleared for herself by her antics; there wasn't another horse within thirty yards. Now she stood stock-still, but with a dramatic stillness, and the pale-faced weaselly man who was in charge of her stood stock-still at her head, and both of them looked as if they were aware of a time-bomb's ticking and had been frozen into stillness as they waited for the bang.

"Four white socks," said Tony. "Isn't there a rhyme?"

" 'One, buy; two, try; three, shy; four, fly!' " Janet said. "It's supposed to be unlucky if a horse has four." She was turning over the pages of her catalogue. "Here she is. 'Lot 11. Black mare 5 years, 15.3, sound in wind and limb. A spectacular performer.' I bet she is! Her name's Nightshade, by the way."

Susan remembered the wicked fruit she had found once when she was a child, by a damp ditchside at Doddington. She'd perilously nibbled one before Janet cried "Deadly nightshade!" and took it from her. Glossy as that berry was the black mare's coat in the sun. When she moved, the light and shade in quick alternation ran along the muscles which Leonardo loved to draw, little flickering impulses ran down her shoulder or rippled along her flank, like catspaws upon a shimmering sea.

Meanwhile Tony, who loved to pretend he was a likely customer for a horse so that he might enjoy the lies which its owner told about it, had detached himself from Susan and was talking to the furtive-looking fellow who held the black mare's bridle, but who eyed her as warily as if she had been a Black Widow spider poised to strike. He whispered to Tony from beneath his little whiskery moustache, so Susan and Janet could only catch a sentence now and then, when hyperbole took hold of him and discretion was thrown to the winds. Oh, she was a flying machine! She'd lep a haystack, lep a house, lep the course at Aintree with her legs tied together. The word 'active' recurred several times. Apparently she was somewhat too 'active' for the chicken-hearted folk one met nowadays. She'd given evidence of this activity in the ring when she came under the hammer; so nobody would bid her price and she'd been withdrawn from sale. Weasel would send her to the knackers, and then cut his own throat, rather than accept the miserable sum he had been offered.

Janet nudged Susan's arm. Tony had noticed some fault or blemish, and he took a step nearer to the black mare. Yes, there was a long jagged scar running down the off hind from stifle joint to hock. Tony bent down to have a look, and as he did so the mare nervously swung round and turned her hindquarters towards the sun, which showed up some smaller scars on her near hind leg as well. Tony, having spotted the injuries, pressed his advantage to the full. "Accident in traffic?" he enquired casually, but in a tone which suggested all sorts of dark suspicions: that the mare would shy at every motor-bike and bolt a mile if she met a bus. Weasel raised his voice in passionate denial; he waved his free arm too, and this so alarmed the mare that she went back on her hocks, heaving him towards her by the reins. It seemed to Susan, as she watched the little drama, that at last the truth was being dragged out of him, painfully and against his will, as he braced himself against the mare's tugging, and the admissions came from between his teeth in little breathless gasps.

TRAFFIC? SHE WOULDN'T turn her head to look at the Lord Mayor's Show. Wouldn't take no notice of a regiment of tanks.

It was in the Show Ring, Mister.

We tried to make her into a jumper. She'd clear a five-barred gate as if it was no more trouble than steppin' over a thrippeny-bit in the roadway.

But she hadn't got the temperament for it: hotted up in the ring.

My kid brother was on her back. Suddenly she was bilin' over and leppin' into the elements.

Over the ropes as if she was flying Becher's.

Into the car park, kickin' spots off the cars. And my kid brother took to 'Orspital.

Tore the skin off her legs, but I got a vet's certificate, here it is, Mister, sound in wind *and* limb.

If anyone wanted her for a show jumper I'd shoot her, Mister, I'd shoot *meself*, rather than sell her to him.

But if a young gent like yourself, who I can see by the look of you *likes* 'em a bit active, wanted a good-lookin' young hunter that'd lep a haystack——

TONY AT THIS POINT began to run his hand down the mare's near fetlock. She put her ears back and edged away. Susan could hear Weasel swearing at her under his breath, and she thought how that vicious small sound would frighten you if you were an animal in his power. Then suddenly she noticed some-thing extraordinary. Over the mare's glossy neck a dark matt patch was slowly spreading; wet streaks from it seeped down her shoulders. Tony had spotted it now, and was staring at it in surprise. He laid his hand on the sweating shoulder, gave Weasel a look, wiped his hand ostentatiously on a handkerchief, and came back to Janet and Susan.

"What do you make of that, Cousin Janet?" he asked.

"At some time or other, she's been beaten up."

"She might have been quite something," Tony said, glancing back at her. "She's perfectly sound as far as I can tell."

"Well, they've certainly ruined her now. There's big money in show jumpers, so I suppose you get these fools on the fringe of the business who imagine you can make a horse jump by frightening it to death."

The mare still twitched and trembled. Raw with pity, Susan went up to her. Tony and Janet watched as she put her hand on the high withers, stretched out her fingers and began to tease out the long mane. The ears, that had been laid right back like a squatting rabbit's, began to flex forward at last.

"Goodness, look at that!" Tony said.

Janet smiled. "Seems it's men she's frightened of."

The sweat-patches still showed like charcoal smudges against the shine, but the panic which engendered them was dying down. The twitching and quivering ceased. Susan, looking pleased with herself, cocked an eye at the saddle, as if to say "Shall I?" Tony recognised that look—Susan at the age of nine or so looking up the trunk of a just-climbable tree: Shall I, shan't I, yes I must! For some reason the recognition delighted him; and now she turned her head and gave him a grin, inviting a dare. "May she?" he said to Janet, who laughed; "She can look after herself." The Aunt, Ferdo's sister, whom Susan had stayed with during the war, was one of the wilder Seldons; she went in for young Irish horses, straight from the bog. Susan had spent most of her holidays on and off their backs from the age of seven until she was twelve.

"Up you get, then!" Tony called.

Weasel, whose pinched face and tremulous moustache reflected all his emotions, turned from Susan to Tony in dismay; he had few principles, but murder was not in his commission, the look seemed to say. At last he offered the reins to Susan as reluctantly as if he were the apothecary of Mantua handing the poison to Romeo. He then retreated rapidly, muttering "Mind you, she's

active" in admonition or excuse. Tony went forward to give
Susan a hand. She'd collected up the reins, and already the mare
was beginning to dance. " 'Matthew, Mark, Luke, and John,
Hold my horse while I get on!' " she laughed, pleasing him again
with a reminder of their childhood, when she used to say that
rhyme. He caught hold of the reins and stood by the mare's
head.

"Want a leg up?"

"No, I'll jump. Hang on." Then she was in the saddle crying,
"I've got her," was feeling for the stirrups, had gathered the
reins. Weasel's moustache twitched and 'his nose was as sharp a
a pen' as he gazed up at Susan, casual and collected in her old
blue jeans, which she'd nearly grown out of and were rucked up
to her knees.

THE MARE STOOD STILL; but it was a dynamic stillness.
Susan was conscious of a sort of suppressed panic *rippling* as it
were underneath her seat. It struck her for the first time that this
Fair Ground must appear to Nightshade just as alarming as the
Show Ring from which she had incontinently bolted. The crowd
made a pattern of continual menace as it surged this way and
that, converged, scattered, receded, advanced and performed
small purposeless antics like a hive of disturbed ants. Now from
one quarter, now from another, rose raucous inexplicable sounds.
Yahoos! thought Susan getting a Houyhnhnm's-eye view of
them.

Sitting there, patting Nightshade's neck, altogether possessed
by compassion for the wild misused thing, she didn't hear the
thudding hoofs until they were almost upon her, until Tony was
raising an arm in warning and Nightshade like a rocket was
going up in the air. Then Susan heard the thuds, looked over her
shoulder and saw that peaceable galumphing roan, prodded at
last into some semblance of activity, coming full tilt at Nightshade from the rear. The owner, himself alarmed by his unaccustomed speed, was shouting, "Out of my way!" while the prospective buyer continued to utter his strange poetic abracadabra,
Light her up for me, set her alight! as he raced along with wildly
flapping arms, like a plump bustard inadequately winged that
tries in vain to get up enough speed for a take-off.

Susan felt Nightshade rising up between her thighs, and thought: She's going to bolt and nothing I can do will stop her. She'd never been afraid on a horse before; now for a moment she had the same odd feeling of purely physical fear which she had when she climbed to the top of Elmbury Abbey Tower and dared herself to lean over the parapet and look down. The feeling had been right down in her stomach, almost sexy. It was uncomfortable but there had been a temptation to tease herself with it, to look over the parapet again and again.

For two or three seconds, now, Susan's body knew this extraordinary fear-feeling that lay halfway between pleasure and pain. During that brief space the roan passed within feet of her, Nightshade's sideways leap sent Weasel scurrying, and the mare got her head down, so that there was nothing in front of Susan at all. For a moment it was touch and go. Then, feeling her mouth as she shortened the reins, Susan collected her together, imposed her authority, took command, and turned her in a wide circle, cantering delightfully on the razor edge of fear.

She came back to Janet, and pulled up so gently that Nightshade, shortening the pace of her canter, seemed to be doing a series of small diminishing bucks without moving forward, an agreeable rocking-horse motion which made Janet laugh.

"We didn't expect to see you back for quite a long time," Janet said.

Tony was confabulating with Weasel. They both looked very earnest. Susan heard the word "guineas" and thought Tony was amusing himself at Weasel's expense, by pretending that he was going to buy.

FORTY GUINEAS A LEG then, said Weasel, and it's givin' her away. His morale had been boosted by Susan's safe return. You saw how a slip of a girl could handle her, he cried gleefully. I'll be lookin' for a hook to hang meself on, if I part with her for less than forty guineas a leg.

Some mysterious taboo, such as primitive tribes have, forbade him at this stage to state his price in so many words. Tony, bargaining for the fun of it, fell in with the convention and remarked pleasantly that considering the animal's history anybody who offered more than twenty-five guineas a leg his head would want looking at. Weasel edged closer, and putting his tiny mouth within inches of Tony's ear, hissed passionately: *Thirty-five guineas a leg and for God's sake don't say yes or I'll be shootin' meself tomorrow!*

Tony thought that if he were a horse-dealer he would always put up a pretty girl on any animal he was trying to sell. Susan, flushed and excited, her hair all over the place, tossing back her head, added fifty pounds to Nightshade's value.

Suddenly the idea came into his mind: Well, why *not* buy her the mare, now she's so beautifully shown us how to ride her? He could well afford it: he'd had a good bet last week, nine to four in tenners. Rather fun to give Sue a little surprise. He was still puzzled, surprised, amused and a little bit excited by her growing-up.

He whispered to Weasel, whose secretive ways seemed to be catching: I'll bid you a hundred guineas, take it or leave it.

A hundred and thirty, Weasel whispered back.

Not on your life, a hundred and ten.

Look here, Guv'nor, breathed Weasel, make it a hundred and twenty-five, and I'll give you back a fiver for luck.

At the mere prospect of his having to do so, a sort of sacrificial spasm shook his meagre frame. Shake hands on it, Guv', he wheezed in agony, shake hands before I changes me mind!

SUSAN DIDN'T UNDERSTAND what it was about. How unpleasant for Tony, to be shaking hands with Weasel.

She was still on Nightshade's back, determined to remain there until the last moment, appalled at the prospect of handing her back into Weasel's charge. Love and pity tore at her, for she could still sense the ripples of suppressed panic going on under the saddle, and she knew that she was still personally engaged with that panic, as she tried to send messages of encouragement along the reins. She knew that if she relaxed for a moment, and some small untoward occurrence took her unawares, Nightshade would be off again, madly bolting away from some invisible in-audible Terror galloping at her heels. It was lovely to feel that she held the whole spirit of the mare in her two hands. She hummed to herself, because she was still happily afraid.

Tony with a final nod to Weasel came back to them.

"What on earth have you been up to?" Janet asked him.

"You don't really mind, Cousin Janet, do you?" He always

used that old-fashioned style, Cousin Ferdo, Cousin Janet, taking
pleasure in the quaint formality yet half-mocking at it. He had a
way, which Susan loved, of affecting rather elaborate manners,
kissing your hand or helping you out of a car with an air, while
at the same time he seemed to be laughing at himself for his
affectation. "Dear Cousin Janet, *please* don't be cross. But Sue
rides her so beautifully; it suddenly struck me that she might
make something of her,—something really good: and after all,
her birthday's not very far off."

"You dear absurd boy." Janet was laughing. "You mean to say
you've gone and bought her?"

Still Susan could hardly believe it. For me, for me, this
princely present shining in the sun? Oh, glory, he loves me he
loves me he loves me! she sang to herself as she dived off Nightshade's back, threw her arms round Nightshade's neck, pouring
out love on her, loving her mother as she pressed the reins into
her hands, Hold her please, Mummie, for just a minute,—loving
everybody, above all loving Tony as she rushed up to him and
threw herself into his arms. Great splendours of giving and receiving love opened up ahead of her and stretched forever and
ever, so that she was sure she had never been so happy in her
life before. Then the silliest thing happened to spoil it. She was
about to kiss Tony, she had put up her face to him as she'd often
done before, when all at once something told her that it was
different now, different because of the way she loved him and the
way she assumed he loved her: they could no longer kiss in front
of other people like that. So at the very last moment she turned
her face from him; and even as she did so she realised too late
that *that* was the give-away,—if only she'd kissed him right on
the mouth in front of her mother it would have been natural and
accepted, it was her hesitation and change of mind that made a
fool of her and told them all! And now, the thing she always
dreaded, now she began to blush. You little fool, you little fool,
she thought,—the blush got worse,—Tony was looking surprised
at her—oh if only God would send an earthquake to swallow her
up! He didn't; but instead there came with ungainly speed the
returning roan, in a foamy lather, more or less out of control;
Nightshade fly-jumped sideways with Janet hanging on to the
reins, the roan walloped heavily by like some ponderous palfrey

at a joust, and Susan thought thankfully that perhaps her silly blushes might be forgotten, as Tony lifted her up and swung her out of the way, and the weird cries of *set her alight* rang loudly in her ears.

¶ 2

MEANWHILE FERDO POTTERED away his morning.

First he made his way to Ferdinando's Oak, because from that point of vantage he might be able to work out where the new road would go, if Daglingworth had been telling the truth about it.

During a restless night he had dreamed of huge trees tottering against the sky, acres of desolation when they fell, stumps new-sawn and table-topped standing in rows like tombstones. But this morning when he woke up he could not at first remember what it was that made him unhappy. Gradually through his hangover loomed up a recollection of what Daglingworth had said after dinner; then he remembered the surveyors, and the fear of the new road came down on his mind like one of those formless black summer clouds which countryfolk call blight, and settled there, blighting the morning.

H E S A W N O W that if the road were to run from Doublegates Farm to the Ferry, as Daglingworth had hinted, it would be bound to pass within a few hundred yards of Ferdinando's Oak; or perhaps it might find Ferdinando's Oak standing right in its path. Would a motorway made for cars which could do a hundred miles an hour turn aside out of respect for a tree four hundred years old, he wondered?

He walked round in the shade of the tree, peering up into the darkness, hoping for a sight of the red squirrel. No doubt somewhere up there Ferinando's Owl blinked away the long daylight; within the cleft that ran half-way up the tree, bats rustled and creaked their leathery wings; among the branches magpies, jays, and scores of smaller birds went about their affairs; within the crevices of the bark hid beetles, woodlice, earwigs, insects innumerable; upon the leaves myriad caterpillars munched. A

glimmer of wonder struck through Ferdo's gloom as he contemplated the vast hospitality of such a tree to creatures great and
small.

Ever since he was a boy the Oak had fascinated him, ever since
with his first pocket knife he had carved his initials on a smooth
patch where the bark had fallen away and left an area of bare
and weathered wood. They no longer stood alone there. Shelter-
ing soldiers, when Doddington Park was a military camp, had
whiled away their boredom by scratching their names and those
of their units. Lancashire Fusiliers, Somerset Light Infantry,
Sherwood Foresters, Green Howards, Berkshires, Devons, Chesh-
ires, Middlesex Die-hards, Ox. and Bucks known as The Green-
jackets, East Kents known as The Buffs: it touched Ferdo's sense
of history to find the roll-call of those foot-slogging men upon the
tree which three hundred years ago had seen Cavalier and
Roundhead skirmishing in his Park. He spent half an hour at
Ferdinando's Oak, deciphering the weathered scratches left
behind by the men who marched away; the men of the old
County Regiments whose names strung together added up to
the sum total of England.

WALKING ON, he followed the course which he supposed the
new road might take: across the Park and alongside Cuckoo Pen:
by Sexton's Spinney, skirting Honeysett Farm; below Seven
Men's Tump with its plume of ancient, ragged elms, then down
the slope to the river and, on the way there, slap through the two
little woods which he loved best, the ones called Trafalgar and
Waterloo. Their tall oaks, straight as soldiers, dated respectively
from 1805 and 1815. If the new road were going to cross the river
anywhere near the Ferry, it would mean the end of Trafalgar
and Waterloo. Could the Powers That Be really do such things
upon a man's land nowadays? Of course they could; for that was
the way the weather was, that was the way the tide was running.
You could fight against men, thought Ferdo, but you couldn't
dispute with the weather and the tide.

ON HIS WAY HOME, he came by Huntsman's. It was Fenton's dinner-time, and the man was rigging up a clothes-line between two posts which he had erected in a narrow strip of garden

at the side of the cottage. Ferdo thought he had better give him
a word of welcome. Going down the path, he caught a glimpse of
Mrs. Fenton's pale sharp face at a front window, took off his cap
to her, and got a surprised stare in return. Fenton, preoccupied
with his job, hadn't seen him; the clothes-line was operated by a
series of blocks and tackles and, as Ferdo approached, Fenton was
in the act of hoisting, as if it were a signal, a row of homely and
utilitarian garments,—aprons, skirts, long combinations, short
combinations, woollen pants, and black bloomers.

"Avast heaving," laughed Ferdo, and Fenton turned round to
gaze at him resentfully. Ferdo knew exactly what he was thinking: 'You'd better not treat me as if I was still in the bloody
Navy!' Obviously he was going to be an awkward cuss; but there
was some quality about him, of pride or independence, which
Ferdo had liked when he offered him the job; and now he liked
the sudden change of expression, from a scowl to a quick satur-
nine grin which Fenton gave him over his shoulder, as he belayed
the line to a cleat which he'd bolted on to the pole.

"Very seamanlike," said Ferdo; and then he felt rather disloyal
to Janet for praising the clothes-line which, he reckoned, must
have introduced those combinations into the view from her
bedroom-window.

"I hope you're going to be happy here," he said.

"Hope so," Fenton grunted.

"Northover's shown you round the garden?"

Fenton nodded.

"And fixed you up with tools and things?"

"Yes." Fenton clearly wasn't going to say 'Sir' as if he were still
a rating speaking to an officer. Ferdo noticed that his large hands,
hanging by his sides, were nervously opened and shut. There was
nothing furtive about him: he looked you straight in the face;
but when he did so there was fear, defiance or resentment in his
eyes. It occurred to Ferdo that he would have seen Daglingworth's car rolling up the drive within a few hours of his arrival;
he would have guessed that Daglingworth was likely to pass on
that story about a conviction for theft; in any case, he would
imagine the bosses ganging up on him, he'd feel persecuted, bitter and insecure. Ferdo wished he hadn't listened to Daglingworth's tittle-tattle and half-believed it; and for a moment he

was as embarrassed as Fenton, who was shuffling from one foot to another, still opening and shutting his hands.

"Well, if there's anything you want, don't hesitate——" And Ferdo hurried on his way. When he got to the garden-gate something, perhaps a tiny rustle, made him look up into the tree where he had spotted the squirrel yesterday. The glint of sunlight on spectacles caught his eye; then Carolyn moved, and he saw her face peering down at him, then another face, then a third. The Fenton children were learning to climb; but though he shouted "Hello" they did not wave or shout in reply. They lay along their boughs watchful as animals, pretending perhaps to be spies or pythons, seeing Ferdo as their enemy or their prey.

AFTER LUNCH he went down into the cellar to see if the water was still there.

It had risen half an inch since yesterday, and the match-stick which he dropped into it swam round in circles, so presumably it was still on the move. There was something almost sinister about it; the way it had stolen into the cellar though there'd been no recent rain. A sense of ill-defined uneasiness, which had troubled Ferdo all the morning, now grew sharper. He climbed back up the steps and set out in search of Egbert, who was more likely than anybody else to be able to explain the mysterious flood.

Egbert was a kind of handyman. He lived alone in a cottage at the back of the stables, rent-free for no particular reason, where his father before him had lived rent-free. His job, for which he was paid the current agricultural wage, was purposely undefined; for if one tried to tie him down to anything he would wander off into the woods and do nothing at all. There was a tacit understanding that he cleaned the shoes every morning. After that, according to how the spirit moved him, he would find for himself useful jobs of carpentry, outside painting, or tidying-up. Sometimes Ferdo would ask him: "What are you going to do today, Egbert?" and he always made the same answer:

"Take a look around and see what wants a-doing."

He would never dig the garden; that was beneath him; but he would repair the rose-pergola, mend a stone wall, put a drainpipe in a soggy corner or build a little bridge over a stream. He loved to do small craftsman's jobs; but he must do them at his own pace, and when he thought they wanted a-doing. Sometimes

he would take a day off without asking; on others you would find
him still working at dusk on a summer evening. No one was
prepared to make a guess about his age. He looked about seventy; but he had looked seventy to Ferdo as long ago as 1926, the
year of the General Strike. At Doddington the strike was remembered chiefly on his account. Although he belonged to no Trades
Union or political party, he had struck. He had not announced
he was doing so; he had simply absented himself from work. The
shoes were put out as usual; but from the 3rd to the 14th of May,
1926, Egbert did not turn up to clean them. (Ferdo, who loved
leather, did the job himself, and rather enjoyed it.) On the morning after the strike collapsed, Egbert returned to duty, and took a
look around to see what wanted a-doing. When they happened to
meet later that morning, neither he nor Ferdo mentioned the
strike. Neither of them had so far forgotten his manners as to
mention it since.

FERDO FOUND HIM at last in the stable-yard, muttering
over some complicated carpentry. Egbert scarcely looked up
when he greeted Ferdo with the single word "Aartenüne." Like
Fenton, he would call nobody 'Sir'; but unlike Fenton he'd never
had to. When he was better-tempered he would sometimes address Ferdo as 'Squire.'

Ferdo watched him for a minute or two in silence, then asked
him what he was making.

"A jump," he said. "Jack Northover asked for it for your
darter. Break her neck, likely. Dussunt thee blame I."

He was fixing hinged legs on to the uprights to the jump, and
making a craftsman's job of it despite his strong dislike of horses
and everything associated with them. He refused to have anything to do with horses, to feed them or clean out their stables,
even when Jack Northover was laid up with 'flu. Ferdo had
amused himself by inventing a theory about this: that it was an
atavistic resentment, something to do with the traditional attitude of the peasantry towards the superior person who went on
horseback. For once you jumped up into the saddle you lost
contact with those who had their feet on the ground. You became
arrogant towards them or oblivious of them; while they, tramp-
ing through the mud, splashed by your passing, became envious
or servile. You had to lean down to speak to them: an act of

condescension; whereas they had to look up to you. Perhaps, thought Ferdo, playing with the idea, this ancient grudge of Egbert's went back to Saxon versus Norman, to serf versus feudal lord, to footsoldier versus knight!

He leaned against the paddock gate and told Egbert about the water in the cellar. Egbert went on hammering and showed no sign that he had heard. He always took a long time to answer questions. His thoughts mustn't be hurried as they roved back into the past.

"Happened before," he said at last.

"When?"

"Often enough I dessay. Last time as I knows on was in thy father's day. Fust it came in a little trickle like as you said——"

"Rising slowly?"

"Riz and riz till it was nigh three foot deep; then suddenly went away. When the floor dried thy father told my father to lay cement six inches thick——"

And then Egbert, who was a good storyteller, put down his hammer, slowly straightened himself, and began to recite a dialogue which he must have had from his father long ago, but which was as fresh in his mind as if he had heard it with his own ears only yesterday.

THAT wun't kip it out, my father tells un.

Then make it nine inches.

Nor nine inches wun't kip it out either. Thee carsn't hold water down, 'tis a strong and furious thing.

Then make it TWELVE inches thick! says thy father to mine; for he was a self-willed man.

Thee might as well save thy money and my time, my father says, but all the same he lays best cement twelve inches thick, and all round the cellar walls a foot thick too. Arter that came a dry time, and one day thy father says to mine, *Well, it did the trick in the cellar,* says he, *dry's a bone.*

That's as may be, my father says.

Seeing's believing, says thine.

Thee carsn't see through twelve inches of cement.

God damn it, says thy father, tetchy-like, *we've kep' the water out, an't we?* .

It bides its time, my father says.

And one night next winter there came a crack so loud it woke up the servants and they was scurrying round to see who'd a-gone and shot isself; for it was just like a gun going off.

‘‘THE WATER BROKE THROUGH?’’ Ferdo said.

"Thee ought to a-sin it. Shooting up from the crack in the floor as if it come out of a fire-hose. And then a lot of little fountains started, and soon the cement was all cracked up into lumps, and it took my father two–three days to carry 'em up the steps and wheel 'em away."

"Did the water stay for long?" Ferdo asked.

"Maybe. I dunno exactly how long. But one summer it seeped away slow, and left a bit of slime on the floor. And next winter, though that were a wet one, the water didn't come back. And next summer the slime dried into a sort of musty dust. Far as I know, the water's never come back till now."

"What makes it come and go?"

Egbert shrugged his shoulders. "Springs down there, maybe a stream underground. There was a well once by the kitchen door and sometimes 'twas empty, sometimes 'twas full—you never could tell which it would be, for it weren't according to the season." Egbert paused and pondered. "Water's a funny thing," he said. "Thee's got to go along with it, thee carsn't hold it down against its will, any more than thee can hold rubbub down. It comes and it goes. Maybe for as long as a man's lifetime it'll lie there quiet as weed-seeds in winter; lie there so still thee'll forget all about it. Then sudden-like it'll come to life and run wild and rampage."

Ferdo had a vivid momentary glimpse of what was in Egbert's mind, he saw the water as a Presence, potent, elemental, laired deep down in the earth beneath the Manor, long quiescent, now suddenly aroused . . .

"It comes and it goes," said Egbert again. "There was a saying about it. My father used to tell it to thine——"

Egbert's head was full of old sayings, mostly in rhyme. Rhyme was the mnemonic by which country folk remembered such things. But Egbert could not recollect this one, though he fell into one of his long silences and sent his thoughts burrowing

down like tap-roots into the secret springs of the past. At last he
shook his head.

"Maybe I'll mind it one day," he said. "Maybe I wun't."

ALTOGETHER it was an uneasy day. Forebodings about the
road lay like a shadow across Ferdo's mind, he was not altogether
happy about Fenton, the news from Korea had been grimmer
than ever when he turned on the wireless at lunch-time. Some
politician had spoken of 'the risk of a wider conflict,' and Ferdo
remembering the H-bomb had shuddered at the phrase. This
afternoon, as always when he was dismayed, he sought comfort in
small familiar things. He watched the spotted flycatchers in the
wistaria at the back of the stables, as they taught their fledglings
to hawk for flies. They must be the great-great-grandchildren (he
couldn't work out how many 'greats') of the birds he'd watched
here in 1939. Soon they'd be off, to Natal or wherever it was they
wintered, but they would fly north again in May, just as they'd
done for thousands of years and would do for thousands more,
whatever catastrophes might befall mankind.

Ferdo pottered down to the bottom of the garden, saw that the
Worcesters were colouring up on the neat little apple-tree which
was like a Kate Greenaway illustration, heard a party of greenfinches twittering in the hedge where there always used to be
greenfinches, came across a clump of Turk's-cap lilies in the place
where he remembered them growing when he was a boy, and
found as always a sort of reassurance in the seasonal recurrence of
things.

SO HE WENT UP to the Lily Pond to have a look at the
Tropaeolum speciosum burning bright against the almost-black
cypress-hedge. He always found it difficult to believe that this
spectacular thing was first cousin to the homely dull nasturtium.
It looked as if it had set the tall hedge alight; yet all this
pyrotechny sprang from two or three fingerling roots, no thicker
than lobworms, which he and Janet had planted here in the days
of the otter. That would have been in 1936, thought Ferdo, as
he sat down on the wrought-iron seat in the sun and, helped by
the claret he'd drunk with his lunch, dozed himself gently back
into the past; for 1936 was the summer when Janet took on the

Mastership of those detestable hounds which reminded him of the shoughs, water-rugs and demiwolves in *Macbeth*—the summer when she learned to blow frightful sounds out of a hunting-horn, and wore a dam-silly blue-and-scarlet get-up like a female version of a French *chasseur*. Janet was a great one for killing the things she loved: but having pursued otters relentlessly for half the season, the contradictory woman got herself bitten in the course of *rescuing* a young one from the water-rugs' jaws, brought it home, patiently tamed it, and actually sold out some shares in order to build the pond for it! Ferdo in his half-dream remembered how he and Janet would have their tea in the newly-built summerhouse, and eat warm apricots just picked off the high garden wall, while they watched the otter playing in its private swimming pool. When it swam just beneath the surface it looked almost silvery because of the little air-bubbles clinging to its coat . . .

"DADDY," SUSAN WAS SAYING, "wake up wake up wake up he's bought me a horse."

She was carrying a bathing-dress and a towel, and she stood in front of him swinging them and jigging up and down. "He bought me a horse he bought me a horse at Stow Fair."

Ferdo, confused and with a dry mouth, said, "Who?" and she put her hands on his shoulders and shook him.

"Tony of course and she's called Nightshade black wicked like the Deadly I don't know why he did it what she cost must have cost the earth he just bought her suddenly on the spur of the moment because I'd ridden her and she didn't have me off though she's mad as March hares because some brutes have beaten her up trying to make her into a show jumper but she shines like those black Nightshade berries goes like mad jump anything." She took a deep breath. "Isn't it glorious blazing hot we're going to have a swim."

Ferdo finally heaved himself out of his doze and said,"Where's Tony?"

"He's changing in his bedroom." Susan gave another gasp and looked all round her at a world which Ferdo, fully awake now, knew was brighter by many shades than his. "Isn't it beautiful here, that creeper and the water-lilies, and the statue of the Boy.

I wonder if the man who made him knew how lovely he'd become when he was tarnished? You ought to make him pee again, Daddy.—Look, Tony will be here in a minute, I must get changed."

FERDO WENT WITH HER to the summerhouse and pushed open the door.

"I don't suppose anybody's been in here for years," he said. He'd forgotten about the soldiers. It was a curious thing about the military, he thought: their movements were planned with meticulous care, typewriters tapped away, orders were issued, rear-parties detailed—all so different from the casual coming and going of ships; yet the debris they left behind them always gave the impression that they had decamped precipitately in the face of surprise attack by a superior foe. Ever since he came home he'd been finding abandoned gas-masks, tin-hats, blank cartridges, webbing equipment and haversacks all over the place; and there had been so much waste-paper littered about in the Park that he got Egbert to fit a sharp spike to the end of his walking-stick, with which he went bumph-collecting and gradually cleared up the mess.

The summerhouse must have been some minor functionary's office. There were pin-ups stuck on the walls, almost all of them redheads, as if the owner of the office had specialised in that line. Although the pictures were only a few years old they were as out-of-date already as war-time slang and war-time tunes. "I wish I knew," said Ferdo, "how girls can become old-fashioned-looking when they haven't any clothes on."

Hanging on the wall among the redheads was a notice-board with Battalion Orders pinned to it. Across the roneo'd sheet someone about to be demobilised had scrawled his exultant valediction: AND BALLS TO YOU REGIMENTAL SERGEANT-MAJOR! Nearby a Chad, chalked by perhaps the same nonconformist hand, remarked plaintively: WOT NO PEACE?

"You're too young to remember about Chads?" said Ferdo.

"Oh no. We used to see them on walls everywhere. Why are they called Chads?"

"Nobody knows." They had always fascinated Ferdo. They were strange manifestations of the English spirit, and disconcerting—rather like Shakespeare's Fools, for their comments were pertinent though their expressions were inane. During the war they had sprung up wherever there were service-men who could lay hands on a stump of chalk: idiot faces with long noses poked over imaginary barriers, and captions demanding WOT NO BANGERS? when there was a shortage of sausages; WOT NO FRATTING? among the rubble-strewn streets of Hamburg; WOT NO BEER? amid the vineyards of Italy.

But this Chad belonged to the post-war. It spoke for the disillusioned; not defiant, but resigned. Its oafish face stared vacuously into Ferdo's as he went out of the summerhouse; and its plaint found an echo in his mind as he followed the path beside the Lily Pool to the gap in the cypress-hedge. As he went down the steps beyond it, his eye was caught by Mrs. Fenton's proletarian washing bellying out in the light wind, only thirty yards away from the courtyard entrance-gates. Through the gates, just then, came a telegraph-boy on a bicycle. Somebody's belated congratulations on our Annie, he thought? But he was conscious at the same time of a just-perceptible qualm; it reminded him that he belonged to the generation that had tended to associate bad news with telegraph-boys.

¶ 3

SUSAN TOOK OFF HER SHOES and wriggled out of her tight jeans and felt the floor-dust soft and creepy on the bare soles of her feet. She noticed that the dust was all scuffled up in one spot where Rosemary and her boyfriend had been. What a funny place to make love in, she thought, looking about her with lively interest at the scribbling on the walls and the words she half-knew or guessed at,—some of them looked very odd, perhaps the soldiers didn't know how to spell them! And all those naked girls. She was struck by a sudden awareness of her own shape as she pulled on her bathing-dress; an awareness too, half-dismaying, half-exciting, of the disturbing hunger of men. They stuck up those pictures and looked at them; and the simple silly frustrated ones wrote things on walls and drew things. Goodness. Then she thought about Rosemary. An intense curiosity possessed her, and

became part of her general excitement and of her particular
happiness, which of course was about Tony and about Nightshade. He bought me a horse he bought me a horse he loves me
he loves me! She was too excited to wait for Tony, and she could
no longer bear the feeling of that dry dirty cobwebby creepy dust
upon her soles and toes. So she rushed out of the summerhouse
and dived straight into the reflection of the blazing climber
which struck against her body like cold fire.

A COUPLE OF MINUTES LATER Tony was beside her; his
shallow dive carried him half-way across the pool, with his arms
still close to his sides he glided up to her and his brown shoulder
just touched hers as he came to rest. There were pink water-lilies
all round them. She said:
    "Is pink champagne that colour?"
    "I daresay. I've never tried it."
    "I shall one day. I shall try everything."
    They swam round among the lily-pads and she found a small
beetle crawling on one of them like a shipwrecked Crusoe on a
desert island. Dragonflies with delicate blue bodies sailed by on
shimmering wings. The long stalks of the lilies brushed against
Susan's legs and were slimy like octopus-tentacles, so she swam
clear of them and Tony joined her; for quite a long time they
floated on their backs in the sun, and the sky was so bright it
shone pink through the pulsing blood in their closed eyelids.
Then they paddled up to the Boy and inspected him from below,
and crawling out on to the grass lay down at last beside him. As
they lay there Susan glancing sideways at Tony caught him looking at her, she thought with surprise. But why surprise? She was
momentarily put out by something she did not understand.
Then he said:
    "You looked smashing last night. I wanted to tell you. Shakes-
peare had a word for it: something about a fair wench in flame-
coloured taffeta!"
    She didn't know the quotation and it seemed marvellous to
her that anyone who could soldier and shoot and ride and swim
and keep wicket for the Army, and who was also good-looking
and tall and lean and dashing and gay, should be able to quote
Shakespeare too. She closed her eyes in great happiness and when
she opened them, once again he was looking at her, and once

again it was in a way she couldn't understand at all, half-puzzled,
half-amused: agreeably disturbing. He said:

"I don't know why, you make me think of an apricot. I saw
one nearly ripe on the south wall in the garden as I was coming
up here. I think I'll run and get it for you. It's something special
to eat an apricot warmed by the sun."

He got up and strode over her as she lay there, and she
watched him through half-shut eyes, bewildered and perturbed
and excited, as he ran fast for fun on bare feet, over the short
grass towards the gap in the cypress-hedge.

T H E T E R R A - C O T T A B R I C K S behind the apricot tree were
hot as an oven-wall. Tony found three ripe apricots which were
as warm in his hands as eggs taken from under a hen. He carried
them back to Susan where she lay spread-eagled in the sun. Her
growing-up still astonished him, for only last holiday, when he'd
spent Easter at Doddington, she was still a child. They went
birdnesting together, and when he lifted her up on his shoulder
to look at a chaffinch's nest on an apple-bough he'd been no more
conscious of her body than he would have been of a boy's. He was
very conscious of it now, lambent upon the lawn, long legs
stretched out, arms thrown open wide.

He sat down beside her and watched her eat the apricots.

"Yes," she said. "They do taste quite different, exciting, when
they're warm."

"There you are. Another new experience to add to your list!"

The overwhelming richness of life suddenly struck her: new
and unexperienced things to feel, see, hear, taste, find out about,
every week, day, hour, nobody could live long enough.

"Tony," she said, sitting up. "Of all the things you haven't
done, big or small, what do you want to do most before you
die?"

"Oh, ride in the National," he said without any hesitation.
"Not win it; I wouldn't mind about that. But to know what it
feels like just before the start, with the wind blowing cold
through your thin blouse, and no tummy. And then to see one of
those bloody great fences looming up, and to find out how frightened you are, and what *that* feels like. But I don't suppose I ever
shall."

"Why not?"

"Not quite good enough. Not enough practice. Absurd of me even to think of it." He looked almost embarrassed, as if he wished he hadn't said anything about it. "One'd have to be riding hard all the season," he said. "While I stay in the Army I can only manage a race now and then. It was rather a lineshoot I'm afraid."

Susan realised that this was his special, cherished and secret ambition which he'd confessed to her, and it touched her that he should be shy about it, who had always before in her presence been so confident and sure. His diffidence seemed to be a kind of compliment, an admission of their closeness, an acceptance of a special relationship,—and without thinking what she was doing (except that she wanted to show him somehow that she understood) she leaned back against his shoulder. At once he put his arm round her, they both lay back, and blissfully she nestled against him with her head on his chest. Soon he began rather idly, almost abstractedly, to run his fingers up and down underneath her arm; then, inch by inch, he put his hand on her breast under her bathing-dress and she heard herself say most casually "I'm still wet there," in a voice that did not sound a bit like hers because she'd been holding her breath. Among a whole confusion of things Susan was most conscious of her terrifying innocence. She thought that something was expected of her, she ought to say something or do something, and the need became more imperative as Tony went on touching her in that odd abstracted way. She couldn't think of anything to say, so she took her whole fortune into her hands and suddenly rolled over towards him, pulling him to her and pressing against him and worshipping him with all of herself. She opened her eyes for a second and saw the great red streak of the climber against the black cypress and told herself, dramatically, that it would be imprinted upon her mind like a burning brand for ever and ever. She pressed her mouth clumsily to Tony's, and then instead of kissing her he put his hands very strong and firm on her elbows and gently pressed her away from him. Next he was sitting up beside her and half-laughing at her but in fact looking much more embarrassed than he had done when he spoke to her about the National. Then it was Doomsday for Susan, with a voice in her head tolling *You fool, you fool, you fool.* She turned away and stared into the sky that was so bright it helped her tears to come, and she knew what was meant by a bolt from the blue. Out of that awful emptiness, like an H-bomb came the invisible thing which blasted you. He doesn't love me and now because of the hateful thing I've done he will hate me always. It was the end of the world.

"Look," he said gently, "I should go and get changed; your back'll get sunburned if you don't take care." And he touched it, but now she couldn't bear to be touched by him, she got up and ran into the summerhouse and felt again the disgusting woolliness of the thick dust on her feet and saw the sleazy pin-ups and the silly scribbled things. She rolled down her bathing-dress and kicked it off and she was like the horrible readhead on the wall so she gave a tug and pulled her down and scrabbled her up and threw her into a corner.

When she was dressed she went out and Tony was waiting for her with his towel on his shoulders, looking shy and remote and like a stranger now, although it was only three hours since he'd bought her Nightshade. He took her arm and she remembered how she'd pressed his hand to her side at Stow Fair when he'd done that; waves of shame like invisible blushes swept over her. She tried not to look at Tony or to wonder what he was thinking as they went down the garden past the Kate Greenaway apple-tree.

H I S   T H O U G H T S in fact were as confused as hers. He certainly hadn't intended anything much when he'd touched her, or expected any reaction other than a squeak or so; indeed he'd been telling himself that he oughtn't to be doing anything of the kind, for he thought of her as half a child still. So when the powder-barrel blew up, he'd been taken altogether by surprise; astonished, put out, even alarmed. This, in view of his wide experience of girls of all shapes and sizes, now considerably amused him. He simply hadn't thought of Susan in those terms; but already he was beginning to readjust his thinking, and right at the back of his mind, lurking behind the surprise, the amusement and the tenderness for her, was the shadow of a tough masculine regret: Wish I had.

They went past the apricot-bush, and he noticed another ripe

one and its warm skin was satiny like hers as he picked it and
offered it her; but she shook her head and turned away, "Please,
I don't want another, eat it yourself."

COMING IN SIGHT OF the stables, he said:

"Look, when it gets cool this evening, I'll take Trumpeter and
you take Nightshade, and let's ride them through the woods."

But Nightshade didn't mean anything to her any more. The
whole splendour and joy of Nightshade was her being a present
from Tony. She told herself she could hardly bear to look at
Nightshade again because when she did so she would think herself back to the moment when she'd been sitting on the mare's
back and singing in the secret places of her spirit He loves me he
loves me he's bought me a horse. But now in those secret places
the Doomsday bell was still tolling, Finished, finished, forever,
forever, *he'll* never forget, *you'll* never forget the awful thing
that happened, his embarrassment, your shame.

And then just as if the devil had planted them in her path on
purpose there was Rosemary with Goff against the wall in the
shadow at the back of the stables, breathing so hard that you
heard them before you saw them, and Tony said: "What on
earth's that?" Rosemary, with a squeak, scurried away; and Goff
shambled off towards the lane, and a few minutes later his motor-
bike started, bang, roar, shattering a silence.

Tony didn't say anything. He must think I'm just like Rosemary, tolled the bell in Susan's mind.

They got to the house, and went in by the front-door, and the
yellow telegram was on the silver salver in the hall. It was for
Tony, and Susan welcomed it at first because it gave her something to say: "Telegram for you, wonder who it's from?"

He opened it and raised his eyebrows and showed it to her:

REPORT TO ME FORTHWITH STAND BY FOR SERVICE OVERSEAS
ADJUTANT.

PART THREE

Ferdinando's Oak

¶ 1

AFTER A BREATHLESS AUTUMN the wind had come suddenly with a sound like surf in the tops of the trees. That was the day when Tony with his Gloucesters sailed at last for Korea. Their ship, by chance, had a lovely Gloucestershire name. Susan knew that she was called the *Empire Windrush.* Tony's letter which told her so was light-hearted, easy, casual but affectionate; you couldn't call it a love-letter by any means, but Susan reading it over and over again contrived to discover some hints and nuances which persuaded her it might at least be the precursor of love-letters to come. After all (she'd been telling herself lately, for the end-of-the-world feeling hadn't lasted very long) his reaction to her folly by the Lily Pond *could* be seen as a chivalrous thing, verray parfit, self-denying! So now a kind of sad sweet hope was kindled by his letter, and she loved him till she ached. She perched herself on a window-seat and settled down to write him a long letter back, while the wind moaned outside and combed the first brown leaves out of the dishevelled oaks. She thought of the ship's name, *Windrush,* and then of that Cotswold village called Windrush. They had noticed its name on a signpost, going to Stow Fair: the never-to-be-forgotten day when Tony bought her Nightshade.

"I TOOK her cubbing for the first time yesterday, they met at the Ferry and drew Trafalgar Wood . . ."

IT HAD BEEN THE LAST of a score of still days with little hoar-frosts which nibbled but didn't cut down the flowers. There was such a hush over the countryside that even pigeons' wings sounded loud. Nightshade's quick hoofs danced on the white crisp grass, all the tinsel spider webs were glittering. The mist hung late, and the horn of the invisible huntsman blowing through it seemed to give out a queer quavering misty sound. Nightshade too was all a-quiver. For weeks Susan had been riding her twice a day, cherishing her because she was Tony's present, striving with the devils which possessed her still. It was adventurous to take her out cubbing; and Susan kept her well away from the other horses as she went fly-jumping crabwise down the lane.

Oh, but she could gallop! They found a cub in Trafalgar and raced him across two long meadows to Waterloo. Shortening the reins, sticking in her knees, ever conscious of the devils, Susan let her go; and she 'trod as on the four winds'!

Breathless and elated, when they came to a check at Waterloo woodside, Susan had slipped her hand into her pocket and brought out Tony's letter: just a glance at the awful round boyish handwriting which hadn't changed much since he was at school.

Then the horn was blowing in quick short bursts and the hounds in Waterloo began a new clamour. A sleek young dog fox slipped out of a hazel brake at the corner of the covert and went streaking by Susan, so close she could see his white teeth and coral-red tongue. Nightshade stood on end as the pied pack exploded out of the wood and began to race up the bank towards the clump of elms on the skyline . . .

> *"HE HAD a coat as bright as beechleaves and I was glad we didn't catch him, he got into the big earth on Seven Men's Tump where it's too stony to dig. The 7 old elms have gone blonde in patches, they always do in the autumn, you know, like badly-dyed hair. . . ."*

THEN OUT OF one of the blonde patches there was shaken suddenly a shower of yellow leaves like doubloons. Susan felt the awakened breeze gusting in her face, and looked up and saw the mare's-tails in the sky. Afterwards the wind had freshened steadily all day, and in the night she had heard it howling among the crooked chimneys. By the time she sat down to write to Tony it was blowing a full gale, and she thought how shrill it would whistle in the rigging of the *Windrush* going down Channel, carrying Tony away to the far foreign war.

> *"I WONDER if you'll land in Japan? Fenton the new gardener was a P.O.W. there and I got him to tell me all about it. He's a strange obstinate fellow, with an ugly face. It reminds me somehow of a camel's; and like a camel he's all knobbles and knuckles; his knees and elbows seem to stick out, one shoulder is higher than the other, he's got enormous feet which leave tracks like the Abominable Snowman on the garden wherever he's been. He's awkward I think, in his mind as well as with his limbs, but Daddy and I like him very much—Mummy doesn't!"*

SUSAN HAD GOT ALONG with him in the first place because she was interested in his pigeons. She was interested in anything new, curiosity about great things and small filled her days and sometimes kept her awake at night. So she was eager to know how the birds found their way, and how the races were organized; and Fenton's long scowl vanished, his ugly bony face took on a new look altogether, as he explained his fancy to her. "Of course, the wife and kids can't understand what I see in 'em," he happened to say; and Susan wondered whether this was the first chance he'd had to talk about his hobby, except to his pigeon-flying cronies who knew all about it.

A few days later Ferdo said to her: "You get on well with Fenton, see if you can find out a bit about his past." And he told her Colonel Daglingworth's story, that Fenton had a conviction for theft. Ferdo hadn't told Janet. He said: "Keep it to yourself; it might upset Mummy if she knew," and gave her a conspiratorial smile.

She was all for Fenton, naturally, because of her powerful dislike of Daglingworth and his pawing. She contrived the opportunity to have a talk next morning, when Fenton was working in the fruit-cage and she went into pick the last of the raspberries. Within ten minutes she'd discovered the truth about that 'theft' quite by accident. She'd been asking him about Japan. She was curious to know what it felt like to be a human being in confinement, and what happened to you in your mind when you were really hungry. The unshapely fellow leaned on his spade-handle, all angles, like a scarecrow hung upon a wooden frame, and talked; but haltingly, a sentence or two at a time, as if he'd never told some of these things before. After a while he said:

"Funny thing about hunger is what it does to you afterwards."

"Afterwards?"

"Maybe you've a full belly, but you can't get the idea of grub out of your head. My demob. leave, went to a tea-place with the wife. Cakes on the table, sugary jammy ones like we used to dream of, once I dreamt three nights running of treacle-tart three inches deep and a yard across; I was just going to take a bite of it when I woke up crying my eyes out. But when I came home, I soon had enough of such things, I didn't fancy 'em any more; it was cheese and steaks I wanted; so Gawd knows what it was made me do what I did."

Mrs. Fenton had gone to spend a penny; Fenton had paid the bill for the pot of tea and a couple of sandwiches; and he sat waiting for her in front of the plateful of uneaten, unwanted cakes. Having nothing better to do, he stared at them; then suddenly he had to have them, his hand shot out and he clawed four or five of them on to his lap whence, in a panic, he transferred them to the haversack lying by his chair, scrabbling them up and stuffing them in on top of Mrs. Fenton's shopping. He'd been sure nobody was looking; but a waitress must have been watching him through the corner of her eye. She fetched the manageress. It might have been all right even then if Mrs. Fenton, returning from the lav., hadn't indignantly taken his part. *"Of course he wouldn't do such a thing!"* He felt he 'mustn't let her down,' lost his head altogether, and refused to let the manageress look inside the haversack. So the woman rang the police. The policeman, opening the haversack, extracted a squashed sticky mess,—as Fenton told it, the thing was half a joke, half an abiding horror in his mind. "I can see it still: one of those chocolate sticky things sandwiched between two cheesecakes; a doughnut with the jam oozing out of it; bits of sugar icing with hundreds and thousands; and a cherry. I can see the copper wiping his fingers on his handkerchief, and the wife looking at me."

Mrs. Fenton stuck by him, although "she had the worst of it, being the woman she is; 'd never owe anybody a tanner, strict over everything, if she found a bill'd been added up wrong in her favour she'd go back to the shop to hand over the tuppence-ha'penny." She was real good to him: 'you had to give her that.' Susan's ears, sharpened by her curiosity about people and their relationships, got an impression that Fenton did not love his wife though the loyalty or respect or admiration which bound him to her might well be stronger than love. "*Why* did you do it?" Mrs. Fenton kept asking him; and for the life of him he couldn't say why. "I didn't *want* the cakes, that's certain: couldn't have ate 'em: but I suppose something was saying to me at the back of my mind I *might* want 'em later on. That's what I told the doctor. It was the wife got him to speak for me."

Once again Susan's sharp ears detected some undertones. He wished she hadn't got the doctor; and he was ashamed of whatever had been said in Court concerning the state of men's minds when they'd been hungry. In a way he resented his wife's help though he was grateful for it.

The Chairman of the Magistrates was a woman. Lady something, she was; and there were no undertones when Fenton spoke of her: just sheer blazing hatred. At one time he'd been in a prison-camp with the Aussies; they'd have had a word for her, they'd have called her a Fair Cow! She had a la-di-da voice and a smell under her nose. She publicly thanked heaven that nobody in England, who was willing to work, need be hungry nowadays. She asked Mrs. Fenton how many children she had. When she said "Five" the woman said "Oh," as if to imply she'd no right to have so many. "Were they hungry?" she then asked. Mrs. Fenton said no. "Was your *husband* hungry?" badgered her Ladyship. No again. So she turned towards Fenton and gave him a long look which seemed to say: sheer greed. She had a brief consultation with her fellow magistrates, then bound him over in the sum of five pounds. She observed that the war had had a bad effect on people's attitudes to private property. Picking and stealing could not be tolerated in a civilised society. Then out she went and everybody stood up to show respect for her.

WHEN SUSAN TOLD ALL THIS to Ferdo he said: "We'll still not tell Mummy, she wouldn't understand," and she realised, without any diminution of love, that it was perfectly true: her mother, because of some blind spot in her understanding, would not be able to *imagine* why Fenton had grabbed those cakes. It was fun, and flattering, to be in a kind of confidential relationship with Ferdo. They were together a good deal nowadays. He was teaching her to shoot, and to throw a fly on the river. When she fetched down her first flying pigeon (amazed, appalled to see it tumbling out of the sky) and when she brought back from Elmbury Weir her first three-quarter-pound chub to be cooked for Ophelia's supper, Ferdo was as pleased as Punch, and determined, of course, that they must have something special to drink at dinner on the strength of it. He took her down to the cellar 'to help him choose the wine'; and they paddled about in the remains of the flood while Ferdo talked learnedly about claret and Burgundy and port. But this was a man's thing, she thought, a kind of toy they played with; and she regarded with amused tolerance his male solemnity about châteaux and vintages. Nevertheless, in this as in all things, she observed her father with a lively eye, for of late, as she pined for Tony and puzzled her head about the why and wherefore of love, she had been much troubled by her ignorance concerning the ways and the habits and the thinking of men. She had hoped that perhaps she might learn a little from her father. The only firm conclusion she came to, however—watching affectionately, coolly and with surprise—was that men didn't grow up as they got older. They were like boys in this matter of wine, and in their attitude to such a thing as the flood in the cellar, which advanced and receded and in doing so exercised an extraordinary fascination upon Ferdo: he had a measuring-stick marked in quarter inches, and daily recorded in a notebook the rise or fall of the tide. Then there was his boy scout passion for bonfires. It simply passed Susan's comprehension that an intelligent man could spend a whole afternoon happily watching the flames devour a pile of faggots. Ferdo could—and so could Fenton; and it was their shared pyromania, more than anything else, which brought them together in that autumn season when there seemed to be such a lot of stuff to burn. They'd build a pile of hedge-trimmings six feet high; and having lit it they would stand by with pitchforks, feeding it with yet more rubbish whenever it looked like flagging, possessed by a most absurd determination to keep it going as long as they possibly could. On one occasion, running out of combustible material, Ferdo fetched from the potting-shed an old pair of gumboots, which he said had a leak in them. (Susan doubted it; she believed that he simply wanted something exciting to burn.) The rubber sizzled with a clear white flame, and gave out a horrible smell. Fenton meanwhile had run back to his cottage to fetch a couple of perished bicycle-tyres and an old tarpaulin coat which had gone tacky. With this he temporarily snuffed the bonfire, and clouds of stinking black smoke billowed forth from underneath it. Then, as dusk deepened, the flames leapt up again, crackling and roaring. The game now was to heap wet turfs upon the blaze and so confine it that the red heart would smoulder away within the heap of turf, until eventually all was consumed. If you could keep it going for a week this represented a gardening triumph. So Fenton and Ferdo with their pitchforks ran to and fro in front of the blaze looking like devils in old pictures of hell: the one tall, thin and angular, the other stocky and rotund. Sweat poured down their faces, making runnels through the smuts. They were happy as sandboys: and never so happy as when a series of sharp explosions occurred within the heap, throwing sparks and flaming twigs high in the air. . . .

> *"BELIEVE it or not, the bangs were pre-war cartridges which Daddy said had got damp and were too unreliable to use. Those two would burn anything! When they've got a bonfire going Daddy goes prowling round the place with a sack, looking for things to burn. He had a clean-up in the summerhouse by the Lily Pond and put all those pin-ups on the . . ."*

SUSAN DIDN'T FINISH THE SENTENCE. At the very thought of those pin-ups she felt again the creepy-crawly dust on the soles of her feet and a sort of imaginary dust just like it, grey and mildewy, creeping over her spirit. And she didn't want to say anything to remind Tony of the Lily Pond: so she tore up that page and started again. She knew about Ferdo burning the pin-ups because a change of wind after dark had carried the smoke from the bonfire towards the house. With it came a shower of small fragments of half-charred paper falling like manna from heaven. This confetti had lain in the courtyard until morning, when Susan, trying to tidy things up, had discovered the members and morsels of nude redheads, enough to make a jigsaw for an anatomist.

They had even flown into the house through an open window; while across the courtyard Mrs. Fenton's washing had been blackened by the smoke. Mrs. Fenton and Janet made a joint protest; and thereafter no bonfires were permitted within two hundred yards.

THAT WAS PROBABLY the only time Janet and Mrs. Fenton had agreed about anything. Mrs. Fenton was what Janet called spiky. It wouldn't have mattered her disapproving of so many things if only she hadn't been subject to puritanical promptings which commanded her to Speak Out about them. Janet at a distraught moment had written down in her diary a list of some of the things Mrs. Fenton disapproved of. It had filled the whole day's space and overflowed into next day:

> *Vivisection smoking America meat monarchy Winston drink armed forces South Africa colour bar makeup vaccination horseracing gambling House of Lords lords baronets bishops bikinis boxing Franco foxhunting keeping pets Prince Philip all cheese except mousetrap debs and H-bombs.*

To make matters worse, about almost everything except foxhunting she was better informed than Janet, who recognised this and refrained from arguing with her. So she argued in the kitchen with Mrs. Northover. The very first morning she came in to help she got up against Mrs. Northover. It was about a contrivance called a bell-board above the kitchen mantelpiece, which had been modern perhaps in Edward the Seventh's day but had since fallen into disuse and was kept as a curiosity. Each of its twenty-two bells, one for every important room in the house, hung beneath the appropriate caption: DINING ROOM, LIBRARY, BATHROOM 1, BEDROOM 1, 2, 3, 4, and so on up to 10. (The servants' bedrooms did not possess bells, of course.) Mrs. Fenton was interested in the bell-board, which she saw as a kind of sociological relic, and she asked Mrs. Northover how it worked. Mrs. Northover, who remembered the thing in operation thirty years ago and was proud to have experienced those palmy days, hastened to explain it to her:

"Supposing her Ladyship was in the bath and she suddenly

thought of something she'd forgot to tell cook about the vegeta-
bles for dinner, she'd ring the bathroom bell—dreadful whirring
sound it had, made you jump out of your skin—and then you'd
look up at the bell-board and you'd see BATHROOM TWO, that was
the one on the second floor——"

"And then," said Mrs. Fenton, "I suppose some poor little
skivvy jumps up and tears panting up two flights of stairs to find
out her Ladyship's will and pleasure?"

"If you're referring to me," said Mrs. Northover, who saw herself in retrospect by no means as a little skivvy but as a junior
member of a well-ordered and very high-class establishment,
"—If you're referring to *me*, I did."

She and Mrs. Fenton were at odds ever after; and Janet would
have been only too glad to end the arrangement by which Mrs.
Fenton came in to help for four hours a day. But with all those
clever children going to Grammar School and needing school
clothes and pocket money for extras and special books because
they were so extra specially clever, the Fentons needed every
penny they could lay hands on. And certainly Mrs. Fenton
earned her three bob an hour. She scrubbed and polished as if
she thought she was cleaning up the world. Her own cottage
was spotless, orderly, a-place-for-everything-and-everything-in-its-
place. The regiments of jamjars on her shelves were dressed by
the right as smartly as guardsmen. On each of the three or four
occasions when Janet had reason to go to the cottage she found
Mrs. Fenton bottling and jamming; for she was one of those
provident squirrel-women who love to fill their larders with an
autumn hoard. Janet said to Susan: "Mrs. Fenton is the Perfect
Housewife as conceived by the Women's Institute. What's the
betting that next week we see her there?"

JANET, WHO WAS PRESIDENT, took Susan along to the
Annual General Meeting; and sure enough there was Mrs. Fenton sitting in the back row. Everybody stood up and began to sing
"Jerusalem." If only William Blake could have seen them, opening and shutting their mouths like that chub gaping on the bank
after Susan had taken the hook out of its mouth!

> *"Bring me my bow of burning gold!*
> *Bring me mine arrows of desire!"*

Straight as arrows Susan's thoughts sped to Tony. She looked about her in wonder at the singing women, the sad sour spinster who kept the village shop, the puddingfaced wife of Hipkins the blacksmith, Olive Turberville the cobbler's daughter, who was dismally pious and played the organ dismally in church, fat Mrs. Trent who kept house for the Rector, full-throated like a pigeon with all her double chins a-quiver—and she wondered what images came into their minds when they sang once a month about the arrows of desire. The only woman who looked as if she might know what she was singing about was Mrs. Fenton, standing right at the back under the notice which said NO INTOXICATING LIQUOR MAY BE SERVED ON THESE PREMISES. The soft September sunlight came in through the window just behind her and lit her pale tense face and her frizz of auburn hair, so that she looked transparently luminous like one of those pre-Raphaelite red-heads in a stained glass window. And she was singing as if she really meant it, *"Bring me my chariot of fire!"*

At last everybody sat down and the business began. Janet more or less took the Minutes of the Last Meeting as read and hurried on to the next item. Susan, who was staring about her instead of attending to what was going on, observed that Mrs. Fenton was on her feet again; but because she was right at the back of the hall nobody else noticed her for at least a minute. Janet meanwhile had got on to the subject of the Rector's kind offer to give an Address on the History of the Parish Church. At last Mrs. Fenton managed to catch her eye. Janet, looking surprised, said, "Is anything the matter?" and Mrs. Fenton, whose hand holding up the Agenda was twitching as if she had St. Vitus's Dance, gasped desperately:

"I wanted to speak please on Matters arising from the Minutes."

Janet, putting on her glasses to look at the paper in front of her, said: "That doesn't seem to be on the Agenda."

"I know it isn't, Madam President," said Mrs. Fenton, still trembling but in a way assured; Susan guessed that she knew a lot more about Meetings than Janet did. She paused, and there was a few seconds' dead silence. Then Mrs. Fenton added:

"But, with respect, I submit that it ought to be."

The Doddington branch of the Women's Institute had probably never heard anybody use that phrase "with respect" before: their equivalent would have been "begging your Ladyship's pardon." Mrs. Fenton's use of it put the whole meeting against her; and all at once they were giving themselves cricks in the neck as they turned round to scowl or raise their eyebrows. Janet, trying extra hard to be patient, said:

"Well, I'm sure we're all very pleased to welcome the new member. What was the point she wanted to make?"

"Arising out of the Minutes," began Mrs. Fenton, taking a deep breath, "I see it is proposed to hold a Fowl-plucking Competition and it says Fowls must be alive when brought into the Hall. Well, if that is the case I should like to make a strong protest on the grounds——"

But nobody heard what were the grounds of Mrs. Fenton's protest; because suddenly the women sitting in the back row began to shush her, for her own good if for nothing else, for they obviously thought it was crazy to get up against her Ladyship if you lived on the estate and your husband worked for Sir Ferdo. Put out by the shushing, she hesitated and was lost. Janet very quickly said: "Well, that was settled at the last meeting and I don't suppose we want to discuss it all over again—" at which the occupants of the front rows, craning their necks uncomfortably as if they were old turtles trying to look back over their shells, began to cackle like a gaggle of geese, telling Mrs. Fenton to sit down. For quite a long time she defied them, standing wanly in the pool of sunlight like a Burne-Jones woman under her aura of bright hair. Susan was desperately sorry for her; but she was sorry for her mother too, who was getting into a fine old muddle over Item Number Three and whose hands were trembling just as much as Mrs. Fenton's were because she realised she had managed the whole thing badly,—even though Mrs. Fenton had at long last subsided into her chair and all the gaggling geese-women in the front rows were still firmly on her Ladyship's side.

"MUMMY is determined to get me involved in all the local goings-on. She wants me to be Secretary of the Elmbury Young Conservatives. I told her: 'I don't know if I am one,' and she looked at me as if I'd said I didn't know if I was English. 'Of course you are, my dear, don't be absurd.' But I

*shan't be one much longer if I see much more of Col. Dag-
lingworth. It turns out he's Chairman of the Elmbury Conservative Association; and his daughter's just been made
Chairman of those Young Conservatives. I haven't met her
yet. She's called Sandra. But Col. Daglingworth came to tea
to persuade me to be Secretary. I like him less and less. He
looked as if he wanted to sit by me on the sofa but didn't
dare. I gave him hot scones and he had awful tummy rum-
bles which I think cramped his style. He kept wriggling on
his chair to try and keep them quiet; and he talked very
loudly so that I wouldn't hear them. He said it was very
important to build up the Party because there was sure to be
another Election soon and this wasn't a safe seat any longer
because of the housing estates and new factories at Elmbury.
He said: 'Do you know the Member, Le Mesurier?' and I
said I didn't. Then the gallant Colonel goes on: 'Very clever
fellow. I think he's a Jew. Of course I like Jews, but—' and I
knew the tone of his voice so I got in very quickly and said:
'Yes, I like them too' and gave him a stare which shut him
up.*

*"He doesn't like cats either. Ophelia jumped up on his lap
and purred, I can't think why. He didn't just put her down.
He sort of threw her. I swear I'll go Labour if he ever does
it again."*

SUSAN COULD HEAR OPHELIA, who was shut in to keep
her from the farmyard Toms because she was in season, wailing
like a woman for her demon lover in the old nursery next door.
You wouldn't think a small Siamese would be capable of such a
noise. By turns she howled like a banshee and barked like a dog.
Sometimes it was as if all the anguished longing of all the cats in
Christendom was pent up in the nursery and was expressing itself
in apt and terrible terms through that hoarse hysterical voice.
And Susan on the window-seat with her knees drawn up to her
chin, in torment because she could not decide whether to end
With love or *With lots of love* or *With all my love,*—Susan
confessed to herself that she felt at least a little bit like Ophelia,
she had such an ache and longing for love. For weeks she'd been
trying to assuage it with poetry; but that only made it worse,
poetry to lovers was like drink to drunkards, she supposed! She'd
been taking it in reckless immoderate draughts, Tennyson and
Keats and Shelley and Coleridge, and Shakespeare's Sonnets and

Romeo and Juliet. She had read the "Gallop apace" speech to herself over and over again until she knew it by heart and began to understand what it really meant and realised how powerful it was and was almost frightened by it and heard her heart thumping. Then one day, going shopping with Janet to Cheltenham, she bought on the strength of its title an anthology called *Love* by Walter De la Mare; and again she took it like a drunkard in gulps until her head swam. She found in it a strange anonymous fragment which went:

> *And my breast it pricks me so*
> *I may not endure it,*
> *For I meddle me to know*
> *Love, and naught can cure it.*

She read it just once, and it went whispering through her mind thereafter and she couldn't keep it quiet. So now she burnt her boats and put *With all my love,* and she was going to put *Yours Sue* when it occurred to her to cut out the 's' in 'yours' and she daringly did so.

Your Sue. She sealed up the letter quickly before the doubts crept in; and just then there was a knock on the door and it was Rosemary. She shut the door carefully behind her and Susan had the impression there was something the girl wanted to say; but she seemed to change her mind, flushed, said "Beg pardon" and turned to go. "Yes, what is it, Rosemary?" asked Susan. Rosemary hesitated for a moment, said "Nothing, Miss Susan" and fairly scuttled out. Goodness, Susan thought, I wonder what's the matter with her—*Love and naught can cure it?* Then we're a pair. And next door Ophelia began to howl and to yelp again, Ariadne's weeping for Theseus, Thisbe's for Pyramus, Hero's for Leander, all translated into terms of Siamese cat!

¶ 2

THE WIND, STILL BLOWING NEXT DAY, ripped from a telegraph-pole in Doddington Lane a mustard-coloured handbill, which came flapping towards Nightshade and sent her bounding sideways into the ditch. It was a remnant of the crop of handbills which had proliferated over the village three weeks ago, rather like the yellow toadstools which just then were breaking out like a rash all over the autumnal woods.

Janet had been furious about them. Under the heading '1950 NOT 1850' the letterpress ran:

LABOUR PARTY!!
High time we had a Doddington Branch
All Welcome at Public Meeting, Village Hall
2nd October
Further particulars from Ben Fenton
Huntsman's Cottage.

"'HE ACTUALLY HAD the cheek to give the address of our cottage!" said Janet to Ferdo, who replied mildly:

"I don't know what other address he could have given, my dear."

"Oh, it makes fools of us!" she said. They were having tea in Ferdo's study, on the day after the posters had appeared. Susan with a long toasting-fork crouched in front of the fire. Ferdo was enjoying his buttered toast spread with Gentleman's Relish.

"I cannot imagine what the Committee was thinking of," Janet went on, "to let the Hall to a schoolboy! The shop and the pub and the Turbervilles and old Hipkins all refused to stick up the notices, of course. Hipkins threw his on to the fire in his smithy, and said: That's the place for rubbish like that. So the boy tacked them on to the telegraph-poles instead. There's one just outside our drive. There's even one on that big oak on the Green."

"Ah well," said Ferdo, half-way through his fourth slice of toast, "I don't suppose that'll do it any harm. The old tree must have seen a lot of political ups and downs in four hundred years."

His complacency irritated Janet.

"I've a good mind," she said, "personally to pull them down!"

Suddenly Ferdo sat up. "You'll do nothing of the kind," he said, with an access of authority which astonished Susan. One was apt to forget that he'd captained warships. She put down her toasting-fork and looked over her shoulder just in time to see an extraordinary thing. Ferdo fairly roared at Janet; and suffered a sea-change as he did so. He looked ten years younger, and much like his photograph in Janet's bedroom, taken early in the last war, in which he was wearing a duffle-coat and a muffler, his cap on the side of his head, and the expression of a man happily and eagerly looking for trouble. The picture had always puzzled Susan, because she hadn't known that side of her father.

"By God, Janet," he blasted off, "I hate politicians, the whole bloodstained lot, I hate their guts and their flaming Parties too. But if there's anything I believe about politics, it's that everyone's got a right to have a go. Have *you and I* got to be reminded it's 1950 not 1850? Good luck to the lad, I say."

There followed an ominous quiet, during which time Susan glanced rather nervously at her mother. The broadside having been delivered, the smoke was blowing away; and Janet was not only unharmed but a small smile was coming upon her face as she stared at Ferdo and recognised (Susan thought) that old photograph come to life. So Susan turned round again to look at Ferdo, and he had helped himself to another piece of toast and was smearing it with his beloved Gentleman's Relish. He glanced from Susan to Janet and grinned at them both before he took a bite at it. He munched happily. At last he said:

"Janet: sorry I blew my top. But you must admit, to take on an old battleaxe like you, that boy's got some guts, anyway."

AND HERE WAS BEN FENTON walking along the drive as Susan trotted home after Nightshade had shied at the piece of paper.

She hadn't seen much of the Fenton children lately. The two girls went to Elmbury High School; and she'd noticed the boy called Willum, the one with the lowering looks, with a Grammar School cap which looked much too small for him perched absurdly on top of his thick black thatch of hair.

Mrs. Fenton was always annoying Mrs. Northover by talking about her children's 'C' levels and 'A' levels. Rosemary, remarked Mrs. Northover, got on very well without such things.

Susan had imagined Ben was at the Grammar School too. However, this afternoon he was capless and was wearing a horrible cowpat-coloured sports coat, which didn't fit him anywhere, with obviously new greenish corduroy trousers. He looked shy, as he always did when they met. She had the impression that he avoided her, though she couldn't think why, unless it was something to do with that brief, odd encounter when she caught him letting the air out of Colonel Daglingworth's tyre. Walking towards her, he took his hands out of his pockets, put them back, took them out again.

Nightshade, still upset by the sight of that handbill, stamped and fretted when Susan pulled her up.

"Hello. Did you have a good Meeting?" she said.

For a moment he seemed put out. Then he gave her a dubious and endearing smile, rather like his father's. He wasn't at all like his father otherwise; nor like his mother. You could recognise bits of both in him, only in his case Mendel's Law had worked very kindly to result in a happy mean. He was nearly as tall as Fenton, but as tidily-built as Mrs.; Susan thought he was nice-looking, with his grey eyes, hazlenut-coloured hair, prominent cheekbones and rather severe mouth, which nevertheless turned up at the corners when he smiled.

He hadn't answered her question.

"How many?" she teased him.

"All the family," he said, giving her another doubtful smile. "Except Adam and Eve, of course." They were the two little ones, aged nine and eight.

"Nobody else at all?"

"Yes, there were one or two." He looked a bit embarrassed, and Susan realised that he wasn't going to say who they were, lest, presumably, it got them into the Seldons' bad books. He must think we're pretty feudal, she thought; still, when one remembers Mummy, perhaps he's not far wrong!

Nightshade, who'd been scraping a new hole in the drive with one of her forefeet, suddenly decided to dance round in circles. Her hindquarters nearly barged into Ben. Susan asked a silly question, "Do you like horses?" because she couldn't think of anything else to say. After a pause he said gravely: "I think they're beautiful; but I'm scared of them." Why then, Susan wondered, hadn't he skipped out of the way of Nightshade's business end? Bravado? Somehow the boy embarrassed her, although she liked him; his shyness made her shy, so that she was apt to say silly things to him:

"I thought you were at school still?"

"No, I finished last term."

"Oh. Yes. I suppose you're—looking for a job?"

He gave her an odd look then, at once shy and defiant and diffident and truimphant.

"No. Not yet." Again his mouth twitched up at the corners in that uncertain smile which Susan found curiously touching. "You see, I've been lucky enough to get a scholarship; and the day after tomorrow I'm going up to Oxford."

¶ 3

FERDO HAD INVITED LE MESURIER to stay when he came down to address the Young Conservatives: 'to save the poor fellow from a night at the Daglingworths'' was his excuse. But notwithstanding his prejudice against politicians, he admitted to Susan that he'd liked the look of the M.P. on some occasion when he'd heard him speak. Ferdo was inclined to like people who were opposites to himself; and Stephen Le Mesurier was his opposite in almost every way. Colonel Daglingworth would surely have described him as a Hairy Intellectual if he'd been Liberal or Labour. His longish black hair made him look a bit like Disraeli, Susan thought; but that was perhaps because he told her Disraeli was one of his heroes. He was about forty, and had somehow managed not to get married, which Susan found surprising. He certainly wasn't a pansy, you knew that from the way he looked at you! She had encountered that look when Rosemary brought him into the sitting-room before dinner. Ferdo and Janet weren't down, so she introduced herself and asked him what he'd have to drink. She poured out his gin and French, and met the look again, full in the face, when she handed the glass to him: disconcerting but not disagreeable. It wasn't in the least related to those furtive nasty little glances she got from Colonel Daglingworth: but it was frankly and unashamedly appreciative, and it contained an element of amused surprise which seemed to say: How *unexpectedly* delightful! She found this very comforting because at that particular moment she was feeling gauche, ill-at-ease, dowdy and unsophisticated by comparison with Sandra Daglingworth, who'd been asked to dinner, of course, because she was Chairman of the Young Conservatives.

SANDRA WAS A TALL TAWNY GIRL with a splendid body which she boasted was brown all over, yes, everywhere, because she'd just had a month's holiday in the South of France. She was obviously a frightful snob even at the age of twenty-one, and when she chattered to Susan about lords and the sons of lords she somehow managed to convey the impression that she'd gone to bed with them; or that she was hopeful of doing so; or that it was a matter of indifference to her whether she did or didn't. This might have been just silly boasting, but Susan by instinct or intuition guessed that it had a certain foundation in fact. She would probably have disliked Sandra very much, but that from the moment of their first meeting the girl had patently and warmheartedly taken to her. You couldn't continue for long to dislike anyone who liked you, and who showed it in such an open way. So almost against her will Susan had drifted into a friendly companionship with Sandra, forgiving her silliness and her put-on drawling voice, envying her assurance and the way she wore her clothes. Indeed she now became aware, for almost the first time in her life, of a little tweak of jealousy when she glanced across the table, during dinner, and caught Stephen Le Mesurier looking at Sandra in much the same amusedly appreciative way he'd looked at *her*. Well, you couldn't blame him; Sandra was looking so lovely tonight that Susan herself could hardly keep her eyes off her. And of course she was playing up to Le Mesurier, and flirting a bit, and talking politics in quite a sophisticated way, as if she really knew a lot about them. She said something about Nye Bevan; Susan didn't hear what it was because Ferdo was talking to her, but she saw the sudden change in Le Mesurier's expression as he turned sharply to Sandra and said:

"Hold hard, my dear; you're talking about a friend of mine!"

"What, Nye Bevan?"

"But of course," he said, laughing at her surprise. "We were having dinner together the night before last."

Sandra still looked as if she wasn't quite sure if he were pulling

her leg, and now Janet, joining in from his left-hand side, protested that it must have been like supping with the Devil. "I just
can't believe that a person like yourself, loving and serving this
country as you do, could made a *friend* of a man like that."

Enjoying himself now, Le Mesurier leaned back in his chair
and glanced mischievously from one to the other,—Sandra still
incredulous, with her pretty mouth looking a bit petulant and
suddenly reminding Susan of Mrs. Daglingworth's, Janet becoming horsey in her indignation.

"Not make a friend of a political enemy? My dear Lady Seldon," said Le Mesurier, half-mocking, but in such an agreeable
way that Janet wasn't aware of his teasing,—"My dear *Janet*,
if I dare—you surely do not imagine that we in the House of
Commons, with all our faults, are *quite* as uncivilised as that!"
Neither Janet nor Sandra realised that he had most politely
reproved them; indeed Janet smiled as if she thought she'd been
paid a compliment. Susan caught his eye, and he had the cool
cheek to wink, a confession of comradeship which flattered her,
and she blushed. Sandra's pout disappeared—it had made Susan
think of Oscar Wilde's crack in *The Importance of Being Earnest:* "All women become like their mothers. That is their tragedy." You couldn't see Mrs. D. in her at all now, as she laughed
at a story of Le Mesurier's about Winston Churchill and General
de Gaulle. As for Janet, she had obviously been won over by his
use of her Christian name: 'My dear *Janet*, if I dare—'

Yes, you old Disraeli, thought Susan, can't I just imagine you
charming Queen Victoria with love-letters and violets!

THE MEETING TOOK PLACE in the Seldon Memorial Hall
at Elmbury, a gloomy Victorian building which commemorated
the benefaction of Susan's great-great-grandfather, who had
fought in the Indian Mutiny; on the wall opposite her hung his
portrait as a Major in the 61st Foot. The uniform didn't fit very
well; like all the Seldons he'd have been happier in country
tweeds.

For the most part, the Young Conservatives were the sons and
daughters of Elmbury tradesmen and of the farmers round
about, but there was a sprinkling of rather tiresome young men

from the Royal Agricultural College nearby. They'd obviously
been to the pub before the meeting and were noisily appreciative
of Sandra's looks. They cheered and chi-acked whenever she
spoke. She was a hopeless Chairman anyway, and the interrup-
tions made her worse. Then the Treasurer took over, a bespectacled Bank Clerk with the dopey euphoric grin which you see in
the photographs of people who've won Football Pools; but he
only announced a credit balance of one pound one and a penny
ha'penny. Susan began to wonder, not for the first time, whether
she was a Conservative after all. "I will now," said Sandra, "call
upon the Member . . ."

The R.A.C. boys were less approving of Le Mesurier than they
had been of Sandra. Susan heard one of them say: "Sissy type."
Others were still audibly speculating about what they called the
local talent, a term which Susan uncomfortably suspected might
include herself as well as Sandra. A florid young agriculturalist
who seemed to be uncertain which Party was in power fiercely
demanded whether the speaker approved of Giving Away the
Empire. But before long Le Mesurier had charmed away the ill
manners as a gipsy charms warts; and Susan no longer wondered
whether she was a Conservative, she was whatever he was, she
believed whatever he believed! The curious thing was that when
she thought about his speech afterwards, she couldn't remember
much about it. He hardly touched on party politics at all. The
word that stuck in her mind was 'adventure'; by the time he sat
down he'd made you believe that every time you woke up in the
morning you ought to feel as excited as Christopher Columbus,
Captain Scott and Livingstone rolled into one and all starting
out on their explorations! He finished with a quotation from his
hero: "Adventures are to the adventurous." Then Sandra rose to
propose a vote of thanks, and the R.A.C. boys enthusiastically
supported the motion with yells and wolf-whistles.

SANDRA WENT ROARING down Elmbury High Street in her
noisy little sports car, and Susan set off home with Le Mesurier in
the draughty Land Rover.

"I wish," he said, "that I really liked Young Conservatives."

"You don't?"

"I know I ought to. But something at the back of my mind says to me that nobody ought to be Conservative when they're *young;* and that if they are, there's something a bit wrong with them."

"Thank you, Sir, for those kind words," said Susan.

"Oh, *you're* not a Conservative—whatever your mother says," he added, with what seemed to Susan almost supernatural percipience. "You're just looking round for a cause to believe in."

Then they started arguing about what they believed in. He was the easiest person to talk to that Susan had ever met. They were still at it when she swung the Land Rover into the courtyard where drifts of dead oak-leaves stirred out of their sleep and whispered after them as she led the way into the quiet house. Ferdo and Janet had gone to bed; but Susan, who'd been briefed by Ferdo, offered their guest a drink before he turned in, and he said he'd love a whisky and water. She deliberately poured him out a big one because she didn't care how long she sat up talking. He settled himself in Ferdo's armchair and put his feet up on the sofa opposite saying: "This is how we take out ease in the House of Commons!" Susan knelt on the hearth and tried to wake up the fire with a poker.

They went on talking about beliefs. He was the first grown-up person, except perhaps her father now and then, who had ever treated her as an equal in argument. He made her forget that she'd had her eighteenth birthday only last month. She wasn't shy of him in any way at all. They began to talk about God.

"What are you?" she asked him. "Agnostic, I bet."

"I'll tell you how I answered the last time I was asked. It was in the war. I'd been wounded quite badly, and by the time they got me into hospital I was in a sort of haze of pain and dope. A sister bending over me was just a cool antiseptic smell and a face floating in the air. She asked me about next-of-kin, and then she said: 'What's your religion?' I caught a glimpse of a pencil poised over a pad, and I was about to say C. of E., which was down on my military papers, when it struck me that I couldn't bear to have any blessed parson hanging about my deathbed. Also, at that moment I felt it was important to tell the truth. So I said 'Pantheist.' She looked very puzzled, and made me spell it, and then her face floated away like something in a seance."

"What did you mean by Pantheist?" said Susan.

"That's what I asked myself as I lay there and thought I was leaving the world, which despite its cruelties and terrors has always seemed to me very beautiful. If I'd been a Roman I'd have worshipped at any old altar that I passed on the road: 'I'd have wanted to thank Diana for the woods in spring, and Apollo for music and Flora for the flowers and Bacchus for fun and games and Neptune for the sea! So I thought to myself: If there's a God at all, which seems unlikely, surely he manifests Himself in all the things that move me, mountains and little alpine flowers and Beethoven and Shakespeare——"

"Did you ever get a chance to expain this to the Sister?" said Susan.

"She came back, still holding the pad and the pencil. The world was drifting away from me then; I could hardly see her at all. Her voice came through the mists, hundreds of miles off, worried and frustrated by the untidiness of the business. All nurses like things to be tidy. 'I can't find *anybody* who knows how to get hold of a Pantheist Minister,' she said. 'Are you sure C. of E. or R.C. wouldn't do instead?' Then everything went dark gradually."

"And when you got better, you still felt the same about it?"

"Oh, more so! The world was so bright and new, everything had been created specially for my benefit. It still looks like that sometimes. I look around me and see manifestations of divinity in every living thing."

Susan's fire leapt up at last, and set the shadows dancing all round the room, and as she turned away from the blaze she saw his dark eyes in the firelight intently looking at her. "Divinity," he was saying, "in everything that lifts the spirit or delights the eye, in the morning on the Matterhorn or in a flowering apple-tree or in a bugle-call or in a sailing-ship or in a poem or in a primrose or—in you, my dear," he smiled, with a cheerful acceptance that it was right he should find delight in her, and a cheerful assumption that she wouldn't mind.

Then he drank the last of his whisky as if it were a toast to her, and she showed him the way to his room.

OPHELIA, who generally slept with her, was sitting outside her bedroom-door. The grandfather clock on the landing was striking half past one. Goodness, they must have been talking for more than two hours! She went into her bedroom, and Ophelia thankfully jumped up on the bed. Then going towards her dressing-table Susan saw with surprise the piece of pale blue, lined paper lying there. It was folded in two, and 'Miss Susan' was written on the outside of the fold. Rosemary had started to write 'Sue' and then crossed out the 'e'; when they were children she'd always called her 'Sue,' and 'Miss Susan' was a formality she'd put on with her first maid's apron, a few months ago. Neither of them was quite used to it yet.

Inside the folded sheet Rosemary had printed in pencil:

> MISS SUSAN MAY I TALK TO YOU
> MOST PRIVATE MY $\frac{1}{2}$ DAY OFF
> TOMORROW 3 O'CLOCK FERDINANDO'S
> OAK   ROSEMARY.

¶ 4

IT WAS ONE OF THOSE midwinter afternoons when you seem to stand at the centre of a contracting world. The tower of Elmbury Abbey first vanished from view; then Doddington chimneys; then the pewtery glint of the river blurred as the fog breathed upon it; Trafalgar Wood, then Waterloo, then the nearer covertsides became smudged like old photographs yellowing as they fade; lastly the solitary trees in the Park were swallowed up in turn by the fog. From Ferdinando's Oak at three o'clock you could see nothing but a diminishing circle of soggy sad greygreen grass.

The Oak itself was owly and dark. Susan standing against it gazed up into the long narrow cleft where the bats hid and sometimes stirred, so that you could imagine Ariel shut up there by Sycorax.

Not a squirrel; though she stared hard into the branches which were black against the bilious sky.

It was quaint of Rosemary to choose the Oak as a secret meeting-place; but when they were children they used to make assignations here, they built a den in the branches where they gave imaginary tea-parties at which the invisible guests drank out of Ferdinando's acorn-cups. The Oak became the centrepiece of an elaborate fantasy, and the headquarters of their private and mysterious games.

Susan was still trying to remember those games when Rosemary came running out of the murk. She heard her before she saw her, panting as if she'd run all the way from the Manor.

Straight away she blurted out: Miss Sue you must help me please I'm going to have a baby.

I should have guessed, thought Susan, what a fool not to have guessed! But Mrs. Northover, who disapproved of Rosemary's boyfriend, had been telling everybody that he was in trouble or likely to be in trouble with the police; and Susan had jumped to the conclusion that Rosemary had wanted to talk to her about that. Taken by surprise, she couldn't think of anything to say; she put her arm round Rosemary, and they leaned together against the great trunk of the tree, and Rosemary began to cry quietly. At last Susan recovered her wits sufficiently to ask:

"Are you quite sure?"

Rosemary sobbed and nodded.

"How?" persisted Sue.

"Not for more than two months," said Rosemary.

Susan then summoned up all the Facts of Life as she'd scrappily learned them from novels and girls' gossip and from Sandra, who with tantalising flattery always assumed one knew as much about these things as she herself did. In what she thought was a woman-of-the-wordly way she asked if Goff took care; and got the answer: "Generally he did but that time he didn't." There followed an uncomfortable interval during which Rosemary tried to put Susan back on the pedestal she'd just stepped down from: "But you wouldn't know about it, Miss Sue."

"Have you told your mother or your father?" Susan asked.

"I dursn't," said Rosemary, real Gloucestershire in her distress.

"But you'll have to tell them . . . Well, no, of course, you won't. If you marry him soon they'll never——"

"That's it," said Rosemary, "I don't want to."

"—Marry Goff?"

"No, please, Sue," she whispered, dropping the "Miss" now.

"You don't love him?"

But this was too difficult a question for Rosemary; the problem didn't admit of a plain yes or no. She began to cry again, and hid her face in her hands, and at last whispered:

"It's just that I don't love him in that way, Sue, not to marry."

"In that case," said Susan, feeling herself at last in command of the situation, "we can fix things easily, I'm sure. First I'll talk to Mummy."

"Not her Ladyship!" Rosemary cried.

"Don't be silly. She'll be able to find out about homes and things. I'm sure there are plenty of places where you can have a baby, and if you like get it adopted, and come back and start again."

She hadn't meant it like that, of course; but when she heard herself say it she had to laugh, and she watched a very faint smile creeping over Rosemary's pretty face which was blurred with tears.

"Won't her Ladyship mind?" persisted Rosemary.

"She'll help," said Susan with conviction. Mummy was absurd about politics and old-fashioned in some of her attitudes, but she'd always been good and kind in her dealings with people. The Northovers worshipped her; she was the one to talk them round and get them on Rosemary's side.

"Please let me have a word with her," Susan said. "Then she can tell your parents, and get everything fixed up."

Rosemary hesitated, then nodded. She murmured:

"But I'm real frit of her Ladyship knowing."

Something stirred in the branches overhead, and they both started. Then they saw the owl launch himself out of the tree and set off on his blunt wings into the foggy twilight.

"Our owl!" cried Susan. Of course it wasn't; some ancestor of his would have been Ferdinando's Owl in the days when they hid in the den and had imaginary owls and squirrels to tea. But Rosemary remembered, and grinned. Susan still had her arm round her; and now she was overtaken by the tenderest compassionate affection for Rosemary, she pulled her to her and held her tight so that their bodies were pressed close together.

It was queer, awe-inspiring rather, to think that there was a baby already growing down there where Rosemary's belly touched hers.

THAT EVENING when she told her mother she felt sure it was going to be all right.

Janet was writing in what had been called the Housekeeper's

Room in the days when they had a Housekeeper. She had taken it over for her 'study' (though it was difficult to associate Janet with a study) and in the first pride of ownership she had decorated the walls with trophies of the chase. Foxes and otters peered over her shoulder now as she wrote up her diary for the day:

> *Vet to see Trumpeter ? worms—Ophelia howling mad for Toms vet says best to fix her   Filthy* FOG *all day   !! 6 p.m. Ophelia got out! Too late fix her now !!!*

The foxes, with their sly cads' faces, smirked; the otters looked blah and bored. It was the *furriest* room you ever saw, with foxes' brushes and otters' rudders and pads mounted on wooden shields hung up among the masks and the horseshoes and the hunting-caps and photographs of Janet winning Ladies' Races. Above the fireplace were the heads of two stags which Janet when she was a girl had shot in Scotland; and on the hearth was a rug made from a tiger which her father, the late Earl, had bagged when he was staying with a Maharajah. Susan sat down upon this rug in front of the fire, and told her mother about Rosemary. It was cosy in the little furry room and the conversation was cosy too.

"I'm *awfully* glad you came to me about it," Janet said. "That poor frightened child! I'll go and see the Northovers tomorrow morning."

"How will they take it?"

"They're good people. I'm sure I can put things right."

"And you won't blame Rosemary?"

"Of course not! We'll do everything we can for her," Janet said.

Susan leaned back against her mother's knobbly knees and glanced about her at the furry onlookers. A hare, completely haywire, stared back at her with glassy eyes. Mummy's otter-pole stood in the corner nearby, with fifty notches on it. Susan remembered Bella the Otter, and was encouraged by the reflection that although Mummy had leu'd on the hounds to tear fifty otters to pieces, as soon as she had a personal relationship with one she'd become quite soppy about it. In just the same way, she could be tough and unsympathetic about miners striking or girls having illegits but if you confronted her with a miner hard-done-by or a girl in trouble she'd surely do anything possible to help. The contradiction in her mother's character (she was currently campaigning against gin-traps while foxhunting like mad) puzzled Susan and pleased her. She saw no great virtue in consistency. In sudden affection she stretched back her arm behind her shoulder and Janet caught her hand. Then after a silence Janet said: "Tell you what. Let's rope in the Rector, he's so understanding about the Young." And Susan, face to face with that wild-eyed hare, was aware of the first faint doubt, turned her head sharply to look at her mother, was reassured by the comfortable smile.

THREE DAYS LATER, coming home from hunting in a cold drizzly dusk, she saw the Rector's big black Jaguar parked opposite the Northovers' cottage; and not for the first time she asked herself if she was being uncharitable in thinking that a clergyman oughtn't to possess a car like that. He could well afford it: he was a middle-aged bachelor with a private income compared with which his stipend was mere chickenfeed. But if you set yourself up to preach Christanity, ought you not perhaps to go about your affairs in a car which was rather more the equivalent of the donkey on which your Master rode—say a pre-war Austin 7 with the big-ends bumping? Though it would be a bit of a squeeze for the Rector to get into an Austin 7. His name, Mr. Goodbody, suited him rather well: it suggested a sort of fleshiness. Susan's secret nickname for him was apter still: she called him the Reverend Pigling Bland. His voice was bland and so were his manners and the social graces which oozed out of him as if they were squeezed from a tube He had a snouty kind of face, with a big blunt nose and a chin which receded into his dog-collar in a series of small but plumpish ripples running down towards a prominent and energetic Adam's apple. You had to admit he conducted the services beautifully; his rich baritone intoning *O Lord show thy mercy upon us* fetched exciting echoes out of the church roof. He liked incense (so did Susan) and gorgeous vestments and good music. And he ran a Youth Club, and played the guitar in its band, and organised Saturday hops in the village hall, and used the slang words which the young people used, only they were always about six months out of date.

Anyhow, there was his car, so he was inside the cottage; and Jack Northover wasn't waiting at the stables to fuss over Night-

shade and ask what sort of a day it had been: Was there a fox in
the long osier-bed, then, Miss Susan? Did they run alongside the
river and up the slope into Puckrup? That's the way the varmint
always goes; and when he finds the earth's stopped he turns left-
handed and straight as a die for Whistling Down? . . . Jack knew
every cover, copse or clump that was big enough to hold a fox
within twenty miles of Doddington. You had only to tell him
where the Meet was and at once he conjured up in his mind a
map drawn in such extraordinary detail that the very fences were
identified—"Then you went across Lambkins and Lyppiatts,
skirting Naunton Knapp, and you had to jump that nasty post-
and-rails into Pilgrims Piece and the bit of a brook alongside
Starveall? And d'you tell me your little Nightshade took in her
stride that big hedge beyond, with the drop on the far side of it?"

He'd be proud as pie if she had; for that would be one up to
Doddington, a credit to the family with which he had identified
himself ever since he was a child, yet another demonstration of
the excellence of Us. He was a Seldon-worshipper like his father
before him, who had kept the Seldons' game against the en-
croaching world.

SUSAN SAW THE DANGER now: that he'd look on Rosemary's predicament as a let-down not only of the Northovers but
indirectly of the Seldons too: a discredit to the family, a bad
mark against Us. There was a lot of self-righteousness in Jack; his
outlook was Victorian in most things, and this had lately brought
him into hot dispute with Fenton—their marathon arguments,
concerning politics, morals and religion, went on across the wall
between the stables and the vegetable-garden, day after day.
Susan, passing by there, had surprised them as they raised their
voices to argue across the manure-heap which divided them. She
didn't catch what Jack was saying; but as she came round the corner of the stables she received the full force of Fenton's reply. In
his rasping voice rather like a donkey's bray he delivered himself
of one of those rhetorical questions to which he was addicted—
Do you call that justice? Do you call that democracy? he would
ask Jack Northover, always with the meaningless adjective attached.

"Do you call *that* fucking Christian charity?" he demanded

now; and Susan hurrying past dared not look at Jack lest her grin should suggest that she wasn't as shocked as he was by that word.

THE TAP-WATER RATTLED in Nightshade's bucket, so Susan didn't hear Rosemary coming. She appeared out of the dimmit like a small ghost and spoke in a small flat ghostly voice. Susan couldn't hear what she was saying until she turned off the tap.

"Dad said to leave the mare be, and he'll be along to see to her in a few minutes." Rosemary gave a shrug in the direction of the cottage.

"Rector's in there."

"I saw his car. How did your father——?"

"He said he'd rather see me in my coffin but he didn't mean that and Rector told him he shouldn't of said it. Rector says it'll be all right; people don't count up the months on their fingers; and nobody will think about if any more after I'm married——"

"Rosemary!" cried Susan, sensing betrayal, aware already that she was partly to blame.

"It didn't work out like you said," Rosemary went on in that tired, *beaten* voice; not resentful, just dully compliant. "They all got on to me: I ought to marry him; well, the way they put it, *he* must be made to marry *me*. It'd be bad for all of us otherwise. Dad said he wouldn't be able to look you in the face, and Mum wouldn't feel she could go on working at the Manor. Folks'd be pointing the finger at us. . . . Well, you know. They went on and on. I couldn't stick out against them all, could I?"

"My mother too?" said Susan. I should have gone straight to Daddy, she told herself; and now it's too late. But she still couldn't quite believe her mother had let her down.

"She was very kind," said Rosemary, and continued so tonelessly it was as if she recited a lesson learned in school: "Her Ladyship promised she'd see me all right whatever happened; only she said to talk to the Rector 'fore I made up my mind. Rector knows the curate at Elmbury, and sent him to see Goff. And Goff came out on his push-bike, he's not got the motor-bike, there was trouble over it; he pretended to be cross because I hadn't told him but I knew he was pretending. Then in front of Dad and Mum he said: Just name the happy day; but he gave me a funny sort of look when he said it. I think he hates me for it. They've got to call the banns 'fore we can be done. It'll be in the Church three weeks Saturday, Rector said."

Watching Rosemary as she talked, Susan had an extraordinary impression of the change in her. It was a queer sort of optical illusion, she thought: when a person's spirit shrinks the body looks shrunken too. Now Rosemary's spirit was pinched up inside her, she'd gone into her shell like a snail when you touch the sensitive horns; and she looked so small you'd think she was a schoolgirl. There was another, profounder change. That afternoon at the Oak, Susan had felt she was by far the older and wiser one. Absurd, because after all Rosemary had the experience: but that had been the way it felt. Now it was the other way round. Rosemary must have learned a lot in the last three days; her disillusion was as old as the hills. She'd seen through everything and everybody, seen through Goff, seen through her mother's silly respectability, her father's stiff pride—seen through Mummy, trying to tidy things up, hoping the Rector would fix it,—seen through the Reverend Pigling Bland.

"Rector was kind too. I cried a bit. He kept patting me."

Then Susan could hardly believe her eyes. Upon Rosemary's face, pale as a primrose in the drizzly dark, appeared the shadow of a smile. It hadn't got much fun in it; but it was terribly comprehending. She doesn't trust anybody now, thought Susan: perhaps not even me. She came to me because she trusted me, and by going to Mummy instead of Daddy I let her down . . .

But Susan couldn't think of any comfortable thing to say to Rosemary. In her embarrassment she turned on the tap again. When the bucket was filled she looked up. The stable-yard was empty and silent, the little ghost had gone without another word.

SHE TOOK THE BUCKET in to Nightshade, threw a rug over her, and ran all the way to the house. She found Janet in the study, but the Rector was there too. He must have known he'd get a better tea here than at the Northovers', she thought. He was eating a crumpet, and when he got up to greet her, there was butter running down his chin.

"Hello, drowned rat," said Janet. "Sit down and hear about Rosemary. Happy ending."

Susan squatted down on the cosy tiger-skin, but now she hated the cosiness of the little furry room. She took off her hunting-cap and shook out her damp hair. The shoulders of her coat were soaking, and Janet said: "Do take it off, you're steaming like a racehorse when it's unsaddled." So she sat by the fire in her shirt, the Rector beamed down at her, and the butter glistened on his chin in the firelight. It looked like dribble and it happened to be one of the few things that made Susan feel queasy.

"Now," smiled Janet, looking across at the Rector.

"Where's Daddy?" asked Susan, desperate for an ally.

"He had to go across to Honeysett. Something to do with repairs. But about Rosemary——"

"For the happy ending," began the Rector, "we're really indebted to that very dull stick, but earnest do-gooder, the curate at Elmbury." Janet laughed from her deep armchair, and the Rector wiping his chin at last leaned back in his, and the talk went between them so lightly and casually that they might have been talking about the plot of a new novel that had entertained them: not about real people at all. Janet had often said that she liked the Rector because unlike most parsons he was 'so amusing.' Now he was being amusing about the Northovers, and about Goff, and about George Benson the Elmbury curate who came into the story because Goff had once been a choir-boy at the Abbey. "Really a most worthy fellow, George, though he always makes me think of that remark of Sidney Smith's, 'There is something which excites compassion in the very name of a Curate!' " George Benson had 'chased up' Goff and discovered that "he'd got himself into trouble as well as the girl." He couldn't keep up the instalments on his 100-mile-an-hour motor-bike; so he'd sold it without telling the hire-purchase firm and then "in the words of Mr. Mantellini, he went to the demnition bow-wows—literally." He used the cash which he got for the fast bike to back slow greyhounds: so when George Benson went along "to have a quiet word about the maiden in distress" he found him very sorry for himself, very contrite, very frightened, —"in short just the way George likes 'em when he's out to save their souls."

Susan suddenly found in herself a sort of puritanism which she hadn't known she possessed. The Rector's manner shocked her: half-cynical, half-prep-school, speaking of the Bishop as the

'Bish,' seeming to mock at everything he believed in, or pretended to believe in! And she was horrified at the way Goff's problems had been so neatly resolved. The curate had been to see the hire-purchase people and had persuaded them not to prosecute "a lad who was just about to get married"; and Goff, knowing himself lucky to escape the police-court, had readily agreed to pay off the debt at twenty-five shillings a week. The whole thing sounded like blackmail to Susan, and for the first time in her life she had a glimpse of the Establishment in action, not unkindly but loveless, arranging people's lives for the sake of good order and tidiness, using privilege and power and assurance ever so gently, ever so casually, to settle this trouble which seemed so tiny that it was turned into a joke. Susan remembered a poem of Chesterton's called "The Secret People": "They look at our labour and laughter as a tired man looks at flies." Her new unexpected puritanism burned within her, she hated the Rector and she was angry with her mother, whom she loved. She was appalled by their light-hearted asides and their silly banter:

"So off goes the erstwhile Jehu, pedalling a push-bike for a change, to inform the outraged parents that he wants to make an honest woman of the girl——"

"And now I gather everything's *couleur de rose;* except that we've lost a promising parlourmaid——"

While Janet was speaking, the Rector glanced at Susan. She hadn't said a word yet; and he must have sensed she was against him. Terribly wise, as wise as Rosemary now, she watched him tying to win her by being broadminded.

"Morally," he said, "I can't take these little slip-ups very seriously. I was much less shocked, I can tell you, than her Pa and Ma!"

"Poor old Jack," said Janet.

"So delightfully old-fashioned. He always reminds me," said the Rector, "of a russet apple."

"You hardly ever see them nowadays——"

"The sort that gets better the longer they're kept!—Well, I tried to explain to him about the Young Today. They seem to reject everything we older ones believe in; but they have their ideals all the same." The Rector gave Susan a confidential look as if to imply that he knew all about her ideals. She realised she'd

have to say something soon, and she was terrified and longed for
Ferdo. Meanwhile the Rector went on in his rich voice:

"Believe it or not, the poor girl hadn't even *told* him she was
pregnant! But I'm sure they'll be billing and cooing in no time.
We'll be ringing the bells for them three weeks hence; and as I
told the distracted Northovers, by the time the little blessing
arrives, everybody will have forgotten all about the present
contretemps. . . ."

It was that word 'blessing' that set Susan off. The way the
Rector spoke it seemed to her corrupt and contemptuous. She
would have liked to say something awful, something to shock and
outrage them, the four-letter word that Fenton used which she'd
never said or wanted to say before,—if only she had dared to ask
the Rector: *Do you call that effing Christianity?*

She jabbed angrily at a coal with the poker; and she flared up
like the fire.

"Mummy!" she cried. "Rector! You're doing something awful.
I've talked to Rosemary. He doesn't want to marry her; she
knows he doesn't. It's their lives you're mucking about with.
You're playing it like a game! Rosemary doesn't want to get
married either. She doesn't love him——"

"My dear," said the Rector, "you're not going to tell me that
young Rosemary is a tart or a wanton or anything like that, are
you?" Susan had the impression that he was glad of the opportunity to use the word 'tart' to show how worldly he was. "Surely
she's a romantic, sentimental, *ardent* young girl who's come to
maturity a shade too early? Girls like that don't go to bed with
people they don't love, do they?"

"They do, they do!" cried Susan recklessly, knowing it was
sometimes so but not knowing why it was so; blushing as she said
it, not because of what she said but because she was suddenly struck by the embarrassing absurdity of the Rector's
phrase "go to bed with" in connection with Goff and Rosemary. Then she knew that they had seen she was blushing,
and that they didn't know the real reason, and were simply
amused. Her mother said, "Calm down, pet," and the Rector
looked like the beamish boy in *Through the Looking-Glass*,
and she thought he was going to pat her with his fat white paw.
She believed that if he had, she would have hit him; as it was she

only spilt the tea on the tiger-skin, and tried to mop it up with a handkerchief, and bent down low so that they wouldn't see her blushes. She knew they were laughing at her, Mummy affectionately, the Rector in his sophisticated cynical way that perhaps had a bit of sex mixed up with it—she wasn't sure. So she fled. She blurted out that she was soaking, she'd got to go and change. She mumbled goodbye to the Rector, she didn't dare to look at either of them, and she knew she was a coward as she ran out of the room.

¶ 5

THE WEDDING WAS ON A RAW GREY DAY when a small insinuating east wind whispered its midwinter heresy, that nothing would ever sprout or burgeon or blossom again. The church was cold, and the tiny congregation made it seem colder. Janet and Susan were in the second row, just behind the Northovers— Jack hardly recognisable in a dark suit with knife-edged trousercreases, which probably hadn't been taken out of its drawer since his father's funeral, Mrs. Northover wearing a squirrel shouldercape which filled the whole church with a smell of camphor. Goff and Rosemary standing side by side looked less like a couple about to be married than the trivial victims of some political trial; they seemed to Susan to shrink and shrink as the Rector, whose rich voice might have been that of the prosecuting counsel, pronounced the dreadful prologue to matrimony: *"Not to be enterprised to satisfy men's carnal lusts and appetites like brute beasts that have no understanding. . . . Ordained for the procreation of children . . . for a remedy against sin and to avoid fornication . . ."* and so on. Susan shut her mind against the magnificent and monstrous words and found herself, improperly but not irrelevantly, thinking about the marvels of reproduction. She'd looked up in the Encyclopaedia (*"See also* EGG, EMBRYOLOGY, FERTILITY, GERM PLASM, GESTATION, HERMAPHRODITISM, PERIODICITY [ANIMAL] SEX") and she had been flabbergasted by the notion of 300 million spermatozoa rather like tadpoles launched upon their hour-long swimming race through the dark; only one winner out of all those 300 million! And three times every second, somewhere upon the earth, the race was run to completion; and in some woman somewhere the miracle of pro-creation began.

A great awe came over her, nothing to do with the solemnisa-tion of matrimony, which didn't seem nearly as solemn as the wonder of the thing that had happened to Rosemary when she procreated without any blessing from the C. of E.

And now the Rector was saying:

"Likewise the same Saint Paul, writing to the Colossians, speaketh thus to all men that are married: Husbands, love your wives and be not bitter against them."

A draught chilly as doubt blew around Susan's legs; and per-haps because of the draught everybody shuffled.

¶ 6

SOON IT WAS THE SEASON OF THE HUNT BALLS. Sandra got up parties, and invited young men down from London, pro-viding a succession of partners for Susan out of her seemingly in-exhaustible store. They were all very much alike, rather bored and rather boring: Susan didn't take to them at all. In return for driving her to the dance (tickets supplied by Sandra), buying her a couple of soft drinks, stamping on her feet and nearly tearing her dress off her back in the Gallop, they expected to be allowed to fiddle about with her in a cold car on the way home—and got cross if she wouldn't let them. One of them must have carried his plaint to Sandra, who teased her for being a little iceberg. Susan didn't care: these January days she felt as tight-shut to love-making, of that sort anyhow, as the sealed-up buds on the horse-chestnuts were to the winter sun. Her heart was with Tony, some-where between Seoul and that place with a cruel name, which rang like steel upon ice: Pyongyang.

The war swayed to and fro. Early in the New Year she heard on the wireless that the Chinese had crossed the Imjin; Seoul had fallen, then a place called Wonju; and the British Brigade was back across the Han River.

That was the weekend when Stephen Le Mesurier came down for a day's hunting. Susan asked him what was likely to happen

in Korea, and he said seriously: "There won't be any quick end
to it. Everybody's a bit worried about the prospect of a big Chinese offensive in the spring." Then, seeing her expression, he
added quickly: "I'm sorry, Sukie; I'd forgotten about your Tony
being there."

She had told him about Tony. Although they had only met
two or three times she was more at ease with Stephen than she
had ever been with anyone of her own age, and she felt she could
talk to him about anything. He had taken to calling her Sukie;
she'd no idea why, but it was a nice affectionate name.

The Meet was handy, so instead of taking the horse-box they
rode there together, she on Nightshade, he on Trumpeter, which
she had persuaded Janet to lend him. Most of the day was spent
in the big coverts. They cantered up and down the muddy rides,
got splashed and spattered all over, stood now and then at the
crossings listening to the occasional yelping and to the high-
pitched voice of General Bouverie swearing alliteratively. The
hard-riding ones grumbled at a hunting-day wasted, but Susan
enjoyed being with Stephen and showing him the woods she
knew so well. Their talk ranged from Trollope to Teddy-boys
and from Mozart to men on Mars. They spotted a buzzard circling like a sailplane three hundred feet above them, saw three
foxes, a weasel, a stoat and a badger, which looked cross and
sleepy as if it had just been woken up by the hounds. And
standing by a hazel-brake at the edge of the wood they watched a
big flock of long-tailed tits, a score of them at least, flitting from
twig to twig, blown along by the big wind which turned their
tails inside out like ladies' parasols in a gale. They were like
little trapeze-artists upon the swaying hazel-wands, doing extraordinary acrobatics, more often upside-down than right-side-
up: and during a brief blink of sunlight they looked so pretty, in
their brown-and-white-and-rosy plumage, that Susan turned to
Stephen in sheer delight, and saw her pleasure reflected in his
eyes.

"This is surely the nicest sort of fox-hunting," he said.

Then suddenly out of the dark wood, which up to that moment had been as quiet as the grave, came an astonishing ex-
tempore clamour: a kind of thunderclap of hounds' voices, all
speaking together. The cries fused into a single yell. The fox
must have jumped up right in front of the pack; anxious in case

she might head it back into the wood, Susan edged Nightshade close up to the hazels and beckoned Stephen to her side. Knee to knee they waited there; the horses quivered and flexed their ears. Stephen said quietly:

"Which way do you think he'll go?"

"Over the brook by those willows, then straight for the Park!"

"Sukie, I'm scared stiff!" he said.

The admission took her by surprise; he had such an air of insouciance always.

"I wouldn't have thought you'd have been scared of things."

"I am though! Making a speech in the House. Climbing mountains."

"But you love them, don't you?"

"Love them; but frightened all the same."

"What about the war?" she whispered.

"By turns bored and terrified."

"What were you in?"

"Commandos."

Just then the hounds came crashing through the hazels. The fox must have run up the ditch at the edge of the covert; at any rate Susan didn't catch a glimpse of it. She reined in Nightshade to let the screaming pack go by.

"Why *them,* if you were terrified?" she asked Stephen over her shoulder; and there was just time to hear his answer.

"If you were Jewish as well as British you had one *extra* reason for wanting to get at the bloody Huns."

Then they were off. The hounds were well out in the field now, and streaking towards the willows. The huntsman was with them, and General Bouverie on an enormous horse had come crashing out of the hazels like an elephant bashing its way through bamboos. Susan rode side by side with Stephen to the brook; it was only a little one, and both horses took it in their stride. The hounds were screaming mad and their cry drove Susan mad, she yelled to Stephen "Listen to them, oh listen!" but the wind blew away the words when they were scarcely past her lips. Stephen had noticed that the pack was beginning to swing left-handed, and now without a glance at Susan he turned hard left in quick anticipation and galloped for the fence in the corner against the wood. Susan knew that post-and-rails. It was as tall and solid as if the farmer had wanted to confine kangaroos

instead of Hereford cattle. Left to herself she would have gone
for the gate at the opposite corner, trusting to her good start to
reach it and get through it before the rest of the field caused a
hold-up there. But Stephen was pounding hard for the post-and-
rails, so she accepted the challenge,—wouldn't Nightshade jump
the course at Aintree with her legs tied together? (For a fraction
of a second she remembered Stow Fair. She saw Tony bargaining
with the dealer in the bright sun. The memory warmed her
whole spirit; then the wind seemed to blow it away.)

Stephen was over the post-and-rails. Here goes: she was over
too. She had the impression that there had been a lot of daylight
between Stephen's breeches and the saddle. He hadn't hunted
since before the war, but Trumpeter was an armchair of a horse,
unlikely to peck or stumble. Stephen, still with a short cut in
mind, now led the way through a clump of scattered trees which
straggled out from the edge of the wood. He shouted to her over
his shoulder "Absalom my son my son,—look out!" and tucked
his head into Trumpeter's neck as he tore between the oak-
boughs. Then they were clear of the wood altogether, and galloping down the long slope with a good view of the pack racing up
the hillside opposite them. Susan could see a flock of sheep forming themselves into a kind of defensive phalanx, and what she
took to be a collie-dog about thirty yards from the sheep. Then
she realised it was the fox, only a field in front of the pack. He
was going straight for the Park, as she had thought he would.

The next hedge was a hell of a thing, mixed blackthorn and
hawthorn, which looked even taller than it was because it hadn't
been properly trimmed at the top. It was black and solid and
there was a big drop on the far side; and the approach to it was
downhill all the way. It was one of those obstacles where you
have to 'throw your heart over first and follow it as best you can.'
Stephen had already thrown his. He'd decided the place where
he was going to jump and had aimed Trumpeter at it. Susan
prayed that he would guess about the drop on the other side, and
she was angry with him for risking his neck, and risking Trumpeter, just to show off in front of her, or perhaps to try to prove
that he wasn't really as old as it said in *Who's Who*. (Born 1909;
so he was forty-two.)

She took her eyes off him, while she looked after herself and

Nightshade. Going faster than Susan liked, the mare rose like a bird and simply flew the tall hedge. Susan lay right back and pretended she was riding in the National. Nightshade landed neatly, collected herself, and was off up the opposite hill. Susan out of the corner of her eye saw Trumpeter going well; but now with a long grass field before her, and Nightshade's splendid stride lengthening, she easily caught up with Stephen and decided she'd have no more nonsense: "Follow me, I know every inch from here; he's making for Ferdinando's Oak." It was a good half-mile, all uphill, and Susan doubted whether the fox would make it; but the pack had checked when he ran among the sheep, and he reached the big badgers' earth with minutes to spare. When Susan got there the hounds were milling round the tree, General Bouverie was swearing Blast and bloody shipwreck because the earth hadn't been stopped, and there was nobody else except the huntsman within two hundred yards.

"Here comes your perishing politician," the General shouted at her. "I thought he was going to break his bloody neck." He hated all politicians irrespective of party because they were responsible for the Income Tax. Susan had left Stephen behind when they were over the last fence before the Park. He cantered up to her now with Trumpeter in a foaming lather; the old horse had a look in his eye which seemed to be asking Susan what kind of a devil she had put upon his back. As for Stephen, he'd smeared some blood from a thorn-scratch all over his nose, and looking a bit clownish he gave Susan a most endearing grin, composed of guilt, mischief, relief that he was alive and unhurt, and a sort of boyish conceit which he ought to have grown out of long ago, so that she forgave him for showing off and liked him even better than she had done before.

Now the terrier man arrived in a Land Rover which he'd driven round by Elmbury Back Lane. General Bouverie, with oaths, shouted for spades and a mattock. The terriers whimpered on their leash. The First Whip and the Huntsman gathered up the pack and took it away from the tree, which dwarfed the men and the horses standing beneath its gaunt and wintry boughs.

Susan wondered if Ferdinando's Owl was there, his feathers fluffed out, his head turned right round to see what was going on, his great eyes wide open in annoyance at the clamour that had broken into his sleep. Was there a red squirrel there too? she wondered—and hoped it wouldn't jump down in panic, for the hounds were in a mood to tear to pieces any furry thing. Were the badgers at home, grunting at the fox which had sought refuge in their sett? Were the bats waking up in the hollow trunk, their wings crackling like old parchment?

From where she was, on the slope below the tree, she got a fine view of it against the sky, in which ragged dove-grey windy clouds raced each other across a patch of wan cold starling's-egg blue. The pattern of the bare boughs was familiar; she'd been brought up with that pattern, she would have known straight away if anything were different, if one of the boughs had carried away in a gale. The tree was part of her background. She remembered the games with Rosemary, and climbing with Tony, and Rosemary only the other day in the foggy dusk confessing about her baby; and the owl and the bats and the squirrels, and the badgers which she'd once watched by moonlight with Tony at her side. It was a special tree, and she thought the fox ought to have sanctuary there, it wouldn't be proper to dig him out from among the ancient roots and chuck him clay-streaked and bedraggled to the still-whimpering hounds. So she rode up to General Bouverie, much more frightened than she had ever been during the run, and dared to say:

"Please, Master, do you mind if we leave him where he is?"

"Leave my fox?" roared the General, who always assumed that any fox he chased was his personal property. He goggled at her alarmingly, with hot eyes in a windscorched face; then, just as she was beginning to explain why Ferdinando's Oak was a kind of sanctuary (and feeling rather a fool as she did so) he cut her short with another roar: "Well it's your blasted tree and your perishing Park. You'd have had his brush if we'd caught him, so if you want to save him for another day"—and a slow smile spread over his formidable face like a hint of spring upon a winter land. He clambered up on to his huge horse and yelled and swore at his Huntsman and his Whip and his hounds, and the oaths ringing in their ears meant no more to any of them than the crows cawing, or the jackdaws' raucous chatter as they flew overhead towards their roosts in Elmbury Abbey Tower.

Hounds and horsemen trotted off down the long slope. The

wind sighed in Ferdinando's branches. Somewhere in the dark, down among the gnarled roots lay the panting fox, his muddy sides heaving. Susan was pleased by the thought of him lying so cosy there, and she smiled happily at Stephen, as they rode on together up the hill towards the Manor, and heard far below them the long thin quavering day's-end blast of the horn.

¶ 7

ROSEMARY HAD SAID she would like to have one of Ophelia's kittens to remember her by. As it turned out, there was only one survivor of the half-caste litter, which the vet had to deliver by Caesarean section in order to save the little cat's life. Susan christened it Macduff; and one afternoon in late February she made it her excuse to visit Rosemary for the first time since the wedding.

It was another blowy day—surely this had been the windiest winter for years—and because she enjoyed walking in a gale Susan packed Macduff in a fishing-creel of Ferdo's, which she slung over her shoulder. She went through the loud wood down to the Ferry, routed out old sleepy Jakey, and had the fun of crossing the river in his punt. There was a spring tide running, backed up by the wind. Small waves slapped the punt's side and kicked up a knee-high spray. Susan wondered if her pirate ancestor, growing bored in his retirement, ever came down here to get a whiff of the sea. It was only thirty miles, as the gulls flew or the salmon swam, from Elmbury Weir to the estuary in the Bristol Channel. There were no locks in between, so a high tide like today's came racing up with a surge and a splashing, bringing with it the sea-creatures large and small: fresh-run salmon, lampreys and lamperns, elvers all the way from the Sargasso.

Macduff yowled pitifully, but Jakey was too deaf to hear. He kept his head down and never looked over his shoulder to see where he was going as his long sweeps drove the punt along; but he always fetched up at exactly the same landing-place, where it was easy to jump ashore. If you were a Seldon you didn't have to pay: instead Jakey was rewarded with a present at Christmas consisting of a bottle of rum, two pairs of thick

woollen socks and four ounces of tobacco, which over the years
had become established as the proper recompense for his efforts
in ferrying Seldons across the river about half a dozen times in
the year.

SUSAN FOUND ROSEMARY'S COTTAGE in one of the
back streets close to the river. It was a tumbledown place next
door to a builder's yard. Rosemary asked her in rather hesitantly:
"Goff's here, he's only just getting up, he's on nights." She was
delighted with the kitten, which was greyish-buff with faint tiger-
stripes, and with furry tufts rather like a lynx's coming out of its
ears.

"It's not a bit like Ophelia . . . What's it called?"

"Macduff."

Rosemary wouldn't understand why, of course. But she liked
the name. "Macduff. I'll call him Duffy."

Goff, half asleep, wandered into the room. He'd put on a shirt
but no collar. He wore a thin gold chain round his neck, a silly
affectation for a man, Susan thought, and his neck was white
and puffy: how nasty men looked without collars, how disillu-
sioning to think that when you were married you would often see
them so! He grunted some sort of greeting to her, stared at
Macduff, said "What's that thing?" and went back where he'd
come from without waiting for an answer. Susan said quietly:
"How's it going?" and Rosemary made a face as she shook her
head. She picked up the cat and cuddled him. "He'll be a bit of
Doddington. Oh I do miss it all at home." With the merest hint
of a smile she added: "I dreamt last night I was in your kitchen
with my Mum, and ever so happy, me washing up."

When Susan left, Rosemary followed her out into the lane. She
said:

"He's not on nights really. He's lost his job. There was a
bother about something he took from where he worked. He's in
bad with the police, real trouble, I wouldn't stay with him
else."

Susan said: "You mean there'll be a case?"

Rosemary nodded. "Larceny. *Petty* larceny," she qualified,
rather as if she were differentiating between German measles and
the severer sort. "Sue," she said suddenly.

"Yes?"

"I had a miscarriage. Three weeks ago. I was ever so bad." She bent down over the kitten in her arms. "I needn't of married after all. Funny, isn't it? But it's no use crying over spilt milk, is it?" And she gave Susan another of those little half-smiles, which she found so touching and disturbing.

SUSAN BEAT FURIOUSLY upon the bell which summoned Jakey, and wished she were belabouring the cruel stupidities of the world. That fool of a Rector! Stupid, upright Jack, and his stupid, well-meaning Mrs! Mummy too . . . For the first time in her life Susan understood that you didn't have to be wicked to be cruel. The understanding seemed to open a window in her mind, through which flew in a whole flock of batwinged doubts, questionings and perplexities, concerning the attitudes she'd been brought up to and the things she'd been taught to believe.

Jakey woke up at last, came stumbling down the bank and pulled the punt crabwise across the river; as usual he told her where to sit in order to avoid the tar and where to put her feet in order to keep them dry. The bilge-water slopped about as the punt wallowed. She had leaked ever since Susan could remember her, despite Jakey's lavishness with the tar. " 'Fore very long she'll sink, and there an end," he mumbled now, when they were in mid-stream.

"How old is she?" asked Susan.

"Nigh as old as me, and wore out like most else is hereabouts." Her noisy summons had nettled him and he grumbled at her half-humourously: "The rain comes in my roof every time there's a tidy shower, and the floor's as full of dry-rot as hell's full of devils. I'll catch my foot in a hole and break my bloody neck like as not, one of these fine days when you're banging on that bell fit to wake the jud!"

"You ought to have told us," Susan said. "I'll ask my father to come down and have a look."

"He's got enough on his plate by all accounts." Jakey gave a last strong pull on the oars and glanced at her shrewdly. "Hear tell as it takes the builders all their time to keep the Manor from falling down: and Honeysett's wuss'n the Manor——" Just then the bows came to rest against the half-sunken ferry-boat, and

Susan had to scramble past Jakey in order to jump ashore. She only half-heard the last part of his sentence, and could hardly believe her ears.

"—Hear tell he's thinking of selling the farm."

"Selling *Honeysett?*"

"Leastwise that's what folks say." He didn't look up at her as he sat in the punt, keeping the bows against the ferry-boat with little jerks at the oars.

"Of course he isn't!" she cried. "He'd never——" And suddenly she wondered if it were true, and—if it were—why Ferdo hadn't told her. Angry with Jakey, she forgot to thank him for the crossing, as she ran up the steep bank and took the path into the wet and windy woods.

All the way home she puzzled over what he'd said. She knew Ferdo had been worried about the estimate for the repairs to the farmhouse and buildings. The house was nearly as old as the Manor, and built of the same rose-red bricks and charcoal-black timbers. There was a huge barn which archaeologists came to see and artists loved to paint. It would have been much cheaper to let it fall down and build a new barn; but that was unthinkable, because it was so beautiful. Over the years Honeysett Farm had probably cost the Seldons a lot more money than they had received for it in rent; but not much had been done during the war, and now the tenant was making a great fuss about the state the place was in. Tom Taynton was a youngish farmer who'd made money, married a smart girl from Birmingham and grown right out of the old yeoman ways which his father had followed. Susan could just remember his father, trotting cloppity-clop to Elmbury market in a float, with a couple of calves or a sow-and-pigs under the netting. But when you met Tom in Elmbury Back Lane he was generally driving much too fast in an expensive car, and was more likely to be on his way to the races than to market. He always seemed well off, and he had a fine herd of Jersey cows which grazed the Park under some old-fashioned arrangement that gave the tenant of the Home Farm the right to turn out his beasts there. But Susan didn't take to him, and wondered whether he'd made his money out of black market deals during the war when everything was scarce. He might even have got enough, or be able to raise enough, to make an offer for Honeysett Farm.

But if he had, wouldn't Ferdo have told her? Lately she'd been learning to keep the estate accounts and writing his business letters for him. Whenever she had tried to bring up the question of looking for a job or getting herself trained for one—taking a secretarial course for instance—Ferdo had told her: "Have a look at my desk. There's job enough for you there!" So it would be surprising if he had thought of selling Honeysett and hadn't told her; still more so if he hadn't told Janet. But perhaps he was so worried about money that he was *afraid* to tell them?

Susan knew he was worried. He was still drinking too much, and some days he wasn't himself at all: he was always forgetting things, and losing things, and fussing unduly over trivialities while he let important matters go hang. But there were other days when he was easy and happy and just like he used to be; almost schoolboyish in his enthusiasms. He'd bought her a 16. bore for Christmas, and he loved to take her shooting in the woods,—though the poachers from Elmbury had most of the game nowadays, and often Susan and Ferdo walked miles for a brace of pheasants or one or two snipe, or a wild duck put up along the river. When she shot her first woodcock Ferdo was so proud of her that as soon as they got home, although it was tea-time, he insisted on opening a bottle of champagne: Susan and Janet drank half a glass each and he drank the rest! But sometimes, although they carried their guns 'in case anything happened to get up,' they hardly bothered to look for game. Ferdo was happy simply to walk among the trees; and she to relearn the paths through the woods she'd known when she was a child.

But the woods seemed to have changed since then. In her memory there had always been a lot of sunshine, the unfolding bracken-fronds were more golden than green, there were broad clearings where the insects buzzed and the birds flitted in a special sort of honey-coloured light: lakes of luminescence in which every bee and every butterfly became a pinpoint of light as it swam there. And there were pools and rivulets and alleys and tunnels of sunshine going between the trees; and there were great banks of flowers in their seasons, bluebell and bedstraw, wood sorrel and foxglove, and woodruff that smelt as sweet as hay. What she saw when she looked back into her childhood was

like a glade in the Forest of Arden shown upon a bright-lit stage:
Here shall you see No enemy But winter and rough weather.

But now the woods were darker, she was sure of it: and there
were fewer flowers. Birch-scrub and hazel invaded the clearings;
undergrowth filled the spaces between the trees. Some of the half-
remembered paths were grown over, or blocked by fallen trees
which nowadays were hardly ever cut up and carried away. And
surely there were *more* trees blown down than there used to
be?

Walking back through the woods this afternoon, Susan could
see how the windy winter had taken its toll. A fallen oak-tree
used to be rare and remarkable; but Susan counted seven as she
went through Jubilee Wood. They hadn't been uprooted. They
were broken off; and Susan who'd been brought up in the woods
knew that this could only happen when the timber was decayed.
The rot was caused by a fungus; and this year there had been
more toadstools than ever, speckled and leprous-white and tawny
and canary-yellow,—even some bright orange-scarlet ones.

But the yellowish-brown toadstools, the honey fungi, were the
ones which mattered: Ferdo had explained to her that wherever
they showed themselves at the base of a tree, there was the rot
spreading secretly in the root or under the bark. Because this had
been such a mild, wet winter, some toadstools had lived all
through it; and Susan nearly stepped on a whole tuft of them as
she scrambled over a fallen sycamore which lay across the path.
On a silly impulse she kicked at them; bits stuck to her shoe. The
woods were growing darker, and suddenly, away on her left, she
noticed a tree that shone with a kind of death-light, like a ghost.
She knew what it was because she'd met with the same thing two
or three times this winter, when she hacked home late after hunting. The same honey fungus which threw up the toadstools was
at work within the timber, and caused it to be luminous as it
rotted. Even though Susan knew the cause, it was an uncomfortable thing. She was dismayed by the faintly-glowing tree, she
had a sense of decay going on all about her, and she caught
herself hurrying up the slippery path through the darkening
wood. She was even a little afraid, though she knew there was
nothing physical to be afraid of; and suddenly without warning
all the doubts and disbeliefs came flapping back into her mind.

She wished she had somebody to talk to, but she didn't feel very close to Janet, or even to Ferdo now; there was only Stephen— but he hardly ever came down when the House was sitting—and Tony at the other side of the world. She had never before felt so much on her own as she did this evening, coming into the twilit Park through the gate out of Jubilee Wood. The wind had dropped, and all at once there was such a breathless stillness that when Ferdinando's Owl uttered his first hoot of the night, far from being startled, she was glad of his companionship.

B U T A T H O M E on the hall-table there was a letter from Tony, brought by the afternoon postman who would still bicycle all the way from Elmbury into the back of beyond to deliver, perhaps, a single tradesman's bill to Doddington Manor.

The letter had been written three weeks ago from somewhere close to the Han River: for though he didn't mention any place-names Tony wrote of a big river frozen hard as iron, a regiment of tanks could cross it without the ice cracking; and Susan by now knew the map of Korea like the back of her hand.

It was the best letter she'd had from him since he left. He missed her! He thought of her most of the time, he said! He begged her to write him pages and pages, about herself and all her doings, about Doddington. He said he was colder than he'd ever been in his life; and he wished he had Sue in his sleeping-bag to warm him. While he wrote the letter he could hear the guns. They were putting down a barrage far away to the north, and the flashes were like sheet-lightning flickering behind the hills: the sound of them was rather like a pack of hounds woofing and yelping a long way off in an echoing wood. Susan knew what he meant, because she'd heard that noise when she was about eight: the confused bark of the guns defending London that followed the pale flashes as they flicked in the sky. She was curiously pleased and proud, that she'd been there to hear it, and hadn't been sent to America 'for the duration,' as Sandra had. It seemed to bring her closer to Tony in his far-away war.

B U T W H E N S H E C A M E to write her letter back, she couldn't bring herself to say any of the things she really wanted to say. If only she had dared she would have quoted from *Gallop apace* and let Shakespeare say them for her. As it was, she said she'd like to be with Tony in his sleeping-bag and then, suddenly embarrassed, lapsed into chitter-chatter about the Hunt Balls and Sandra's young men and Colonel Daglingworth getting an O.B.E. in the New Year's Honours,—*"Nobody quite knows why, Daddy calls it Other Buggers' Efforts!"* She told him about Rosemary's wedding, and how she hated the Rector, and about the sort of winter it had been, wild and windy with only one short spell of frost when a Meet had to be cancelled because of the bone in the ground . . . Using the old country expression she realised for the first time how vivid it was, 'bone in the ground,' a sort of poetry,—like that other countrymen's phrase she had put in her letter: *"The countryside was blind up till Christmas,"*— blind because you couldn't see through the hedges where the leaves hung late.

And now her pen went easier, as she wrote about Doddington and the woods and the little things which a man at the other side of the world might like to know: about the dying tree that shone like a will-o'-the-wisp in the dark, about Nightshade (*"I'll never never forget you buying her for me, that day at Stow"*), about the run that finished up at Ferdinando's Oak and her daring to ask General Bouverie to spare the fox. *"Stephen Le Mesurier came out with me on Trumpeter—I like him awfully,"* she wrote; then had second thoughts and scrapped that page just in case Tony might be so foolish as to be jealous of her liking awfully a man who was twice as old as herself. Instead she told him about the flock of long-tailed tits which she'd watched that day with Stephen: *"There must have been thirty or forty, all bowled along by the wind. Do you remember how we used to find their nests in the sloe-bushes and how warm it felt inside them when you poked your finger through the little entrance-hole? Mumruffins, we called them. What a funny word, I've just said it aloud to myself, Mumruffin, I wonder why. . . .*

"It was in the same place where I saw the mumruffins that I got my woodcock—on the north side of Victoria Wood where the hazels are and the clump of snowberries, covered all over with their big white camphor balls. It flitted out of the trees silently like a ghost-bird and it fell as soft as a leaf. I couldn't believe I'd shot it and I just stood there hearing the echo of my shot in the

wood on the hill and smelling that queer sharp smell of powder when you open the gun. Then Daddy gave a cheer and ran and picked it up, and took what he calls the pin-feather to wear in his old green hat . . ."

¶ 8

UPON A HILL WITHOUT A NAME, called 235 on the map, Tony reread the letter by the first light of the dawn. The cold of the night had got into his bones, and the wound in his left leg nagged him. Although it was late April there had been a heavy frost, and a thick white mist shrouded the hill. For the moment, everything was quiet. A living man who lay out in front with the dead ones had been howling all night like a werewolf to the moon. Now that he was silent and perhaps dead there had fallen an extraordinary hush in which even the twitter of the first waking bird sounded important. Soon the Chinese would be blowing their bloody bugles again; and after that there'd be no more listening to bird-song. Tony wondered idly what kind of bird the lonely twitterer might be, and ached with homesickness for Doddington and mumruffins.

Already in the sloe-bushes they'd be hanging up those endearing little nests, spidersilk-lined and lichen-encrusted. Pink-tipped buds on the crabtrees, ladysmocks in the snipe-meadow, anemones in Jubilee Wood, kingcups by the river so shiny you'd think the bees could see their faces in them, bumbles blundering along hedgesides, and the cuckoo's voice . . .

But between Tony and Doddington lay not only twelve thousand miles, but a good many thousand Chinese.

THE BATTLE HAD BEGUN three nights ago. It was the Glosters' first big battle, though they had skirmished now and then, and had one sharp fight, in the course of their travels up and down the harsh unlovely land. It seemed years, not months, that they had been here: bumping along in convoy between the frozen paddy-fields, foot-slogging over the frozen hills, bitter bivouacs outside the ruined villages where there were sometimes notice-boards warning DANGER—SMALLPOX! put up by earnest

Americans, concerned as ever with hygiene amid chaos. They had passed and repassed the same unending files of limping refugees, the old men with the faces of philosophers resigned to futility, the old women bearing enormous burdens, the young ones heavy with child, the little girls carryings their tiny brothers, whose heads lolled like those of idiots as they slept.

So they had come for the second time to the broad Imjin River, where they disposed themselves about a village called Choksong, watching and waiting for the expected Chinese attack. It came one night at moonrise, swift and powerful as a flood on the Imjin, sweeping their defences away. Fighting as they fell back, they had climbed up through a gorge with steep sides, which in Tony's eyes seemed to possess the same doom-laden aspect as Glencoe. As flank-guard to the retreating Army, it was their duty to find a good position and there to stand and fight; so at last they set up their defences on a lonely hill, from which they could watch, though they could not prevent, the Chinese on both their flanks filtering through to the southward. The Glosters had left much behind during the withdrawal; they were short of water, food, ammunition and above all batteries, without which communication became impossible and the last contacts would be lost. They were cut off already from Brigade headquarters: and before long they knew that their encirclement was complete. Yesterday two attempts to relieve them had failed; so had an airdrop from Japan. They had heard the throb of the engines as the big "box-cars" flew round and round above the mist; and they knew the American pilots could see nothing beneath them but a cotton-woolly whiteness, goosefeather heaps piled high upon each of the hills. The throbbing faded and died away towards the west.

So the Colonel had closed up his companies into a tighter perimeter at the top of the hill. The Chinese bided their time, while the mist concealed their preparations and prevented attack from the air. In the early stages of the battle the fighters had got through now and then to attack the Chinese with their guns and to drop the napalm bombs, which when they burst raised huge blue-black smoke-shapes, that looked like genii with fiery en-trails, and seemed somehow to belong to the landscape, native demons of these demonic hills. But since the mist had come down, there could be no air-support; and the Chinese were able to creep closer, unseen.

Waiting for the attack upon a long spur of the hill, Tony's company had grumbled in their slow Gloucestershire voices, dursn't this and carsn't that, and cursed whatever bastards had let them in for the war; but when the assault fell on them, and the Chinese scrambling over their own dead drove in the outer defences, Tony had gathered up a handful of these men who dursn't and carsn't, with a Sergeant from Chipping Campden and a Corporal from the Forest of Dean, and had led them downhill in a furious counter-attack to win back the spur. In the course of this fight some splinters from a hand-grenade, which killed the Corporal, had ripped open his left thigh and knee. He hadn't thought much of it at the time and there had seemed no point in going to the Regimental Aid Post, even if he could find it in the dark. Back in the redoubt which was his Company headquarters he'd put on a field-dressing and counted himself lucky that he hadn't lost his leg. (*No Grand National!* had been his first thought, when the metal-fragments hit him.) Only this morning, when the Company stood to at dawn, had he realised that something was wrong with his knee-cap and that he could scarcely hobble along.

Nevertheless he'd still thought of it as a little wound; he hadn't realised its import, which was out of all proportion to the actual damage, until his H.Q. radio-telephone faintly crackled and he listened to the voice of the Colonel, who sounded a thousand miles away instead of a couple of thousand yards. The Colonel said he had just sent a message to Brigade: *From Glosters. Only thirty minutes of battery remain*; and Brigade in reply had given the Battalion permission to fight its way out. "Company by Company," said the Colonel, "as best we can." Then Tony had forced himself to put his weight upon his left leg and to try a pace forward; and he knew he'd be lucky if he could go five yards.

"Then you'll have to stay behind," said the Colonel, "with the rest of the wounded. And me."

HELPLESS AND HAMSTRUNG, Tony waited for the stretcher-bearers who were going to take him to the R.A.P. He

had said his goodbyes. Good luck old boy . . . Good luck Sergeant,
see you back home at Horfield Barracks. . . . Best of luck, C.S.M.,
I'm sure you're going to make it, for once in a way the mist ought
to be a bit of a help . . . He'd watched the men sorting through
their kit, throwing away what wasn't worth taking, pulling down
balaclavas over tingling red ears; stubbly, grimy, dawn-grey faces,
but he loved them and he wondered how he would ever bear to
see them march away. He listened to the Gloucestershire voices,
grumbling still (but no more bitterly than at home they'd have
grumbled about the weather) concerning the United frigging
Nations and the bullshit which the silly bastards talked there;
carsn't do this, dursn't do that: the voices of the men who'd say
mumruffin instead of long-tailed tit.

And he read Sue's letter and thought of Sue.

HE THOUGHT ABOUT THAT AFTERNOON at the Otter
Pool: swimming among the lily-pads and the pink-flushed flowers, Sue with the whole world before her asking about pink
champagne,—"I shall try it one day. I shall try *everything*"; then
Sue eating the sun-warmed apricot; laughing as she wiped the
juice off her face, lying back on the grass with arms and legs
stretched wide; suddenly rolling over to him and making her
clumsy and inexperienced gestures of love, as she tried to say
with her body what she was much too shy to put into words:
Here I am, all of me, take it, the lot.

It wasn't very like him, he thought wryly, to refuse anything in
that direction when it was presented to him on a plate. Life was
short and youth was shorter, so one might as well pack into it
all the happy things that were going. It would surely have
been a happy thing to make love to Sue, and he'd often regretted not doing so. At other times he'd been glad (and surprised at being glad), for reasons which he couldn't explain
to himself but which had little to do with the conventional
decencies. All this had led him to think a great deal about
Sue, to write her a lot of letters, to conjure up her picture at all
sorts of unexpected moments, even in the middle of a battle.
Always he saw her against the background of Doddington, the
cool green woodlands which were all the more beautiful by contrast with this hideous land.

Hideoụs in all respects, benighted and Godforsaken, not worth fighting for, he told himself in sudden bitterness: the mouldering villages, the squalid towns, everywhere war's wreckage which scarcely mattered because it merely piled ruin upon the ruin which was here before; and the ungainly countryside with its treeless plains flat-faced and ugly as the Gooks themselves, with its uncouth dark gorges and its bald bitter hills . . .

The mist was melting away (the weather hereabouts seemed always to be in league with the enemy) and through the rifts the grey-brown slopes revealed themselves. With their patches of scrub and their outcrops of rock they were like mangy skins, the pelts of old beasts wasted to mere bags of bones. There was no greenness anywhere, and there were hardly any flowers other than the dwarf azaleas, which made crimson streaks along the watercourses, looking like trickles of blood.

A wind got up, the old familiar wind which even in April seemed to have a snarl of Siberian wolves in it.

FOR A LITTLE WHILE resentment and despair altogether possessed him. He dreaded captivity. It was the thing he had always feared most in war. He had never been afraid of being killed, because although that fate demonstrably occurred to others he had never believed it would happen to him; and by reason of that disbelief he had been called brave. But to lie in prison and to rot, month after month, perhaps year after year, never knowing how things went in the world outside: he knew only too well that his mind didn't possess the resources to deal with a predicament like that. He had never been able to find contentment within himself. He depended on friends, parties, drinks, games, girls. Now he was frightened not only of captivity but of cracking up in captivity. He thought he might give in, turn his face to the wall and die.

He tried to imagine what it would be like, the brooding bitterness, the harking-back to happy days, the counting-up of all the things you were missing, the knowledge that day by day and hour by hour what remained of your youth was wasting away.

Better to be dead, he thought.

A sudden weird whimper, from the slope below, informed him that the wounded Chinese who'd howled so horribly wasn't dead after all. He was taking a long time about dying. Tony, looking into his heart, couldn't discover the least morsel of pity for him, which was surprising in a way when he reflected that he'd made love to a Chinese girl when he went ashore at Singapore on the voyage out; and that girl, with her pretty face and manners, could conceivably by a football-pool sort of chance be the whimperer's sister!

He let his thoughts leapfrog over her to Sue with her glowing body lying in the sun; then leapfrog again (in panic almost, because the previous image was too immediate for this hour) to an earlier recollection, affectionate and asexual, of the long-legged kid climbing Ferdinando's Oak, glancing up dubiously at the next bough above her, then grinning down at him: Dare me to go higher!

He recognised the grand design of the branches against the sky, and he realised that he would take that tree with him wherever he was going, acorns and oak-apples and Ferdinando's Owl, and Sue just before she grew up laughing at him through the leaves.

TWO STRETCHER-BEARERS came to carry him to the Regimental Aid Post. One said:

"You'll have plenty of company, Sir. There's an awful lot of wounded up there."

"The Colonel's going to stay behind," said the other. "He's walking about up there with his hands in his pockets, puffing away at his pipe."

Just then the Chinese soldier on the slope gave vent to another long howl.

"Listen to that poor bugger." There was another of those silences—it always seemed specially still when the tormented man ceased his crying—and then from several directions at once came the sound of bugles untunefully braying in the village below. There was no sense in the sound: raucous, incoherent, it went on and on.

"No better'n caterwauling," said one of the stretcher-bearers contemptuously.

At last it raggedly ceased. For a moment the whole hillside seemed to be hushed in expectancy; then most marvellously, and with a sort of Old Testament propriety, a single bugle answered

from the very summit of the hill. It blew the long reveille, vali-
ant, defiant and beautiful, and the stretcher-bearers looked from
one to the other, and then to Tony, in wonder and awe.

"The Colonel said he was going to tell the drum-major to blow
it."

The last echoes of the desperate challenge died away; and all
at once such a cheer went up that it seemed the very hill was
shouting, and Tony raising himself up from the stretcher found
himself shouting too. Hurray, hurray! he yelled and waved his
valediction to the cheering men who slung their rifles and
squared their shoulders and in small purposeful groups began to
move down the gulleys into the mist and the menace below.

PART FOUR

Roundheads and Cavaliers

¶ 1

THE NEWS CAME FROM KOREA on a day of April showers when white clouds proud as argosies sailed the blue sky. In Elmbury streets rheumaticky old men straightened their backs, and slummocking young ones squared their shoulders, because of the last stand of the Glosters on the far-away hill. Dustmen and drapers and pubcrawlers and postmen and shop-assistants and spivs recalled what they had half-forgotten, that they had been soldiers too. Each one that day remembered his little Agincourt.

All those, and the women also, who could hear in their memories the terrible tramp of the man who marched away, looked up from the street at the Abbey's tremendous tower, and saw the Cross of Saint George, at the top of its mast, grandly flying there.

FERDO AND SUSAN saw it as they came out from the oaktrees into the feggy wet field called Cuckoo Pen that lay between Sexton's Spinney and the river.

Ferdo had rung up a friend at the War Office to ask if anything was known about Tony. The expected answer was *Missing Believed Prisoner of War*. Ferdo had said to Susan: "Let's go a walk": so they set off on this proud-pied April morning across the Park and through Jubilee Wood where a million anemones tossed their heads in the wind; downhill by a path hardly used nowadays, through knee-high dog's mercury, which felt cold as cucumber when you trailed your hand in it; and out into the brightness by the river, where the Abbey Tower loomed up before them and the white flag with the red cross on it billowed out against the shining white and blue.

In Cuckoo Pen, very properly, the air was full of voices, as unseen cuckoos called to each other from all the points of the compass. The green was coming shyly on the willows, and round about some golden sallies the bees hummed. All this, much more than the flag, Susan thought, seemed to stand for England and for your sadness and your pride. She dared not look at Ferdo as they went across Cuckoo Pen and through a gate into a green lane, still squelchy, where little frogs jumped up like tiddlywinks before their feet. This was the place where she and Tony used to find orange-bellied newts when they were small, and where always at this season frog-spawn floated in the ditches and on the little pools left behind by the last flood, as if a precipitation of tapioca had fallen like manna from heaven there. And along this lane there had always been flowers. Today there were cowslips and kingcups and celandines and of course cuckoo-flowers, lilac sheets of ladysmocks overflowing from the ditchsides into the meadows beyond. The voices of the cuckoos went to and fro; and all at once it seemed too painfully beautiful, and Susan put her elbows on the gate at the bottom of the lane, and her face in her hands, and wept. She hadn't done so since she was a child; and hardly ever then. When Ferdo came up beside her she made a desperate gesture with her hand towards the flowery lane, and understanding at once, he gave her a bit of a grin and nodded. He knew how spring flowers could touch you. With Janet it would have been quite different. If she had cried, it would have been because of the flag.

THAT EVENING there was more about the Glosters on the wireless. They had been given the President's Distinguished Unit Citation, which was the highest honour in the U.S. Army. The American General had said that their stand had allowed the First Corps time to regroup and so had saved it from encirclement and destruction. The Brigadier in his Headquarters Log had written beneath the Battalion's last signal: *Nobody but the Glosters could have done this.* And now, with whatever reserves and survivors it could scrape together, the Regiment had reported that it was operational again. Nothing was known yet of the fate of the men who tried to fight their way out or of the wounded who stayed behind.

Ferdo fetched up from the cellar two bottles of his favourite claret. Janet had only one glass, but Susan decided to try the experiment of getting a little drunk for once in a way, and she drank three glasses at dinner and finished a fourth while she sat with Ferdo afterwards. Over his port he told her how the Regiment had won its back-badge at the Battle of Alexandria in 1801; the French had attacked in darkness and broken through, so that the front and rear ranks of the Glosters, engaged simultaneously, found themselves fighting back to back. "That old boffin," said Ferdo, pointing to one of the ancestors, "fought as an Ensign with the Regiment then; and that one over there was in the Navy, and in command of one of Nelson's frigates just off shore, while the battle was going on . . . Have a glass of port—You might as well be hung for a sheep as a lamb."

After that he insisted on taking her on a tour of the ancestors hanging round the dining-room walls, beginning with the one who'd fought against the Armada and who looked as if he possessed the piratical dispositions of Captain Kidd, Captain Avery, Bartholomew Roberts and Long John Silver all rolled into one. Next they saluted the one-armed cavalier who had ridden with Rupert, and thereafter some of the soldiers who'd fought at Quebec, Corunna, Waterloo, Delhi, Sevastopol and Ladysmith, and some sailors who, according to Ferdo after he'd drunk his port, had fought all over the five oceans and the seven seas.

So Susan went upstairs feeling very pleased to be a Seldon, and the feeling lasted just as long as she stayed upon her feet. The moment she got into bed, and lay back on her pillow, the head of the bedstead seemed to rise up behind her, while the foot of it fell away in front. So she see-sawed for a while as if on the Big Dipper at a Fair, or in Ancestor Ferdinando's barque bucketing about the Atlantic; until at last the nausea became intolerable, and she was sick.

IN THE MORNING she had her first hangover, but half an hour on Nightshade's back was enough to blow it away. There was a place called the Long Gallop, under the woodside at the top of Honeysett Farm, where the Regency Seldons used to race their expensive horses. Susan wished she could conjure them back for a little while and match Nightshade with the best of them! She finished her gallop in front of the farmhouse. Tom Taynton, very much the gent in a new check suit, standing by his car, with a racing badge in his lapel, waved to her and shouted: "If you were running I'd back you for the two-thirty!" She hated him now, because she knew that he had persuaded her father to sell him Honeysett, and after next September she'd only ride here by his grace and favour.

Of course there was no real reason why Ferdo shouldn't have sold it. He'd be better off without it, and would save himself some worry as well as cash. The farm lay right at the edge of the estate, well away from the Park and the woodlands, and indeed jutted out like a peninsula into his neighbour's territory; so you might almost say that it tidied things up to let Tom Taynton have it for what seemed to be a very fair price. "After all," said Ferdo, seeking to justify himself, "it's only right for a go-ahead young chap to own his place, especially when he means to invest a bit of money in it." Tom Taynton had promised faithfully to cherish the old farmhouse and look after the beautiful barn; and he wouldn't build on the land or put it to any different use. Susan thought privately that his promises weren't worth much, and she wondered again how on earth he could have made, or had managed to borrow, all the money he'd need to pay for the farm and to put the buildings in good repair.

She wondered too, although the price seemed a good one, who had really got the better of the deal. She couldn't see Ferdo being very clever over anything to do with money nowadays. She had been troubled about him lately, watching a gradual change which might be due to his drinking, or to his old wound, or to money worries, or most likely to a combination of all those causes. She had begun to notice some disturbing oddities, which were different in kind from the ordinary failings (such as forgetting several times a day where you had left your spectacles) which she sadly concluded must be inseparable from the awful business of growing old. They didn't amount to much in themselves. They were even rather endearing, because in a sense they were extensions into extravagance of the natural quirks of Ferdo's character. For instance he had always been inclined to let the toss of a coin settle small questions for him. Out walking with Sue he'd say: Heads we go this way, tails we go that. But nowadays he seemed to have difficulty in making up his mind about anything; so in cases of doubt he would toss his lucky half-crown and leave the decision to fate or chance or the Almighty. (But that wasn't the end of it: thereafter like as not he'd pretend to himself that for some reason the toss hadn't been fair, and try again!) And there were stranger things. Susan had noticed that he generally appeared at breakfast with bits of cotton-wool stuck upon his chin, because he had scraped it with an old, rough razor-blade. Yet he refused to treat himself to a new one; and by cross-examining him one evening when he'd had a good deal to drink Susan discovered the extraordinary reason. Upon the morning when he had heard on the wireless that the Korean war had started he'd happened to be shaving with a brand-new razor-blade, and on the spur of the moment he had made one of his peculiar bets with God or the Devil: I bet I'll make this blade last as long as the war does! It was half a game which he played in his mind, half a sort of mumbo-jumbo. Added to all the other little oddities, she found it dismaying; and so she began to feel out of touch with her father, at a time when she needed him especially. She tried to talk to her mother about it; but Janet seemed not to have noticed anything amiss, and was unexpectedly cross with her for having mentioned it.

All this made Susan very lonely during the long sad summer when Tony seemed to be not thousands but millions of miles away, if he were indeed alive. She'd had no letters; and writing to him was like talking into a void. It was a dry season, and she matched it with a long drought of her spirit; even the glory of the Glosters had faded with the spring flowers.

FROM TIME TO TIME she sought out Fenton and asked him questions about the life of a prisoner of war. Some of his goalers had been Koreans, and on the whole he thought they were worse than the Japanese; but "Nips or Chinks or Gooks, there was nothing much to choose between 'em" and in Fenton's opinion it took a practised eye to tell 'em apart. His socialism was not of the international kind. As much of any old pre-war Blimp he disliked and distrusted foreigners.

He talked well when Susan got him going, always out of the

side of his big mouth, and with a slow sardonic humour. He liked to lean on something—a tool-handle or a gate—in some posture ungainly as a camel's. Having achieved the right attitude, he would stay still as a gnarled and crooked tree, until the conversation ended.

So Susan learned a little of what it was like to be inside the barbed wire cage. She *saw* through Fenton's eyes; she *felt* through her quick imagination. She began to understand how much a man's body could put up with, in the way of hunger and humiliation, discomfort and disease, yet the moment his spirit broke he was on the way out, nothing could save him. You only lived so long as you were interested in living. You had to care about something. "Even hating kept some blokes alive," Fenton said. "I've seen 'em stop hating and die. And little things kept you going. There was a little queer fellow in my lot who was queer to start with; but he started taking an interest in spiders and he'd lie in the hut for hours half dead of dysentery, watching his spiders eating flies. You might say spiders kept him from packing it in."

"What kept *you* going?" Susan asked.

He gave her one of his sidelong grins.

"I've often wondered myself. Just bloody obstinacy, I daresay."

¶ 2

FENTON'S ATTITUDE TOWARDS THE SELDONS was curious and complicated. Tony's being a prisoner of the yellow men, as he himself had been not long ago, seemed to form a kind of bond with Susan, indeed to put her on his side against the assortment of enemies whom he thought of as Them. "They" were the capitalists, the bosses, the aristocrats, the middle-classes, the shop-keepers, the business-men, the armaments-manufacturers, the Tories, the Stock Exchange, the generals, the admirals, the diplomats; all the people who caused or contrived wars and having done so mismanaged them so that ordinary poor buggers were made prisoner, maimed or slaughtered. Janet, in Fenton's eyes, was obviously one of Them: an enemy of the working-class. He hated and feared her. But Ferdo presented him with a conflict of loyalties. On the one hand, he was the boss and a Baronet and worse still a Naval Officer. Fenton had always hated officers. His service had begun in big ships, when he had little contact with them except as an occasional Defaulter. They were known among him and his friends as the Pigs Aft, and were thought to spend most of their time drinking gin in the Ward Room. So it was almost embarrassing to Fenton to discover that he actually enjoyed the company of this Boss and Pig when, for instance, they built bonfires together and nearly set the place on fire. Resentment against Ferdo contended in his mind with a reluctant affection for Ferdo which came about through the jobs they did together, the handy things, the contrivances and the ingenuities such as the syphoning out of the flood-water from the cellar, over which they spent half a dozen happy afternoons.

In July, after a longish drought, there had been some thunderstorms; and shortly afterwards the still-slimy floor of the cellar became submerged again and the unaccountable flood rose suddenly, this time to eighteen and a half inches on Ferdo's measuring-stick, which brought it to within three inches of the bins containing the wine. Egbert, whom Ferdo consulted, would have nothing to do with the problem. To him it was a visitation, a manifestation of the power of Nature, perhaps an Act of God: in any case there was no remedy. But Fenton, whose thought-processes were somehow ungainly and angular like his body, bent his mind to the business and discovered a clumsy, awkward but workable expedient. He observed that the level of the Otter Pool was a little below that of the flood on the cellar floor. Ferdo, seeing the point, bought a hundred yards of rubber tubing. By means which were laborious, ingenious and absurd they contrived to fill this tube with water while one end of it, plugged with a bung, remained anchored in the cellar. Then they bunged up the other end and lowered it into the Otter Pool. Next they contrived a signalling device by means of a ball of string and a bell. Ferdo wearing fishing waders and standing in the Otter Pool tugged the string as he removed the bung from his end of the tube; Fenton in the cellar heard the bell ring and simultaneously did likewise. To their great joy the water was syphoned out of the cellar to within about two inches of the floor. Having reached, presumably, the level of the water in the Otter Pool, it could not be syphoned any further; and thereafter many things went wrong—it wasn't easy to keep the long tube in position— and the water began to rise again. But a theory had been proved and a natural law demonstrated; this delighted both Ferdo and Fenton and reinforced their mutual respect.

Hydraulics began to possess them. Egged on by Susan, Ferdo decided one day that it would be fun to make the boy's statue pee again into the pool. Fenton, while he realised that this was a wicked waste of labour and material for the sole purpose of gratifying a whim of the rich and foolish, became fascinated by the problem against his will. He and Ferdo collaborated in the installation of a small electric pump and then contrived a tiny urethra within the bronze statue. At last they switched it on, and it worked. They happily experimented with it, regulating the volume of the stream, and from time to time adjusting the angle. They played with it like naughty children; it gave them hours of enjoyment. Ferdo declared that it was his contribution towards the gaiety of the nation at the time of the Festival of Britain, which was then in full swing. Doddington's other contribution was a Fête at which Ferdo was in charge of the bowling for the pig and Fenton won the pig. Ferdo provided a sty for it, and lest it should be lonely bought another weaner for himself, to keep it company. He and Fenton then decided to share the pigs, on the basis that Ferdo would pay for the food, while Fenton would see to the feeding and clean out their sty. This arrangement worked very well, and often the two pig-keepers might be seen together leaning upon the gate of the sty, watching the pigs enjoying their swill.

Both Janet and Mrs. Fenton, for different reasons, deplored this growing friendship. Janet disliked Fenton, Mrs. Fenton dis- liked Ferdo. Neither approved of the pig-keeping (Mrs. Fenton was in any case a strict vegetarian) and neither saw any point in the waterworks at the Otter Pool. Janet thought the whole thing was 'rather silly'; while Mrs. Fenton was surprisingly shocked by it. An eighteenth-century folly was beyond her ken; and she was against making a joke out of what she called a natural function. For much the same reasons she was always shocked by Fenton's swearing; she believed the four-letter words should only be used

functionally, as in *Lady Chatterley's Lover*, which in a somewhat
expurgated version she had earnestly read. But this use of them in
turn shocked Fenton, and would have profoundly shocked Ferdo
too. They had much in common.

¶ 3

LOVE'S NOT TIME'S FOOL, declared that most steadfast of
the Sonnets; it was Susan's favourite, her book always fell open
at its page:

> *Love alters not with his brief hours and weeks,*
> *But bears it out even to the edge of doom.*

Sandra, on the other hand, maintained that love was like a motor-
car, it needed some fuel to keep it going; and Susan as the
parched autumn went by had to confess to herself that her love
drooped a little, even if it didn't wither like a flower lacking
rain. There was still no letter from Tony, though the War Office
had confirmed he was a prisoner of war. She wrote to him every
week, but sometimes she did not post the letters; for it takes two
to make a correspondence, and soon she found she was sending
him little more than a trivial social diary and an engagement list.
*"I rode Nightshade in the Hunter Trials at the Gymkhana . . .
There was a Festival of Britain Ball at Elmbury last week;
Daddy and Mummy took me, I had to dance with the Mayor . . .
Daddy says there's going to be a General Election soon. Stephen
Le Mesurier is coming to stay here when the campaign starts . . .
I went to lunch with Sandra on Saturday; she's rather keen on a
chap at the Royal Agricultural College. She's asked me to a party
to meet him next week."*
You couldn't write like that to a man in a prison-camp. Susan
gave it up and went to Sandra's party.

''WE all thought you were determined to weep your youth
away," Sandra had said, "like that wet girl in that play." If you
knew Sandra you guessed she meant *Twelfth Night*. "Welcome
back, love, to fun and games."
So she invited Susan to cocktail-parties and dinner-parties and

barbecues and midnight-swimming–parties at the big farmhouse which her father had built on to so that it was something more than a Gentleman's Residence if something less than a Stately Home. You had to admit that he'd done it well. Only two and a half miles away he had recently destroyed a little beauty-spot, where bluebells grew in a dingle among beech-trees. He'd bashed and bulldozed it and ripped it open with mechanical diggers to make a new gravel-pit. It was obvious now that he hadn't bought the farm for the sake of its good pasture; he was after the sand and gravel underneath. But he must also have had an eye to the possibility of making a fine house out of Doublegates Farm (which was now more simply and grandly called Doublegates); and as if to make up for his desecration of the bluebell-dingle he had lavished money and care upon his own place, and done everything in surprisingly good taste. The new wing was well-proportioned, and the house looked charming among new-turfed lawns and new-planted shrubberies. The same mechanical diggers which raped the bluebells had been used to excavate a swimming-pool; the bulldozers had shaped the sweeping curves of the garden-terraces. There were three acres of lawns, flowers and shrubs; Fenton's successor was now described not as the gardener but as the Head Gardener, and what was more he had previously been Head Gardener to a peer. He and all the other members of the staff were extraordinarily subservient: like stage retainers, almost. *Yes, Miss Susan, no Miss Susan, you'll find Miss Sandra down at the swimming-pool, Miss Susan.* It was all very lordly compared with Doddington, where hardly anybody ever called you Miss. Stephen Le Mesurier had once made the mistake of asking Egbert whether he'd seen Miss Susan anywhere about. Egbert, who had called her Sue ever since she was a baby, 'had imagined he was being treated as an inferior sort of servant instead of as an established member of the household. He had simply shrugged his shoulders and walked away.

SANDRA GAVE EXCELLENT PARTIES because she had a generous spirit which enjoyed giving for its own sake—whether hospitality or possessions or herself. It was dangerous to admire anything of hers; she had insisted on giving Susan an evening dress which she had bought for £40 at Harrod's and had only worn once; she had pretended she was tired of it. They were exactly the same size and shape, so after that Susan had to be careful not to say she liked anything Sandra was wearing. She was actually offered a horse because "you ride him much better than I do"; Sandra was quite hurt when she refused to take it. Of course she could afford such gestures; but she was so devoted to Susan that she would even have handed over her current young man if at any time Susan had wanted him. She had so many young men that she could well afford that gesture too!

At twenty-two she was in full bloom. She was the only girl Susan had ever found herself compelled to gaze at for the sheer delight of the eye. You could still see a bit of her father and her mother in her; but transmuted and refined. Sunburn suited her; in this golden autumn weather she looked lovelier than ever before. It astonished Susan, and somewhat shocked the little puritan in her, that Sandra should be willing to bestow the sum total of her beauty, long legs, long neck, fine breasts, lissom body, tawny hair, green eyes, exquisite oval Botticelli face, *everything,* upon almost any personable young man who happened to be at hand at a suitable moment. "Mind you," she'd said to Susan, "I never make love with anybody unless I want to." She looked very serious; then the corners of her mouth began to twitch. "But I generally do want to, you see."

Just at the moment she was going in for a succession of agricultural students from the College at Cirencester. They were mostly well-off, having estates in prospect which it was hoped they would learn to manage or to farm. There were two or three Honourables among them; but somehow or other even these, in common with all the rest, succeeded in being not quite gentlemen. Susan never quite made out why; but she thought perhaps it was due to a sort of infection they took from their flashy sports cars. They drove these with reckless arrogance, especially at night when they had drunk about six pints of beer. Sandra really enjoyed going for dangerous pubcrawls at eighty miles an hour; she confessed to Susan that she liked being frightened first and made love to afterwards. Susan also knew well how danger could excite you and set your whole spirit aflame; but she thought that for the present she preferred to take her risks alone, and on a horse.

Nevertheless, Sandra did persuade her to go to some parties with the R.A.C. boys, most of whom were being driven half out

of their wits by a combination of Sandra's looks and her reputa-
tion. There happened to be one whom Susan liked much better
than the others, a tall one from Kenya with hair the colour she
imagined lion-country to be. He was sensible and rather serious.
The farm he would soon be going back to lay high up in the
hills. He had been born there; Kenya, not England, was his
homeland; he thought it was the most beautiful land in the
world. But every night his father and mother slept with a loaded
revolver beside the bed; the Mau-Mau had recently burned down
their nearest neighbour's house and hacked him to death with
their pangas.

The young man attracted Susan. She let him take her out
twice, to the pictures and once to dinner; he talked well, and
she enjoyed his company. The following week, with Sandra and
her Honourable, they went to a country pub and played darts.
At closing-time the Honourable somehow squeezed Sandra into a
bucket seat in his tiny racing car which had the appearance of an
angry insect and looked all the wickeder because it was painted
in stripes like a wasp. She'd be glad to stretch her legs after *that*
journey home! thought Susan, and caught herself grinning; her
puritanism seemed tonight to be in abeyance, or perhaps on the
wane. Her young man had a slower, safer and more capacious
car. Susan did not protest when he parked it under the oak-trees
off Elmbury Back Lane and began to kiss her, not as a right but
with tender humility. It started to rain hard, and the big drops
off the oak-trees rat-tatted on the car roof. Susan wondered about
Sandra, and thanked heaven that *she* wasn't sitting in a racing
car without a hood! In this one it seemed all the cosier by contrast with the weather outside; she was in no special hurry to get
home, and they stopped among the dark and dripping oaks for
more than half an hour.

What small acts of love they did there derived on Susan's part
from her mood of mischief rather than from any real passion. She
had no sense of guilt in the morning, indeed she felt specially gay
and glad to have found a companion in whose company she was
so much at ease. Also she completely trusted him, and she had
learned that for herself it was important to trust people. But the
next time he took her out, to her astonished embarrassment, he
declared that he was in love with her. On the strength of an

acquaintance only three weeks old he said he wanted to marry her and take her out to Kenya. She knew that he meant it.

Her first proposal! She could hardly have had a more gentle or genuine one; and seeking for an excuse that wouldn't hurt him she told him about Tony. After that they were both constrained, and he didn't stop his car under the oak-trees on the way home. She had noticed that he had rather old-fashioned ways; probably Kenya was in some respects a bit formal compared with England, its manners were those of twenty years ago. Now he told her, awkwardly and sincerely, that he didn't think he ought to see her again. Sadly she let him go; and next day she was very much aware of feeling alone once more, and she missed him a little, and half-hoped it was a call from him when the telephone rang. But it wasn't: it was the Bank Manager wanting to speak to her father.

In her loneliness she began to look forward to Stephen Le Mesurier's visit next week when the Election campaign would be starting. She was always a little surprised at how much she liked Stephen. At any rate there couldn't be anything unfaithful to Tony in such a friendship as hers with him.

¶ 4

"COME CANVASSING, SUKIE," said Stephen on the day his campaign started. "You'll learn a lot." One thing she learned was about Stephen himself. She observed with amusement that he liked his supporters in an inverse ratio to their enthusiasm for his cause. He was at his best with the uncommitted, or with his opponents, whom he treated with courtesy and charm. He reacted against his own side, and probably lost a few votes through being sharp with the bigoted or snubbing the over-enthusiastic.

"Conservative women," he told her, "are worse than anything else in politics. They make me ashamed of my Party. They lost us most of the Empire because they despised three-quarters of its inhabitants on grounds of race, religion or colour; and now they want us to hold what's left of it by force of arms, yet grumble like hell if we put sixpence on the Income Tax to pay the soldiers.

They're mad on birching, flogging, hanging and hard labour. When I tell 'em I don't want to flog robbers or hang murderers or even shoot what they still think of as niggers they realise that they've got the wrong sort of Member; but I get their votes all the same because they're even more afraid of the Socialists than they are mistrustful of me. They're as cowardly as they're ignorant: for heaven's sake, Sukie, promise me that you'll never become a Conservative Woman!"

She reminded him:

"You told me you didn't like Young Conservatives either; because you thought anybody who was young ought to be a rebel."

"Well, I still think that."

"Perhaps *you're* on the wrong side?"

"Good God no! I could never be a Socialist because I'm opposed to anything which tends to standardise people. I loathe the cringing fools who proclaim, not in shame or anger but with a ghastly and grovelling satisfaction, that this is the Age of the Common Man." They were driving along a busy main road, and Stephen, who wasn't a very good driver at the best of times, suddenly jammed on his brakes with the idea, presumably, of pulling up so that he could expound his thesis at leisure. A lorry's brakes screeched behind them. Stephen accelerated too hard and stalled the engine. "To hell with the whole concept of the Common Man," he said. "Just think of it: the glory, jest and riddle of the world, a *common man!*" The engine started again, the car jerked forward, the lorry driver angrily hooted behind. Stephen, drifting a little towards the centre of the road, took no notice whatever. "He who is master of his fate and captain of his soul a *comman man!* He who Sir Thomas Browne said was 'pompous in ashes and splendid even in the grave.'—Have you read *Urn-burial?* You ought to.—Listen to that impatient fellow behind.—What was I saying? I don't want a world inhabited by robots. I want a world fit for Falstaff, or those glorious free and funny people in Dickens. I want a world in which eccentrics can come up all over the place and flourish like marvellous exotic flowers.—Oh hell, *overtake* then if you want to——"

Continuously hooting, the lorry at last roared by. Stephen's car was decorated with blue rosettes and ribbons and VOTE FOR LE

MESURIER on the bonnet and the boot. The lorry driver's mate, by no means a common man but goaded into passionate individuality by Stephen's driving, pointed at the favours in derisive rage. "Can't drive a bleeding car and want to govern the bleeding country," he yelled.

Susan laughed:

"Have you ever thought how many votes your driving loses you, Stephen?"

But now they came to the approaches of a village, and Stephen pulled up at a row of new Council Houses. One of them had VOTE FOR LE MESURIER in a front window. Another had a poster displaying the stodgy if honest features of Stephen's opponent, a Union official called Higgins.

"One friend, one foe," grinned Stephen. "Let's knock on the door of the enemy."

"YOU'RE A PRETTY GOOD CANVASSER," he said on the way home, "because you've got an open mind and keep it open. You listen to other people's arguments and see the point of them."

"I see the point so well that I'll probably finish up a Socialist," Susan said. "I do wonder what I really am—what kind of political animal, I mean."

"Cavalier," said Stephen.

"What?"

"By birth, upbringing, tradition and inclination a Cavalier. But it's quite wrong to assume that's the same thing as being a Tory. I've got a theory about the political structure of England——" Stephen had ingenious and complicated theories about almost everything. "I believe that fundamentally it's a matter of Cavalier and Roundhead still. The *argument* ended when the King's head came off; but the *attitudes* remain. I believe that those two opposing attitudes are still the main sources of all out political thought and behaviour. Sometimes the pull is one way, sometimes another; but between them they dictate our policies and legislation."

He was beginning to drift about the road again. It was quite an adventure to drive with Stephen when he was chasing an idea through the labyrinth of his mind.

"It isn't a question of one side being better than the other," he went on. "In the long run I daresay there's been just as much courage, honour and political genius demonstrated by the puritan-nonconformist-practical-do-gooder Roundheads as by the easy-going-laissez-faire-romantic Cavaliers. Allegiance cuts right across Party and class. There are Roundheads on my side of the House and Cavaliers in Labour; there are costermongers and tarts who are Cavaliers like you and peers who are Roundheads. Both sides produce rulers and both sides produce rebels. England wouldn't be what she is if she didn't draw her inspiration from both sources. Didn't you tell me that one of your rakish ancestors married a Quaker girl after he'd reformed? There you are; that's where your dash of puritanism comes from. We wouldn't be the same people if we didn't all of us have a bit of both traditions in our mental make-up. But some have preponderance of one, and you're ninety per cent romantic-Cavalier. Your father's ninety-five."

"Stephen," she said, "I'm listening and I'm fascinated but do let that Jaguar go by."

"O.K.—You can think of it as two streams running all through our history and through our thought and through ourselves. But not obvious, not on the surface. I see them as secret watercourses running underground. Most of the time we're hardly aware of them. Then at unexpected moments they come to the surface and burst forth like—like the flood in your father's cellar! But much more powerful. Oh, terrific, sweeping everything out of their way! And you never, never know what's going to bring them to the surface. It may be something tremendous—like the Abdication or Munich—or something quite trivial, like foxhunting or the Book of Common Prayer."

His rear tyres screamed as he clumsily swung the car round the corner into Elmbury Back Lane.

"The Waters Under the Earth," he said. "Two or three times in every Englishman's lifetime they burst out and go rampaging through the land. Remember what I'm saying; because you'll see it happen, sooner or later, again and again. And whenever it happens you'll know which side you're on. Not necessarily Tory, not necessarily Labour. You'll know you're Cavalier."

TO FERDO'S PRETENDED DISMAY—but secretly, Susan knew, it fascinated and excited him—the Waters Under the Earth had recently appeared in the cellar again.

Aided perhaps by the storms of the equinox, which brought two inches of rain in a week, the flood reached its greatest height so far: two feet four inches. Moreover it came up suddenly in the night and took Ferdo by surprise: some of his wine was under water by morning. The immersion did no harm to the wine; but the labels were washed away. Upon the bottom shelf, as it happened, he'd been accustomed to keep the single bottles and the odds-and-ends which didn't fit into his otherwise orderly arrangement. He had forgotten exactly what was there. The loss of the labels gave him a good excuse to open the bottles, for he pointed out that this was now the only way to find out what was inside them!

So each night at dinner he played a guessing-game with Stephen, who also knew a good deal about wine. They had long and enjoyable arguments about what they were drinking. Once they encountered a couple of bottles of Algerian, which Ferdo had bought in desperation just after the war and which in happier circumstances would have gone to the distillery and finished up in the tank of somebody's motor-car. Stephen delighted Ferdo with a quotation from Disraeli: " 'I rather like bad wine,' said Mr. Mountchesney. 'One gets so bored with good wine.' " Ferdo's own taste was both cultivated and catholic. He loved good wine, but in its absence he had no fine and finicky choosiness, he was only too pleased to try anything once and if he liked it, as he usually did, to try it again. He and Stephen talked as well on the Algerian as they did on Ferdo's best claret. When Janet and Susan left them to go to bed, Ferdo had just finished a discourse on Nelson's tactics at Trafalgar, and Stephen, who turned out to be a keen amateur yachtsman, was beginning a commentary on the shipwreck of Saint Paul as described in the Acts of the Apostles.

HE HAD ORIGINALLY BEEN INVITED for a week but Ferdo, taking to him more and more, now asked him to stay at Doddington for the whole month of the Election campaign. They both enjoyed playing with ideas, and their minds seemed to work

well together, Stephen's steel struck sparks off Ferdo's flint. Susan
had never head such good talk before, and she realised for the first
time, as she listened to them arguing at dinner, what a good
mind her father had, combative but generous, and unexpectedly
wide-questing: he could sometimes be foolish but he was never
narrow. He'd read much more than she had thought. For one
thing he seemed to know the Bible by heart,—Janet had told her
that he used to give Biblical references in his signals during the
war. Once when his convoy was under heavy attack his last signal
to the Admiralty was simply *Psalms Thirty Eight Nineteen*:
"Mine enemies are lively, and they are strong."

On that occasion his own ship had been torpedoed, and he'd
had what he called 'a cold swim'—Susan could well imagine him
bobbing about in the oil-streaked sea, irrepressible as he was in
those days, unsinkable as one of those red round fishing-floats
which schoolboys use. During the last two or three years she'd
seen little of that buoyancy of spirit; but on these evenings with
Stephen, for just a little while—when he'd had a few drinks but
before he'd had too many—she delightedly watched it coming
back again.

As for Stephen, his mind was a ragbag of quotations; whenever
he dipped into it, some unexpected thing came out. He rode his
hobbyhorses as wildly as Susan's madcap ancestors had ridden
after hounds; and he loved nothing better than fantasticating
theories in which a lot of nonsense was mixed up with a little
truth. One night they were talking about Daglingworth, whom
Ferdo detested and when he had nicknamed, for some reason best
known to himself, Colonel Cleverbreeches. Susan told Stephen
how the Colonel had thrown Ophelia off his lap.

"I could have told you," he said, "that he was one of those
dogmen."

"What on earth do you mean by a dogman?"

"He loves having tails wagged at him; he likes being looked up
to. He tends to be quite a good leader for that reason. Your
catman, on the other hand, is always made a bit uncomfortable
by those spaniel eyes and devoted tail-thumps on the floor.
(Shakespeare was obviously a catman; he always used 'spaniel' as
a term of contempt.) Of course, I'm a catman, I couldn't have a
relationship with an animal which humbly looked up to me: or
with that sort of human being either. On the other hand I get on

very well with your Ophelia, Sukie. She pays me the compliment of treating me as an equal and now and then even condescends to put her claws in and out when she's sitting on my knee. No wonder Daglingworth chucked her off."

"You're quite right about him being keen on dogs," said Susan. "He's got a plum pudding dog and a red setter and a Borzoi. I like dogs but I don't like dogmen."

"I can tell you a lot more about them," said Stephen, fantasticating happily away. "They tend, for some reason I've never been able to understand, to prefer deserts to jungles, Mohammedans to Hindus, Arabs to Jews (which is perhaps why I'm not mad on them personally). And the Army attracts them, of course. All your ships have cats in them, don't they, Ferdo? But you don't hear much of cats in officers' messes or Army barracks. On the more homely level, I find the dogmen drink whisky rather than wine, play golf rather than cricket (and of course they simply adore rugger) and smoke pipes rather than cigarettes. Can't you *see* a typical dogman—Daglingworth if you like—striding over the desert in shorts puffing away at his pipe, followed at a respectable distance by a batman or bearer or platoon sergeant or some such devoted chap who happens at the moment to be doing substitute for his dog!"

Two minutes later Stephen was off on a different hobbyhorse—something about America becoming a modern matriarchy—and Ferdo was arguing with him. Susan would have loved to sit up with them. She was much more at home, these days, with the men and their port than with her mother and the coffee! And the men would have liked to have her with them; but Janet was old-fashioned, the women must always leave the table before the decanter was passed round. Susan suspected that she didn't wholeheartedly approve of Stephen; and she wondered if perhaps Janet had inherited from *her* mother an aristocratic-Edwardian prejudice against Jews. She would never have admitted it, of course; she probably didn't realise she had it. But Susan quite by accident had glimpsed an entry in her diary, lying open on Janet's desk:

> *Le M. still with us—quite a visitation!! Most entertaining talker but? too clever by ½—*THEY *often are! Not v. good for F sitting up ½ night talking and drinking . . .*

BUT STEPHEN, SUSAN NOTICED, didn't drink much
really. He was taking very good care not to blunt his sharp mind,
as Ferdo had blunted his. He needed to keep his wits about him.
With the Election only a fortnight away he was speaking at a half
a dozen meetings every night and canvassing all over a constituency which was thirty miles long and a dozen miles broad and
contained about sixty thousand electors. His majority wasn't a
big one—three and a half thousand last time—and this General
Election was going to be a close thing. For eighteen months
Labour had governed with a majority of only six. It was a situation in which, for both sides of the House, it was almost a crime
to become ill; the cartoonists pictured decrepit Members being
pushed into the Lobbies in their bath chairs. Mr. Attlee, driven
to desperation, had decided to go to the country; and Stephen
predicted that whoever won this time the majority would still
be very small.

As polling day approached, Susan against her will found herself becoming fiercely partisan. Whether you liked it or not you
became involved in the battle. People whom in other circumstances you might have detested became likeable simply because
they were on your side: your comrades, fellow soldiers in the
Cause. The other side became The Enemy. Susan had a good
enough excuse to throw herself into the fray, for she was still
Secretary of the Elmbury Young Conservatives whose Chairman,
Sandra, had chosen the time of the General Election to fall in
love with the son of a business tycoon and to go off with him and
his family to the South of France.

So most days Susan went canvassing with Stephen. One day at
a big meeting in Elmbury, Colonel Daglingworth took the chair.
"Long time no see," he leered at her, in the Committee Room
beforehand. "I hear you're kissing the Member's babies for him."
He said it as if there were something compromising about her
canvassing with Stephen. She hadn't quite got rid of her school-
girlish habit of blushing; now she blushed most absurdly and
unnecessarily, and Stephen noticed and looked at Colonel Daglingworth in a cold contemplative way which Susan found most
alarming. She suddenly realised that if Daglingworth had dared
to be unpleasant to her again, Stephen without thought for the
consequences would have been very unpleasant to him, in public

or private, General Election or no. She responded with a renewed loyalty to Stephen, she was determined to stick by his side
so long as he wanted her throughout the Election, whatever anybody might say. Obviously he did want her: she drove him to
meetings in the far corners of the Constituency and came home
with him in the small hours. She could imagine her mother re-
cording all this in her diary with exclamation-marks and queries:
Old enough to be her father but!!??

Susan, happier than she'd been for ages, was astonished and
delighted to discover that she must be growing up at last; because, realising all this, she simply didn't care a damn!

O N E D A Y T H E B A T T L E C A M E T O D O D D I N G T O N and
raged, though briefly, within the courtyard gates.

Mrs. Fenton, of course, spiky as ever, had stuck up a photograph of Mr. Higgins in a front window of Huntsman's Cottage.
She was possibly ambitious for some kind of political martyrdom;
it might do the Cause good if the big landlord tried to intimidate
the tenant by threatening eviction and the sack. But of course
Ferdo did nothing of the sort. He merely commented: "Can't say
I like the woman but she's got guts." Janet had a moment of
sheer fury every time she passed the cottage, and thought with
nostalgia about her mother's time, the Palmy Days, trying to
imagine what would have been the fate of Mrs. Fenton then.

With the working-classes, her mother used to say, it's give 'em
an inch and they'll take an ell. Janet had never known what an
ell was; but she remembered the proverb when she saw the poster
pasted to the wall of Egbert's cottage which was within the courtyard and just round the corner by the stables. It said VOTE LABOUR
VOTE FOR HIGGINS, below the usual photograph of Bill Higgins.
Intuition told her that Ben Fenton must have persuaded Egbert
to put it there. It wasn't the sort of thing Egbert would ever have
done on his own; and the boy had been home from Oxford last
weekend, Janet had seen him talking to Egbert, and had seen
him again at the Conservative Meeting at Elmbury, where he
had heckled all the speakers, in her opinion most ill-manneredly.
Stephen Le Mesurier had been much too polite in his replies.

Now Ben Fenton had gone back to Oxford, where his braininess had got him some sort of scholarship, a fact which reinforced Janet's general mistrust of the brainy.

The poster remained; and all that day there was trouble about it. Northover, even more shocked than Janet, tackled Egbert and told him to take it down. Egbert replied Who be thee to tell I to take it down?

Northover reminded Egbert that he had the cottage rent-free.

"Not from thee I don't," said Egbert.

"Would you take it down if Sir Ferdo told you?"

" 'Tis a free country," said Egbert non-committally.

Then Northover spotted a flapping, unstuck corner of the poster and tugged at it. The poster tore, and part of Mr. Higgins' nose came off; but most of it still stuck in the wall. Fenton appeared, carrying a bucket. He asked Northover his usual rhetorical question: whether he thought tearing down posters was fucking democracy. Northover spoke to him like a Sergeant Major (which he'd been, in the Yeomanry, between the two wars):

"Shut your mouth, Fenton, we don't want your foul language here."

"I've got a handle to my name," said Fenton; and chucked the contents of the bucket in Northover's face. There was a fight, or at least a scuffle, followed by a good deal of argument about what the bucket had contained. Fenton said it was pure water, North-over maintained it was liquid manure. Ferdo was called in to smell Northover's waistcoat, and in the end he settled the argument by giving each of the combatants a bottle of beer.

The poster stayed on the wall; and later in the day the two smallest Fenton children, Adam and Eve, being too young to concern themselves with ideologies, came with crayons and gave Mr. Higgins a pipe in his mouth, a pair of spectacles, and a red nose.

But Janet couldn't get over what she considered to be Egbert's disloyalty. After all, he'd had the cottage rent-free all his life, like his father before him. To Janet his action seemed quite incomprehensible, a betrayal.

"Sheer bosh," said Ferdo cheerfully at dinner. "Egbert and I understand each other perfectly. He's not a Red but a Radical, which is about as English a thing as an old encrusted landowning

Tory, incidentally." And he told the story of how Egbert had struck, all alone, in the year of the General Strike.

That delighted Stephen.

"There you are, Sukie," he said. "I bet he's a Roundhead. Remember what I said about the Waters Under the Earth, bubbling up to the surface suddenly? Two jolly good examples— a General Strike and a General Election!"

"In his case it goes back much farther than Roundhead and Cavalier," said Ferdo. "It probably goes all the way back to William the Conqueror and Hereward the Wake."

"Next time I meet him I'll treat him with proper respect," Stephen said. "I begin to realise why he was so angry when I spoke of *Miss* Susan to him."

"You couldn't know; but it was quite the wrong thing to say. He really does regard himself as one of us; although in his obstinate independent way he resents us, and all we stand for."

"A love-hate relationship?" Stephen said.

"I daresay his ancestors have hated and loved their bosses ever since the Conquest."

"*The Secret People?*" cried Stephen, with the delight of a sudden discovery.

Ferdo grinned approval. He wasn't very well read in poetry but he liked the rhetorical stuff: the sort of thing Archie Wavell had put in that anthology which came out during the war, *Other Men's Flowers*. G. K. Chesterton was exactly Ferdo's cup of tea, his poems went with a swing, you could shout them aloud when you were alone in the woods; Ferdo knew this one almost by heart.

So it seemed did Stephen. He dipped straightway into his ragbag of a mind:

"Smile at us, pay us, pass us; but do not quite forget,
For we are the people of England, that never have spoken yet."

"Go on, Stephen," Susan said.

But Stephen turned deferentially to Janet; and poetry meant nothing to her, she was against it because she didn't understand it, and she failed to see what it had to do with the ill-behavior of Egbert, which still deeply troubled her.

She shrugged her shoulders; and Stephen with a smile said: "Not now. It's much too long. Another time, Sukie. Tomorrow, perhaps, walking in the woods I'll say it."

THEY'D PROMISED THEMSELVES a long walk in the woods; and by convention there was no active electioneering on a Sunday, owing to the sensible English determination to keep God out of politics. "Perhaps an overdose of Cromwell taught us *that* lesson," Stephen suggested. "Once again we get back to Roundhead and Cavalier!"

So while Ferdo and Janet went to church, Susan led Stephen across the Park and alongside Trafalgar Wood to the top of Seven Men's Tump with its wind-tortured elms that were going blonde in patches as they always did at this time of the year. And there she made him recite Chesterton's poem about the secret people of England who have watched so long with patient eyes their kings go up and their kings go down, their masters flourish and their masters fall,—

And a new people takes the land; and still it is not we.

She wasn't sure whether it was a very good poem, though it went at such a gallop you felt the winds of the world blowing in your hair; and every now and then a couplet made her heart leap and she knew she'd remember it for ever,—for instance:

We saw the King as they killed him, and his face was proud and pale;
And a few men talked of freedom, while England talked of ale.

and again:

In foam and flame at Trafalgar, on Albuera plains
We did and died like lions, to keep ourselves in chains . . .

Down there was Trafalgar Wood, with Waterloo beyond; and as Stephen fairly shouted the last verses it was as if she had a view down the long vista of English history and suddenly glimpsed as in a glass darkly what it had to do with Egbert and Northover and the Fentons and Daglingworth and Ferdo and Janet and Doddington and the General Election and herself. It was only a glimpse; the glass in her mind went cloudy; and Stephen was

laughing at the absurdity of it, "Tory Candidate recites revolu-
tionary poem on eve of Election."

"I wonder what Colonel Daglingworth would think of us,"
said Susan. He took her arm, for the very first time, and they
went down the hill together into the tawny October wood.

I T   W A S   A   D A Y which Susan knew she would remember just for
its happiness without knowing precisely why it had been so
happy. They walked for miles in a pale sunlight which lit the
bracken and the branches in much the same way as an invisible
flame on a bright day astonishingly sets a light to bonfires. Late
gnats danced, ragged butterflies fluttered, in its shine. The last
valedictory flowers, ragwort and tansy and golden-rod, blazed
with an *après nous le déluge* air along the woodsides and in the
clearings. It was too late for the rarer ones which Stephen had
wanted to see; Susan showed him the spinney where she used to
find Solomon's Seal, and the mossy patch between the hazels
where the herb Paris grew. He made her promise she'd take him
there next summer. "I adore it," he declared, carried away by one
of his endearing enthusiasms. "It's an elegant eccentric, there's no
other plant like it in England. Promise you'll show it to me! And
the deadly nightshade, I always get a kick out of it—it's not only
wicked but determined to show that it's wicked, like Aleister
Crowley . . . And your orchids. I'm mad on orchids. I think I'll go
and hunt for them in jungles when I'm too decrepit to hunt for
alpines on mountains. But I'll always love the alpines best, I
don't mean that dull vulgar Germanic edelweiss, but the little
precarious precious things, high-up saxifrages and primulas and
campanulas with the tiniest bells, and gentians shining blue
like bits of the Med. on a mountaintop!"

He interrupted himself suddenly.

"I think I'm talking too much," he said.

Susan laughed.

"So long as it's not in the car, and you driving!"

So after that pause for breath he set off again, rapidly descend-
ing from the mountains to the Mediterranean, which turned out
to be another of his passions.

"—Everything I know and am, everything I love and believe
in, comes from round its shores—almost everything *you* love and

believe in, Sukie, unless you care for those horrible hygienic Scandinavian countries and their ghastly cruel Sagas, and Wagner and the Valkyrie and things like that. You don't? I knew you didn't. But you've never been to Italy or Greece or Spain, never set eyes on that blue sea? I'd love to take you there," he said, with a curious change of tone which seemed to say, But I know, alas, that I shall not.

Then he talked about sailing, which next to climbing mountains seemed to be the pastime which delighted and frightened him most—"I've got to be frightened every now and then; I'm scared stiff of getting smug, of my mind getting constipated; fear for me is a purge of the spirit. Especially when fear is mixed with awe. To be alone with just the sea and the huge sky, and a storm coming!"

The sea possessed him, its beauty, its terror, its moods, its monsters little and great——

"Everything from sea-horses to whales! I wish I wasn't an M.P., I wish I was a marine biologist!"

But a few minutes later he was wishing he was a mycologist.

"What's that?"

"Fungi." The woods, as usual at this time of year, were full of toadstools. They found a beautiful scarlet fly agaric which would kill you if you ate enough of it but like a sympathetic executioner would make you as drunk as a lord before you died; and a death cup of which quite a small quantity, said Stephen with a grin, would be enough to put paid to Colonel Daglingworth.

But it annoyed him that he couldn't name all the kinds.

"If only one had lives enough!" he said.

"You haven't done so badly so far," said Susan, wondering how on earth he'd managed to learn so much about so many diverse things; to read so much and enjoy so much, to climb and sail and fight in a war and go in for politics and collect old herbals and alpines and to travel and—have love affairs? Naturally, she said to herself; and as she began to wonder about them she experienced a just-perceptible twinge of jealousy which amused and surprised her.

¶ 5

ELMBURY DESPITE ITS GROWING POPULATION was a
sleepy old place as a rule. It had seemed to Susan quite apathetic
during the week before the Election. But on Polling Day it suddenly came to life, remembered some ancient grudges, revived
some tattered loyalties, and seethed with political passion suddenly. Susan was astonished by the change in it. She had brought
her father into town to vote, and when he'd done so she took him
to visit his little tailor, from whom he'd decided to order a couple
of new suits. The shop was discreetly hidden away in a sidestreet,
with TREMLETT BESPOKE TAILOR AND BREECHES-MAKER in small letters above a window which contained a length or two of tweed arranged around a damp-stained print showing a lady and gentleman dressed for hunting in the style of fifty years ago. Indeed
Mr. Tremlett was so extremely old-fashioned that he would not
dream of having a telephone upon the premises,—"Why, Sir
Ferdo, we'd have all sorts of persons ringing us up!" Susan remembered him as a small deferential man with a tape measure
hung round his neck, who inhabited the shadows at the back of
his shop and blinked owlishly whenever he stepped forward into
the light.

But this morning his shop window was decorated in blue,
Stephen's photograph had pride of place in the middle of it, Mr.
Tremlett himself wore a blue rosette and stood bold as a lion
in his doorway glaring at any passers-by who happened to be
wearing red rosettes.

"I always get worked up on Polling Day, Sir Ferdo. There goes
Councillor Walker. He's Labour. I make his suits for him. If he
came into my shop today I believe I'd ask him to take his custom
elsewhere. But by next week we'll both be good friends again."

Mr. Tremlett, who must have been well over seventy, began to
talk about elections long ago. "In your Dad's day, Sir Ferdo, I
can tell you we used to have some fun! I've known Town Councillors—solid, respectable men—paint each others' houses in a
night, blue or red, according to their political loyalties: a Radical would paint a Tory's house red, and vice versa! Such goings
on; and heads broken sometimes; and both the candidates fork-
ing out their half-crowns real handsome——"

"You mean there was *bribery?*" asked Susan in astonishment.

"Bless you, Miss Susan, I don't know if you would call it bribery, but there were plenty of half-crowns. The candidates would send to the Bank, quite openly, the day before the poll, and ask for bags of new-minted bright ones. Then they'd send their men round the Alleys inviting anybody who had a vote to drink their health—you could buy a great deal of drink for half a crown in those days. I suppose it was bribery, but it didn't make a jot of difference to the result; for a man would accept half a crown from each of the candidates, you see, and then vote according to his conscience; unless, of course, he got so drunk that he didn't vote at all."

Today the schoolchildren all had a holiday because their schools were being used as polling stations. Entering into the spirit of the thing, the boys and girls had formed themselves into little bands of six or eight and were already marching about the town beating on tin cans and singing:

"*Vote vote vote for Billy 'Iggins!*" ("*We* used to do that," said Mr. Tremlett in a tone of awe, "when we were kids sixty years ago. Who told them, who taught *them* to do it?") Susan, having parked the Land Rover, walked the length of Elmbury High Street, but she didn't meet with any children singing *Vote vote vote for Stephen Le Mesurier*. His name would have been too much for them anyway.

She found him standing outside the Town Hall, which was the main polling station. He and Bill Higgins looked equally absurd, she thought, with their enormous rosettes which seemed to give them sickly complexions. Stephen was being especially civil to Mr. Higgins, who was obviously resenting his civility. Their respective supporters exchanged sidelong and uncomfortable looks —uncomfortable probably because they were fellow Buffaloes, Masons, members of Rotary, British Legion, Bowling Club, Choral Society, all dedicated to brotherhood; but for today they were sworn enemies, the ordinary badinage was out of place, they glimpsed in each other's homely faces the bloated Capitalist or the destructive Red.

Another gaggle of little boys marched raggedly by.

"*Vote vote vote for Billy 'Igg-ins!*"

Susan saw them as her enemies, even though none of them was

more than ten years old. She turned to Stephen and caught him
looking at her.

"Democracy in action," he said.

"It's silly——"

Suddenly he did one of those quick changes, from being gay to
being deadly serious, which always took her unawares.

"No, Sukie. No! It sometimes looks silly. But it works. Not
perfectly by any means; but a bloody sight better than any other
system that's ever been devised. The plain fact is that civilised
man has never found a *better* way of governing himself. Until he
does so I've got to believe in this Parliamentary democracy of
ours, with all its absurdities, because the alternatives are so frightful."

Then quick as a flash he was merry and mocking again.

"Now I'm going to play my part in the democratic exercise
by going into the Town Hall and voting for myself. I wonder if
anybody has ever been so altruistic as to vote for his opponent.
What do you think, Mr. Higgins?"

Mr. Higgins looked shocked.

Susan went off to the Party Headquarters. She'd promised to
spend the day driving voters to the poll. As soon as you got inside
the Headquarters the climate of hot partisanship struck you, it
was the mental equivalent of opening the door into a bakery. Or
it was like the inside of a beehive, where the bees generate their
own heat by angrily buzzing. If a Labour supporter had acci-
dentally strayed in there he'd surely have been stung to death!

A succession of young helpers kept dashing in with slips of
paper. They had the air of despatch-riders who through shot and
shell brought desperate tidings out of the smoke of the battle. In
fact the slips were simply lists of the people who had already
voted. Other helpers sitting at desks marked them off on copies of
the Electoral Roll. The names in this printed list had been
ticked in blue or red according to the results of the previous
canvass. Those without ticks were presumably Floating Voters,
undecided, dithering, maddening, incomprehensible to parti-
sans: unless of course they simply happened to be on holiday or
in hospital or in prison, like Rosemary's husband, whom Susan
had attempted to canvass yesterday. He was doing three months
for theft.

The Headquarters staff whose job it was to mark off the names of those who had voted had worked themselves up into such a state of fervour that you could hear their little grunts of satisfaction when a name had a blue tick; of annoyance when it had a red one.

"We're doing well!" one of the girls whispered to Susan. "Even among the Council Houses, it's three to two for our side."

Leaning over the girl's shoulder, Susan ran her eye down the long column in which some unknown *Smith, Geoffrey Joseph* was a good chap, your heart warmed to him, because he happened to be ticked in blue and had been so public-spirited as to record his vote at eleven o'clock in the morning; whereas *Smith, George William*, whose name was ticked in red, must be a bigoted crank to take time off from his job in a factory in order to go to the poll so early.

Susan's job was to collect from their houses as many as possible of the crippled, decrepit, senile and failing Conservative supporters, to take these decent, sensible, right-minded true-blue people to the poll, and deliver them safely back home as soon as they had done their duty. As the day wore on she warmed to her task, she went without lunch, she fetched voters from remote farmhouses and cottages reached only by way of muddy lanes, she lost herself three times, got stuck in a quagmire, had a puncture and changed the wheel even though the car was an unfamiliar one, and by the time dark fell she caught herself driving much faster than was safe, because there was so much excitement in the air that the whole world seemed to be spinning faster.

She snatched a cup of tea and a bun at six o'clock and was off again. Only two hours left before the poll closed! She had a feeling of splendid urgency, and drove faster still. Once, twice, outside the Town Hall she caught a glimpse of Stephen, waved, got a wave back, wanted to cheer.

Just before eight o'clock she fetched from an outlying hamlet her last passenger, an arthritic and half-witted crone whose joints creaked and cracked alarmingly as she helped her out of the car.

"I wouldn't have done this for anybody but you, dear," said the old lady; and Susan felt as pleased as Punch, alone she'd won a valuable vote for Stephen and the Cause. But driving the poor old thing home, she became less pleased with herself, as she began to realise that her senile passenger would have been quite incapable of knowing where to put her X, and it was an even chance that she had voted for Bill Higgins.

❡ 6

FERDO, MEANWHILE, had spent an uproarious morning, and had an adventurous journey home.

He chose two tweeds at Mr. Tremlett's, one greenish-brown and the other brownish-green. They talked about old times. Mr. Tremlett said he was getting old and would shortly have to retire. He regretted that he had no one to come after him in the tailoring business; his only son worked in one of the new factories.

Ferdo and Mr. Tremlett sadly agreed that times had changed.

Mr. Tremlett then said that although it was his rule never to set foot into a public house during working hours, he nevertheless by custom and tradition had always broken this rule on the occasion of a General Election. He suggested that Squire might care to take a drink with him at the Swan Hotel. The bar was full of farmers and local tradesmen whom Ferdo knew well and who were as glad to see him there as he was to be among them. Everybody was in a mood to have an extra drink because of the excitement in the air. Everybody was talkative and reminiscent. Ferdo, when he'd had three pints of beer, became somewhat reminiscent too and to the amazement of the locals was moved to show the barmaid how to compose a drink which he'd invented in order to while away the time when his ship was in harbour at the horrible and teetotal port of Halifax, Nova Scotia. It consisted of two small measures each of Grenadine and Creme de Menthe, poured out alternately with a very steady hand, so that they formed four distinct layers or strata in the glass: red, green, red, green. It tasted a bit sickly, but looked wonderfully exotic. Ferdo called it the Port and Starboard Lights, and quoted as he drank it from the *Manual of Seamanship:*

> *"Green to green or red to red*
> *Perfect safety, go ahead!"*

He was so uplifted by good talk and good company, plus a sort of effervescence of the spirit induced by the Election, that he drank three of these concoctions, on top of all the beer.

The bar emptied at last; and Ferdo accompanied by a body-guard of uplifted locals made his way down Ferry Lane, taking pleasure in every familiar thing, from the Abbey Tower looming up vastly on his left to the ancient rusty bell hanging on its white post. Imperiously he smote it three times. He also shouted for Jakey in a great voice which carried across the water. Jakey appeared, stumbling down the bank, rudely awakened from an old man's catnap, not quite sure whether or not he was dreaming. The tarry black punt came crabwise across the river and nosed into the bank. Ferdo bade farewell to his friends and saluted the quarterdeck as somewhat unsteadily he went aboard. Jakey, still half in a dream, paddled off with his cormorant's wing-flap.

A chugging sound, unnoticed during the noisy farewells, became suddenly loud as a barge called the *Pisgah,* carrying grain upriver to the flour-mills at Elmbury, suddenly appeared round a bend.

Ferdo, from long habit, at once took command. He told the still-bewildered Jakey that he had the right of way: steam, or in this case, stinking diesel oil, had to give way to oars or paddles. The evil influence of the Port and Starboard Lights now asserting itself, Ferdo gave orders as if from his own ship's bridge, and assured Jakey that he had nothing to fear:

"Perfect safety, go ahead!"

Jakey, who could do little else, having a seagoing Squire in command, held his course unwaveringly. So did the helmsman of the *Pisgah,* whose unexciting job was conducive to slumber, for there wasn't much traffic on the river, and he was accustomed to lie back in a deckchair while steering, holding the tiller lightly in an outstretched hand.

The two vessels approached one another on a collision course, watched by the awe-stricken onlookers in Ferry Lane.

In fact, they did not quite collide. The helmsman was startled out of sleep by Ferdo's huge "Ahoy!", Jakey recovered his wits in time to back-paddle at the last moment; but the bow-wave of the *Pisgah,* crisp and creamy, poured itself over the port-side of the punt and nearly swamped her. She'd been leaking so badly that the water was over her bottom-boards already. This new incursion was altogether too much for her. The bank was still twenty-five yards away when the punt began to go down by the stern.

Ferdo, up to his ankles, declared that he'd been down the plug-'ole once in the Arctic Ocean and once in the North Sea, and he was so-and-so'd if he wanted another cold swim in the River Severn. "Can *thee* swim, Jakey?" he asked, slipping into Gloucestershire. "No? Then thee'd best paddle as thee never has paddled before."

And Jakey paddled with huge flaps like a swan trying to get up flying-speed. Slowly, slowly, the punt went down, until there was only an inch of black freeboard showing at her stern. Ferdo, nearly up to his knees, moved forward to midships, where like a galley-slave master he exhorted Jakey to still more strenuous efforts; and at the very moment when the last of the stern disappeared beneath the brown waters, the bows grounded safely on the mud. Jakey, followed by Ferdo, scrambled ashore and together they tried to pull the punt up the bank; but she was full of water and stuck firm on the bottom; there was no shifting her.

"There she'll lie, I shouldn't 'oonder," said Jakey in a valedictory tone.

Ferdo squeezed the water out of his trousers-legs, waved cheerfully to his friends across the river, and marched off into his brown woodland. They watched him go with a swaying gait (three-quarters a sailor's roll, one-quarter due to the Port and Starboard Lights?) up the slope into the oak-trees. Then suddenly he vanished before the eyes of the watchers—where the devil had he got to, they asked, inclined now to question their own sobriety. The Squire of Doddington had performed the family disappearing-trick. In the old russet suit that he'd had for twenty years, he'd become part of the landscape, he'd melted into the trees!

¶ 7

BECAUSE ELMBURY was a large constituency with scattered villages and hamlets up in the hills, the result of the poll wasn't known until noon on the following day. Then the returning Officer came to the top of the Town Hall steps and announced that Le Mesurier, Stephen, had been elected by a majority of six thousand and one. Susan wondered whether her old lady had provided the odd one, by voting the right way after all!

Meanwhile the results from the rest of the country showed that the Conservatives were in; by a majority between a dozen and a score; so the supporters gathered outside the Town Hall had a double victory to celebrate. They yelled and jeered and looked so unpleasing in their triumph that Susan immediately began to be sorry for Bill Higgins, who had obviously thought he was going to win and who now in his disappointment made a stupid, resentful speech which embarrassed everybody. She thought what a generous, self-mocking, polished little speech Stephen would have made if he had lost; and she realised for the first time that the world had been unfair to Bill Higgins, his discomposure, his bitterness, his lack of polish were in a way an argument for his side. As for those Conservative workers who were screaming their heads off and making fun of Bill 'Iggins as they called him, they who only yesterday had been a band of brothers to her now seemed a lot of ill-mannered louts, oafish as Mr. Higgins but with less excuse for being so.

At the back of the crowd a familiar bright cowpat-coloured jacket caught her eye. Ben Fenton had a friend with him, a lanky bespectacled young man in a flaring scarlet tie. She noticed that when Bill Higgins finished speaking they glanced at each other and the red-tied young man made a face as if to say "He stinks, doesn't he?" Mr. Higgins turned to go, and Stephen leaned across and shook his hand and said: "Well, I expect we'll meet again. You'll have another go at me next time." But Susan was sure he wouldn't. He was done for, finished, he'd go back to being an old ineffectual Trades Union hack, and he'd stay like that to the end of his days. His wife, who was dolled up in glad rags which didn't accord with defeat, gazed at him without pity, as if she saw through him at last. Susan could hardly bear to look at them or think about them. She was glad when Stephen caught her arm and said: "Quick, let's slip away."

Somehow or other he'd managed to shake off the Mayor and Colonel Daglingworth, and running the gauntlet of some hearty and shoulder-slapping supporters he led Susan through a side-door into the Swan Hotel yard and across it into the bar. It happened to be the public bar which was practically empty because its regulars had gone out to join the group in the street. Anyhow, it would be quieter in here, thought Stephen, less chance of being discovered by those triumphant supporters whose *bonhomie* somehow seemed to turn victory sour.

Susan had a glass of sherry, Stephen ordered a pint of beer, —"It's hardly the stuff for a celebration, but champagne is the only drink I really hate."

"Look," said Susan. "Now isn't that typical of Colonel D.?"

On the wall above the mantelpiece hung a monthly calendar advertising DAGLINGWORTH QUARRIES. "Stone, sand, gravel, delivered anywhere." It had seemed to the Colonel that the best way to drive home this message was with naked girls. The October girl had tawny hair to match the season, but lay on her back upon a fur-rug in front of the fire stretching herself like a sleepy cat.

"One for every month," said Stephen. "Can't you imagine what fun he had choosing the pictures?"

Just then the door opened and in came Ben Fenton with his friend.

Susan had noticed that he always looked embarrassed when he met her; she had no idea why. Now he went quickly to the other end of the bar, pretending that he hadn't noticed her. But that was silly, so she called out to him:

"Ben! I thought you were supposed to be at Oxford."

"Oh . . . Yes, we shouldn't be here at all," he said. "We just came down for the day on Tim's motor-bike."

"You know Stephen Le Mesurier?" she said.

"We've met," grinned Stephen. "He heckled me. Please do let me buy the drinks. I can do it today. If I'd bought you one yesterday you could have had me unseated."

A shade reluctantly, Ben and his friend came across to join them. Stephen asked for two pints of beer.

"The other night," he said, "you put some good, sharp questions. I did try to answer; but you know what it is at a meeting like that, you don't get much time."

"Yes," said Ben shortly. Susan sensed his annoyance that Stephen was good-mannered and intelligent whereas Mr. Higgins was neither. The young man called Tim studiously avoided

Stephen's eye and with an air of boredom shuffled over to the mantelpiece, where he stood with his hands in his pockets and examined the October girl.

Ben said at last:

"Well, I ought to say congratulations . . . Your side's in, I suppose? I haven't heard any figures this morning."

"Yes, we just scraped home."

"Well, there it is. I didn't think you'd win," said Ben. "Still, no point in arguing."

" 'A majority is always the best repartee,' " quoted Stephen mischievously.

"Who said that?"

"Benjamin Disraeli."

Susan noticed that Ben's face lit up as if he'd been wondering who Stephen reminded him of and now he knew. For the first time he smiled.

"He said a lot of things. I can remember three."

"Go on," said Stephen.

"I think he said: 'A Conservative Government is an organised hypocrisy.' "

"All square," said Stephen.

"And he said something about there being Two Nations—the Privileged and the People? That's what *we* say."

"One up to you so far," smiled Stephen.

Ben shuffled from one foot to the other, still not quite at ease in the world where you hobnobbed with political enemies.

"And—and didn't he say to somebody: 'Damn your principles, stick to your party'?"

"He did. Two up to you," said Stephen. He leaned back against the bar and seemed to take a long look at Ben: amused, surprised, approving. "What are you reading at Oxford?"

"Classics." Susan had thought it would be economics.

"What are you going to do afterwards?"

"Like you, I hope."

"Parliament?"

"That's what I want."

They were getting on better now; Ben was asking questions about the House of Commons and Stephen's face had that look of extraordinary intensity which it always had when he was talking about something he loved or believed in. Susan saw how Ben responded—at first he'd been shy and rather gauche, and something awkward in his stance had reminded her of his father. But now he was quite at ease, and she was surprised how good-looking he was. She liked his small ready smile, and his grey eyes, and the colour of his hair, which reminded her of the ripe hazelnuts she'd found with Stephen on Sunday. Briefly she remembered cracking the nuts with Stephen, in the clearing where the squirrels used to be: the pale sunlight, the toadstools, the tawny leaves; everything glowing still in her mind.

Ben caught her looking at him, and quickly turned away. She thought he didn't like her, or at any rate resented her—perhaps you were bound to resent someone from the big house if you lived in that cottage? Suddenly she wondered where he'd managed to do his work in the evenings, when he was reading for his scholarship. And all the other young Fentons, crowded together there? We must do something about it, she thought, find them a room at the Manor to work in. She was appalled that she hadn't thought if it before.

Ben's friend, meanwhile, had exchanged a few words with her and returned to his contemplation of Colonel Daglingworth's calendar. She had never met a young man with so many chips on his shoulder before. She sensed his angry resentment at her voice, her clothes, her manners and her presence in a pub, which she thought he would have described as slumming. He hadn't the guts to be as rude to her as he would have liked to, so he chose a peculiar and roundabout method. He took down the calendar off the wall and began to turn over the pages slowly, from January to December, pointing out to Ben the more distinctive features of the various girls and commenting upon them nastily. His purpose, presumably, was to demonstrate that if U-class people with U-class voices came into working-class public-bars, they must be prepared to put up with working-class conversations. His curious behaviour didn't worry Susan, but she was unhappy because of Ben's obvious embarrassment. Also Stephen was getting angry, and she thought that at any moment he might explode.

"—And how'd you like *this* bit of crumpet for a Christmas present?" demanded Tim, having at last reached the month of December. He waved the calendar in front of Ben, who noticed for the first time the name of the firm, and being glad to talk about anything but naked girls, blurted out:

"Daglingworth Quarries,—Good Lord, that's the Colonel!" He looked at Susan and then back to Stephen. She saw the beginnings of his small quick smile, and she couldn't help it, she giggled.

"The Chairman of your Conservative Association, I think?" said Ben. He did it beautifully, his grey eyes all innocence and only the hint of a smile, the corners of his mouth just twitching up. Having made his point, he let it be; no comment whatever that might spoil the effect of it. Stephen gave him an appreciative grin. But two could play at that game.

"You must have noticed," he said, "that it's often your own side that lets you down."

He could have meant the Labour Candidate, or he could have meant Ben's friend in the red tie. The score was all square again anyhow; and Ben acknowledged the fact with his smile. Susan didn't smile for she'd had a brief uncomfortable recollection of Bill Higgins, turning away from the microphone, meeting the eyes of his wife.

"Ah well," said Stephen, "you never know, when you come down from Oxford you might get yourself adopted and take *me* on, if I last long enough."

"I'd like that," said Ben. He gave an unhappy glance in the direction of Tim, hoping that now he'd reached the year's end he would put away the calendar; but no, he was turning it back to January again.

"We'd better be going," said Ben in desperation. His look implored Susan to forget the episode quickly and to realise that it wasn't his fault. She contrived to give him a friendly grin and a shake of the hand simultaneously, and thought that perhaps he didn't dislike her after all when she saw his look of relief.

Tim said goodbye with a grunt and a shrug of the chips on his shoulders. But Ben took Stephen's outstretched hand.

"Goodbye, Sir," he said surprisingly.

"I will see thee at Philippi," smiled Stephen.

AND THEN IT WAS TIME for Stephen to go. It was important for him to be in London during the formation of the new Government. Susan went out with him to his car.

"Oh, I hope the phone goes," she said. " 'Winston Churchill speaking.' "

"At best it'll be his private secretary," Stephen said. "I'm much too unreliable for a Minister; but I think they might offer me some little job . . . Sukie, thank you for all you've done. I don't think I could face another Election without you."

Then he took her by the shoulders and kissed her in the street. She saw the surprised look on the face of the Mayor, who by chance came out of the Town Hall at that moment.

Stephen let his hands stay on her shoulders.

"Whatever happens, I'm going to be jolly busy for a bit. I've got that lecture tour in America at Christmas."

"I know." And she thought what a long winter it was going to be without him,—or with only a brief meeting now and then when he came down to the Constituency to make a speech. They'd been together all day and every day for the last three weeks. It was extraordinary, her feeling of closeness to him.

"Promise you'll show me the anemones in the woods in the spring," he said.

"Promise!"

"And the herb Paris in the summer?"

"Promise!"

"And the Solomon's Seal. And the orchids?"

"I will, I will!"

Just then there came along the High Street a whole rout of Stephen's supporters wearing blue rosettes and singing and shouting. As soon as they caught sight of Stephen they changed whatever tune they were caterwauling and began to yell:

> "For he's a jolly good fare-low!
> For he's a jolly good fare-low!"

Stephen hurriedly got into the car. "Can't wait or they'll catch me!" He started the engine which rattled horribly because of the ill-treatment it had from him. He put his head out of the window. "Don't let anybody make you conform, Sukie. Don't *ever, ever,* shut your mind like those silly sods over there!"

He let in his clutch, the car jerked forward. Driving appallingly as usual, he just avoided mowing down his supporters as at high revs in bottom gear he roared away.

PART FIVE

The New Elizabethans

¶ 1

ON A RAW DULL MORNING at the beginning of February Susan with youthful optimism was looking for the year's first violet along a sheltered hedgeside at the edge of the Park. There were plenty of snowdrops, and she was reminded of the description of them in Gerard's *Herball,* which Stephen had given her for Christmas: ". . . A small and tender stalke of two hands high, at the top whereof commeth forth of a skinny hood a small white floure compact with six leaves, three bigger and three lesser; the smaller are fashioned into the vulgar form of a heart, and prettily edged about with green."

But there were no violets, so at last she straightened her back and turned for home. Across the Park she saw an extraordinary and ominous thing.

Upon the roof of the Manor, between the crooked chimneys, the flag upon its pole became suddenly agitated, but not by any wind. In three jerks it came down the pole to half-mast and hung there. Susan had no idea what it meant, and was terrified. She ran with long strides over the cropped turf of the Park, up the last slope and through the little gate at the bottom of the garden, panting past the Otter Pool where the sedge was withered and all seemed as sad as *La Belle Dame Sans Merci.*

She rushed into the house and her mother was in the hall, Ferdo was coming down the stairs and he'd got dust and cobwebs all over his shoulders, having crawled through attics to get to the rope which raised and lowered the flag.

"Oh S-susan," he said. "S-such a shock. The K-King is d-dead." He always stammered when he was upset, and now it made Susan think of the King's Christmas broadcasts, and the agony of sitting round the wireless and praying that he'd get the words out. So Ferdo's stammer made it seem still more of a shock, somehow, to learn suddenly that George the Sixth had died.

They all three went rather aimlessly into the sitting-room, and through the window that looked across the Park to Elmbury they watched the flag on the Abbey Tower come slowly down; and they heard the far-off bell tolling.

Then Mrs. Northover came in to say that lunch was served. She spoke in a whisper appropriate to the solemn occasion; and her eyes were red from crying. However, it turned out that her tears were only indirectly due to the King's death. She had had 'a mortal quarrel' with Mrs. Fenton, who being asked why she didn't seem sorry about the King had answered with her maddening truthfulness that she was indeed sorry about anybody who died but was no more sorry about George the Sixth than about any Tom Dick or Harry. So there was a row, and Mrs. Northover had shed tears of rage and indignation, and the soup was cold and the stew was so overdone that bits of it stuck to the bottom of the casserole.

FERDO AND JANET hardly spoke during luncheon. They were telling themselves that it was the end of an era; and when you're growing old every such finality seems to say to you, *Respice finem,* Look to the end.

Janet's thoughts went back to the Palmy Days, and she remembered the mourning for Edward the Seventh, when she was a small girl in her mother's great house. That was when the world began to change for the worse, her mother had told her. With each King's death those Palmy Days (which Janet had not known but had glimpsed through the eyes of her mother) seemed to be one remove farther away.

Ferdo was preoccupied with a more recent memory; a day in June, 1944, a brisk wind and a choppy sea off the Normandy beachhead, sunshine glinting on the little lively waves, and the

cruiser *Arethusa* coming into view with the Royal Standard flying at her peak. First from one ship, then from another rose a
cheer which was taken up in turn by all the scores of great and
little ships that stood offshore about the new-built Mulberry
Harbour. The King had come across the sea to Arromanches.

It was tremendously exciting to see that Royal Standard, with
its rampant lion and its lithe lean leopards, fluttering against a
clear blue sky. When the cruiser had passed by they'd spliced
the mainbrace and drunk the health of the King, God Bless
Him.

So Ferdo was reminded—it was surprising that he hadn't
thought of it before—that an unopened bottle of claret stood on
the sideboard. He got up and pulled out the cork and filled all
three glasses. He went back to his place but didn't sit down. He
glanced from Janet to Susan, gave them each a little smile—
Ferdo had a great sense of occasion—then lifted his glass and
said:

"The Queen."

IT WASN'T THEN, it was in the middle of the afternoon as
she was running upstairs to fetch a book from her bedroom, that
Susan suddenly realised "We're Elizabethans now!" She stopped
on the wide staircase and looked about her. You couldn't be born
and bred at Doddington Manor without acquiring a sense of
history. The whole house spoke to you of the past. Upon the
heavy oak door that opened on to the courtyard there were deep
scars made by axes. Susan when she was very small had run her
forefinger along them, and she had been told they were made by
the Parliament troops trying to get in, when some of Rupert's
soldiers took refuge here after the defeat at Worcester.

Then the dark place under the stairs, where she used to hide
from Old Nanny, was still called the Priest Hole; crouching
there, she had thought with pity of the poor hunted priest concealed in it. Actually there was no good reason to suppose that it
had been a Priest Hole; the Seldons weren't a Catholic family;
though possibly the first of them, that pirate with the defiant
grin, might have clung to the old faith, he was an obstinate-
looking fellow; and even if he hadn't, he'd have given sanctuary
to a person in danger, Susan thought, supposing Ferdinando was

in any respect like her father. He would have sheltered a fugitive murderer, partly out of cussedness, partly out of pity, partly because he always liked to fight upon the losing side!

The staircase on which Susan stood had been built when the house was built, by that first Ferdinando. It was eight feet wide, and made of dark oak, almost black, with great square end-posts and carved balusters. The treads were very wide and the risers were very shallow; it was the perfect staircase if a girl wanted to run up and down in a long dress, as Susan had discovered. You could imagine a great lady coming slowly down it followed by pages holding her train; or men with swords fighting their way up it from floor to floor. It was a dramatic staircase; but most of the interior of Doddington Manor had this dramatic quality. It was marvellous by moonlight when the dim light came in through tall narrow windows and lay upon the landings and gleamed upon the panelled walls. And even in broad daylight the house often surprised you, because on the ground floor and first floor there were arches through which you got exciting views of enormous pitch-black timbers, vertical or horizontal or diagonal—they sometimes looked as if the massive oaks had themselves been growing there, and had been hacked and hewn into service while the house was built around them. On all those timbers you could see the marks of the adze which had shaped them out of the original tree-trunks.

Susan continued on her way upstairs, across the landing and along the dark corridor where the floor wasn't flat—there was a distinct hump in it, she used to call it the dromedary corridor. But hardly anything was straight or symmetrical at Doddington. Going into her bedroom now Susan had to duck under an enormous oak beam that sagged from the ceiling. It always looked as if it was about to fall on top of you. In fact it hadn't shifted a fraction of an inch in four centuries.

This was a part of the house where the architecture hadn't been altered, hardly anything had changed at all, since the time of Ferdinando. Some of the panes in the leaded windows were probably the original ones; for they had odd little whorls in them, which strangely distorted the view, so that if you squinted through them on a bright day you got a glimpse of a world shot with pink and yellow shafts of light which sparked like a Catherine wheel. Susan took a peep through one of them now, and had an impression of the Fentons' washing weirdly fantasticated and merrily revolving as it danced in the wind. It pleased her to imagine a girl like herself, Ferdinando's daughter, playing the same game of peeping through the whorls to turn the courtyard topsy-turvy. There *had* been such a girl, her name was Benedicta, she'd been the only daughter, and according to family legend she'd run away from home and married a rich wool-stapler at the age of sixteen. Her portrait was in the sitting room and one could see that she might have proved a bit of a handful to the wool-stapler as well as to her father. Elizabethan to Elizabethan, Susan saluted her across the centuries. She wished she knew what her ancestors were *really* like, those first successful Seldons, the sea-captain who dared to cheat the Queen out of a fortune and got away with it, his lady who wasn't a lady at all but a farmer's daughter from a village five miles down river, the enterprising Benedicta, the son who sailed with Raleigh to the Orinoco, the prodigal who was killed in a drunken brawl . . . "What were we like in those days?—We were rough and tough and ungentle and upstart," Ferdo had said to her once. "We probably had awful accents and awful manners. We were elbowing our way in. We didn't give a damn for anybody or anything, not even the Queen's Majesty."

A bit like the Daglingworths? she wondered now. But no, he was too smooth, his wife's social climbing was altogether too genteel. We were surely much tougher than the Daglingworths . . . Then the Fentons' assorted washing caught her eye again, impolite and indiscreet and infuriating to her mother as it fluttered in the breeze just over the courtyard wall; and she thought of the young Fentons bursting out of their cottage and into the great world, brash and angry and ambitious and adventurous, and none of them giving a damn.

¶ 2

THEY WERE CERTAINLY bursting out: Ben at Oxford, Caronly at teachers' training college, and the sinister Willum, of whom Janet not long ago had written in her diary '*Am told he had* PENCHANT *for dissecting frogs!! Queer streak??* NOUS VERRONS' —Willum was at Medical School, Birmingham University.

As for Gloria, supposedly the one without the brains, on the day after she left school, being then sixteen and a bit, she had plastered her face with a great deal of make-up, including mauve eye-shadow, had confined her large bosom in a spectacular brassiere, put on a very tight jumper and a tight short skirt, marched into the office of the *Elmbury Intelligencer* and asked for a job. There happened to be a new Editor, who came from Manchester, had left-wing sympathies and was ambitious to 'wake up' the fuddy-duddies of Elmbury. Gloria's extraordinary appearance and engaging cheek must have persuaded him that heaven had sent him the very instrument for his purpose. He engaged her then and there as the paper's first woman reporter.

With only Gloria and the two young ones at home in term-time, Huntsman's Cottage seemed very quiet; but they were all at home in the holidays, and although there were enough bedrooms (because Huntsman's had been two cottages originally) the pokey downstairs rooms could hardly contain such a horde. On Christmas morning, Susan paid a seasonal visit and found the whole family packed into the front room. Its windows were small, its ceiling was low, so that by contrast the Fentons looked enormous; Susan had a fantastical impression that if they grew any more the ceiling would be lifted up, the walls would bulge out, the door would collapse, and the Fenton family would literally explode into the world.

It was an uncomfortable visit. She had already been to the Northovers, who gave her a glass of the very sweet brown sherry which they only drank at what they called the festive season: one bottle presumably lasted four or five years. She'd been to see Egbert, and to take him a Christmas pudding, and down to the ferry to give Jakey his usual Christmas present of socks, tobacco and rum. (Why rum? Janet, most likely, had thought it suitable for one who did after all voyage upon the waters, and had instituted the custom long ago. But the long black punt still lay half-submerged against the landing-stage where it had sunk on Election Day; and Jakey had declared, Baggernation take him if he ever worked the ferry again.)

It had seemed natural to Susan, having paid these traditional calls on Christmas morning, to visit the Fentons too. But to her great embarrassment they did not at first understand what she had come for. She squeezed herself into the room and unhappily stood there, while they all gazed at her in surprise. There were no Christmas decorations, probably because Mrs. Fenton thought they harboured dust, which she dreaded; however, there were plenty of Christmas presents, books and brown paper all over the floor, so that it was difficult to find anywhere to stand. Gloria, still in her nightdress, was lying on the floor playing a new record on a gramophone. She had a rounded trim buxom body—you could see most of it—and was going to be pretty, Susan thought, when her puppy-fat disappeared. She stopped the gramophone when she saw Susan, hitched up her nightdress, and gave her a cheerful grin. But that was the only welcome Susan got. Ben looked astonished and a bit alarmed. Willum, with forehead villainous low like Caliban's, seemed to scow at her, but perhaps it was his normal expression. Carolyn's pale eyes peered at her through spectacles without any expression at all. Adam and Eve hardly glanced up from their new toys. Mrs. Fenton looked defensive, as perhaps she had a right to because her hair was still in curlers. From the back of the room Fenton himself rose up, huge, angular and awkward, and in the course of doing so knocked some small ornament off a shelf and broke it.

Oddly enough this little accident made things easier. Gloria said:

"Goodie goodie there goes that gnome with a toadstool with spots on."

"You bought it for Mum's birthday," said Carolyn. "Before you went in for Good Taste."

"I didn't, Adam did."

"I didn't, mine was a cat with green eyes," said Adam.

Meanwhile Fenton smiled in his crooked way and having got over his surprise at Susan's arrival was looking quite pleased to see her. Speaking across the room to him she said:

"I just looked in to wish everybody a happy Christmas."

There was a short silence while this sank in, and Susan thought how silly and superior it had sounded, and felt a fool; then various voices said "Happy Christmas" in various tones. Mrs. Fenton, who probably had thought Susan was going to ask her to help with Christmas dinner, modified her expression of resentment. Another silence fell. Susan pretended to admire the air-gun which Adam had just taken out of its wrappings. She thought it must have been a present from his father, because Mrs. Fenton, obviously seeing it for the first time, said "Oh!" and looked hard at Fenton. She didn't approve of air-guns.

Susan thought the time had come to edge her way out. There were a few faint murmurs of farewell, and Gloria, crouching on her haunches by the gramophone once again hitched up her nightdress, waved and gave her another pleasant frank smile.

Ben followed her to the door and down the garden path. At the gate he offered her a cigarette.

"I'm afraid we're a bit of a crowd," he said.

"You're all getting so enormous . . . Are you sure you wouldn't like a room at the Manor to work in?" She'd asked Ferdo to offer him one when the holidays began; but Ben had said he wasn't very busy, he'd only got a bit of reading to do this vac. . . . Possibly he didn't want to accept favours; or he simply felt more at ease working in his bedroom. You couldn't tell. It made Susan unhappy, liking him so much yet having no understanding, no real contact with him. And for some extraordinary reason it was much worse to think of him trying to read his Latin and Greek, his Martial and Thucydides or whatever it was, in cramped discomfort, than if he'd been reading something in the nature of social history or economics. So it seemed to Susan, anyway, who'd learned only a little Latin and less Greek, and had a feeling of slight awe about them.

Ben was searching frantically through his pockets for a match.

"Never mind," she said. "I'll hardly have time to smoke it anyhow, if I don't hurry I'll be late for church."

"I'd forgotten about that." At last he gave her one of those smiles which pleased and amused her: they were little self-deprecatory twitches at the corners of his mouth. "I suppose we're about fifty-fifty, agnostic and atheist. Not counting Adam and Eve, of course. They go to Sunday School because they like the Rector."

"Do you?" said Susan on the spur of the moment.

"No, I think he's awful."

"So do I," said Susan, and just for a moment they were both being themselves, unembarrassed, companionable, unconscious of any awkwardness. It was an unexpected, happy thing, and Susan couldn't have explained why she was so glad to be at ease with him.

But it didn't last, because Ben having found a box of matches tried to light her cigarette and was overtaken by shyness again. He struck the first match so hard that it broke in two, and the next was blown out by the wind, and when he said: "Third time lucky" she could hear the nervous tremor in his voice, and saw his hand shaking. She didn't smoke much, and she wasn't very good at puffing: at last she had to take the match from him and it scorched her finger before the cigarette was alight.

"Well . . . merry Christmas," said Ben awkwardly. He shut the gate behind her and hurried back down the path.

¶ 3

JANET WOULDN'T HAVE CONFESSED to anybody, wouldn't even admit in her diary, that she was afraid of the growing-up Fentons; but during the Easter weekend, when once more they were all at home, she caught herself making a deliberate détour in order to avoid passing by Huntsman's Cottage lest she come face to face with them over the garden fence. The fear was a quite irrational one, like her fear of thunderstorms. Of course she knew they couldn't do her any harm; but they were at odds with what she saw as the natural order of things, they represented the kind of unexplained phenomena which were frightening (like thunder and lightning) because they were incomprehensible to her . . .

> *MET the v. plain bespectacled one in drive couldn't avoid offering lift to Elmbury—Carolyn?? affected silly spelling Trying to be friendly asked her what she'll do after Teachers' Coll.?   She said (little prig) I want to do some GOOD in the world   Looks at me as if I didn't (Touché all the same !) She wants teach black piccaninies darkest Africa, 'do something useful' (?? more useful than teaching white kids Glos??) . . .*
>
> *Shaggy dark one home too, William, studying medicine, Goodness What a bedside manner!!!!   However says he'll*

be surgeon so n'importe! *his manner will go v. well with sharpening knives scalpels probes scowling down at yr stomach before opening up under Nat. Health . . .*

Ben F. socialist one at Oxford (Really almost imposs. think of one of THEM dining in Hall with learned Dons going Bump Suppers May Balls   Remember one at Magdalen 1914   HOW TIMES CHANGE! He is quite polite even shy but makes me uncomfortable because of a je ne sais quoi—*'I do not like thee Dr. Fell' etc !?!? . . .*

Adam F. cracked our bedroom window shooting with airgun   Nice to find at least 1 Fenton human normal natural child!   Mrs. F. in Cleft Stick over a.g.   If he shoots at sparrows = bloodsports if at target = militaristic   She deplores both . . .

Mrs. F. has friend Trudy absurd distraught neurotic stays sometimes w/e's Mrs. Northover says she is VIOLENT League v Cruel sports whatever-it-calls-itself woman Plans carry Banners next season's Meets (In Mummys day unthinkable tenants servants anti-hunting, we were not undemocratic everybody entitled express views but if on estate wd. have notice get job elsewhere where views not unacceptable.   Fair enough? . . .

Confess I wd. like send them packing but Ferdo would not hear of it   Says Fenton good gdnr but I think only for utillitarian (?) things E.G. he hates lawns because you cannot eat them hates asparagus because the rich eat it loves Savoy cabbage parsnips ugh carrots potatoes . . . V. few tomatoes in ghouse do not trust him suspect nips off buds Hideous thumbnail!!! . . . Am sure he Liquidated Lilies of Valley at btm of veg gdn and planted artichokes vulgar kind of couse   Ferdo says he dug them up by accident but then F. will not hear a word against him They keep pigs together 2 v. fat Large Whites called Hailsham (Hogg!) and B. Braddock they lean together over gate of stye watching them eat and arguing politics Extraordinary but whole world topsyturvy   Imagine what Mummy would have thought!! O for the Palmy Days but fear they are gone forever . . .

¶ 4

FERDO IN THESE DAYS was apt to hark back to the past too. But his past had the salt tang and the tall green seas in it, Greek islands and West Indies, pirate junks in the Yangtze, sailing races in Malta's Maramuscetto Bay, Scapa Flow, the Rock of Gibraltar, Their Lordships' commendation, Their Lordships' view with concern . . . It had Atlantic spume and whales and petrels and albatrosses in it, the dull red far flash of the guns and the sound of them seconds later; the *wumph wumph wumph* of the depth-charges, and the wolf-howl of the wind in the shrouds.

''s o *you* were on that run, Greenock to Halifax?" he said to Fenton as they watched the two pigs gruntling in the trough. "They always used to route us right up north, towards the Newfoundland Banks. Brass monkey country, we called it."

"It'd freeze the nose off your face," Fenton grinned.

Ferdo was remembering how the wind came snarling down from the North Pole carrying with it a sort of mad snow, swirling, whirling, demoniac, coming at you from all directions at once, pricking your eyeballs whichever way you turned. The seas in those parts, grey-green alternating with inky-black, seemed to heave in perpetual distress, as if they had made themselves sea-sick . . .

"To my mind, Bessie's putting it on a bit quicker than Hailsham," he said. But the surge of the sea and the whoosh of the wind wouldn't go out of his mind.

"In one of my convoys there was a little collier from Cardiff called the *Welsh Primrose*. Black as your hat and scruffy as her Skipper: she was a proper primrose! It was a slow convoy, ten knots, but even that was too much for her. At the conference before we left Halifax I'd asked the Skipper if she could make it; and I'd known he was lying when he said Yes. Ianto Jones, his name was; sticks in my mind. Character with shifty eyes but a good grin, and he said he wanted to be home for Christmas because his Missus was having another baby, and that'd make it half a dozen. He was another like you! Well, I warned him I'd had my orders: there must be no stragglers. But I could see behind his eyes what he was thinking, Didn't want to wait for the next convoy, told the Missus he might be home for Christmas, might just manage ten knots if it was calm, and so on. "Don't you worry, Commodore, she's bet-ter than she looks, she'll steam easy at ten knots if we have the weather."

The pigs slopped and gurgled. Ferdo didn't want to say what happened next. He'd never told anyone before, not even Janet. He hated thinking about it. Anyhow he'd started on the story and he'd better get it over.

"She couldn't, of course. Couldn't steam ten. Before long she was three miles astern of us, making a lot of smoke, off those blasted Banks of Newfoundland. It was what I daresay they call a bright day in those parts: the fog turned into a sort of bilious murk. All day I watched that *Primrose* smoking like a chimney on fire and falling further behind. I couldn't slow the convoy. On my chart there was a semicircle of little pencilled crosses lying right in our course just ahead. They meant sinkings of ships or sightings of U-boats. We were steaming right into a bunch of 'em. So before it got dark I told the *Welsh Primrose:* Sorry, return to port. I could somehow imagine that scruffy Skipper on his bridge, a shrug and a grin as he acknowledged my signal. We watched the poor little bugger go about, the murk got a bit thicker and a bit yellower, and then it was dark.

Ferdo broke off and watched the pigs again, and was silent for so long that Fenton looked at him enquiringly.

"She just vanished," he said at last. "One of my look-outs thought he heard a bump in the night; but the destroyer escort didn't report anything. I checked up when we got home. Re-ported overdue, no wreckage, no survivors, nothing. Often think of that chap Ianto Jones. He didn't mean a lot to the war effort. I'd got three troopships, ten tankers, in the sixty-ship convoy. Couldn't afford to wait for him and maybe lose a couple of tankers or a Brigade of Canadians. But I wish I hadn't done it all the same."

"I'll tell *you* one," said Fenton, shifting his unwieldy elbows for better comfort as he leaned on the gate of the sty. "Same run as yours, but early on, late Nineteen forty, when the blitz was on in London. I'd bin on leave and there wasn't an 'ouse standing in our street, looked like most of London'd be flat before long.

Our kids had been evacuated, but the Missus wouldn't go because her Ma wouldn't go, you know what it is; she was just
about to have our Evie and she used to say that every time the
syreens went she felt the baby give a kick. You can imagine I
didn't feel very happy, going back to sea and leaving her.

"Anyways we was on this Halifax convoy lark and one of the
escort—Canadian destroyer I think it was—sank a bloody U-boat
and we was picking up the survivors. Patch of oil as big as
Doddington! We'd got a rope-ladder out astern and as soon as
those Jerries came up we'd help 'em over the rail and give 'em a
smoke and send 'em along to the sick bay to be cleaned up and
seen to.

"There was a poor little bloke down there clinging on to the
end of the rope-ladder, but he was bloody near all in, it was all
he could do just to hold on. You could see him opening and
shutting his trap, he reminded me of a fish on the end of a line.
All oiled up and friz stiff he was, you know what it was like up in
those seas.

" 'Come along up, Mate,' we said; and we give 'im a bit of a
cheer.

"Then like as if he was swimming the Channel along comes a
great hulking Nazi bloke who'd somehow kept his head out of
the oil-patch, you could still see his straw-coloured hair. He must
have been a Petty Officer or something, because he shouted what
sounded like an order to the little feller. Something like You get
up that ladder quick or make way for them as can. He copped
holt of the rope-ladder, and when the little un wouldn't let go he
gave him one with the back of his hand across his throat, Out of
my fucking way!—and the little un went down like a stone.

"Then the big un came up the rope-ladder smart and quick as
if there was an Admiral watching. There was about a dozen of us
on the poop, but none of the P—— I mean none of the officers
were there; only the Chief Gunner's Mate, and I think it was him
said something like This is one of the buggers we *don't* want
aboard. And we was all flaming angry, any one of us might've
done it, but it was me. There was a bit of a batten lying on the
deck, dunno where it come from, but it was just by my feet and
when I bent down and picked it up I caught the eye of the
Gunner's Mate and he nodded his head.

"So when the tow-headed bloke caught holt of the rail to climb aboard I brought down this batten whang on his hands; and he let go and fell back into the sea. We all leaned over the rail, but nobody ever saw him come up again, there was just the greeny-brown oil with some bits of rubbish floating in it.

"And all our lot said Serve the bastard right.

"But I keeps on thinking about it, wishing I hadn't. Funny thing, I never told anybody else about it till now. Not even the Missus," Fenton said.

They both fell silent. The pigs were getting to the bottom of the trough, and Ferdo smiled at their windy gulpings.

"Like to see 'em enjoying it," he said at last.

"Ar. But I'm not sure as you ain't wrong about Bessie."

"What?"

"About her putting it on quicker than 'Ailsham."

Hailsham was Fenton's pig. Before long he would have it killed and cured and would eat it; Ferdo would eat Bessie Braddock. So it had seemed fitting that each should name his own after a political enemy.

"To my way of thinking," said Fenton obstinately, "it's 'Ailsham as is the better doer."

"No, you can see Bessie's the heavier."

"Maybe she's broader, but 'Ailsham's deeper. Look at 'is 'ams."

They had this argument almost every time they fed the pigs together.

"Well," said Ferdo, "with all that family of yours, those hams'll come in handy."

"Missus is vegetarian; the young uns'll make short work of 'em, though."

"Those young ones. Must surprise you sometimes?"

Fenton grinned and nodded.

"I look at 'em now and then, Gawd, what have I gone and done, I says to meself!"

"Six of 'em," said Ferdo, and wished he could forget that Captain Ianto Jones had said he'd got his sixth coming.

⊄ 5

ONE DAY DURING THE SUMMER HOLIDAYS Janet overtook Willum as she drove back from shopping in Elmbury. He
was carrying a heavy rucksack, so she stopped and offered him a
lift. He was shaggier than ever, he hadn't shaved for about three
days, or had his hair cut for six weeks. On top of his hair he wore
one of those little round knitted hats, which looked very silly.

Almost any encounter between Janet and the young Fentons
nowadays was fraught with embarrassment and misunderstand-
ing. This was no exception. She thought Mrs. Northover had told
her that one of the children had gone to a Holiday Camp; in fact
this was a mistake, Mrs. Northover had been talking about
somebody else in the village. Janet knew little about such places,
but Willum's appearance accorded with her preconceived idea of
the state in which a person might return from one. She said
brightly:

"I expect you hitch-hiked home?"

"Yes."

"How long did it take you?"

"Five days."

Janet thought she must have misheard him.

"*Where* was your Butlins?"

"My what?" glowered Willum.

"Haven't you been to a Butlins Holiday Camp?"

"No," said Willum. "I've been to Andorra."

That more or less ended the conversation, because Janet
wasn't quite sure where Andorra was and didn't want to confess
her ignorance to one of the Fentons. A few days later she learned
from Mrs. Northover (who held that England ought to be good
enough for anybody, let alone folks like them at Huntsman's)
that Ben had gone to Italy and Carolyn was in Jugoslavia.
Remembering the trouble, expense and anxiety involved in
transporting herself, Ferdo and Susan to Aix-les-Bains for their
only post-war Continental holiday, Janet was bewildered and in
a curious way affronted by the ease with which these young up-
starts got themselves about Europe. How could they *afford* it, for
one thing? Mrs. Northover had thought of that too; but Mrs.

Fenton had explained to her that they did casual jobs for part of
the holidays in order to pay for their trips; and sometimes they
eked out their funds by working in bars or cafés when they were
abroad. "They cadge lifts everywhere, so they've no fares to pay.
If the weather's fine they sleep rough. If they run short of money
they even wash up dishes in hotels! That Gloria spent her holiday being a waitress in France or somewhere so as to learn the
lingo."

Janet's mind went back again to the Palmy Days when (it
seemed to her) Continental travel had been for the well-born and
the well-off. Dimly she began to perceive that the financial sanc-
tions as well as the social ones had ceased to operate any more.
The Fentons and people like them were breaking through all the
barriers which in Janet's youth had separated class from class.

> *In drive met Gloria F. just back from CONTINONG!!*
> she wrote in her diary. *V. sophisticated though only 17*
> *prob speaks better French than me!!!!   Make-up and*
> *clothes as usual* outre *but* autres temps autres meours (??)

She always mis-spelt that one.

¶ 6

FOR A FEW DAYS BEFORE THE END of the holidays they
were all at home together: sunburnt, travelled, toughened, full of
tales, experienced in all sorts of new things, from currencies to
coffee-bars, from cheap wine to the ways of long-distance lorry-
drivers. Citizens now of the wider world, they discovered an unexpected affection for Doddington. Its green shade welcomed
them; its cool leaf-smell was pleasant in their noses after the
strange hot smells of places abroad. They told each other their
travellers' tales as they walked among the oaks and the bracken;
and since they were all so broke after their holidays that they
couldn't afford so much as half a pint at The Green Man, they
were content to sit around in the evening and dispute about
every conceivable subject, but chiefly about sex and God.

Meanwhile Mrs. Fenton washed their jeans, shorts, shirts and
underclothes in strong disinfectant to destroy the foreign germs,
and even as the flag flying over the Manor proclaimed that the

Squire was in residence, the oddly-assorted garments on the clothes-lines alongside Huntsman's Cottage said to the Seldons that the young Fentons had come home.

The lawn in front of the cottage was their favourite debating-place. These warm dry evenings, because the small rooms could no longer contain them and their expanding arguments, they would move out into the garden where the hollyhocks once again had seeds like green halfpennies all the way up their stems, and only two or three wan wretched blossoms at the top. Stretched out in all kinds of abandoned attitudes, long-legged, spread-eagled, they more or less covered the lawn.

It seemed to their mother now that they were not so much growing up as rising up like yeast. Their turbulence was extraordinary. When they were arguing they not only all talked at once but displayed the ability to listen on several different wavelengths, as it were. What was Babel to Edith Fenton made sense to them. Sometimes they lost their tempers and shouted each other down, using words which she didn't think she would ever grow used to, such as balls and cock. They quickly made up their quarrels, changed the subject and in no time were arguing again.

Their mother sat with them and listened, but did not often take part in their debates. They frightened her a little and puzzled her a lot; and she conjured up a comparison, not without humour, between herself and a Rhode Island hen, much of her colour, which had belonged to the gardener at Doublegates Farm, where her husband had worked for Colonel Daglingworth. The gardener had been a part-time keeper as well; and finding in the pond some orphaned wild ducklings—a fox had killed their mother—he slipped them at night under the broody Rhode Island, which took to them and brought them up as her own. But oh! her agitation when instead of behaving like chickens they behaved like ducks and launched themselves upon the pond. She would squawk and cackle and run to and fro along the bank; she would even paddle a little way in pursuit of them, only to flutter back in terror of the unfamiliar element in which they were so surprisingly at ease. But worse was to come: in due course they took to the air. In vain the miserable hen squawked and flapped her wings. They flew away, and she could not follow. It must have seemed to her as if the whole natural law as she understood it had been suddenly set at naught.

So with bewilderment Edith Fenton observed her fledged young ones, in whose growing-up she had expected to see a reflection of her own. It hadn't worked out like that at all. *Her* rebellion had been founded on certainties; theirs seemed to be based upon doubt. When she was about seventeen socialism had given her a whole new creed. She'd marched for what she believed in, borne banners, been rude to policemen, dodged the hoofs of their horses, and had even thrown things (but always soft ones, such as tomatoes) at Sir Oswald Mosley's Blackshirts in order to demonstrate more forcibly what she believed. For every old shibboleth which she cast away, she had put a bright new belief in its place. For instance she had replaced God with a sort of concept of Rectitude. But this brilliant brood of hers did nothing of the kind. They had no more use for her brave new world then they had for the rotten old world of the Seldons. Rectitude was all very well, but it depended what you meant by Right. They questioned, mocked, mistrusted, doubted, loudly demanded proof. Their mother was not only frightened of them but frightened for them, because it seemed to her to be a desperate and fearful thing to face the world without the comfort of convictions and fortifying faith.

The young Fentons, however, were no more frightened of the unknown than those ducks had been of the untried water and the uncertain air.

THE SMALL ONES, meanwhile, were still in the process of knocking down some of the more elementary Aunt Sallies.

"Adam had an argument with the Rector at Sunday School," said Eve.

"Who won?" Ben asked her.

"Adam, I think. Old Goodbody couldn't answer. You ought to have seen his face."

"I thought you were mad on the Rector," Carolyn said. "You and Adam." He'd made a special fuss of them, presumably because they came from an atheistical and socialist family and were therefore to be regarded as valuable prizes: just as the Salvation Army used to give the biggest welcome to the greatest sinner.

"I don't like him any more," said Eve.

"Why?"

But Eve wriggled and wouldn't say why.

"Well, what was the argument about?" asked Gloria.

"The Resurrection of the Body," said Eve, and giggled.

"Go on, Adam," said Ben. "You tell us."

Adam sat up in the middle of the lawn and looked round at everybody with his big eyes.

"I said, What if Eve is run over by a bus and her legs cut off and her tummy squashed and dies. Will she be resurrected with her legs on and unsquashed just as she is now aged nine? He said Yes. So I said, What about you then, suppose you die sudden will you be resurrected just as *you* are now? He thought for a bit——"

"He wasn't so sure about himself," Eve put in.

"—But in the end he said Yes, he expected he would be resurrected like that."

"The Resurrection of the Goodbody," said Gloria. "All flabby, and those chins that wobble."

"Please listen," said Adam earnestly, as he came at last to his point. "So I said, What about me? What if I live to be a hundred with white hair and a beard and half-blind and deaf and walk with two sticks like that old man who used to be a roadman and lives in that cottage by the Green and has got a thing in the side of his neck that gets bigger and bigger because he's too old to have it out? If I live to be a hundred will I be resurrected like that, and with a thing? Because I don't think that would be fair."

"It certainly wouldn't," said Ben with his grave smile. "For ever and ever world without end. But what did he say?"

"He wouldn't answer."

"He sort of cheated," said Eve. "He said God couldn't be unfair."

"Oh, can't He?" said Ben, half to himself. " 'God is always for the big battalions'?"

"What I still want to know," said Carolyn, who was always inquisitive and persistent, she went on goggling at you until she got an answer, "what I want to know is *why* our Evie doesn't love the Rector any more."

Eve turned away and said quietly to the hollyhocks against the wall:

"If you must know it's because he will put his fat hand on your knees."

Everybody laughed except Mrs. Fenton and Ben, who said: "Does he now?" in the hard tone which he used very rarely. Eve didn't say any more, and there was a rare moment of silence before Gloria announced: "I've thought of a limerick." She was in the process of acquiring a remarkable collection of limericks, mainly from the middle-aged, harmless, drunken and disillusioned Chief Reporter of the *Elmbury Intelligencer*.

Sprawling on her back, relaxed as a kitten, she recited happily:

> *"There once was an amorous friar*
> *Who was smitten with sudden desire.*
> *The immediate cause*
> *Was the Abbess's drawers*
> *Which were drying in front of the fire."*

THEN ALL AT ONCE the episode was over, thrown away, half-forgotten, and they were arguing again. They were being angry and fierce and disputatious and doubtful about Hiroshima and nuclear disarmament and pacifism and civil disobedience and the right of minorities and Could Democracy Work? They went on arguing oblivious of the midges which drove their mother to distraction because her pale skin was vulnerable to all biters and stingers. As for Fenton, the midges in conjunction with an argument about Existentialism had sent him back into the cottage long ago. Alone in the front room he was reading *The Pigeon Racing News and Gazette*.

Literally, they argued themselves to sleep. One by one they stopped talking and leaned back or fell back on the lawn; and as they lay down their eyelids closed like the eyelids of dolls.

Then their mother who was always the last wakeful one went round waking them up in turn and urging them to go up to bed. When the last of them was upstairs she closed the front-door and put out the light in the hall and stood still in the dark thinking about them each in turn with tenderness and bewilderment. She loved them in a puzzled and painful way—painful because she was so made that the overt expression of love came hard to her.

The heroines of her school-teacher days were always unsentimental ones; such as Mrs. Warren's daughter in Shaw's play. She hardly ever kissed her children because of her dislike of soppiness. Tonight, because of her great hopes and her great fears for them, she had caught herself wishing that she could make some little display of her affection, before they went up to bed. But she had not dared.

¶ 7

IN CONTRAST WITH ALL the bustle and excitement at Huntsman's Cottage, the Manor was very quiet.

The house was so big, and there were so few people in it. Sometimes Susan would be sharply aware of the quiet, as she went up the big staircase on her way to bed and listened to the grandfather clock ticking on the landing; as she walked along the dromedary corridor and heard the boards creak; as she lay in bed and listened to Ferdinando's Owl hooting in the Park, or a mouse scuttle behind the panelling.

She got the impression that there were more mice than there used to be; and that the floorboards creaked more often under your feet. You could feel them move sometimes; and Susan wondered whether there might be dry-rot or something of the kind. Now and then she thought she smelt a curious, sweetish but unpleasant smell. She asked her father about it, and he said: "I must get the builders to have a look." A fortnight later she asked him again, and he said: "Bless your heart, I must have got dry-rot in my memory!" But Susan's sharp eyes could see through him; and she knew that he was afraid to ask the builders to rip up the boards, for fear of what they might discover there.

Helping him with his letters and the Estate Accounts, she saw his Bank Sheets now and then. Slowly but steadily the overdraft got bigger. Meanwhile Ferdo pottered more vaguely, forgot things more often, procrastinated more tiresomely, was less in command. But it was all as slow as the ruin of the woodlands, which you hardly noticed save when the toadstools reminded you of it, or when you saw rotten branches strewn about, and fallen trees here and there after the first winter gale.

BACK IN THE SPRING she had had a letter from Tony. It
was a strange, short, oddly formal letter. He was in a prison camp
in Manchuria somewhere beyond the Yalu River. It had been
written in the winter, and he said he was very cold. Otherwise he
was well 'considering everything.' He'd been wounded in the leg,
but it was healing. He sent his love to Susan and to Cousin Ferdo
and Cousin Janet. Otherwise he did not mention Doddington at
all.

It was such a letter as a tired man might write at the end of a
very long day. Of course he had to be careful what he said,
because of the Chinese censorship; but what dismayed Susan was
an impression that he hadn't *wanted* to write the letter; for some
reason which she couldn't understand he'd had to force himself
to write it. She thought it was as if he had deliberately put her
out of his mind, with all the other things which stood for home,
and having made that effort he was afraid to let her come back
into his thoughts again. She had shouted for joy when she first
caught sight of the letter lying on the breakfast-table; now she
wished she had never received it. She remembered what Fenton
had told her, that hope and despair both became blurred when
you had been for a long time in prison; in your mind's eye the
brightness and the darkness merged into grey; nothing lifted
your heart very high, nor cast it down into the depths any more.
And when at last you ceased to care very much about anything,
you turned your face to the wall.

But at least Tony was still alive! The Korean war dragged on;
and Ferdo, faithful to his foolish vow, scraped his face each
morning with a blunter razor-blade. But surely it would end one
day, and when it ended Tony would come home. So once again
Susan reminded herself of Sonnet 116 ('Love is not love Which
alters when it alteration finds'!) and resigned herself to waiting.

Her cloistered spirit was quiet as a nun's during that quiet
year which followed the death of King George. But sometimes
she had a sense of waiting in a pregnant silence, waiting for
something to happen to her.

AND WHILE SHE WAITED she was watchful.

Across the courtyard she watched the Fentons growing up.
Often she longed to make contact with them, but was unhappily
aware of their mistrust of her. In their eyes she belonged to the

opposite camp; when she and they met, it was like an encounter
of foes at a truce-line, they exchanged embarrassed half-smiles,
awkward, perfunctory waves.

She watched her parents growing older. With love and pity she
observed her father, with love and something less than comprehension she studied her mother, as each began to improvise a
defence against the events and circumstances which seemed to
threaten them. Ferdo's way was to take no notice of anything
that appeared to be difficult or unpleasant. Sometimes when his
Bank Sheets arrived he would hide the envelope unopened in a
drawer; and then (quite genuinely, Susan thought) he would
forget where he had put it. Janet, for her part, had an increasing
tendency to escape from the disagreeable present by retreating
into the past. "It wouldn't have happened in Mummy's day";
and in no time she'd be back in her mother's day, remembering
and reminiscing.

All change frightened them now. Susan noticed how more and
more they clung to routine, and how the little upsets, much more
than the real misfortunes, seemed to put them out. Against her
will, and more or less by accident, she became caught up in their
routine; and with dismay she watched herself becoming part of
the pattern of their lives. Against this integration she made a
brief unsuccessful rebellion: she told them she was determined to
get herself trained for a job: or to leave home and try and find
a job that did not require much training. But her revolt petered
out absurdly. They didn't forbid her to go; they even agreed it
might be a good thing; they encouraged her now and then to go
up to London, stay with her aunt, and see a couple of plays. But
all the time by subtle and perhaps unconscious means they
demonstrated their dependence upon her and made her realise
how much they needed her at home. Janet was going through
what Mrs. Northover, who was about the same age, described as
'a difficult time for the likes of us.' Therefore they had dreadful
rows, Janet sacking Mrs. Northover, Mrs. Northover tearfully
giving notice, and they were both inclined to call Susan in to
settle their quarrels, which with smiles and sympathy she was
generally able to do. Ferdo had a neighbour's quarrel with Colonel Daglingworth about a boundary fence in which as it happened he turned out to be in the wrong. Janet begged Susan to
put things right, which she tried to do through Sandra; but in

the end she had to go and have a drink with the Colonel, who was horribly good-humoured and under the guise of a hearty magnanimity somehow succeeded in slapping her on the bottom.

Next Ferdo got into a muddle over his Income Tax; and although Susan wasn't very good at figures he pretended to be ill and sent her to see the Inspector of Taxes on his behalf. She got on so well with the Inspector that he took to ringing her up whenever he wanted to talk about Ferdo's affairs. In the end she found the pile of unopened letters which Ferdo, like a dog with a bone, had deliberately buried under a quantity of wine-lists and then forgotten where he'd buried them. When she opened the letters she discovered among the Demand Notes three cheques for rebates of tax which came to more than the total demands.

"You see how helpless he is without you," Janet said. "*Of course* you must go away from home if you feel you've got to; but put it off for six months and have another talk about it then. By then everything may be different: Tony may have come home."

Janet didn't say how Tony's homecoming would affect the issue; but Susan knew very well what she was thinking: "One of these days Tony is sure to ask Susan to marry him": and that, in some mysterious fashion, would solve all the Seldons' problems at what Janet (who never used phrases very accurately) would describe to herself as 'one fell swoop'!

DURING THIS YEAR when so little happened, and what did happen was mostly ominous or sinister or so slow it was almost imperceptible, such as the ruin of Doddington Manor creeping on at its petty pace from day to day,—during this year of waiting and watchfulness Susan looked forward all the more to Stephen's infrequent visits. She told him in fun that he was the only man in her life; she didn't tell him the reason: that because he was so much older she could enjoy his company without feeling that she was being unfaithful to Tony in his prison-camp!

But he couldn't come down very often now that he had office as a Parliamentary Secretary in a Government that had a majority of seventeen. The Labour Party was taking its due revenge for the torments inflicted upon it by the Conservative Opposition, during the year when it tried to govern with a majority of only six. It was war to the knife in the Mother of Parliaments, which meant for the Members late nights, perpetual frustration, precious little leisure, and the Whips like scourging beadles ever at their heels. It was one of the mad moments of democracy, Stephen said; on the face of it a lunatic way to run a great country; yet *"Somehow or other it works,"* he insisted, his faith unimpaired. "By means of some mystical mathematics it contrives to express the people's will. Pretty soon after it stops doing that, we'll be out on our necks and the voters will be able to have another go."

The ways of democracy, however, permitted him to match his visits to his constituency to the times when the best of the flowers came out in Doddington Woods. During the Whitsun recess Susan took him orchid-hunting, and they found a scarce fly orchis and an early twayblade. The same day she made good her promise to show him the Solomon's Seal and the herb Paris, which memory led her to find in the very spot where she'd first seen it, that last summer before the war, when she was six. It had seemed to her then a quaint and goblin flower. It was still so today; like a giant four-leaved clover carried on a foot-high stem, not graceful but with a sort of ingenuous charm, and the untidy flower atop bearing shaggy green reflexed petals like the trimmings on a jester's cap. Stephen showed her how the pattern of the leaves had got it the name of true-lover's knot. There were only four or five plants growing in that mossy place between the hazels, but he'd said it would do no harm to pick one if she wanted to. Because he'd told her it was his favourite flower she pressed it in the copy of *A Shropshire Lad* which he'd given her last Christmas.

But by now she possessed almost a shelfful of books from him. Knowing Stephen was rather like taking an Extra-Mural Course at a University. As his quick mind danced from one subject to another he was liable to ask: "Haven't you read this?" —"But surely you've read that!"—and when Susan said she hadn't he would profess to be very shocked and horrified. Three or four days later a parcel would arrive. At various times he'd sent her the *Religio Medici, Crime and Punishment* and *The Brothers Karamazov, Le Rouge et Le Noir* and *La Chartreuse de Parme,* the Collected Works of Thomas Love Peacock, two Trollopes and *A Shropshire Lad.* He had written a different inscription in each—"Sukie, you *must* read this because . . ." and then he'd explained why he thought she ought to read it.

All that quiet year she read prodigiously, not only Stephen's books, but Dickens almost all the way through, and *Anna Karenina,* and Jane Austen. The stories possessed her, so that sometimes she seemed to be living only half her life at Doddington; the other half at Barchester or at Longbourne with the Bennets, or wherever else a story might happen to be set.

WHEN PARLIAMENT ROSE AGAIN it was foxglove-time, and wherever they went in the woods the hum of high summer was in their ears, and the light seeping through the trees was as green as the light in a goldfish-bowl.

That was the time when they found two wicked flowers, deadly nightshade and henbane, both in the same afternoon. *"Fleurs du Mal!"* said Stephen. "Mean to tell me you haven't read Baudelaire? Not that marvellous poem about the cats?"

Two days later the little book came. For Sukie. Damnation to all Dogmen like Colonel You-know-Who. Baudelaire wasn't one. *Please* read the one about *'Les chats puissants et doux'* . . .

Curled up in her favourite window-seat, where Ophelia slumbered and dreamt and twitched upon the warm sill, she read:

> *Ils prennent en songeant les nobles attitudes*
> *Des grands sphinx allongés au fond des solitudes,*
> *Qui semblent s'endormir dans un rêve sans fin . . .*

STEPHEN CAME DOWN for a Saturday morning's cubbing just before the House reassembled. Janet once more was persuaded to lend him Trumpeter. Nightshade was looking splendid because Susan had been working her hard in order to get rid of the belly she'd put on during a summer out at grass. On the way home, Stephen remarked that he was friendly with a young painter who had just had an exhibition in London and was beginning to make a name for himself as a sporting artist.

"Really black thoroughbreds aren't very common, are they?"

"I don't think they are," Susan said.

"If he wanted to do a picture of Nightshade would you let him?"

"Of course. So long as he wouldn't expect her to stand still."

The young man came down next month and put up at The Swan at Elmbury. He painted for three hours a day, four days running; Northover, proud as pie, spent much of his time trotting Nightshade up and down in the stable-yard. Then the young man departed without showing Susan his picture. Janet, who'd taken against him, said she thought he was a very ungrateful and ill-mannered young man.

But Stephen, when he came to stay at Christmas, arrived with a large parcel: not books this time, but Nightshade's portrait, a canvas three foot square. Somehow or other the painter had caught what Susan called her Deadly Nightshade expression. He must have got a glimpse of her at one of her moments of near-panic; and when she was most distraught she always looked most beautiful. It was an extraordinary picture, with more than a hint of danger in it. It made Susan realise that one reason why she loved riding Nightshade was the knowledge that you could never be smug and cosy, you could never ease yourself in the saddle and say to yourself "I'm safe," so long as you were on her back.

Janet as a rule was mad on pictures of horses; her study was full of them. But to Susan's surprise she didn't seem very enthusiastic about this one. "It's certainly generous of him," she said doubtfully.

It was Ferdo who had suggested asking Stephen down for Christmas. "Not much fun spending it in a bachelor flat in town," he'd said. "And after all, he's more or less one of the family now."

> *WISH in a way F. hadn't asked him for Xmas Suggests special status somehow "One of the FAMILY"!?! Of course I know F. amused by his talk & company (Good men often amused by little MONKEYS e.g. Winston by Brendan and Max B!!) And of course anything that pleases F. poor dear so v. worried abt finances, I.T. and repairs and High c. of Living . . .*
>
> *Susan wants to know where she can hang picture Though brilliantly done I DO NOT WANT TO SEE IT Books are 1 thing but this v. expensive present???? Am told artist is on the up and up—100 gns?? Obviously clever*

as cartload of Cats but most of "Them" are (obvious from his looks he is same Lot as Le M.   "They" stick together !!) . . .

Hunted Boxing Day Trumpeter no scent S. did not ride came to Meet in Landy then went off with Le M   Am really CONCERNED as she is so young only 20!!   Hope and pray Tony safe and well soon released and home Have not said anything to F. about mistrust of Le M and naturally try to be agreeable, friendly—Pense ce que tu veux, dis ce que tu dois !!!!

SOON AFTER CHRISTMAS the dark of the winter set in, the weather worsened, and Egbert noticing that "the wind was going uphill" (by that he meant it was veering round to the north) quoted with grim satisfaction an old rhyme:

> "As the days do lengthen
> So the cold do strengthen."

The Fentons one by one departed to University or College. On the clothes-line at Huntsman's where the jeans had hung in a row Fenton's long combinations, his wife's flesh-pink vests and fawn Celanese bloomers, froze stiff as boards in the keen nor'-easter. There was no hunting because of the frost. Egbert sawed up a fallen ash-tree and brought in the logs with another rhyme on his lips:

> "Ash new or ash old,
> Fit for a queen with crown of gold."

And the logs in the hearth burned so bright that Ophelia turned away her speedwell-blue eyes. Ferdo sitting by the fire read Scott's Last Diary. Janet read Jorrocks for the twentieth time and still laughed aloud when she came to "Come hup I say, you hugly beast!" and "Hellish dark, and smells of cheese!" Susan began to read *War and Peace* because Stephen had told her she ought to.

At last the frost broke and the wind turned downhill and blew from the south so that the little chiffchaffs riding on its back arrived three days early. Egbert muttered:

> "March damp and March warm
> Allus doeth much harm."

Then all at once there were primroses everywhere, and you could go for a long walk after tea, the yellowhammer sang 'A little bit of bread and no cheese,' the pipistrelle bats squeaked at dusk round Ferdinando's Oak, and the spring was running like green wildfire up the sunny woodsides and along the hedgerows. Even the slow oaks hung out a gauze of green, and Egbert predicted a dry summer:

> "If the oak's before the ash
> Us'll only get a splash."

Cuckoos shouted reveille all over the land.

¶ 8

UPON A DAY BETWEEN THE PRIMROSE and the dogrose, Susan taking a glance at her face in the looking-glass caught herself unawares as it were and was astonished by an unwonted and quite wicked little smile. She hadn't the faintest idea where it came from, because despite the cuckoo's call her quiescent spirit had slumbered on like those black-budded ash-trees in the Park. Now it was nearly summer, the may was like split milk upon the hedges, even first thing in the morning it was warm enough to wear a sleeveless dress.

Searching in her thoughts for the source of the smile, she traced it to Sandra's homecoming. Sandra had always been a wakener-up of mischief, as far as Susan was concerned. Lately she'd been abroad with her rich young man: Susan had had postcards from Spain and Morocco. But yesterday evening in her little scarlet sports car she'd turned up unheralded, straight from town in two hours five minutes, merry as May in her London rig, a black and white printed silk dress, a shocking-pink coat, and an absurd but enchanting sailor hat.

"Give us a drink, love, I've got something to celebrate!"

"You're going to marry him I bet," said Susan.

"No, I've given him the sack."

Janet was out at the Women's Institute but they found Ferdo and asked him to recommend a drink suitable for a girl who'd just jilted the son of a millionaire. Ferdo fetched a bottle of

champagne from the cellar, but explained that he personally
didn't think much of it as wine, only as soda-water for brandy.
So he made champagne cocktails, had a couple himself on the
principle that a good excuse for a drink should never be wasted,
then tactfully left them so that Sandra could tell her tale.

"I adore your father because the more he drinks the nicer he
gets," she said. "With Dominic it was just the opposite . . ." She
sat on the arm of the sofa, swinging her beautiful legs, and
explained that the trouble with Dominic was not only his drinking but the fact that he never wanted to make love until he was
three-quarters tight: a practice which she found conducive to
ennui. So at last out of sheer boredom she turned him down;
whereupon, being as she put it oafish when pickled, he had
chosen to remind her that he had recently taken her to Cannes,
Monte Carlo, Antibes, Madrid, Ibiza, Marbella, Tangier, Casa-
blanca, Fez and Marrakesh ("The list went on for ages") and
that his father was a millionaire, and she'd better mind her p's
and q's. "Those were his very words," said Sandra, wide-eyed.
"So I told him where he could put his million pounds, and
swep' out."

She leaned back and stretched out her arms which still had the
brown of Marbella or Marrakesh on them. "D'you like my hat? It
expresses my mood. This is when I'm always happiest. When
something's over. When I'm free to start again. When I'm looking around."

"You don't waste much time, do you?" said Susan.

"Oh, I don't mean that I'm consciously on the war path, or
anything like that. Nothing may happen for weeks or months.
But I've got a fine free feeling, that at any moment it *might*. You
know, love, to tell the truth I don't think I like the sort of affair
when you become steady and possess each other and belong. I'm
not made that way. I like to go into a ballroom, say, and feel I'm
looking nice, without any tie or obligations to anybody, and say
to myself: 'Now I wonder who?' and then just let things happen
to me . . ." She grinned. "And by the way, isn't it about time *you*
had a bit of a look round, love? Gather ye rosebuds while ye
may?"

"A clergyman wrote that," laughed Susan.

"Did he now? Then I think we should heed him, don't you?

I'll be home for a bit. Let's do something exciting. What *can* we do at Doddington, for goodness' sake?"

"I can't imagine," said Susan. "Unless you're mad on the Coronation Day Sports and Fête next week. It's in our Park. I'm in charge of the donkey races. You can help Daddy with the Bottle Stall. Five-bob hop in the big barn at Honeysett afterwards. You can come too and dance with the young farmers."

"After Dominic," Sandra grinned, "to have my feet stepped on by honest sons of the soil would be absolute bliss."

When she'd gone Susan began to feel very light-headed; and Ferdo forgetting that he'd had a couple of glasses himself said: "What do you expect? Between the two of you, you finished the bottle!"

This morning, though she felt very well, some trace or repercussion of the light-headedness remained; she discovered with surprise that she had what Sandra called 'a fine free feeling.' She put on a summer dress for the first time this year, and took some trouble over her make-up, and it was after that, taking a quick last look in the glass, that she saw the smile which surprised her. She certainly had no immediate intention of 'having a look round,' but it was agreeable and rather exciting, on this perfect spring morning, to think that she *could* do so if she chose. She put Tony out of her mind for the time being, and bundled Stephen away into some cosy avuncular corner there, and decided on the spur of the moment to go shopping in Cheltenham and buy herself a new dress.

ON THE WAY THROUGH ELMBURY she remembered that she hadn't seen Rosemary lately and that she had heard things weren't going very well with her. Mrs. Northover, forgetting how anxious she'd been to get her daughter respectably married, had told Janet: "He's no good to himself or to her, that Goff or whatever she calls him." Susan had tried to find out from Northover how the land lay. "How's Rosemary getting on?" she'd asked casually, while he was grooming Nightshade and hissing like an angry snake. The hissing stopped and he turned his little nutty face sharply towards her.

"She's made her bed and now she must lie on it."

"But Jack—she's your daughter!" said Susan, very shocked.

"Yes; and if she went wrong it wasn't for the lack of good advice from me. I told her where her latewalking would lead her. Young people *think* old people are fools; but old people *know* young people are fools, I used to say to her."

Then his small mouth, like a lizard's with hardly any lips showing, closed tight.

He had seemed to think that in his axiom about the old and the young he was stating some irrefutable fact; and this had enraged Susan, to whom the follies of old people, however beloved, were only too apparent every day. She was all for Rosemary against those sanctimonious old Northovers whom her mother loved because they were old-fashioned and 'loyal.'

So half-way down Elmbury High Street she turned off down the lane that led towards the river. She found Rosemary at the door of her cottage, looking very pretty and dolled-up for an outing. It must be something in the air today, Susan thought!

"I've got to catch a bus, Miss Sue." Rosemary generally started with 'Miss'; she always dropped it later.

"Where to?"

"Chelt."

"I'm going there. I'll give you a lift."

Duffy on the doorstep was purring round Rosemary's legs. Rosemary picked him up and slung him round her neck so that his hind paws and forepaws were touching. As if he were a plastic cat, he stayed like that, still purring.

"I think I love him better than anything else in the world," Rosemary said.

There was a pause in which the purr sounded very loud. Susan couldn't find anything to say, except, at last, "How are things going?"

"You mean about Goff?"

"Yes."

"He goes his way, I go mine."

In the Land Rover, on the way to Cheltenham, Susan said:

"It was partly my fault, telling Mummy. I wish you hadn't married him. Is it no good at all?"

Rosemary shook her head.

"It wasn't his being in clink. When he came out I tried again. I did try, Sue, honest. But it didn't work. Two or three times he's hit me. And he's got other girls."

"What about you?" Susan said.

"The one I'm going to meet? He's a Yank. Staff Sergeant in the Air Force."

"Fond of him?"

"So-so," said Rosemary, who seemed to be developing a tough little character of her own. "He's kind. He takes me shopping."

Susan looked sideways at Rosemary. People who are very much alike do not often recognise the likeness; Susan certainly hadn't realised how like she was to Rosemary before. But the slantwise view she got of her now was from much the same angle as the glimpse she'd had of herself this morning, when she was going out of her bedroom and had glanced over her shoulder into the glass. With amusement she identified in Rosemary's mischievous little smile the very twin and image of her own.

¶ 9

CORONATION DAY, June the second, would have been thought pretty chilly if it had happened in March. Ferdo muttering about brass monkeys mixed a heartening cocktail with rum in it, to drink the health of the Queen who was about to be crowned, and of Hillary and Tenzing, who had yesterday climbed to the top of Mount Everest.

Janet had arranged an early luncheon; Susan had invited Sandra, the Rector had 'looked in for a drink' and stayed on until he had to be invited, and Stephen had driven down from London. He was wildly excited by the news about Everest; being himself a mountaineer and also of course a great romantic, he saw the climb as a sort of Coronation present to Her Majesty. Ferdo took the wireless into the dining-room so that they could hear the Coronation Service, which caused Mrs. Northover to weep as she waited at table. "It's the change of life makes you feel things so," she whispered in Susan's ear as she helped her to potatoes. But those boys' voices singing *Zadok the Priest* in the great Abbey were enough to move anybody to tears, Susan thought; except perhaps that great fat slab of a Rector, who was making Stephen squirm with his own special brand of cultivated facetiousness.

Then Ferdo produced a bottle of cherry brandy, and they all

had a nip to fortify themselves against what the Rector excruci-
atingly called a Fête worse than Death. Then they wrapped
themselves up and set forth into the Park to brave the untimely
nor'easter.

OUT THERE, IRON-GREY CLOUDS that made you shiver
even to look at them grew darker and more ominous as they sped
towards you over the treetops on the skyline. They passed overhead with a windy hurroosh and a little brief patter of rain.
Then the sun blinked, and you had a momentary impression of
its warmth, just enough to emphasize the cold of the next cloud-
shadow and of the wind which came with it. Now and then there
splashed down a spargefaction of large raindrops which were not
quite liquid nor yet quite solid: a sort of pre-hail.

On the slope of the Park the stallholders shivered. Fancy-
dressed children ruefully felt their goosepimples. Runners and
jumpers slapped their red knees. The Rector strode about in his
cassock which he wore perhaps for warmth, perhaps because he
thought he looked like a jolly fat friar in it. Two professional ox-
roasters, hired to roast a fallow-deer in Ye Olde fashion, stoked
their fire and basted furiously, spattering their hired Robin
Hood costumes with grease. A pig, about to be bowled for,
squealed loudly in its poke. Three donkeys, which Janet had
borrowed to give sixpenny rides to the children, with dissonant
ee-aws prohesied rain. As for the public, there seemed to be only
a dozen or two in the whole of the big Park. Most of these made
their way towards the beer tent, outside which they were inter-
cepted by the most depressing woman in Doddington, Olive
Turberville, who asked them to guess the name of a peculiarly
hideous doll which she was raffling in aid of the Organ Fund.

"Oh Stephen, isn't it frightful?" cried Susan as she surveyed
the scene. "I'm so ashamed of myself for getting you down here."
He had to drive back to town in time for a dinner at the House
of Commons; she knew he'd only come down to open the Fête
because she had specially asked him to.

"No," he said. "Not frightful. It's quintessential England: the
weather, the social set-up, the touch of absurdity going along
with a fierce determination to see the thing through . . . You can
laugh at it a lot, Sukie, but you must love it a little, because it's
part of the pattern of England today. The Queen's being

crowned with pomp and circumstance at Westminster Abbey: and all over the place people are bowling for pigs and running potato races and having tuck-ins and giving mugs to schoolchildren. It all fits in together, the high drama and the comic relief. But of course you don't see it as I do: you're too much part of it. You belong."

"So do you, surely?"

"Not half as much as you think. I worked it out that about one-sixth of me comes from Herefordshire; half's Jewish, a sixth is French and the other sixth belongs to Wales. Being so un-English I can observe the English; and I think I know you better than you know yourselves. As for Fêtes, I'm the living expert——"

He gave her one of his mischievous grins which always meant that he was about to get on to some hardly-manageable hobby-horse.

"I know everything about them. For instance I can tell you that the name of that revolting doll which looks like a Mongol baby will turn out to be either Marina or Marlene. I can tell you that within the next half hour I shall be invited to guess the weight of a cake and to guess how many boiled sweets there are in a glass jar. I can tell you that as soon as I get up on that platform about a dozen determined women will take up station within twenty yards of the Jumble Stall. They're never allowed to buy from it until the Fête's officially open; so they'll keep their eyes on me as if I were the starter of a race and the moment I end my speech they'll all make a dash for whatever they've set their hearts on. When I'm opening a Fête I always watch 'em out of the corner of my eye: lined up ready for the sprint like fillies about to run in the Oaks. You watch. I'll tell you another thing. When somebody tots up the takings at the end of the day you'll all be astonished to find that you've rooked the public of twice as much money as you expected, in aid of the good cause—what is it, by the way? Here comes Ferdo; he wants me to make my speech and get it over."

"Half to the Village Hall," said Susan. "And half to the Lifeboat Institution. I expect that's because Daddy's a sailor."

"There you are again, absurdly English . . . Well, here goes," said Stephen.

As always, he did his job beautifully. He made jokes but he didn't make fun. He took the occasion seriously, and treated the

small and inattentive audience with as much respect as if they'd
been Members of the House of Commons.

Susan had caught sight of Rosemary, and while Stephen was
speaking, she went and stood by her.

"I felt I couldn't bear to miss anything that happened at
Doddington," Rosemary said. "I say, Miss Sue, I wish I'd put
my winter woollies on!"

Another of those dark scudding clouds was coming up over the
treetops. Raindrops spattered, umbrellas went up, a gust of wind
blew half of Stephen's last joke away. He caught Susan's eye and
grinned at her as if to say: I could have told you that would
happen, too: it's all part of the pattern!

"I say, Sue," whispered Rosemary, "I do like Mr. Stephen!"
Perhaps she couldn't pronounce 'Le Mesurier'; 'Mr. Anthony'
was the only other person she spoke of in that way. She gave
Susan a sideways glance, demure but disconcerting:

"I think he's nice-looking, don't you?"

Just then Stephen's speech ended, everybody clapped, the sun
came out from behind a cloud and, exactly as Stephen had predicted, the women made their dash for the Jumble Stall.

Rosemary said:

"I think I ought to go along and see Mum and Dad before
they turn up here and find me. They'll be hurt else. Mind if I
have a walk round the garden while I'm up there? It's heaven to
be home," she added, with a rather forlorn smile.

NO SOONER had she gone than Colonel Daglingworth appeared at Susan's side. He was wearing of all things a Teddy
Bear coat that made him look even larger than life.

"Long time no see."

As usual he was full of quips and clichés. "Cold as Christmas,
what a day! Still England Expects and we must all do our duty, I
suppose . . . Good speech, clever devil. You get on well with him,
I know."

"Yes," said Susan, defensive and if necessary defiant.

"M'yes. Who was that you were talking to, looked just like
your sister, only I know you haven't got one?"

"Rosemary? Oh, she used to be our parlourmaid," said Susan
with a sweet smile, taking pleasure in his discomfiture. But of

course it didn't last long, the old rhinoceros was only put out for a couple of seconds!

"Of course," he said. "I remember now. Pretty kid. Didn't I hear something about her getting married to a bad 'un? Wasn't he sent to jug for pinching things not long ago?"

"Yes, he was." Whenever she was talking to Colonel Dagling-worth Susan had to avert her glance from those large pores in his nose, which horribly fascinated her. Yet you had to admit he was handsome in his Roman way: if you sculpted him with his eyes out, she thought, he'd look like one of those busts they used to stick up on pillars in eighteenth-century gardens: Claudius or Augustus or Nero.

"Poor child," he murmured, sententious about Rosemary. "Well: there's my Sandra over there. I gather you two will be tripping the light fantastic this evening. Enjoy yourselves," he added, with a bit of a leer: as if he knew or guessed about Sandra's goings-on and was pruriently wondering about Susan's. He went off shrugging rather sadly, perhaps because he wouldn't be tripping the light fantastic and feeling Susan's shoulder-blades with his big paws; and the Teddy Bear coat made his shrugs look grotesque and gigantic.

SUSAN DULY JUDGED the Children's Fancydresses, and awarded the prizes, rather for fortitude than originality, to a small girl with a bare tummy who represented Salome and to an Ancient Briton aged eight whose motheaten furs left him half-naked to the elements. Next she gave her mother a hand with her donkey-rides, watched Fenton bowling for the pig and had a look round the Produce Tent in which the Women's Institute displayed their cakes and buns and pickles and jam. Mrs. Fenton had consented to take charge here, for however much she might disapprove of coronations she was very enthusiastic about such things as bottled gooseberries and home-made lemon curd. She was wearing an extraordinary dress which she'd probably made for the occasion, of glazed cotton in black and yellow stripes. There seemed to be an argument going on about honey, and she was buzzing about the trestle-tables like a persistent little wasp.

Ferdo had left his Bottle Stall in charge of Sandra, and he and

Stephen were acting as starters for the races. "I believe it's because they like letting off pistols," said Sandra percipiently; and
Susan thought that was true but extraordinary: with all their
war service they ought to have got it out of their systems.

Sandra told her that she hadn't been able to resist ringing up
some of her old friends at the Royal Agricultural College.

"I asked them to come along and stay for the hop afterwards.
Actually I rang three. I expect they'll bring dozens."

"Goodness, then they'll want dozens of girls," Susan said.

"I expect they'll find some. There's a jolly pretty one over
there."

The pretty one turned out to be Gloria, who was going round
the stalls taking notes for the *Elmbury Intelligencer*. She'd got
over her period of gaucherie when she experimented with absurd
make-up and tried to confine her plumpness in the tightest of
jumpers and skirts. (*'Saw Gloria F. looking a Fright! !'* [Janet
would write in her diary] *'Bosoms bottom bulging like Pillows
tied up in a clumsy parcel with tight string ! ! !'*) Most of her
puppyfat had disappeared anyhow; and today in a simple
straight dress her figure looked neat and trim, yet had just a trace
of the young plumpness left; the brown arms and legs just a little
rounded, brown hair, brown eyes, a slightly snub nose in the
pretty brown face,—you got an overall impression that was quite
delightful of brownness and roundness and innocence and cheek!

"She's not a local?" Sandra said.

"Jolly local! That's Gloria Fenton——"

"Honestly? One of *his* brats? There seemed to be dozens of
them when he worked for us. What's she doing?"

"She's reporting for the *Intelligencer*. She's quite bright, I believe. She writes a cheeky column every week called 'Gloria's
Gossip' or something."

"Does she now?" said Sandra. "I find that fascinating."

"Why?"

"Daddy told me that column had a crack at him a few weeks
ago. Something about his new gravel-pit being a blot on the
landscape and how did he manage to get planning permission for
it. Then it said sort of casually that he'd got on to the County
Council. He wrote to the paper threatening libel but they said
they'd taken Counsel's Opinion or something and more or less

told him to go to hell. Daddy was furious. He says the Editor's a
bit of a bolshie anyhow. He'd have been still more furious if he'd
known the piece was written by one of the Fentons. I wouldn't
like to be in that Editor's shoes, though. Daddy's like an elephant
——" ("You're telling me!" thought Susan. "The old pachyderm!"
But of course Sandra didn't mean anything of the kind.) "—He
never forgets and he never forgives," she grinned half-admiringly.
"There he is, by the way. Trust him to be talking to a pretty
girl!"

He was, in fact, in the process of introducing himself to Rosemary, whom he had just encountered at the entrance to the
Produce Tent. Rosemary seemed surprised and amused as she
smiled up at him. Then he motioned her to go before him,
propelling her forward with a huge hand pressed into the small
of her back; and vast as an Abominable Snowman in his Teddy
Bear coat he somehow squeezed himself after her through the
tent-flap.

THE SUN WAS WINKING between the clouds, and there was
a patch of blue sky, enough to make a Dutchman a pair of trousers, over the top of the slope towards the north-east. That was
where the weather was coming from; perhaps after all it would
turn out to be fine! All at once there seemed to be a sizeable
crowd in the Park; and a steady stream of people came along
the Back Lane from Elmbury, which in its usual sleepy fashion
hadn't thought of arranging any Coronation celebrations until it
was too late. A few customers began to turn up at the Bottle Stall.
Jack Northover won a bottle of brown sherry which Susan
thought she'd see again on a good many Christmas mornings.
Then Sandra was suddenly surrounded by a lot of young men
from the R.A.C., who looked as if they'd spent most of the morning in the pubs that lay between Cirencester and Elmbury. They
put up Sandra's takings by three pounds in a quarter of an hour,
and at last won a bottle of rum which they carried off in the direction of the Beer Tent, where they hoped to get hold of some
glasses and buy something suitable to mix with it. On the way
they swept up Gloria, who with notebook in hand chanced to
stray into the path of their noisy rout. A big strong fellow caught
her by one brown arm, another great Rugger forward caught her

by the other, and they bore her along in triumph, their by no
means unwilling captive, and pulled her into the Beer Tent
with laughter and with cheers.

FERDO AND STEPHEN came back together, both a little
contrite when the races were over. Ferdo spent ten bob at the
Bottle Stall in order to expiate his neglect of Sandra in favour of
starting-pistols; but all he won was a bottle of tomato ketchup
and a jar of pickled walnuts. Then Susan took Stephen off to be
the judge of a matter which he really knew about. The local children had been invited to go into the woods and see how many
different wild flowers they could find; there were prizes for the
greatest number. The fading bunches, stuffed into jamjars, stood
in a long row upon a trestle in the Produce Tent. Stephen had to
take each bunch apart, disentangle the different species and count
them; it took him more than half an hour, and he did it with
sheer joy, discovering some little obscure things which he had not
guessed were to be found at Doddington, astonished that the
kids' eyes were sharper than his trained ones. At last he chose the
winner, and they came out of the marquee into unexpected,
blinding sunshine and on to a field full of folk. It looked as if
half Elmbury had decided at the last moment to have an afternoon out at Doddington. Susan and Stephen, because they always liked being alone together, walked away from the crowd
and out of the Park into the fringe of woodland; but even in the
green shade they looked in vain today for solitude. Susan
couldn't imagine where all the courting couples had come from.
Two by two—an arm clutched round a waist, a head laid sideways upon a shoulder in the delightful discomfort of love—the
boys and girls from Elmbury walked among the late-leafing oaks.
The cold didn't seem to make any difference to them. Susan
looking about her with wonder perceived that there was hardly a
large oak-tree that didn't have its own particular couple, who
either sat and cuddled with its truck as a windshield, or stood
and embraced, using the tree to lean against, or who lay down
and kept themselves warm in their own way—you didn't look too
closely at them, you tactfully turned away your head!

Stephen walked at Susan's side and didn't offer to touch her
at all; for the first time she was acutely aware of his constraint.

She wondered, as she had often done before, whether it was possible that she was in love with him; whether a girl could really fall in love with a man who was more than forty. Try as hard as she would to be straight with herself, she still didn't know the answers.

Although he didn't say anything or do anything she was conscious all the time, as they went along the path past the loving-couples, of his unconfessed desire and unhappy forbearance; something which she'd never even considered before, because he had always seemed to her so sophisticated and assured. Now in a way his deliberate not-touching her became more meaningful than any physical contact would have been. She was uncomfortable for the very first time in his company; and she was glad when he said suddenly: "Let's go and have a drink together before I start back to town," and they went out of the dubious shadows into the frank brightness of the Park.

A R O U N D T H E B E E R T E N T, where you could feel the sun on your back and you had a sense that the crowd was beginning to liven up like sun-warmed bees, the R.A.C. boys were getting a little tight and wolf-whistling at anything in the nature of talent. They always used that phrase, displeasing Susan, to whom it was extremely puzzling that any young man should set out, as these quite frankly did, with the simple objective of getting himself a girl, any girl who happened to take his eye, and making love to her before the evening ended; as if love were something to be undertaken in the same spirit as a shooting or fishing expedition! It wasn't as if they just let things happen to them, took a chance when it was offered; that wouldn't have been so bad. It was the deliberate intent against which Susan's private puritanism rose up in anger. For this and many other reasons—a certain brash arrogance, a certain loutishness, but above all their collective insensibility—she disliked R.A.C. boys, and she told Stephen so.

"I know exactly what you mean," he said. "At first sight they always have that effect upon me; then I remember that chaps just like them were flying the Hurricanes and Spits which won the Battle of Britain thirteen years ago!"

They went into the tent, and there was Gloria with her

Rugger forwards, four or five of them now; apparently they'd been experimenting with a variety of soft drinks to see which went best with rum, and Gloria had discovered a taste for rum-and-blackcurrant, which the boys found amusing. One of them was filling up her glass, and sloshing the rum into it out of the bottle they'd won from Sandra. Gloria perhaps had never before drunk anything more powerful than half a pint of beer or cider; she'd got to the giggling stage, and when she saw Susan she waved and shouted "Hello there!" rather wildly. Stephen had gone to the bar to buy himself a whisky and Susan a lemonade. When he came back they moved out of the way of the young men who were apt to tread on your feet or jog your elbow. Standing apart from the crowd round the bar, they were witnesses of an odd little drama.

Somebody must have told Mrs. Fenton, in her Produce Tent next door, that Gloria was being 'led astray'; she would never have come into the Beer Tent otherwise. You could tell by her air as she entered that she wasn't accustomed to bars: that she disapproved of them and feared them. In her striped black and yellow dress she looked fiery and waspish; but Susan knew she was scared, was touched by her courage, and prayed that she wouldn't make a fool of herself as she confronted Gloria and the R.A.C. boys. From where she was standing Susan couldn't hear what was being said, but obviously Mrs. Fenton was begging Gloria to leave the bar and come away with her; she seemed to be remonstrating with the young men as well. The whole scene, played in the half light of the marquee, was absurdly reminiscent of an illustration to a Victorian temperance tract. Gloria resented her mother's intrusion. Encouraged by the rum, her natural cheekiness became defiance. She waved her glass of rum-and-blackcurrant under Mrs. Fenton's nose, as if to say: "You ought to try one too!"

And then the young men laughed, in their stupid, neighing way, with mockery in their laughter. Mrs. Fenton looked about her, aware suddenly that people were watching and listening. She blushed till her face was as red as her hair, turned to Gloria as if to make a last appeal,—and Gloria laughed at her too. She gave a little choking cry, and ran out of the tent.

"Oh *damn* them!" cried Susan, torn with pity. She wondered

whether she ought to take a hand: try to get Gloria away from the young men and have a quiet word with her alone? Indeed she took a step or two in her direction; then suddenly funked it. Gloria was leaning back against a tall boy's shoulder. He slipped his hand under her arm and tickled her. She squeaked. The one who held the rum bottle cried: "Three cheers for the Rum-and-blackcurrant Queen!"

Susan turned back to Stephen, who said: "Look, Sukie, I've got to start back for London or I'll be late."

She went out of the tent with him and they walked up the slope towards the house. She said:

"I was a bit of a coward then. I ought to have done something about Gloria."

"I don't see what you could have done," he said. "How old's the girl?"

"Eighteen, I suppose."

"She'll look after herself, I daresay."

"Oh, hell, yes, I hope so."

"So do I," said Stephen. "I like the look of that cheeky little face." He thought for a moment and brought a quotation out of the lucky dip of his memory. He said it half to himself, and Susan asked him where it came from.

"Chaucer?" she guessed.

"Not quite; but Kipling imitating Chaucer. It comes in one of his short stories. Isn't it good?" And he repeated it:

" 'Dayspring mishandled cometh not again.' "

❡ 10

THE BARN AT HONEYSETT had been built during the fifteenth century presumably to accommodate the Rector's annual tithe, for the glebe-land adjoined it, and the Rectory was only a couple of fields away. Susan thought that the Rector in those days must have been a very greedy and optimistic fellow: rather like a child who hangs up a bolster-case instead of a stocking on Christmas Eve; for the barn was so huge it would have needed the produce of half a dozen parishes to fill it. Tonight the powerful lamps rigged up by an Elmbury electrician could only light three-quarters of it; round the edge of the vast floor you danced into the shadows. It was exciting to look up into the high roof and catch a glimpse of the dim-lit kingposts and the cobwebbed trusses that had been hewn out of Doddington oaks four hundred years ago.

Susan as a small girl had played games in the barn, where unseen cats hunted unseen mice with mysterious and ghostly patterings. She felt sad that it didn't belong to the estate any more. Tom Taynton and his good-looking, hard-faced wife were very much the proud hosts tonight. He'd asked Susan to have the first dance with him: "Late owner's daughter and new owner take the floor together, don't you think that's proper?" They waltzed three times round the floor—each circuit seemed to take ages— and Susan didn't like him any better than she had done on the strength of their brief encounters in the lane. He was what Janet would have described in the social sense as 'neither flesh nor fowl nor good red herring.' He'd grown away from his yeoman class but hadn't yet found a niche for himself elsewhere. He struck Susan as a bit flashy and slick; he boasted about his hundred mile an hour car, and the racehorse which he'd just bought and sent to a trainer. Susan, who'd met him two or three times when she was riding Nightshade, guessed that he was scared stiff of horses and knew precious little about them; it unreasonably annoyed her to think of a man owning such a beautiful thing as a steeplechaser without cherishing it as she, for instance, cherished Nightshade. She wondered where on earth he got his money from: nine months ago he'd bought and paid for Honeysett Farm, and now he'd become a racing owner! You couldn't, surely, make all that money out of a hundred and fifty acre farm? She was thinking about this all the time she was dancing with him. He was obviously a great snob, and she only half listened while he talked about the rich racing people with whom he claimed to be friendly.

Thank goodness, a few more couples were on the floor now! Susan caught sight of Rosemary, dancing with a farmer's son, and Sandra in the arms of one of her Cirencester boys. Sandra grinned at her, and Tom Taynton said:

"Very pretty girl, Sandra. I've got a lot of time for her father too. First-class business man, must have made a lot of money. Real bit of luck for the village, him settling down here."

Something in his tone suggested to Susan that he wasn't showing off this time, that he really did know Colonel Daglingworth quite well, and in perhaps a sycophantic and tail-wagging way he greatly admired him. There was no reason why he shouldn't, of course, but nevertheless it surprised her. She wouldn't have thought they had anything much in common. Tom Taynton wasn't involved in business, and Daglingworth, she knew, hadn't any enthusiasm for horseracing.

"He's a chap who looks ahead," said Tom Taynton. "He's got ideas."

Susan for some reason—the new dress she'd bought the other day in Cheltenham, or Sandra's company, or the awakening of her spirit which seemed to have begun with that smile in the looking-glass—Susan was feeling a little excited tonight; and when she was in such a mood, not only were all her senses sharpened, but she felt as if she had one or two extra ones, little probing antennae which picked up the meaning behind a tone of voice or glimpsed the significance of a fleeting expression. Watching and listening, while Tom Taynton talked about Colonel Daglingworth, she had an odd sense of 'something going on,' of some small tantalising mystery, of what her mother would have called 'wheels within wheels'!

But then, as she began to puzzle her head about this, something happened which put it clean out of her mind.

Near the entrance to the barn, which was the best lit part, she caught sight of Gloria. At once she realised that there was something wrong. The girl wasn't drunk, at least not obviously so, but she looked a bit dazed and the lively spirit seemed to have gone out of her. She was still with the same crowd; they were standing in a group near the door with Gloria in the midst of them, there was a good deal of horseplay, and Susan as she watched got the impression that Gloria was being passed from one to another in a casual and careless way as if she were something to be played with. One young man tugged her towards him, then another came up from behind her, put his arms round her with his hands on her breasts and pulled her away. Gloria seemed neither to resent this nor to enjoy it; she had an air of being quite indifferent to whatever might happen to her. Her hair was all over the place and her lipstick smudged. As soon as the band stopped, Susan excused herself to Tom Taynton and went quickly to Gloria's side. She had to run the gauntlet of the young men and she came out of a good-humoured scrimmage with her dress off one shoulder and minus a shoe. However, somebody returned it to her, and once she'd got hold of Gloria she was allowed to lead her away.

"What about letting me run you home?"

She'd expected Gloria to be obstinate. However, she just pushed back her hair off her forehead with a tired gesture and said: "O.K." Susan wondered where she'd been since six o'clock; apparently she and her R.A.C. boys had only just arrived at the dance. In the Land Rover she leaned back and shut her eyes; Susan thought she'd gone to sleep, but when they were turning into Doddington drive she whispered suddenly, "Stop please." She scrambled out and knelt down and was sick. Susan went and crouched by her, and held her head.

Back in the Landy, she borrowed a handkerchief and remembered that she'd lost her bag. Susan promised to look for it when she got back to the barn.

"It probably isn't there. I don't know where I lost it," said Gloria.

Susan drove her right up to the garden-gate of Huntsman's, and Gloria said: "Thanks for the lift. No, you needn't get out. I'm not tight at all."

Susan's antennae perceived that Gloria at this moment hated her, and she couldn't understand why, because Gloria was the one she'd always got on best with, of all the Fenton children; the only one with whom she'd made any real contact, across the Iron Curtain which seemed to lie between Huntsman's Cottage and the Manor. Bewilderedly and in distress for her she made the clumsy beginning of an affectionate gesture—stretched out her arm to put it round Gloria's shoulder and give her a sort of goodnight squeeze. But she felt her stiffen and edge away.

"I'm quite all right, thanks." Gloria moistened her lips with the tip of her tongue and wiped them with the handkerchief. Susan in pity for her could almost taste the sour tang in her mouth and in her mind. "Please leave me now, and go back to your friends."

On the way back to the dance it occurred to Susan that by 'your friends' Gloria might have meant the R.A.C. boys:

not because she really thought they were her friends, but because superficially at any rate they had the same sort of accent, the same assurance, perhaps even some of the same attitudes as she had.

B A C K I N H O N E Y S E T T B A R N the band was playing but nobody was dancing and people were standing in groups, very still, all round the floor. As soon as she went in Susan realised that something was wrong; the two men who'd been selling tickets must have got up from their seats in a hurry, because there were half-crowns piled on a ten-bob note left lying on the table. There were a lot more people in the barn, and most of the new ones were young men in tight trousers and drape coats: presumably an Elmbury version of the Teddy Boys that Susan had heard of but had never yet seen. Her first reaction was to make them welcome: the more the merrier in a huge place like Honeysett. Indeed, she said "Hello" to a gangling youth whose sooty-coloured jacket had a peculiar pattern of lozenges done in silver thread. He gaped at her but didn't reply. Squeezing herself past him, anxious to know what was going on, she saw Rosemary standing face to face with her Goff. Rosemary looked frightened. Behind Goff in extraordinary clothes stood about half a dozen of these Teddies or whatever they might be. Goff was wearing a striped open shirt like a pyjama top, and once again the thin gold chain round his suety white neck aroused Susan's distaste.

Rosemary saw her and cried out, "Oh, Sue—!" as if in warning. Susan went straight to her side and said to Goff:

"What's the matter?"

He dropped his glance when she stared at him. At last he said:

"She belongs to our lot and she ought to stick to our lot."

"That's up to her," said Susan.

"She better."

"Better what?"

"Not dance with other blokes," said Goff, who looked as if he was torn between bravado and alarm at his own daring. He was breathing rather quickly, and this gave him that wolfish look Susan had seen on the occasion when she opened the summerhouse door.

"I imagine she'll dance with whoever she wants to," Susan said. Goff looked over his shoulder to make sure his friends were listening, and said loudly:

"She better not. My lot might take the place apart, else."

Rosemary tugged at Sue's arm in agitation, and whispered: "Please, Sue, you might get hurt——" The possibility hadn't even occurred to her; and now Goff's threat made her so angry that she wasn't the least afraid. She blazed at him, and he wouldn't meet her eyes. Then she saw a sudden movement among the youths behind him. Their hands went to their pockets. At the very same moment she saw on her right two of the R.A.C. boys who'd been with Gloria. The one nearest to her was the very tall one who'd won the bottle of rum and helped to carry her off to the Beer Tent. He hadn't yet realised what was going on, but he was quick in the uptake, and he gave Susan an urgent look, half a question, and as the group behind Goff began to move forward she'd only time to say "Yes please!" but that was quite sufficient. The young man, who had seemed foolishly drunk when Susan had last seen him with his arms round Gloria's waist, sprang to action instantly. With all the power of his lungs he yelled over his shoulder what was clearly a battle-cry: *"Out dogs of war!"* Susan learned later from Ferdo that it was a war-whoop of the Navy, traditionally used in the course of gun-room horseplay; apparently a Midshipman, invalided out of the Service, had brought it to the R.A.C. But it sounded extraor-dinary at the time and its effect was extraordinary too. It seemed to Susan that several more of these tall, quick young men mani-fested themselves out of thin air. She had the briefest glimpse of Goff's terrified face before it disappeared from view: the young men broke over him like a wave. There was hardly any noise: just a thump or two, and briefly the crackle of a splintering table or chair. The band went on playing, and the episode was over so quickly that only the people close at hand realised what had happened. There were nine or ten R.A.C. boys against a couple of dozen Teddies. But the Rugger forwards weighed about thir-teen stone apiece, they were broad-shouldered and athletic and fearless and devil-may-care. Goff's lot for the most part were weazen, scruffy and unassured. The wave that had overwhelmed Goff himself carried them before it to the doorway, in which they jammed. This gave the Rugger players time to form a scrum. They packed themselves tight in two rows and with a total weight of more than half a ton pushed slowly and steadily. During this phase of the business there was almost complete silence broken only by occasional grunts and one agonized squeal. Then something gave way, the scrum with a roar of triumph burst through the door, and once again everything went quiet. After a minute or two this silence in turn was broken by a series of most peculiar metallic sounds as if tin cans were being jangled together. Susan found out later that they had been caused by the Rugger players first jumping up and down, then playing leapfrog, on top of the bicycles which belonged to the Teddies.

ROSEMARY DIDN'T KNOW why Goff and his gang had invaded the dance. She thought he hadn't expected to find her there, but having done so had realised that she provided him with a good excuse to kick up a row. "You don't know them, Sue; they just want to break things. It's like a sort of bug that's got into them. They never want to do anything else. Just spoil everything and smash things and hurt people. Some of them have got knives. You were brave! I'm real frit of them sometimes."

Luckily Rosemary had arranged to stay at her mother's. She didn't have to go back to Elmbury tonight.

"What about tomorrow?" Susan said.

"Oh, he'll be sober tomorrow. I'm not a bit frit when he's sober. If he went for me I'd clout him back. But he won't say nothing about it tomorrow. Sometimes we don't say anything to each other for days and days."

SANDRA, IT TURNED OUT, had actually danced with one of the Teddies. She told Susan that when the gang arrived there was a Paul Jones going on and some of them joined in. She'd found herself in the arms of a young man in a bright blue suit with padded shoulders.

"How did you get on?" laughed Susan.

"It was most extraordinary. I smiled at him but he didn't smile back, he glared, we danced about half-way round the room without either of us saying anything, then as if he'd suddenly made up his mind to break the ice he said in a very determined way:

'Are you a virgin?' Funny thing, nobody's ever asked me that before."

"What did you say?"

"Nothing. If I'd told him No he'd have said That's fine, and if I'd told him Yes he might have said Time we fixed you. So I just looked shocked."

Susan was delighted with the idea of Sandra looking shocked.

"Heigh ho," said Sandra. "I don't know how it is with you, love, but fights always make me feel wicked somehow." The R.A.C. boys were coming back into the bar in ones and twos. One of them asked Sandra to dance and she went off with him, looking very wicked indeed. Then the tall young man who'd saved the situation came up to Susan to claim his reward. They did a quick-step at a hell of a pace, then they jived, then another quick-step, after which another of the Rugger players claimed Susan, and as soon as the band stopped she was taken over by a third. In her new dress of buttercup linen which she'd bought at Cheltenham she was feeling fine, and she wondered whether there might per-haps be something in what Sandra said, about fights having that effect on you. During the next couple of hours she waltzed and quick-stepped and jived and sat out in cars and was cuddled and pawed and kissed and pulled about, and the touching and the pressing awakened a little wickedness in her body which some-what surprised her. This was a new thing for Susan, and she thought perhaps it was part of her growing up, at any rate it was something she needed. It was a gay, free-and-easy but never hazardous wantoning. There wasn't a hint of trouble except towards the end of the evening when she had a second waltz with Tom Taynton. He was rather drunk by then, and once again he seemed anxious to talk about the Daglingworths—

"That girl Sandra, you're great friends with her, aren't you?"

"I like her very much."

"Her father and me, funny thing, different as chalk from cheese, yet we get on like a house afire."

Interesting how he harps on it, thought Susan. Something going on? Something just a shade fishy? Her antennae were sud-denly very alert. But Tom had no more to say about Colonel Daglingworth, and Susan became aware that she was being rather professionally manoeuvred towards the door. Just as the band stopped she caught a glimpse of Tom's wife, that pretty tough girl, in a low-backed dress a bit out of place at Dodding-ton, looking through half-closed eyes rather cynically at Tom.

He said, not very coherently:

"New owner and late owner's daughter take the air together? Let's go outside."

"Not on your life," said Susan cheerfully.

"Just for a minute. Come along," he pleaded. "It's stopped raining."

"Really? I wonder how you know!" laughed Susan.

Then he put his arm round her and began to push her towards the door. His wife was still watching, and Susan was furious.

"No!" she said; and was quite ready to slap his face. He dropped his arm immediately and she knew from the way he looked at her that the conceited silly ass didn't understand why she wouldn't have dreamt of going outside with him. He was stupid enough to think it was something to do with class. He was also drunk enough to say what he thought:

"You snooty little bitch," he said; and slummocked away.

SUSAN HAD INVITED Sandra to stop at the Manor for a drink on the way home. They looked up at the grandfather clock on the first landing and were amazed to find it showed a quarter to four. Sandra had a whisky while Susan, to Sandra's vast amuse-ment, brewed herself a cup of cocoa.

"It's somehow just like you," she said. "But I must say you let your hair down tonight! Honestly, love, I didn't think you had it in you."

She leaned back in the sofa and smiled at Susan sleepily.

"Don't know about you, I feel as if I'd been pulled through a hedge backwards. Bedraggled. That's a funny word when you think of it."

It was a quaint, unexpected, and rather endearing aspect of Sandra that although she hardly ever read anything but gossip-columns and fashion-magazines, she was curiously fascinated by words. She had a way of looking at them from unusual angles and discovering quirks and absurdities in them. Sometimes she invented rather nice ones of her own. One day she was hacking home with Susan after a long day's hunting and her horse was all in, his ears laid back, his neck thrust forward, his head carried low. "He looks a bit hangdog," said Susan. "Hanghorse," laughed Sandra; and the word went straight into Susan's own vocabulary, it described so well the attitude and appearance of a horse that was unhappy or out of sorts.

Sandra said again:

"Bedraggled. Did you ever misunderstand words when you were young?"

"Yes, I always thought misled was mizzled."

"Well, one of mine was bedraggled. I pronounced it 'bed-' raggled. It made sense that way; you know, the blankets and sheets all tumbled and awry. When I grew up it got a new meaning. Now whenever I feel bed-raggled in the morning I know I've done wrong somehow."

Sandra stretched herself.

"God, I was fed up with Dominic. It got to the stage when I felt bed-raggled every time after I slept with him. It's gorgeous to be free again . . . Goodness, what's that?"

Susan had left the sitting-room door open, and they could hear the grandfather clock groaning as if its innards writhed in some agonizing peristalsis, while it worked itself up to strike the hour.

"Four o'clock! I must go," said Sandra. "See you soon, love. I must have made a dozen dates tonight; but I'll never keep any of them because I didn't write any of them down. Oh, isn't it fun to be free!"

One of the nicest things about Sandra, thought Susan as she went out into the courtyard with her, was the way she made you feel adventurous. Somehow she always managed to communicate to you her own sense of lively and excited anticipation: a kind of "You never know what you will find round the next cor-ner, you never know what unexpected thing may happen to you tomorrow morning!" In Sandra's case what she found round the corner, what happened tomorrow, was generally a man. But it might equally be any kind of new experience, discovery, explora-tion, delight.

When the noise of Sandra's engine (like ripping calico when she revved up to change gear) had died away down the drive, Susan stood still in the hush before dawn and enjoyed this feel-ing of anticipating the unexpected, of standing on the brink of things, you-never-knew-what. There was just a little light in the east, and the trees in that direction were huge black blurry shapes. Not a leaf stirred. You could have heard a mouse's footfall, a moth's wingbeat, you could almost have heard the missel thrush drawing breath into his speckled breast before he began to sing his aria to the new, exciting day.

❡ 11

ON THE MORNING AFTER THE FÊTE Ferdo slung a sack over his shouder and carrying the special walking-stick-with-a-spike-on-the-end which Egbert had contrived for him he went off into the woods round the Park to clean up the mess. He speared the cigarette packets, and the discarded wrappings of picnic food, and yesterday's papers with pictures of the Queen, and transferred them to his sack until it bulged, then stuffed them down to the bottom and resumed his litter-hunt. You begin to have obsessions as you get older, he thought, trying as always to be honest with himself. Litter was becoming one of his. He discovered that he took actual pleasure in filling the sacks, he might have been just a shade disappointed if there hadn't been enough litter to fill it! When he got home he'd pile the whole of his morning's collection, the sack and all, on to Fenton's rubbish heap at the bottom of the garden, and they'd have a jolly good bonfire; which perhaps was another of his little obsessions, he cheerfully reminded himself.

He went along the edge of the woods where at the foot of every oak-tree the browny-green bracken fronds were crushed and broken. Ferdo loved these little fronds of early June, which opened in the sun like the feathered feet of owls, when their claws at twilight are sleepily unfolding. Then he quartered the rough field on the Elmbury side of the Park, which had furze-bushes and hollows and hawthorns and tufty grass. The name of this field on Ferdo's six-inch Ordnance Map was The Rampings, but he'd often thought that might have been a corruption of The Rompings, a name which would certainly have suited it yesterday. What extraordinary objects people nowadays left behind them! Ferdo picked up gingerly the distasteful detritus of Elm-

bury's love-making on the end of his stick and added it to the
rubbish in the sack. When he chucked it on to the bonfire it
would certainly sizzle.

Lucky Janet wasn't here! She'd suggested coming along with
him, but he'd put her off because he wanted to potter alone and
give himself a chance to think. He had plenty to think about,
God help him, what with the state of the Manor and the state of
the woods and the state of his bank balance! At any rate, he told
himself, it was just as well old Janet wasn't with him now: she
was very much on the side of the old-fashioned conventional
morality, especially where the lower classes were concerned. She'd
have been outraged by what had gone on in The Rampings
yesterday. It struck Ferdo as very remarkable, in this year of
grace 1953, that Janet, whom he deeply loved, was nevertheless
able to think of people collectively as the lower classes, though
she didn't actually use the term. Her mother who'd been troubled by no such inhibitions, had used it freely and comprehen-
sively, to include everybody who wasn't aristocratic or professional or rich. In the very feudal village where Janet grew up
there was no Middle Class and everybody belonged to the Lower
Class up to, but not quite including, the curate and the Agent,
who were of equal degree and stood as it were betwixt-and-
between classes. You asked them to dinner once a year as a duty,
and now and then to a glass of madeira and a slice of seed cake
after church on Sundays.

Ferdo had a lively recollection of the old battleaxe, Janet's
mother, whom he had detested as heartily as she had detested
him. From the beginning she had baulked at the prospect of
having a naval Lieutenant for a son-in-law, even if he was the
heir to a Baronetcy. Unlike most sailors, however, Ferdo rode
well to hounds; he wouldn't have been a true Seldon if he
hadn't. Janet in those days was a tall grey-eyed girl with high
cheekbones and long legs and bright chestnut hair. She looked
fine on a horse and she rode as if the devil were after her. During
the course of a long courtship, interrupted by spells of service
abroad, Ferdo had galloped hell-for-leather in pursuit of Janet,
as she in turn had ridden hell-for-leather in pursuit of foxes, all
over the patchwork fields and tall fences of Worcestershire and
Warwickshire. The chase had cost Ferdo two broken collar-bones,

three cracked ribs and a dislocated shoulder. Janet's mother accepted him at last (her father had died some time before) but she somehow contrived to make it clear that his good horsemanship had outweighed such obvious disadvantages as his not being a Lord.

The old lady used to hunt six days a week during the winter, and went to church twice on the seventh day. She was very strict and conventional in her religion and in the hunting-field. She wore the right clothes for the opening Meet and the right clothes for church, and looked with scorn upon anybody who didn't. Her Establishment consisted of the Monarchy, the C. of E., and the M.F.H. Association. She was also very fond of animals and was a great supporter of the R.S.P.C.A. In her latter days, as her wits began to fail her, she believed that she would meet again in heaven all her favourite horses and most beloved dogs. Ferdo suspected that she thought all the foxes she had killed might be waiting there for her too, to be happily hunted through the Life Everlasting.

'Old Janet,' as Ferdo affectionately thought of her, had certainly inherited or caught a good many nonsensical notions and prehistoric attitudes from her Mama; and Ferdo had noticed that she was more and more inclined nowadays to run away from the world as it was and turn her thoughts back to the world as it used to be, or as she imagined it used to be, in the Palmy Days of her girlhood. This caused her to say some silly things and to take up some foolish attitudes; and Ferdo laughed at them, but with tolerant understanding. Janet in her turn put up with his own kinks and quirks; Heaven knew, he had plenty! As we get older, he said to himself, we become habituated to each other's absurdities; maybe we even cherish and enjoy them. But we must seem pretty odd sometimes to other people: Susan, for instance— wonder what she thinks of us, really?

SHE WAS RIDING NIGHTSHADE this morning, schooling her over some new difficult jumps which she'd somehow persuaded Egbert to build for her. Ferdo had noticed that she got on particularly well with proud independent awkward characters such as Egbert and Fenton, and he thought it was because she had courtesy, which implied a great deal more than civility and good manners. It meant that while being completely *your*self, you were all the time helping the other person to be *him*self, through your appreciation of his point of view, your respect for his individuality, your sensibility and your quick awareness of how he thought and felt and what he was. You could show courtesy to animals too. When Susan picked up a hedgehog off the road, to save it from being run over, when she handled a kitten or a toad or an injured bird or a grass-snake, she seemed to know how it liked to be held, to be aware of its special fears and discomforts, in fact to appreciate all the things which made that particular creature different from other creatures. It sometimes seemed to Ferdo that courtesy was an uncommon thing nowadays, and welcome as a spring flower. He was all the more proud of Susan because she possessed it.

Before he set out on his litter-hunt, he had leaned upon the paddock gate and watched her exercising this courtesy towards her beautiful, panicky Nightshade, who still refused sometimes because of inexplicable terrors and would then stand abject in expectation of the beating she used to get when she refused. It was fascinating to see the look of concern and concentration on Susan's face as she leaned forward and tried to communicate with Nightshade through her mind, through her body, through her hands and through her voice.

Then as if they had come to a happy understanding suddenly, Nightshade whisked round, back to the starting-point purposefully—Susan collected her and set her going, ears pricked, long tail swishing—then over the in-and-out without fear or fault, lengthening her stride as she cantered away . . .

That was the last jump; Susan had finished for the morning; but the ground was soft after yesterday's rain, it'd do Nightshade no harm to stretch her legs in a short burst round the paddock. The mare fairly leaped into a gallop; Susan settled down into the saddle, shirt-tails flying, jeans rucked up to her knees! When she went hunting she was always spick and span, but at all other times she liked to ride in these awful old faded blue jeans which seemed to have shrunk in the wash, and in a loose shirt which for some reason or other was never properly tucked into the trousers, so that you got suprising glimpses of her midriff now and then. In this haphazard rig she nevertheless managed to look superb on

Nightshade because she had the sort of witchcraft horsemanship which Shakespeare described in *Hamlet:* Janet had had it too— 'Incorps'd and demi-natured With the brave beast' was the phrase which stuck in Ferdo's mind. That was how she looked now as she galloped up to him, she was one with her Nightshade, girl and mare were marvellously fused together as they took the bend at racing pace only a few yards from Ferdo's gate. Little bits of muddy turf spattered his forehead; and Susan turned round to wave, and laughed at him over her shoulder as he wiped them away.

S H E W A S M E R R Y A S A S P R I T E this morning, though she'd confessed at breakfast that the missel thrush had just started singing in the oak-tree outside her window when she went to bed. Janet over the coffee-jug had raised her eyebrows at that. Later when Susan went out of the room she said:

"What on earth could they have been up to? What do you make of Sandra—is she all right?"

Ferdo privately thought she was a most attractive little tart, but all he said to Janet was: "Don't worry. Susan can look after herself." He was quite sure of that. In any case he had a bluff naval attitude to these things, that there was a lot of unnecessary fuss made about sex. Generosity and gentleness, honesty and humour, courage and that rare, precious courtesy, were the virtues which mattered most in his opinion; a combination of three or four of them would look after your sex-life for you reasonably well, he thought, and the rest of the dismal dogmas could go hang. Susan certainly wasn't going to follow Sandra's example! In fun or in frolic she might give a little of herself now and then; but there'd be nothing much to it, nothing that mattered, unless and until she really fell in love. *Then* it would be look out, Ferdo thought; no reserves or hesitations then!

Janet said, as she'd often done before:

"If only Tony could come home! It said on the wireless that there were talks about an armistice."

Ferdo, who loved Tony and was sometimes kept awake at night by thoughts of him rotting away as a prisoner in that far cruel land, was quite sure all the same that he'd be wrong for Susan. It would be difficult to explain why to Janet, and he'd never really tried. His lack of enthusiasm always puzzled her, because in her eyes it was so obviously the ideal arrangement and solved everything. It would mean that Doddington stayed in the family, there'd still be Seldons there!

"—Ferdo, there's nothing *wrong* about second cousins marrying?"

"Of course not."

"I'm sure Susan adores him. And his father left him so well off, they'd be able to run the estate as it ought to be—I mean, the way you'd like to if we could afford it."

This was always Janet's theme. The estate wasn't entailed. Tony was heir to the title, but Doddington went to Susan; therefore her future husband must have enough money to help her maintain it. Janet was much troubled by apprehensions lest some penniless ambitious upstart, seeing Susan as an heiress, might marry her for the sake of laying hands on Doddington.

Ferdo reckoned that Susan had enough sense to see through that kind of suitor. But if any such bounder succeeded in his courtship, and married Susan because he fancied himself as the future squire of Doddington, he was in for a nasty shock, and serve the bugger right; he was going to find himself with a pretty little problem on his hands, thought Ferdo grimly.

THE PROBLEM INVOLVED the paradoxical situation of being simultaneously both handsomely rich and devilish poor.

You could take a pencil and paper and work out the value of your land at so much an acre, and then reckon the worth of the timber over and above the value of the land—those huge and heartlifting oaks reduced to terms of three bob a cubic foot, as Daglingworth had suggested on that Anniversary night when he came to dinner. If you could do the sum, you would then discover that you were very well-off indeed, and deservedly the envy of all the people whom Janet thought of as bolshies, though their only offence as a rule lay in their wishing they'd been born into your shoes instead of their own.

But if on the other hand you believed that those oakwoods were not to be sold and cut down, but to be enjoyed and cherished, and that you had a special duty and obligation to conserve them because you happened to have had the stupendous one-in-a-

million football-pool luck to inherit them and all that they implied,—*then* when you took up your pencil and paper you could
easily prove that if you weren't quite broke you jolly soon would
be! On Ferdo's current account that overdraft of £1066, which
once upon a time had worried him, seemed now as remote and
unimportant as the Battle of Hastings. It had built itself up to
five or six thousand. On the Estate Account, which carried the
burden of maintenance and repair, the overdraft was twice that
figure; and there was precious little coming in to prevent it getting bigger all the time. The builders continued expensively, not
to put the Manor in good repair (which would have cost a fortune), but to save it from falling to pieces. They hadn't yet sub-
mitted an estimate for dealing with the dry-rot, for the simple
reason that Ferdo himself hadn't yet formally admitted that the
dry-rot existed. He knew it was there, of course; but as a man
who knows he has a cancer, yet is afraid to let a doctor translate
his personal intuition into objective diagnosis. He hadn't talked
to Janet or to Susan about the dry-rot or the debts or the overdraft. He didn't dare.

He had staved off a crisis by selling Honeysett Farm. Both his
lawyer and his Bank Manager had advised him to sell, partly
because the cost of the repairs to the house and buildings was so
enormous—the tithe barn alone needed £3000 spent on it—and
partly because the price offered by Tom Taynton was a surprisingly good one. Ferdo had invested the money in Government
Bonds because although the interest was low he'd always understood they were 'safe' and of course he wanted to keep the capital
intact for Susan. However, as it turned out, those gilt-edged
stocks had been going down ever since he bought them; and he
wondered whether after all he should have taken the advice of
Colonel Daglingworth, who had called to see him round about
the time when the farm was sold. Daglingworth had mentioned
casually: "I've got a damn good stockbroker if you happen to
want a bit of advice how to invest the money." Then he'd suggested various shares which he particularly fancied. It struck
Ferdo as rather strange that Daglingworth should know so soon
about the sale of the farm; but of course it would be all round
the village if Tom Taynton had been boasting about his pur-
chase.

Ferdo thought to himself that he wouldn't trust any stock-broker Daglingworth recommended, any more than he trusted Colonel Cleverbreeches Daglingworth himself. He said:

"Thanks very much, but I think I'll get the Bank to buy me some War Loan or something."

Daglingworth snorted.

"Government Bonds are the biggest swindle out. In any case what's the use of three or four per cent to a chap like you? If you put the money into equities and sell 'em when they go up you'll get a tidy bit of capital appreciation, and tax-free, my boy!"

"Yes, and what if they go down?" said Ferdo, who hated being called 'my boy' in that jocular way by Daglingworth.

But they hadn't gone down. Ferdo looked in the *Times* occasionally and saw that the shares Daglingworth had recommended had gone steadily up. And when he met Daglingworth in Elmbury High Street one day, the oaf said:

"What about your gilt-edged two-and-a-half per cents now, looking a bit sick, ain't they?" That 'ain't' was another of his tiresome jocularities. Ferdo detested the fellow. A month or two later they'd had their neighbours' row, about the ownership of some elm-trees in a hedgerow which formed a boundary-fence between them. Daglingworth had them cut down because, he said, they were rotten with elm-disease and he wanted to stop it spreading. Ferdo maintained that the hedgerow belonged to him, because he'd always had it laid and trimmed in the days before Daglingworth came to Doublegates, and therefore the trees which grew up in the hedge belonged to him too. But when their respective lawyers got down to the argument, it turned out that Daglingworth was right, and Ferdo had to apologise. Magnanimous in victory, Daglingworth came to pay what he called 'a neighbourly visit,' had a couple of whiskies and casually let drop that he intended to apply for planning permission to open up a new gravel-pit on a piece of his land at the top of the village, just over the boundary from the Doddington woods. He said, as if it were a great privilege for Ferdo to be let into the secret:

"Since you're in a way interested I thought I'd tell you before I told anybody else."

"But—but how would you get the gravel away?" asked Ferdo in astonishment.

"Stuff don't fly, my boy."

"You mean—there'd be lorries going to and fro through the village all the time——?"

"King's Highway. Beg pardon, the Queen's. It's not a private road, after all."

The road through the village was quite narrow, and you couldn't widen it because of the big oaks which stood along the edge of the common; one every twenty yards or so. There had never been much traffic along it—just the tradesmen's vans and a few picnickers' cars at weekends in the summer. The picnickers often lit their fires and had tea in the field which Daglingworth was going to turn into a gravel-pit. It was a pretty place, with a stream running through it and masses of foxgloves along the edge of the woods which stood in a semicircle round one side of it.

"I should think there'll be lots of objections," Ferdo said.

"Always are. Mostly by crackpots. Up on the Cotswolds I wanted to make a new quarry, and blow me if a *bearded bug-hunter* didn't come along to the enquiry to say I was destroying the only breeding place in Gloucestershire of some perishing bug! It was war-time and the Ministry didn't go much on *that* lark, I can tell you. Well, it ain't war-time now, but if we're going to make anything of the peace we've got to have roads, houses and whatnot, and that's where my sand and gravel comes in. You'll understand that, I know. I can't see *you* being one of the objectors."

Then suddenly he changed the subject. He did it so quickly, it was like a conjuror's sleight of hand. "And talking of roads," he said, "have you heard any more about this M-something or other which was supposed to be going to cut right through our Dodd-ington?"

"No, no, nothing new," said Ferdo miserably; he hated even to think about the road.

"Well, I have. Of course you realise it's a Ministry of Transport job. We—the County Council—only come in on the side." Ferdo had forgotten that Daglingworth had got himself onto the Council; it was very useful, no doubt, in his line of business.

"But we do get a few snippets of information now and then," he went on, "and of course they condescend to consult us about local problems occasionally. I can tell you they're getting

just a bit worried about the cost of the viaduct to carry the road
across the flat fields when the river's in flood. There's just a
chance they may re-route the whole section, to cross the river a
bit farther upstream. I can't do much to influence things I'm
afraid; but naturally I'll do what I can."

Daglingworth downed his second whisky, grinned, nodded as if
to say 'Thought that might cheer you up, my boy' and got up out
of his armchair.

"I must get back to my office. Sacked one idle bastard, and now
all my lorry drivers are threatening to go on strike unless I rein-
state him. I'll see 'em in hell first. They want their heads looking
at, chaps who are taking home eighteen or twenty pounds a week
. . . Well, that's the way things are today in England's green
and pleasant land!" Ferdo saw him to the door, and Daglingworth shook hands rather formally—he always did it yet somehow it always took Ferdo by surprise.

"Thanks for the drinks. I thought I'd better come clean with
you about that little new pit we're thinking of digging . . . And
of course I'll keep you in touch about the motor-road."

He couldn't have put it more plainly if he'd actually said:
"You scratch my back, I'll scratch yours."

WALKING THROUGH THE WOOD this morning Ferdo was
possessed as ever by the grandeur of his trees. Here at the edge of
the Park he was among the great ones, the oak three centuries old
which had perhaps been planted by the first Ferdinando, for the
delight of his great-grandchildren and for the defence of the
realm. There had been some heavy felling towards the end of
the eighteenth century. Maybe the huge crooked boughs of some
Doddington oak had formed the stern-post of a ship that fought
at Trafalgar!

The survivors from that felling, which had been left presumably to form a shelterbelt for some new plantations, stood at
intervals along the fringe of the woodland, from the top of the
Park nearly down to the river. There was a whole clump of those
mighty ones half-way down the slope—right in the path of the
new road, if indeed the road was going to come here.

Perhaps after all it wouldn't come. Daglingworth had said
there was just a chance that it might be routed elsewhere. How
good a chance? Ten to one, four to one? Ferdo's hand went to his

pocket and brought out a fistful of small change. He didn't open his hand for a few moments. He said to himself: This is silly, you must be in your dotage, softening of the brain. Thus sometimes he frightened himself into a recognition of what he was about to do, and put the coins back into his pocket. Sometimes he told himself: What does it matter, it's only a game? This morning he leaned against one of the oak-trunks for quite a long time, watching the little green caterpillars swinging on their silk threads and the tomtits busy among the foliage collecting caterpillars for their nestlings. At last he said to himself: Here goes: if it's heads the road comes this way, if it's tails the road goes elsewhere. He willed that it should be tails. Then he opened his fist very carefully and sorted out the coins lying upon the palm of his hand.

Four tails. Six heads.

Then he wished he hadn't done it, because it made him miserable even though he told himself that it was all foolishness anyway, how on earth could the fortuitous arrangement of sixpences and half-crowns laid on your hand foretell events or influence them? Don't be a bloody old fool.

Then he saw the magpie.

It flew out of the wood and into the Park, probably making for Ferdinando's Oak, which was a perching-place for magpies. 'One for sorrow.' But they certainly seemed to go by pairs, you could often see another if you waited for a few minutes in the same place.

Ferdo waited, and remembered that he'd read somewhere that the word 'auspice' came from *avispex;* an *avispex* was a soothsaying bird-watcher, who deduced omens from their flight. I'm a hell of an *avispex,* thought Ferdo ruefully: I can actually kid myself that it would be a good auspice if another magpie were to come into sight now, so that I could say 'Two for joy.'

Ferdo stood very still, and listened to the faint humming of small winged things, which passed for silence in the woods in summer. This silence was suddenly broken and Ferdo was startled by a *Phutt!* quite loud and close, followed by a fainter *Flippp!* right overhead. A moment later the hoped-for second magpie appeared, lurching clumsily after a hurried take-off, crosswind, with its long tail blown awry. It just cleared the treetops and vanished behind them.

Hurray! thought Ferdo, and took off his hat to it. But where

had that *Phuttt-Flipppp!* come from? It was an unmistakeable
noise; it had been made by an air-gun. Now he heard a scuffling
among last year's dead leaves, and peering round the trunk of
the trees he saw the two youngest Fentons, Adam and Eve. Adam
carried the gun which his father had given him for a Christmas
present. Ferdo remembered Fenton telling him that he'd had a
bit of a row with the missus about it, she'd thought it might
encourage the child to enjoy blood-sports, and had tried hard to
interest him in shooting at tin-cans hung from a tree at the
bottom of the garden.

"Hello," said Ferdo. Adam started and looked rather guilty.
He'd probably come all this way from home so that he might be
unobserved when he took a pot at a living target. Ferdo had a
good deal of sympathy for him.

"Any luck?" he said, as if to a fellow sportsman.

Adam shook his head.

"You had a go at that magpie?"

"Yes," said Adam at last: hesitant, wondering if he was going
to be in trouble.

"That's all right. They're vermin. You can shoot 'em any old
time. How far away were you?"

Adam looked up into the trees and made a serious calcula-
tion.

"If I was *here*," he said, "he'd have been just *there*"—and he
pointed.

"He was sitting on a branch?"

"Yes, I could see him against the sky. His tail sort of bent
down at an angle. He looked enormous."

"I expect you *pulled* the trigger," said Ferdo.

"Yes, o'course," said Adam. "O'course I did."

"Well, you shouldn't. You've got to *squeeze*. If you pull, the
whole gun moves and you're off the target. Let me show you."

"What shall we shoot at?" Adam said.

"My hat'll do."

"It'll make holes in it."

"If you hit it."

"Don't you mind?"

"They'll let the hot air out."

Ferdo handed his hat to Eve. "Stick it up over there." He
pointed to the post-and-rail fence which divided the wood from

the Park. Eve trotted away obediently. She didn't say anything. It occurred to Ferdo that he'd hardly ever heard her speak; she was like one of those seen-but-not-heard Victorian children. How old was she? About eleven, he thought; and the tousleheaded Adam must be twelve or thirteen. They both looked younger than that, because they were very small by comparison with the other Fenton children. Perhaps being babies during the war-years had made the difference?

Eve duly hung Ferdo's hat on a post, and he called to her: "Keep well out of the way while we're shooting." She ran off into the wood and didn't return until about twenty minutes later, by which time Ferdo's hat had five holes in it and Adam had learned to keep the target in his sights, hold his breath, and *squeeze . . .*

"Do you think I could hit a bird?" Adam asked anxiously.

"If it was as big as my hat. If you held the rifle straight."

"When you were a boy," said Adam, did you have a gun?"

"No, I had a catapult."

"Could you kill things with it?"

"I certainly could."

"I wish I had a catapult."

"I'll show you how to make one."

"Honest?"

"Honest. By the way, why aren't you at school?" Ferdo asked.

"We got two days off for the Coronation."

"Did you win anything at the Sports?"

"Our Dad won the pig." Ferdo knew that already. He'd had a look at it in the sty where they kept their pigs: Lord Hailsham the Second.

"But what about *you?*" Ferdo persisted.

"I don't much like running and jumping," Adam said, and gave him a dubious, endearing smile, not quite sure if such a view would be acceptable. "I like shooting and—and——"

"What else?"

"I caught an eel last Sunday in the river."

"How big an eel?"

Adam held out his hands about two feet apart; then scrupulously adjusted them to eighteen inches. "It swallowed the hook," he said. "It was a terrible job. I had to cut its head off." Ferdo wondered briefly how Mrs. Fenton would react to the decapitation of eels; but Adam went on breathlessly: "Then I brought it home, it was dead of course, and I nailed it up on a door in the stables and skinned it."

"Whoever taught you to do that?"

"Egbert. You can make shoelaces out of the skin. Did you know?"

"Yes, I did know."

"You let the skin dry and then you oil it and cut it into laces. Egbert's going to make me some out of my eel."

As it happened, Egbert had made a pair for Ferdo, about forty years ago, when Ferdo was a young man and Egbert already seemed an old one.

Very much at ease and talkative now, Adam continued:

"I like the stables. Mr. Northover showed me how to groom Trumpeter. I fill the haybags for him sometimes when he's got the horses in. I love horses."

"But you've never been on one?"

"I want to."

"We must see what we can do about it," Ferdo said, half-committed to a pony already. He spared a fraction of a thought for his overdraft, but the cost of a pony would be a drop in the bucket to that. Janet might be able to buy a cheap one at the next Stow Fair. Susan would enjoy teaching the boy to ride . . . He again remembered Mrs. Fenton, and speculated with enjoyment on what she would think about the huntin' shootin' fishin' proclivities of her youngest son.

"What's the time?" asked Adam.

"Goodness—half past one!"

"We'll be late."

"So will I." Ferdo put on his hat with the five holes in it, and just then Eve appeared as if from nowhere. She had collected a fistful of assorted wild flowers. She seemed to know the names of all except three or four. She spoke so quietly that Ferdo had to lean down to hear her. Fenton had told him that she'd been born in the blitz, amid the bombs and the barrage and those blood-chilling syrens mooing like sick cows. Perhaps it had taught her the virtue of quiet!

Under what lowering skies, Ferdo thought, these two had been conceived. There couldn't have seemed to be much of a future for a kid who would be born in England during the years 1940 and 1941!

This small silent Eve sorted out the flowers in her hand.

"What's this one called?"

"Woodruff."

"Yes, of course. Mum got me a book. What's this one called, please?" she whispered.

It was that yellow dead-nettle thing, archangel—but why the devil was it called archangel? Then Ferdo remembered that it had another, better name.

"I've heard it called weasel-snout."

"Weasel-snout!" It was the first time Ferdo had ever heard her giggle. Then Adam repeated "Weasel-snout" and they ran away laughing. Eve's untidy blonde head reminded him a little of Susan's when she was a kid. Adam shouted over his shoulder:

"You'll make me a cattie—promise?"

"Promise!"

On the way home he kept his eyes open for a good forked twig. He wondered if you could still buy that heavy black elastic, square in section, which he got from a little shop in Elmbury when he was a boy. Then he'd need the soft leather tongue from an old shoe; and some waxed thread.

He didn't give another thought to the motorway, or to his overdraft, or to ominous magpies, as he made his way along the edge of the woods and across the top of the Park to the Manor.

¶ 12

THE GREAT GRAVEL-PIT ROW blew up a few weeks later, when the *Elmbury Intelligencer* drew attention to the fact that a local beauty spot and favourite picnicking-place was threatened with destruction. The curiously breathless prose in which the piece was written pointed plainly to Gloria, who probably bore an ancient grudge against Daglingworth because he had sacked her father. She followed it up with a paragraph about the alarm in Doddington village at the risk to schoolchildren when the gravel lorries started using the narrow roads. The lively young Editor of the paper, whom Daglingworth not long since had threatened with a writ for libel, ran the story for all it was worth. Elderly Elmburians, who probably hadn't picnicked in the 'beauty-spot' since they were children, and who looked back upon its foxgloves through rose-tinted glasses, penned impassioned Letters to the Editor about wicked vandalism. Daglingworth, bewildered as well as furious, wrote to Stephen, as his M.P., asking for "his public support against the fuddyduddies of Elmbury who oppose all progressive developments designed to provide full employment and a high standard of living for your Constituents." Stephen scribbled 'What a sentence!' at the bottom of the letter and sent it on to Susan:

'Sukie, you know the local situation, what sort of a line are we going to take about this?'

She couldn't help feeling a bit flattered by the way he put it; but she thought she'd better have a word with Ferdo before she replied. She purposely didn't show him the letter, because of course Stephen should really have written to him. She chose a good time after dinner, just as her mother was going out of the room and Ferdo was pouring out his second glass of port. She stopped at the door and said:

"About old Daglingworth's beastly gravel-pit—I suppose you'll have to give evidence at the enquiry, won't you?"

IT WAS THE QUESTION Ferdo had been dreading for weeks. Ever since Daglingworth's visit he had funked this problem, hoping against hope that it wouldn't arise. Even now he tried to avoid making a definite decision.

"It's all a bit complicated," he said.

Susan seemed surprised. She came back from the door, sat opposite him at the table, and looked at him in her direct and disconcerting way.

"Why's it complicated?" she said.

"The damn fellow came to see me. He was talking about the new road. He's on the County Council, you know, and they're naturally concerned about the route the road will take. He said there was just a chance it might not come through Doddington after all. He might have a bit of influence, I think. He also talked about his gravel-pit. He seemed to—er—assume I wouldn't object."

Ferdo had, in fact, hinted about his difficulty to Janet, and the only comment she made had cheered him up a good deal: "Obviously the gravel-pit will do less harm to Doddington than the new road; so if it really *were* a choice between the two——"

That had seemed a fairly good excuse for not being one of the objectors at the enquiry. But Susan, he could see already, wasn't going to take this line. She gave that little toss of her head which she always gave when she was combative, and said:

"He actually put it like that? As if his influence about the new road would be a kind of *quid pro quo* for the gravel-pit?" Indignation blazed up in her. She said: "There really is something in what they're saying about the danger to children. The way they have to walk back from school there are some awful bends. In any case the village could never be the same with those great yellow lorries roaring through it. I suppose you told him to go to hell?"

Ferdo would never have believed that Susan's brown eyes could discompose him so, as she faced him across the table, straight and still as the candle flame that burned between them. He avoided her question.

"It's going to be devilish awkward," he temporised.

There was just a little pause before Susan said: "You mean socially awkward?"—and then Ferdo knew that whether she had meant it or not she had made his decision for him by her assumption that there couldn't possibly be anything awkward in the choice *itself,* it was a clear-cut issue of conscience: You *had* to object at the enquiry if you thought it was right to do so, even though it might cost you the support of Daglingworth over the road. All at once Ferdo felt immeasurably relieved, because an ever-present nagging temptation had been removed from him. He smiled across the table at this surprising girl, his daughter, and the little tension between them snapped.

Susan burst out:

"And who's to say the bugger *has* any influence about the road in any case?"

It always surprised him a little to hear Susan using that word as light-heartedly as a man would use it. Tonight, because of the sudden lightening of his spirit, it made him laugh. And she was quite right, of course: the odds were that Daglingworth *didn't* have any influence, but only pretended he had. Ferdo was quite certain now that he must stand up to Daglingworth, indeed he was surprised and rather ashamed that he'd ever had any doubts. But it was going to be socially awkward, as Susan had said.

"—Your mother," smiled Ferdo, "has accepted an invitation from the so-and-so for us all to dine there next Thursday."

"I expect he intended to put the pressure on you then. You won't weaken," she said, a shade doubtfully.

"No. No, no. I'll tell him to go to blazes. Have a glass of port with me."

He filled a glass which Janet hadn't used, and passed it across the table to her. She raised her eyebrows, thinking of the last time she drank port, when the news had just come from Korea about the Glosters at Imjin. As she sipped the port a shade doubtfully, remembering her hangover, Ferdo poured out another glass for himself and drank it; he began to feel brave, even belligerent, and happier than he'd felt for ages.

IT WAS A VERY GOOD DINNER at the Daglingworths, cold lobster and then roast guinea-fowl. Susan sat between Sandra, who was merrily flirting with Ferdo, and the Colonel, who in common politeness was bound to address most of his remarks to Janet. So she had very little to do save to enjoy the excellent food and look about her. Through the corner of her eye she watched and marvelled while Daglingworth poured mint sauce over both lobster and guinea-fowl in turn—a little on the lobster, a huge dollop on the guinea-fowl so that the whole dish was swimming in it. He made no bones about this, having a kind of honesty in some things however dishonest he might be in others.

"If I enjoy a thing," he said to Janet, "I don't ask myself whether it's right and proper for me to enjoy it; I have it. If I wanted to drink champagne with kippers at Claridges I should tell the waiter to bring me champagne with kippers; and if he had the impertinence even to *look* surprised I'd send for the Management."

He was very genial and expansive tonight, and had seemed even larger than life when he greeted them on the lawn, where a white-coated manservant stood ready to pour out drinks. The lawn was greener, soften and finer than any Susan had seen before; better than the lawn at Buckingham Palace where she'd once been to a garden-party, and by comparison with it the poor lawn at Doddington was almost a hayfield. No daisy, no plantain, no dandelion would dare to poke up its head on Daglingworth's lawn. This was his realm, here he was king, and here he demanded absolute obedience. When the two Dalmatians ran boisterously towards the Seldons on their arrival, he had shouted in a great voice "Sit!" and immediately they had sat, with slobbery mouths wide open, still faintly wagging their tails. It was most impressive. Daglingworth was certainly the perfect Dogman. Mrs. D, thought Susan, with her pendulous cheeks and rather squashed-together features, was herself beginning to look a bit doglike,—you could see her as a chow or a peke, her small eyes followed her husband all the time as if she were looking for orders from him.

The last course consisted of devils on horseback. Daglingworth stretched out his big paw for the mint sauce; but this time he carefully unrolled the rasher of bacon, removed the piece of liver from inside it, applied the mint sauce to the liver, and rolled it up in the bacon again.

Susan was fascinated by this operation, which she was able to observe at leisure since Daglingworth was discoursing to the table at large on How to Succeed in Business,—at least it sounded like that. She herself was hardly listening to him; instead she was thinking about a most strange little conversation which she'd had with Rosemary yesterday.

She had gone into Elmbury on a mission for her mother: to try to persuade Rosemary to come back and work at the Manor for a month or two, because Mrs. Fenton didn't want to help during the holidays, when her children were home.

"I'd have loved it, Miss Sue," said Rosemary with real disappointment. "It'd be just like old times. But Goff's out of work again and I had to do something—even when he's in work he spends all his money with that Teddy crowd. So I've got a job regular in the town."

Susan asked her what it was; and Rosemary looked at her a shade doubtfully, as if she were not very anxious to tell.

"It's in an office."

"But what do you *do?*" said Susan, who couldn't see Rosemary in the context of an office at all.

"Funny thing, Sue, it was your Fête begun it. Colonel Daglingworth spoke to me, he remembered me waiting at table, so he said, and did I want a job? Well, the pay was all right, I can tell you, so I said Yes. I clean up the offices first thing. It's a big place now, more'n a dozen work there. And I make the tea. And some days he has a business lunch in the office, just cold of course,—I fix it for him, and when he has company I make his coffee and do the drinks."

Rosemary was quite breathless after this long recital.

"It doesn't sound a very hard job," Susan said; and Rosemary, with a small, faint and fleeting smile, said:

"Well, no, Sue. No, 'tain't."

Daglingworth was still lecturing, it seemed. He turned to Susan, catching her unawares, and startled her considerably with a precept for success delivered in his harsh and hectoring voice:

"Know exactly what you want, go for it, and get it."

Luckily no comment seemed to be called for; and at that moment Mrs. Daglingworth looking for orders managed to catch his eye, and he said something across the table which Susan didn't quite hear but which was delivered in much the same tone as if he had said "Down good bitch!" to one of his Dalmatians. At once Mrs. Daglingworth seemed to fly into a tizzy; she nearly knocked over a wine-glass as she jumped up from the table.

"Come along, girls, time we left the men to it."

On her way out Susan glanced back over her shoulder at Ferdo, and was much encouraged by his cheerful and piratical grin. In the hall at the Manor, just before they started, she'd whispered to him:

"Whatever you do, Daddy, stick up to the old horror."

"Pro bono publico. No bloody panico," Ferdo had said "Don't you worry my dear. If he's going to be okkard, we'll part brass rags."

''THOSE TWO, they'll be talking for ages," said Mrs. Dagling-worth, as she scraped the spoon round her coffee-cup in search of the last grains of sugar. "I'm sorry we've got no young man for you, dear. But Dags specially wanted it to be—just a quiet neigh-bourly party, he said."

It occurred to Susan that she didn't know what Daglingworth's Christian name was; you could have an amusing guessing game about it. Mrs. D. always spoke of him as Dags, which perhaps she wouldn't have done if she'd been brought up in the country. Dags were the tangles of wool and hard lumps of excrement which you cut off the hinder parts of sheep.

"Sandra dear," Mrs. Daglingworth suggested: she always pronounced it Sarndra—"Why not take Sue upstairs and show her that pretty dress you bought last week at Harvey Nicholls?"

So they went up to Sandra's bedroom, which was rather like the bedrooms you saw pictures of in women's magazines, and Sandra put on the new evening dress, in which she looked so enchanting that Susan momentarily forgot the dangers inherent in saying so.

"D'you like it?" Sandra pouted at herself in the looking-glass. "I think it'd suit you better than me, somehow."

It was an unusual colour, a sort of mermaid sea-green.

"Don't be silly," said Susan. "You look marvellous in it."

"I'm wondering if it's just a shade tight for me across the bum. I'm bigger than you are in that direction . . . I say, d'you think Ferdo and my Dad are arguing like hell about the gravel-pit?"

"I daresay."

"How quaint to have a row about it," Sandra said, in her rather agreeable drawl which concealed the trace of her mother's accent. "I do like Ferdo. I bet he was a hell of a chap with the girls when he was young. I hope to goodness he doesn't get up against Dad. It's no good, you know."

"How do you mean it's no good?"

"You can't win. He's too tough. You're out of touch, love, all of you. It's a tough world. What does the old gravel-pit matter anyhow?"

"*I* think it matters," Susan said.

"But then *you're* quaint, aren't you?" Sandra began to take off the dress, pulling it over her head not in the usual gauche skin-a-rabbit fashion, but with a grace and gaiety: the way she'd undressed for lots of young men, thought Susan suddenly.

"Do try it on," said Sandra.

"No."

"Just for fun?"

"No, I won't. Why are you always trying to give me things?" said Susan almost crossly.

"Only because I love you, love," laughed Sandra, getting back into her old dress and peeping out of it merrily as she pulled it on. "You won't hate me if our fathers have a row?"

"Of course I won't."

"Even if Dad gets tough and turns nasty?"

"No, never," laughed Susan.

"Let's go down," said Sandra. "If they're no-speaks by now we'll be needed to keep the party going."

"MUSTN'T HAVE THOSE nasty noisy lorries running through *our* pretty village," Daglingworth was saying. He gave Ferdo a tigerish grin. "Mustn't spoil the pretty foxgloves with those beastly bulldozers. Good God Almighty, what sort of a world do you people imagine you're living in? The *real* world, my dear feller, runs on lorry wheels and caterpillar tracks. Have another brandy."

"Thanks," said Ferdo. He'd drunk champagne at dinner; there had been no other choice. He despised all fizzy wine, and there was a sharpness about champagne which soured the spirit, he thought. But perhaps at the same time it sharpened the wits. All through the argument with Daglingworth his ears and his eyes had been keen, his mind had been wonderfully clear. He'd seen right through Daglingworth, the bad in him and, surprisingly, the good. There was a bit of good. For instance, Ferdo perceived now that when Daglingworth had tipped him those shares, just after Honeysett had been sold, he had genuinely wanted to help him. Why he'd wanted to help him was anybody's guess; but they'd been good tips, and Daglingworth had been disappointed and even hurt because he hadn't acted on them. Now he was hurt again, as well as angry, because Ferdo was going to give evidence at the enquiry and object to the gravel-pit near Doddington village. "But how does it harm *you*, how does it affect *your* interests? Don't you know I'd have never undertaken anything which might have done that?" He'd turned his hard, handsome, Roman face towards Ferdo with an *Et tu, Brute* look. God help me, I believe he really *liked* me, Ferdo thought. After to-night he's never going to like me again.

"As for our precious Member of Parliament," Daglingworth went on, as he poured out a generous glass of the *Grande Cham-*

pagne Cognac which cost a fiver a bottle, "—as for our Stephen Whats-'is-name who nobody knows how to pronounce, he seems to forget that I'm the Chairman of his Constituency Party, and he coolly writes to say that he's by no means convinced of the merits of my case."

There was something almost innocent, thought Ferdo, in the way Daglingworth expected everybody to be motivated by self-interest and never by anything else. He thought Stephen must be mad to go against his own interests by putting the back up of his Party Chairman. He'd be reminded of that, perhaps, when the next General Election came along . . .

"Calls himself Conservative," said Daglingworth, "but always bollocking about *planning*. He's not what I mean by Conservative, I can tell you here and now. I'm not the least anti-Semitic. I've got a lot of good friends who are that persuasion, they're O.K., they're fine so long as you watch 'em. But between ourselves over this glass of brandy I'd describe our precious M.P. as a bit of Ikey who thinks he's jumped on to the right band wagon. That's not what *I* call a Tory."

"Hm. Of course we mustn't forget," smiled Ferdo, who felt much happier now that he could really loathe this man,—"we mustn't forget it was a Jewish dandy, with a Jewish imagination, who *invented* the modern Conservative party, must we?"

Daglingworth gave him a hot, angry stare. At last the penny dropped and he said:

"Oh, Disraeli, yes, but what the hell's he got to do with us nowadays." My complaint against these so-called modern Tories is that as soon as you put 'em in power they start legislating just like the damn Socialists or even worse."

"Yes," said Ferdo, who was somewhat inspired by the champagne even though he hadn't much enjoyed it. "That was just what Disraeli said, wasn't it? 'A sound Conservative Government: Tory men and Whig measures'?"

Daglingworth gave him a rather surprised look over his brandy glass. Ferdo with his clear mind, which he knew wouldn't stay clear much longer, discovered in that look a kind of backhanded compliment: "You're not quite the old fuddyduddy I thought you were, and I don't think I'm even *sorry* for you any longer."

The realisation came to Ferdo, almost with exhilaration, that he was looking across the table at a relentless foe.

This foe, meanwhile, for the very first time addressed him by his Christian name.

"Here's to us, Ferdo," he said. "We'll see who wins."

⊈ 13

IT WAS SOON AFTER THE DINNER-PARTY at the Daglingworths that Stephen came down for a weekend, and walking in the woods with him Susan had a strange little adventure. She found a ghost orchis.

On this Sunday morning they had decided for some reason to go a different way which took them right out of their usual territory into the only part of Doddington woods where there was a preponderance of beech over oak.

Now the glossy beech leaves tend to be less destructible and to lie about longer than any other leaves; and as Susan walked upon a thick carpet of them in a glade between the beeches where nothing green could grow, her attention was attracted by a humblebee's loud buzzing. It was right at her feet, and looking down she spotted this bumble and wondered what it was so excited about; because she didn't, at first, see the flower. She bent down, the bumble flew away, and then she noticed the small undistinguished-looking thing, a plant about four inches high that had a straw-coloured stem without any leaves. Instead of leaves it had two or three little brown bracts attached to it; and the sparse flowers which hung down from it were sad, wishy-washy pale yellow and pale mauve,—but unmistakeably orchid-like things.

She had never seen anything like it before, so she called Stephen and he looked down and cried: "Good God, you must be a witch or something." Then he told her it was a ghost orchis, and one of the rarest flowers in Britain. It had another, duller name: the spur-lipped coralroot. Less than a dozen plants had been seen in the last hundred years; and by a most remarkable chance all but one of them had been found by women!

Stephen said it nearly made him believe in magic; and indeed about the plant itself there seemed to be something magical and mysterious, for while its root remained underground for many years, and got its nutriment with the aid of an associated fungus out of the decaying leaves, the *flower* only poked up its head at long, irregular intervals—once every five or six years, perhaps. "A sort of comet of the plant world!" was how Stephen put it. Obviously the odds were millions to one against anybody finding a ghost orchis, because in the first place it was so rare, in the second it hardly ever showed above ground, and in the third its combination of colours—drab brown, pale yellow, faint mauve—served as a very good camouflage, merging into the leaf-carpet out of which it sprung.

"It's like a ghost in its comings and going," said Stephen. "It's like the flood in your cellar, the waters under the earth, popping up unpredictably. But goodness, what luck you had, what sharp eyes you have, to find it!"

He went down on his knees beside the precious drab egregious thing. He said: "Smell it," and Susan crouched down beside him: it smelt of vanilla, faintly and unexcitingly, to others than bumblebees.

"Think of this," said Stephen. "More people have got themselves close to the summit of Everest than have seen a ghost orchis growing. What you've done is rather like discovering an extra Shakespeare first folio among the junk at a furniture-sale, when there are only about sixteen first folios in the world!"

Her finding of the orchis had its special consequences in her relations with Stephen. Kneeling down to look at it, in the excitement of seeing it, he'd kissed her. There was nothing much to the kiss itself but it removed at one go a tiresome barrier which lately had seemed to lie between them and which was becoming an obstacle to their closer companionship. Susan knew that she was specially sensitive about touch. Physical contacts meant a great deal to her in both directions: of distaste or of delight. In all her relationships they had been liable to cause diffidence and disquiet, awkwardness and uncertainty. Probably Stephen through his tenderness had recognised this; a mutual embarrassment had been engendered. But now the spontaneous and unselfconscious kiss under the beech-tree had put things right. After that it seemed quite natural that she should sometimes slip her arm in his, or that he should put his hands on her shoulders and kiss her goodbye when he was going back to London. And although these actions were trivial in themselves, they were in a sense cumulative. They brought Stephen and Susan into a closer and more understanding relationship; and there were occasions when she discovered that they awakened a lively response in her body, very much to her surprise.

WHETHER OR NOT THIS FEELING about Stephen was the cause of it, Susan at this time became more and more aware of a quickening tempo in her spirit. Perhaps this was something which had started with that tiptoe-feeling and mood of expectancy which had come upon her at Coronation time. But following her finding of the ghost orchis life seemed to speed up somehow. there was change in the air like a wind which comes from nowhere and stirs the leaves, dies down, gets up again, sends the dead leaves scurrying, rat-tats a twig on your window as if to wake you up, then falls light once more in a sudden last hush before the great *hurroosh* bursts upon you and the gale begins to blow. Susan had no idea whether the changes which shortly would catch her up and bowl her along with them would be agreeable or otherwise; but she had a strong anticipation that they were going to be exciting, and that when they began to happen nothing thereafter would ever be the same again.

All this coincided with the approach of her twenty-first birthday. Stephen, who had gone abroad with his Minister for a long series of trade talks in Denmark, Norway, Sweden and Finland, expected to be back in time for it and had promised to come down on the day if he possibly could. She had decided not to have any special celebrations at Doddington. Her favourite aunt had promised to give a party for her in London; and Sandra was determined to make her birthday the excuse for a dance. But when Janet had asked her what she wanted to do on the day itself, and had brought out her diary at the back of which she kept a formidable list of the County,—"We ought to ask the Fortescues and the Barrington-Wills, haven't they got two nice boys?"—then Susan began to have visions of a birthday spent mostly in being polite to bores. She said: "Please, Mummy, let it be just us. But it'd be nice to have Stephen, if he gets back to England in time."

Janet said: "Of course, it shall be exactly as you want it, it's your birthday, after all . . ."

WISH failing dear Tony we cd. find a YOUNG *man for her Hoping and praying T may be home soon   Truce delegations have been mtg so long at* PANMUNJONG *even I can spell the place !!!   Of course if she wishes S Le M for her Bday she must have him also F. likes him so much must always think of Ferdo . . .*

His worries v. bad See no way out   He thinks I do not know   Even bkeeping a problem now because of H.C. of L. but I dare not ask him for more wd. so much distress & upset him   Over money he lives in the past pre-war ideas re prices wages etc V difficult get Help tried Rmary in vain (Northover and Mrs. HINT she is GOING TO BAD ?!? how sad if so ! poor child !! NB see Rector abt her) No village girl will do domestic work now high wages Elmbury more 'freedom' they say ! Well look at Rmary !!?

Daglingworths manage somehow because they pay the EARTH understand they are going in for Spaniards now but even if cd. afford it wd. not like Foreigners in house and Mrs. N. says she wd. not have them in her clean kitchen so wd. leave.

So face prospect no HELP only Mrs. N. next 2 months Mrs. F. will not work here when her children home Cannot blame her they bring friends heavens DOZENS *!! all v.* AV-ANT GARDE *!!! Long hair filthy jeans counted TEN of them this mng outside courtyard gates thought of BASTILLE !!! Made me almost sorry for Fenton who is not Intellectual is perfect Piltdown Man actually and for Mrs. F who perh. was* AVANT-GARDE *when little schoolmistress 20 yrs. ago so is up to date as dodo   Do wonder how she feeds that Horde she herself lives on wholemeal bread peanuts yoghert (??) raw carrots . . .*

Went to Stow Fair bt. Pony 13.1 dun g. 8 yrs nice action think it cheap at 45 gns but MAD of us in view of worsening sit. I.T.   H.C. of L. etc.   But F. so keen for S. teach that boy to ride did not care to argue for fear he thought I guessed abt appalling Fin. sit. wh. he tries so hard poor darling to keep from me   In any case pony will not lose money and S. may enjoy teaching those kids both the boy and the girl V. different kettle of fish from older ones Less gauche more savoir faire and more normal Outlook Yester-

day loud crash tinkling glass found landing window broken
by shot from catapult boy Adam v. nicely came to apologise
F made him the catapult POOR MRS F how funny if he
asks to go cubbing on the pony   According to Mrs. N. she
has her friend Trudy League Against Cruel Sports woman
coming to stay again and liable carry Banner at Meets Gen
Bouverie has said he will PERSONALLY HORSEWHIP
anybody doing that   Can understand how he feels but you
cannot go on like that nowadays . . .

Latest news PANMUNJONG (!?!) v. encouraging but
even if Truce is fixed up no certainty T. will be back yet or
at all   No word from him after that 1 letter and Red X say
they have no information   Alas how diff. all mt. have been
for S. if he had not gone to Korea sheer tradegy (?!) whole
affair . . .

THE TRUCE WAS SIGNED at the end of July and soon after
that the first prisoners were handed over. The authorities warned
that it might be weeks or even months before all of them were
free. Although it was called a truce it was really the end of the
Korean war; Ferdo who had kept his absurd vow not to use a new
razor-blade until the war finished went to the village shop and
bought a whole packet. They were so sharp by comparison with
the edge like a hacksaw which he'd been using on his face that
every morning he cut off a whole lot of minor blemishes blains
and pimples as if they had been daisies on a lawn; and went
about for most of the day decorated with tufts of cotton wool.

Meanwhile, there had been no news of Tony, or of anyone
who had been in touch with him recently. Susan asked Stephen if
he could help, and being Stephen he 'had a word over a drink
with the Minister of War.' The Minister wrote him a chit a few
days later and he sent it on to Susan. Two officers in Tony's
regiment who had just been released 'had heard he was very ill
more than a year ago.' They thought he might have been taken
to a prison-camp deep in China. The Minister was 'pursuing his
enquiries.' '*P.S. Sorry old boy will let you know straight away if*
we hear . . .'

It upset Susan for a day or two; but the sense of shock did not
stay with her very long. After that short tired letter she had
waited anxiously for another; but the months went by, a year

went by, and gradually she had come to accept at first the possibility, then the likelihood, that she would never hear from Tony
again, indeed she might never learn what had happened to
him.

> *F. rang his Adjutant says he's not v. optimistic If only Mira-*
> *cle cd. happen and T. cd. be home for S's Bday!!! Too much*
> *to hope for but prayed for it hard in Ch. Sun. He wd. find*
> *things v. different here Fenton kids at Universities (1 at*
> *Oxford) all things topsy turvy and changing for worse*
> *morals manners politics newspapers esp Elmbury RAG used*
> *to be so sensible content with local news weddings etc now*
> *critical of EVERYTHING incl US wonder what it will all*
> *Lead To but perh F and I may not live to see Worst . . .*
>
> *Yesterday old Hipkins bsmith died Elmbury Hosp.   No*
> *one to carry on smithy   Poor Turberville ill with Parkin-*
> *sons (says he must give up cobbling soon both his son killed*
> *in 1st war) centre of village will never seem same again . . .*

TRUMPETER WAS the very last horse old Hipkins shod.

Generally Janet herself took him to the forge; she and the
blacksmith were the greatest friends, she always enjoyed talking
to him. This time she asked Susan to go instead of her, because
she could not bear to see the old man in such a state. He had a
cancer in his throat and he couldn't speak at all, he just nodded
when she gave him the halter, and she thought of Felix Randal
in the Manley Hopkins poem. He blew up the fire, he made the
sparks fly, he smote upon the anvil so hard it seemed to Susan
that by making a great deal of noise he was trying to break the
horrible silence which his malady imposed upon him.

When he had finished the job, and Trumpeter was shod all
round, he handed him back to Susan and she looked into his eyes
with terror and dismay. Then he made a clumsy dismissive gesture with his left hand, as if to say, That's the lot, that's ended,
that's the last, and his huge shoulders turned slowly away. He
didn't go back into the smithy, its fire blackened as he went
towards his house.

And it was at this same season that Turberville the cobbler
finished; though he didn't die, he simply shook like that springy
quaker-grass that grew in the woodland clearings. Susan took

along to him a bridle that needed repairing. He came shuffling towards her, with back bent and head thrust forward, and received the bridle in his poor agitated hands. He said he'd mend it as soon as he could. A fortnight later she went back but he looked at her in a sick expressionless way and said he hadn't had time to get down to it yet. She left the old bridle with him but she hadn't the heart to go back again.

Doddington was much changed thereafter. For one thing it seemed, on these autumnal days, uncomfortably quiet. Old Hipkins had been kept pretty busy right up to the end; mending farm machinery, doing a bit of wrought-iron work, and shoeing the hunters and the children's ponies which were brought from near and far. From within his smithy there had gone forth a clattering and banging and neighing and shouting and hoof-scraping and cursing and laughing from morning till night; and upon the few occasions when he hadn't any work to do he would generally stand outside the smithy in his stiff leather apron and looking like a giant with a club would wave his hammer in salutation to any passers-by. In between times he would exchange badinage and prognostications about the weather with little Mr. Turberville his next door neighbour who sat outside his shop with his mouth full of nails. Mr. Hipkins was huge, Mr. Turberville was almost a dwarf. Mr. Hipkins had a deep bass voice, Mr. Turberville a penetrating treble. Their dialogue was like an operatic duet. Mr. Turberville spat out his brads into the palms of his hand and said there was tempus coming: Shouldn' 'oonder if us doount get a bit of a starm like. Mr. Hipkins roared back that 'Twas nothing of the sart, 'twasn't tempus, 'twas only Blight. So they'd argue for a bit, then Mr. Hipkins would go back to his forge and bash away at a piece of hot iron, Mr. Turberville would fill his mouth with nails again and angrily beat the shoe upon his last, and it sounded exactly as if they were continuing their dialogue through hammering.

But now that all had fallen so quiet you had the feeling that a heart had ceased to beat at the centre of Doddington village; and the very air seemed changed because it no longer carried along with it a sweet whiff of new leather, bootpolish and neatsfoot oil mixed with a sharp one of burnt horse-hoof, dying sparks, coke fumes and red-hot metal.

ELMBURY WAS CHANGING TOO. One by one the old-fashioned tradesmen were disappearing: the 'sweet wholesome men,' as Janet had called them in her diary, who were so anxious to please her and who had manners like Northover's or Hipkins' or Turberville's: "May I have the pleasure of putting the goods in your Ladyship's car?" They went the way of all flesh, and their shops were bought by multiple stores which had a peculiar passion for nation-wide conformity. Elmbury High Street, which had been characteristic and unique, soon became indistinguishable from all the comparable High Streets from Worcester to Weston-super-Mare. Meanwhile an Elmbury Development Corporation Limited (of which Colonel Daglingworth was a Director) was buying up all the back-street premises that it could lay hands on. The Corporation had big schemes afoot, and was prepared to pay a tempting price for immediate possession. One of those tempted was Ferdo's little tailor. A friend of his who owned a taxi brought him out to the Manor to deliver the two latest suits which Ferdo had ordered from him. Ferdo asked him in, of course, and together they recollected the times when he used to go round on his bicycle, 'waiting on the gentry' as he put it.

"Better try 'em on, Sir Ferdo," he sighed now. "There won't be another opportunity."

Ferdo tried them on, and for the last time he and the Elmbury tailor exchanged jokes about his waistline.

"There's a man in Cheltenham," the tailor said, "who's bought the goodwill of my business, what's left of it. I've got his card——"

"Don't bother," said Ferdo. "You always made 'em to last. These two, with the others I'm still wearing, will just about see me through, I reckon."

Because it was a nippy morning he gave the tailor and the taxi-driver three or four nips of cherry-brandy each, and sent them away with flushed faces, half-happy, half-sad.

THE WHOLE ATMOSPHERE OF Elmbury was affected by the big military vehicle depôt which had grown up during the war-years on the outskirts of the town. But for the Korean affair, it would probably have been closed. But now it was badly needed for the repair of tanks and transporters, lorries and DUKWs, and it ensured that there was full employment at Elmbury, because for every soldier who worked there at least two civilians were recruited and provided with brooms (so the joke went) for the purpose of leaning upon! 'He's gone for a Rest Cure' was the phrase people used when somebody got a job at the depôt. Susan wasn't at all surprised when she heard, from Mrs. Northover, that Goff had gone for a Rest Cure; but apparently he was a little more astute than his fellows, for he quickly found out that as a civilian employed by a Service department he was entitled to a maximum of three months' sick leave per annum without losing his job. So he discovered a pain in his back which his doctor could neither diagnose nor dispute. Susan found him at home when she called with a birthday present for Rosemary. She hadn't seen him since the dance in the Tithe Barn.

"She's out," he said. He added truculently:

"What d'you want with her, anyway?"

He looked at her with real hatred, and since it was the very first time in her life that she had met with hatred, she was taken aback, and momentarily silenced by it. Then, growing angry, she answered back: "What the hell's it got to do with you?" and looked at him so fiercely that Goff, to her amazement, immediately dropped his glance. Exactly the same thing had happened during the encounter in the Tithe Barn. Now he meekly took the parcel from her, muttered without looking up that he'd see Rosemary had it, and hurriedly closed the door.

How extraordinary! Now isn't that how *lion-tamers* are supposed to exercise their power? thought Susan gaily. They stare at the beast until it can no longer endure their gaze, and then they've won! But she knew that in that moment of triumph she'd spoil it all by feeling sorry for the lion; and if Goff hadn't closed the door so quickly she'd have spoilt the whole effect by feeling sorry for him too. Hatred was so horrible, it made you sick with revulsion and pity, as leprosy would do.

AS IT TURNED OUT, she was to come face to face with hatred once again before the week was out.

On Saturday morning there was a cubhunting meet at Doddington. She had set her alarm for five o'clock and it was still dark when she went on tiptoe along the dromedary corridor; in the silent hours its boards creaked louder than ever under her tread. She let herself out of the front-door, which anciently groaned and moaned upon its rusty hinges. The sky was grey behind the black velvet trees. In the stables she had to light a hurricane-lantern, and as she swung it marvellous shadows danced—she was almost glad that owing to some old-fashioned obstinacy or fear of expense on Ferdo's part the electricity had never been laid on to these outbuildings. In Nightshade's loosebox, as Susan groomed her and she played up as she always did when she was tickled under the belly, her image cast upon the wall sometimes had long rabbit's ears and sometimes a giraffe's neck; in turn she was a steed of the Valkyrie, a charger for one of the Four Horsemen, and a prehistoric horse painted on a cave wall in the Dordogne!

By the time Susan had got a saddle on the mare's back she was feeling as excited as Nightshade. She trotted past Huntsman's Cottage and noticed a light in one of the windows. Somebody was getting up early,—she wondered if young Adam in defiance of his mother had decided to go cubbing. The morning was misty and the sun came through slowly. At the Meet on the village green the hounds in the half-light still looked like Hounds of the Baskervilles.

They found a litter of cubs in Jubilee Wood and hunted with a wonderful cry for an hour and a half up and down the length of it. Susan was keen on getting Nightshade fit for the hunting season so she stayed on the outside of the covert and let the mare enjoy herself in a gallop or two up the slope of the Park. She saw little of the hounds, but listening to the cry she knew that they killed twice,—once at the edge of the wood and once in a thicket in the middle of it. By nine o'clock she decided that her sweating Nightshade had had about enough, so she made for home. Halfway along the drive she overtook a small, dejected, middle-aged woman in gumboots and mackintosh, and realised that this was Mrs. Fenton's friend Trudy, who was reputed to be militant against hunting. She was a schoolmistress in London, who stayed at the Fentons' now and then during the holidays. Susan had never spoken to her before. As she trotted up beside her she wished her good morning.

Turning round, the woman threw up her arms in a gesture which terrified Nightshade, who jumped sideways and came to rest facing Trudy with forelegs wide apart, tail swishing, and nostrils flared.

"I saw them kill one," she cried. "Oh, how can you do it, on a morning like this, so beautiful? The blood and the smell and the beastliness!"

Her pale face staring up at Susan was all twisted with horror and hate.

"I saw them catch it and tear it down there at the edge of the wood. Oh, I wish you could die too!"

Then Susan saw that the woman was crying, and feeling that this was something she couldn't cope with from Nightshade's back she jumped down and upon a sudden impulse put an arm round Trudy's shoulder while she slipped the other through the reins. She did this partly because it was so painful to see a grown-up person crying and partly because she was appalled at the distress of someone who could wish another person to die. The impulse surprised her even as she obeyed it, and she began to feel a fool; for Trudy was even more surprised and seemed at first to think she was about to be hit. She put up a hand to protect herself. She would probably have much preferred to be hit than comforted; for now she broke down altogether and wept on Susan's shoulder.

It was a very absurd situtation; for while Nightshade loudly snorted on one side of her, Trudy choked and snivelled on the other. Susan slipped a hand in her breeches pocket for a handkerchief and gave it a flick to open it, whereupon Nightshade stood up on her hind legs and nearly pulled the reins out of her grasp. This new alarm, however, had the effect of quietening Trudy, who blew her nose and wiped her eyes and breathed:

"I don't wish you to die. It was wicked of me to say it."

"Of course you didn't mean it," Susan said.

"I meant it when I said it. If you lived in Brixton you'd see this place as paradise. You'd go down on your knees to look at the flowers and you'd do ridiculous things like *stroking* the cool grass." Susan felt her grow tense under her arm, and she guessed that some sort of confession was coming. "You think I'm neurotic? All right then, I am. I let my side down by it because I spoil our case. I suppose I even let that fox down. I've never seen one actually killed before, close to . . . Oh God. You're so pretty, and you've got everything and yet you want dead foxes too . . .

Sorry, that's not fair, I don't suppose you give it a thought really
. . . I don't want you to die, please believe that. God ought to kill
me for wishing it. He won't though. He'll just let everything go
on as it was before, that's the way He pays us all out . . . Will you
please do something for me? It won't hurt you. *Don't tell anybody about this.* About what I said."

"I won't tell anybody."

"Not make fun about it?"

"Never."

"Thank you. Goodbye."

Susan scrambled up on her fretful Nightshade, and trotted
away quickly. She dared not look back over her shoulder in case
she should catch Trudy crying again.

The encounter had an odd sequel next day. Susan had written
a letter to Stephen, and she'd given herself only just enough time
to catch the post which went at half past three on Sundays from
the letterbox by the drive gates. She was hurrying along the drive
when she saw Trudy, presumably returning from an afternoon
walk, coming towards her. Trudy must have noticed her at the
very same moment, and the same acute embarrassment affected
them both simultaneously. Trudy turned round and strode rapidly back in the direction she'd come from; Susan decided that
her letter wasn't very important, stuffed it into her pocket and
turned towards home.

GLORIA'S GOSSIP in the *Elmbury Intelligencer* next week recorded that the unspeakable was in pursuit of the uneatable once
again. The column made Janet so angry nowadays that she refused to read it, which was just as well, because Gloria had
invented a character called Lady Bountiful in whom she might
have glimpsed a reflection of herself; for Lady Bountiful was apt
to say the kind of things which Janet often thought but did not
quite like to put into words; for instance, she regretted the Good
Old Days 'when people were so much more charitable, and
nobody minded us having everything we wanted.'

Susan had to admit that Gloria's column was often funny and
always lively. She didn't write particularly well, but her personality and her emotions came through. You could almost feel the
shock to her innocence when she came face to face for the first
time with some injustice or cruelty which she hadn't believed to

exist until that moment; you were scorched by her blazing anger
which succeeded the first shock. Her liberal Editor let Gloria
have her head and seemed to chance his arm now and then in the
matter of libel. Janet regarded him as the quintessential Bol-
shevik. He was a shockheaded untidy ill-dressed young man who
shaved only when he felt like it, had a cigarette dangling from
his lower lip (like Dylan Thomas), ash all over his tie, dirty
nails, inkstained hands and cigarette-stained fingers. But he
knew how to edit a local paper, and he knew that one way to sell
it was to *épater les bourgeois.* Gloria was therefore encouraged to
have a go at all established things, whether national or local: the
Bomb and the Archbishops, the House of Lords, Big Business,
Grouse Moors, the local Council, British Legion, Territorials,
Boy Scouts, the County . . . She spared nobody, and Susan noticed one day a sharp little aside concerning the agricultural
students and their devotion to blood-sports; Gloria wondered
how they ever found time to do any work 'what with beagling by
day and barmaid-hunting in the evening.'

Susan wondered, not for the first time, what had happened to
Gloria on Coronation Day. She would probably never know; and
perhaps it was only her imagination that saw a change in Gloria
since then. After all, as we grow up, thought Susan, we all shed
our innocence bit by bit. But she still had a vivid recollection of
Gloria as she had been on the afternoon of the Fête, so pert and
so gay in her brownness and roundness; and she fancied that she
would never set eyes on that particular Gloria again.

In fact, she had hardly spoken to her since that day; and in
each of their casual encounters she'd been very much aware of a
constraint. She was sad about this because at one time she'd had
great hopes of making some real contact with Gloria and,
through her, with the rest of the Fenton children. Some understanding, liking, mutual sympathy, had seemed to be growing up
between them. On the night of the dance in the Tithe Barn, for
whatever reason, it had faded and died.

SHE SPENT A GOOD DEAL of time during the summer holidays teaching Adam and Eve to ride the new pony: but the older
Fentons were not much in evidence, being away on their wander-
ings north, south, east and west. Carolyn had got herself to Israel

under some exchange scheme and was teaching children at a
kibbutz; Gloria went hitch-hiking in Erie; Willum joined a University expedition to study the tundra in Iceland; Ben set off
with three friends in a very old car with Russian visas and audacious ideas about driving to Moscow; but the car irreparably
broke down in East Germany and they had quite a job to get
home.

It was soon after this adventure that Susan and Stephen met
Ben on a Saturday morning in The Green Man. Stephen had
flown back from Sweden for some discussions at the Board of
Trade and had a weekend to spare before he rejoined his delega-
tion at Helsinki. He said he'd been drinking too much akvavit
with the Swedish business men, and he had a craving for a pint
of English draught bitter. In The Green Man he drank three
pints, and so did Ben, and they argued agreeably about politics
and international affairs. At a quarter to one they were still so
obviously enjoying themselves that Susan on the spur of the moment asked Ben to lunch. He looked shy and doubtful at
first, but Stephen said: "Please come, it's so rarely we meet,"
and that settled it. Janet had gone off to have a new hunting coat
tried on at Cheltenham. She wouldn't be home to lunch—otherwise Susan might have had second thoughts about inviting Ben!

But Ferdo was delighted as ever to have company, he went
down to the cellar for a couple of bottles of claret, and Ben's
initial nervousness quickly disappeared. It occurred to Susan that
he would have been completely at ease in any big house except
this one, where one would expect him to be shy. He had pleasant
manners and an engaging diffidence which didn't get in the way
of his frankness—she felt that here was someone who would
never trim his expressed opinions in order to please, and who'd
never, for effect or for a laugh, say anything he didn't believe.

Ferdo had obviously taken to him, and with Stephen only too
happy to exercise his whole string of hobbyhorses, the conversation went so quickly from one subject to another that it reminded Susan of opening the Encyclopaedia at random, a game
which she played sometimes when she couldn't find anything else
she wanted to read; her only rule was that she had to read the
whole article wherever she had opened the book, even if it was
about the Cardiovascular System or the Liquefaction of Gases.

The three men turned over the pages of their mental encyclo-paedias so swiftly that Susan could hardly keep pace with them. One moment they were arguing about Disraeli's proposition that 'Increased means and increased leisure are the two civilisers of man.' Stephen and Ben were in favour. Ferdo was doubtful.

"What about those luxurious Romans? Surely unlimited means and unlimited leisure produced chaps like Tiberius and led to eating nightingales' tongues?"

Quick as beagles that have put up a fresh hare right in front of their noses, they all three turned to pursue this new idea. Ben knew a great deal about the Romans, and seemed to be an expert concerning the curious habits of their Emperors. He said they ate as a delicacy the fat white grubs of a moth called Cossus, and he quoted Pliny to prove it. Stephen said:

"Have a heart. Let's get back to civilisation. What about the Greeks?"

So off they went at breakneck speed to ancient Athens. Stephen held that it was the perfect democracy, Ben pointed out that it was easy enough to give your mind to civilised matters if you had slaves to do the hard work for you.

Stephen quoted from Plato's *Republic,* and from Plato some-how or other they got on to Greek tragedy, and Ben produced out of his classical learning a strange snippet of information, that Aeschylus died 'though being hit by a tortoise dropped by an eagle on his bald head.' "At least, that's the story," he said. "It's supposed to have happened in Sicily." That set Stephen off on a gruesome discourse concerning strange modes of death; but soon they got back to Aeschylus and he led on to Aristophanes, and Aristophanes led on to frogs, and in no time Ferdo was explain-ing why frogs were becoming scarce at Doddington, Ben was observing that he had never heard frogs croaking like the ones in Aristophanes, and Stephen was telling him:

"Of course not. The Mediterranean frogs are a different species and speak a different language from the English ones. If you went to Greece or Spain or Italy you would hear them chanting *Brekekekekex ko-ax ko-ax* on any warm spring evening . . ."

And so they went on! Towards the end of lunch, when Stephen was momentarily exhausted by riding his hobbyhorses and every-body else was out of breath from pursuing him, there was a short lull, during which Susan caught Ben looking at her, she thought, with interest and pleasure. This didn't displease her at all, for she'd already decided that she liked his looks and his manners and everything she knew about him; so she acknowledged his glance with a quick smile. Immediately he smiled back, then suddenly became shy again and turned away. Anxious to get the conversation going, he said to Stephen:

"I say, Sir, what are the chances of persuading you to come down to Oxford to debate at a meeting of the University Labour Club? I'm President next term."

"Do you really want a Tory?"

"Yes, we try to get one victim every term. It's not all that easy."

"So I imagine," said Stephen. "Not everybody wants to be butchered to make a Roman holiday . . . Do you give the condemned man a decent meal before the execution?"

"We reckon," said Ben, "that we're a bit more civilised about food than the University Tories. They're sort of mixed grill chaps mostly."

"Very well," said Stephen. "Your Club will give me the best dinner it can afford to put me in the right mood to be your victim. I'll have to get in touch with you about the date—they work us bloody hard in this Parliament. By the way, d'you ever come to London?"

"Of course."

"I'd like you to have lunch at my club. I wonder if you'd care to meet Nye——"

"To meet——?" Clearly Ben thought he couldn't have heard right.

"Nye Bevan. I think he'd like you."

Susan was amused to see that Ben actually flushed with pleasure. Then she looked across the table at Stephen's face, dark, intent, excited by his sudden inspiration that it would be a good idea for those two to know each other.

Ben said:

"Well, of course I can't think of anybody living I'd rather meet, in the whole world."

"Done," said Stephen. "I'll see when I can lay it on. I know he'll come. You're the sort of young man he's looking for."

Ferdo chuckled:

"My dear Stephen, it's wonderful to watch you actually re-cruiting for the other side."

"I'd like him on my side," said Stephen, "but he won't come. Already today he's told me my party is decadent, decaying, dilet-tante, dinosaurian—he goes in for alliteration rather—and a dilapidated hangover from the old days of *Imperium et Libertas.* He mixes his metaphors a bit, but one gets a general impression of where he stands."

That started another argument, and Susan, taking no part in it, thought what civilised men were sitting at her table, all three of them, and she was pleased with herself for instituting this luncheon party. Stephen, of course, always seemed to bring with him an air of a larger and more generous world. She'd often heard him describe Aneurin Bevan as his 'beloved enemy.' He must think a lot of Ben if he wanted them to meet.

The men went on arguing until nearly three o'clock, with Susan happily listening and putting in a word now and then. They'd have probably gone on for much longer, but Janet ar-rived home and somehow or other—it wasn't altogether her fault—she spoilt it and ended the party.

She didn't show any surprise at Ben being there; she was much too well-trained socially to do that. But somehow she failed, by the narrowest margin it seemed to Susan, to achieve a casual acceptance of a situation which must have seemed extraordinary to her: the luncheon-table still not cleared at five past three, two empty bottles, and her gardener's son happily arguing with her husband, her daughter and her guest.

Janet tried hard, and Susan didn't blame her at all; but some-thing went wrong, and suddenly all the warmth seemed to go out of the room. Ben's shyness returned, he made his excuses rather clumsily and left. Stephen looked disappointed; he'd been in the middle of a good argument. Ferdo in silence finished the last of the wine.

Susan, conscious of disloyalty, caught herself wishing that her mother hadn't come back so early or that Ben had decided to leave before she arrived.

Oddly enough Janet never asked how Ben came to be there. Perhaps she herself was aware of some awkwardness when she came into the room, realised that she hadn't managed as well as she should have done? At any rate, much to Susan's surprise, she did not mention Ben's visit again . . .

SUSPECT S. le M. invited him (More and more convinced Le M. a MOUNTEBANK tho gt. charm & clever as Cartload Made discreet enquiries his mother a Levi (??Levy?) v. well off BUT!! . .

He (Ben) must admit most PRESENTABLE little Accent apart from his clothes off Peg and haircut if I had not recognized him might even have thought him a poss. young man for Susan!!!! This shows extraordinary state of world??!!

Little hope Tony now Adj. says we must fear worst strong suspicion he died of his wound in P.camp S seems to have ½ forgotten him Cannot blame her You heal quickly when you are Young!!

Worried abt many things not only Susan & Stephen but Ferdo finances owing I.T. tradesmen builders ? dry rot tho F. will not admit it Only real pleasure these days (other than beloved F. & S.) hunting when forget ALL troubles my dear old Trumpeter 19 still in 1st 20 much of time But how much longer can it last?? Changes everywhere changes in vill. Above all dreading forthcoming A.G.M. of W.I. Know there are Factions Antis New Brooms New People from housing estate nr river bridge pt of wh. comes in our Parish everyone now so niggling formal diff. kind of membership Expect one to know everything Am v. nervous and do not understand Procedure never did we never bothered our own people made Allowances expect difficulties Thursday but NOUS VERRONS . . .

SUSAN BY THIS TIME disliked the Women's Institute so much that she knew she would henceforth never encounter Blake's *Jerusalem* without dismay. But she went with Janet to the Annual General Meeting because her mother confessed it would be a comfort to have her there. "I'm much more nervous than I ever am before the first fence out hunting. Being President is such a responsibility nowadays. I used just to muddle through, and everybody was so nice I rather loved it; and I honestly think they liked me for not being too *professional*. It didn't matter two hoots to any of us which came first, the Apologies for Absence or the Minutes of the Last Meeting."

And Agenda was anathema to Janet always. At a meeting back

in the summer Susan had watched in helpless embarrassment while her mother made a complete muddle of everything and finally got herself into such a state of agitation that she announced: "Will the entrants for the Baking competition please come up to the Platform to collect their Scones?" while Mrs. Fenton was still on her feet taking advantage of the item 'Any Other Business' to make some tiresome procedural complaint. Utter confusion followed, Janet lost her head, raised her voice more than was necessary and became through sheer nervousness bossy and dictatorial. During a moment's silence she was heard to shout:

"Have you got that down? We will bring that up later."

This unfortunately provoked a giggle, because it occurred to somebody that it might be thought to refer to the scones. The giggle was followed by others at the back of the hall, and suddenly the whole meeting burst into roars of laughter. It was half-sympathetic, and Janet could have turned the situation to her own advantage if only she had laughed too. She didn't, and the laughter ended, abruptly and uncomfortably.

This morning she had said to Susan:

"It's not our own people I'm worried about. It's the new ones." Recently the boundaries had been altered, to bring into the parish a small housing estate on the Doddington bank of the river. Also, Daglingworth had sold some land for building at the far side of Doublegates Farm. The inhabitants of these houses were the ones Janet described as 'the new people.' Until recently she had known not only the faces but much of the life-histories of every member of the Institute; now nearly half of them were strangers. Some of these had come from other Women's Institutes which, they seemed to think, were better-managed than Doddington's was. One woman in particular, a Mrs. Trent, whose husband was the Managing Director of a small factory in Elmbury, was always jumping up to criticise, to correct and to argue. Janet had noticed that Mrs. Fenton generally applauded her.

She anticipated trouble from Mrs. Trent if she got into a muddle over the Agenda.

"—And an A.G.M. is so much more complicated than an ordinary meeting," she whispered to Susan as they went into the hall.

She began well, however. She welcomed the visitors from other Institutes. She gave out a couple of notices. She managed the election of the new Committee, which had to be done very democratically by means of a secret ballot conducted by two 'tellers,' husbands of Members, imported into the Annual General Meeting for this special purpose. (How extraordinary, thought Susan: the idea must be that women can't trust other women not to cheat!)

The names of the new Committee members were duly announced. Then Janet said cheerfully:

"Now we come to the election of President for next year. So I must step down from the platform and hand over temporarily to the V.C.O.——"

As Janet got up from her seat Susan realised her appalling mistake. It was that word 'temporarily.' There was a sudden perceptible change in the whole atmosphere; Susan could feel the chill of it. But Janet was simply unaware that she had said anything she shouldn't. She came down the steps from the platform and gave Susan a smile as if to say 'I'm not doing too badly so far' as she sat down by her side.

The V.C.O. took the chair. (The W.I. were great ones for initials; Susan gathered that these meant "Voluntary County Organiser.") She was a very businesslike woman with a quiet voice, who said:

"Ladies, we now proceed to the election of your President. May I have your nominations, please?"

Silence; but then there was always a little hesitant silence on these occasions, wasn't there?

"Any nominations?" said the V.C.O. "If there should be only one, I shall of course put that name to the meeting. If there is more than one we will conduct a ballot as usual with the kind help of our tellers."

She smiled at the two men sitting at the side of the hall.

Still nobody spoke. Susan felt herself blushing for Janet's sake. At last the silence was broken by a shuffling sound at the back of the hall. Susan didn't look round, but she heard a voice she didn't recognise saying:

"I should like to propose Mrs. Trent as President."

Susan felt Janet stiffen at her side. After a longish pause there was more shuffling, and a familiar voice this time—it was Mrs. Turberville's—said rather indignantly:

"I want to propose Lady Seldon. We've always——"

"Thank you." The V.C.O. cut her short. "Any more nominations?" But there were no others, and soon the tellers were busily handing out their folded sheets of paper. There was a general stir as people hunted in their bags for pencils. The V.C.O. was asking the Secretary meanwhile to announce the winners of the competition for baking scones.

Susan hardly dared look at her mother. At last the papers were collected and examined and counted as carefully as if it were a Parliamentary Election, and the V.C.O. announced with maddening formality:

"The result of the ballot for President is as follows: Mrs. Trent, thirty-one votes. Lady Seldon, sixteen. Mrs. Trent therefore is duly elected."

Then Mrs. Trent went up to the platform and took the Chair, and said some nice things about Janet which she obviously didn't mean. The meeting went on. Susan put out her hand to touch her mother's, but Janet drew hers away.

At last it was 'Any Other Business,' and Mrs. Fenton had her little say about the wickedness of keeping hens in batteries, and Mrs. Trent suggested tactfully that they might debate the whole question later in the year. The meeting was over. The helpers handed round the coffee and cakes; and everybody was trying to be specially nice to Janet, either because they were sorry for her or because even in this microcosm of democracy the people who had disliked her when she possessed power felt their sympathy swinging towards her as soon as she was shorn of it.

Janet stayed for just as long as was decent; then she invented some excuse about the vet coming to see Trumpeter, and she and Susan left the village hall.

They went out into the first chilly wind of the autumn. Janet didn't speak, and Susan thought it best not to say anything unless her mother did. They took the usual short cut over the Village Green, and when they were about half-way across it six or seven geese which grazed there, with the old gander in front, ran towards them with outstretched necks, hissing. This always happened if you walked across the green, and nobody as a rule took any notice of it. But now Janet walked so quickly that Susan had to hurry to keep up.

Beasts!!   BEASTS!!!   Can hardly believe it after all these yrs.   Know I wasn't v. good not my métier but did my best and LOVED it (Why???) Have not yet told F. he said How did mtg. go I said A lot of talk as usual He still doesn't know unless S. had told him   Wish she wd. Why do I mind   ??? could not easily say   Despite myself S-pity most horrible . . .

¶ 14

IT WAS BIRTHDAY WEATHER FOR SUSAN, blue and still. The clearing where she stood with Stephen, which was almost circular and walled by the wood, was brimful of cider-coloured light that spilt over and splashed into the surrounding trees as if it had been poured with careless generosity out of the shining sky.

"This was always the best squirrel-place," she said. "It was from those big oaks that they peered down at us. When I was a child I used to *feel* them looking at me even if I couldn't see them."

A whim of Ferdo's had sent her out with Stephen on this quest for squirrels, which had become a small obsession with him lately. Susan knew that only last week he'd let Egbert take a day off and had promised him a fiver if he could come back and say he had seen a red squirrel in the woods. He couldn't; and he knew all the quietest places, all the secret paths. It was more than three years since anybody had seen one. The exact date was remembered because it had been Ferdo's and Janet's wedding anniversary: July the 31st, 1950. That a red squirrel should appear to them on that occasion had seemed to Ferdo most fitting, a special favour almost. Now Susan, who could see through him, realised that he'd been thinking it would be equally fitting if one should show itself to her on her twenty-first birthday; and from that fancy there had grown up in his mind the absurd belief that a squirrel would actually do so.

"He's worried and unhappy about that old rhyme," said Susan. "I told it you, didn't I?"

"Yes, but I've forgotten."

She quoted:

> " 'Should squirrels be gone and oak-trees fall,
> Then down go Seldons and down goes all.'

"Daddy's awfully superstitious. Haven't you noticed?"

"Tossing up and all that? That's just a kind of game, isn't it?"

"It is and it isn't. I think it began by being a kind of game. Now it's—something different. It all ties up with a change in him: as if the edges of his mind were getting blurred, almost. You know what I mean?"

"Yes, I do. But he's still better company than most of the people I meet," said Stephen.

"For a bit. Then he gets tired, and seems to fade out. I don't know if it's just the claret or that old wound in his head. It worries me a bit."

"It's against the rules for a girl to worry about anything on her twenty-first birthday," Stephen said.

STEPHEN HAD GOT BACK only just in time for it. He'd flown from Helsinki overnight and arrived at Doddington in the late morning. He'd had no sleep other than catnaps in the aeroplane, but he was a person who thrived on catnaps, he always said too much sleep made you smug. Susan could see that he was a bit keyed-up today, a bit taut and tense—because of his tiredness, she supposed. The effect was to make him more talkative, quicker-witted, even more perceptive than usual. For once his eyes and ears were sharper than Susan's, his sensibility to what he saw was more acute. The beauty of the woods, which she accepted as a familiar joy, kept taking him by surprise; he found something to delight him round every turning: One of his favourite quotations was from Walter De la Mare, "Look thy last on all things lovely, every hour." He was reminded of it again today.

"My *God*, Sukie, look at those elephant-grey tree-trunks, half in the sunlight, half in the shade, with the green and the gold all round them! If we're lucky and we live long enough we may see *something like that* but never that exactly, a moment never comes again——"

He was in one of his Pantheist moods, he told her. If he'd been a Roman he'd have worshipped Faunus, or whichever deity looked after the groves. Not being a Roman, he had what he called intimations of divinity, very disturbing.

"You do seem to have a lot of difficulty with your agnosticism, Stephen," Susan laughed.

"No, not as a rule. Most of the time I live by reason, I judge by reason, I am convinced that reason works. It's the unexpected beauty of things that undoes me, when it catches me unawares. 'Just when we're safest, there's a sunset-touch, A fancy in a flower-bell' . . . You know."

He'd only recently persuaded her to read Browning; and much to her surprise she had enjoyed those conversation-pieces, "Bishop Blougram," and "Fra Lippo Lippi," though he'd warned 'her that Browning was a man's taste in poetry. But she didn't like all the books, by any means, which Stephen recommended in urgent scribbles on their fly-leaves or their title-pages. '*I know Kipling was a Dogman and sometimes had the dreadful sentimentality of Dogmen; but you* MUST *read these short stories . . .*' Unfortunately she began with "The Brushwood Boy," and Kipling remained a blind spot as far as she was concerned. As for Byron— '*As a woman you'll learn a lot from him even if you hate him*'— she had told Stephen that if she read much more of him he'd put her off men for good. Stephen agreed that would be a pity; and so he had started her on Browning as a corrective. He still showered books upon her for the nicest of reasons: that in each case he wanted to share an experience with her. Among the assortment of parcels, some of them book-shaped, which he had brought for her birthday and which she was going to unwrap after tea, was an L.P. record of Sibelius' Fourth Symphony. He had bought it in Helsinki yesterday morning. He hadn't enjoyed Scandinavia (it was too hygienic, he said, for a Mediterranean type who refused to equate civilisation with efficient plumbing) but Finland had been fun, and he thought the Finns must be very civilised because when their Sibelius grew old and famous they provided him with as much good claret as he could drink at the expense of the State. Stephen had learned this from a Finn who

had also less credibly assured him that the great man had drunk
half a dozen bottles of the free claret every day.

"Daddy would approve of both Finland and Sibelius," Susan
said.

"Yes, he would. Well, this Finn and I—we met in a hotel bar
just casually—thought it would be a good idea if we drank a
couple of bottles ourselves to the old boy's memory. After dinner
—we were both a bit tight by then—the Finn said: 'If you wish
to understand Finland you must listen to his Fourth Symphony.
There's the spirit of the birch-woods in it.' So we went back to his
flat and drank some whisky and played the record. The Finn
wept all the way through it and passed out at the end. It was a
marvellous evening."

Stephen grinned; and she knew he'd bought her the record
because he wanted to share with her a bit of the evening, just as
he always wanted to share his favourite books.

"IF ONLY WE COULD FIND YOU a red squirrel for your
birthday!"

They gazed up into the trees round the edge of the clearing.

The place was exactly as she remembered it when as a child she
used to picnic here. The days had always been golden then; and
windless, like today. There was the same hectic butterfly-flutter
where the sunlight shafts struck down between the trees. There
were the same tufts of feggy grass and the same clumps of
bracken along the banks of the little stream.

"Which is the orchis which smells of tomcat?"

"The spotted one," said Stephen. "Comes out in May."

"That was the one I used to pick here. I had to wash my hands
in the stream afterwards."

The trees stood round the clearing in a reverential calm. They
hadn't begun to change colour yet, but Susan fancied they always
grew a little darker at this time of year, and acquired an air of
grave expectancy.

Sometimes if you clapped your hands you used to get a glimpse
of a squirrel's tail as its owner skedaddled away.

Susan clapped hers loudly. Two jays flew out, making their
smoker's-cough noises. She watched their white rumps undulating against the dark trees. Stephen cried:

"Look! Oh, look!"

A squirrel,—but alas, only a grey one! He must have jumped
down from his bough when Susan clapped. He hadn't spotted
them, however; he came rippling across the clearing with an
action rather like a fish jumping on the end of a line. At last he
stopped and stood up on his hind legs to take a cautious look
round. Then he saw human beings twenty yards away; he froze
solid for a fraction of a second, a statuette of a squirrel, then
magically melted, trickled through the bracken and was gone.
His grey coat was almost silver in the sun.

"Daddy calls them tree-rats," Susan said.

"Oh, but he was charming!"

"Yes, but not *one of ours*. The red ones are different altogether. They've always been here. They belong."

Stephen looked at her with amusement and affection.

"As you do," he laughed.

"Yes, of course . . . I was thinking this morning," Susan said,
"when I first woke up on my twenty-first birthday, that I belong
too much. It's partly Daddy and Mummy; he relies on me for lots
of things, she's got into the habit of having me around. But it's
partly *me*. I'm quite frightened sometimes at the way I'm getting
all wrapped up in Doddington. I said to myself, lying in bed,
You're twenty-one, if you don't take care you'll become a stick-in-
the-mud and a cabbage, nothing will ever happen to you at
all!"

"To a girl who can find a ghost orchis," he laughed, *"anything*
might happen, I should think. But I wasn't blaming you for
belonging. I was envious in a way. It must be nice to have a place
where your roots are. If you were at the other end of the world,
and something went wrong for you, life turned sour, you'd make
a bee-line for home."

"Naturally. Wouldn't you? Haven't you got a place?"

"Not where I belong. I'm not made that way. If I belong
anywhere it's probably in one of those old ports around the Med.
that you come across in Saint Paul's journeys. I've no special
reason for thinking that, except that I feel so much at home
there."

"You love that sea," she said. "You're always talking about
it."

"Yes. And in sterilised Sweden I was always thinking about it,
I was thinking how much I preferred smells to no-smells! There's

a special Mediterranean port smell; the hot breeze smells of oranges and garlic and tar and drying fishnets and coffee and fish all mixed up with the salt-and-seaweed smell of the sea. When I was about your age I used to go off to Spain or Italy or Greece for my holidays; and with that whiff in my nose, and the shine so bright I had to screw my eyes up, I'd go down to the harbour and look for an old dirty ship and I'd hitch a lift from its Master without asking where he was going!"

Susan caught a gust of adventure, almost as if it were that sea-breeze in her nose. Stephen talked so well that he made you feel you were a born traveller even though you'd hardly been abroad at all; in the same way he seemed to assume you were *cut* out for a climber though you'd never been on a mountain,—that you'd enjoy orchid-hunting though you'd never seen a jungle! So although she knew little or nothing of physical adventure, Susan's spirit leapt to match his. She could accept and understand that drunken evening with the Finn, she could appreciate the rightness and the propriety of joining a ship without first asking where she was bound. And because it was her twenty-first birthday she felt the world was at her feet.

"To think," she said, "that I've been no farther than France, and then it was only to Aix-les-Bains with Daddy and Mummy after the war because they always used to go to Aix-les-Bains!"

"That's easily put right," said Stephen. "One day we'll——" He broke off so suddenly that she turned to him in surprise.

"We'll what?"

"Tell you later."

"Why not now?"

"Because there's a time and a place," he said, half-laughing, half-cross with her for her insistence. "I've got lots to say to you. We promised we'd be back for tea. Talk later." He caught her hand in his and started to walk fast across the clearing. He fairly swung her along. The clearing had soft and springy turf, you felt light-footed. Susan with long strides bounded from tuft to tuft. Out of the corner of her eye she glimpsed Stephen's face, dark and eager and edgy, and just as she had caught from him a sense of adventure so did she catch a queer excitement from him now. When they came to the little stream, which had high banks, he said "Jump!" and in one motion slipped his arm round her

waist and lifted her across. He had ceased to be shy of touching
her, ever since the episode of the ghost orchis, and there was no
embarrassment between them any more. His hand on her hip was
firm and authoritative, and Susan not for the first time was conscious of her body's response to his touch. Mischief and curiosity
and a sense of *something going to happen* prickled her all the
way home.

THE HEAVY FRONT-DOOR had been getting more and
more stiff on its hinges lately, and when Stephen tried to open it
today it stuck. "No wonder it kept the Roundheads out," he said.

"Yes, you can see the marks of their axes." She put her finger
into one of the grooves, as she had done when she was a child. "I
don't know why, it has always been exciting to do that."

"You little Cavalier," he laughed. "Help me, give it a push."
He put his shoulder to the door and heaved. With a cronking
groan the door gave way suddenly and they both nearly toppled
over into the hall. As he caught her by the shoulders Susan
thought he was going to kiss her; and she wouldn't have been
surprised, a birthday kiss, it would have seemed quite right and
proper at that moment. She wasn't sure which of them it was who
first saw the telegram on the hall table, nor why that trivial
distraction kept them apart.

"Bet it's for you," she said. "Perhaps it's from Winston asking
you to be Chancellor of the Exchequer or whatever you'd like
best to be——"

"Foreign Secretary!" he laughed.

But it was for Susan Seldon. As she was opening it Ferdo and
Janet came down the stairs into the hall. Apparently they hadn't
seen the telegram, for Janet said: "Had a good walk?" and Ferdo
asked anxiously:

"Did you see a red squirrel?"

She was slow in reading the telegram because the word at the
end of it was 'Adjutant' and it threw her at once into confusion
and alarm. It took her right back to that other telegram on the
hall table, the last time she had seen Tony, on the occasion of her
wretchedness and her shame. That one too had been signed
'Adjutant.'

MESSAGE JUST RECEIVED FROM PUSAN KOREA DATED 25/9/53
CAPTAIN ANTHONY SELDON HANDED OVER SAFE AND WELL ON
WAY HOME VIA JAPAN URGENTLY REQUESTED ME INFORM YOU
IMMEDIATELY ADJUTANT HORFIELD BARRACKS . . . !

"Oh, it's Tony!" Susan cried, as at last it sank in. "Hurray hurray Tony's coming home!" Ferdo and Janet had come close to her to see what was in the telegram; she kissed them first because they were nearest, then she ran to Stephen and threw her arms round him and kissed him too. She hugged him tight, and felt his shoulders stiffen a little and only then—You fool, you fool, you insensitive little fool! she said to herself—she remembered that he had said he wanted to talk to her tonight, he'd lots of things to say—and whatever they were this telegram had surely changed everything for him and her! She was only just beginning to realise how profoundly it had changed everything. She let go of Stephen and for a moment she dared not look at him. In the little silence she could hear her heart beating. Ferdo said:

"Well, well, we must open a bottle of champagne to celebrate this."

He stumped off towards the cellar. Then Stephen said, very easily:

"I should certainly think so . . . Oh, by the way, may I use your 'phone, Ferdo? I want to put a through a call."

He went away, and Janet hugged Susan and said:

"Oh pet, what a marvellous present for your twenty-first birthday."

Susan was going back in her mind to the things that had happened this afternoon, and bit by bit she was beginning to understand about Stephen; but even in her distress for him she was aware that her whole spirit like one of those radar screens that turn questingly like blind faces this way and that—her whole spirit had turned towards Tony. And that her excitement and her sense of adventure-round-the-corner which had been engendered by Stephen, even the quick tremulous awakening of her body, had turned that way too.

Stephen came back and she was in agony on his behalf but she knew she couldn't do anything to comfort or cheer him; and in her eyes he looked much older than he had done before.

"You got your phone call?" said Janet solicitously, who now for the first time perhaps felt kindly towards Stephen.

"Yes, thanks."

Ferdo brought the bottle and four glasses. He was bad at opening bottles, which was surprising in view of the practice he had: the cork shot out, the champagne fizzed over, he made the fatal mistake of pressing his thumb where the cork had been, sending two powerful jets in opposite directions. One hit Susan in the face, the other spattered against the wall.

Stephen said "Let me," and wiped Susan's face with his handkerchief. She noticed that when he'd done it he quickly looked away.

"Well, here's to Tony," said Janet, "and his safe return."

Then the telephone rang.

"I'll go," said Susan, glad of the excuse. She ran to answer it. She knew the voice. It was Stephen's secretary.

"Miss Seldon?"

"Yes."

"Can you give a message to Mr. Le Mesurier? I'm so sorry about this . . . He'd expected to stay with you till tomorrow. But something's turned up about those trade talks he's been engaged in. The Minister wants to see him urgently."

"Oh!—you mean he's wanted back in town tonight?"

"I'm afraid so. You'll tell him? I'll hang on here and explain everything to him when he arrives."

She was a very good secretary, and it wasn't until Susan got back into the hall and began to give the message to Stephen that she remembered about his phone call and realised that he'd put the girl up to making this excuse for him.

"—And the Minister wants to see you urgently." As she said that she understood, because they were still so close in spite of everything, that *he* knew *she* knew the message was a faked one.

He looked straight at her now, and lifted his champagne-glass in salutation, and smiled.

PART SIX

Soldier from the War Returning

⁋ 1

THE COCK PHEASANT SEEMED TO DUCK its head into its breast as it started to fall. Turning over and over, its long tail bent almost into a semicircle by the wind of its own speed, it hurtled to the ground and came down, thump, fifty yards from where Tony stood. Feathers exploded from it like a puff of smoke from a little bomb.

Susan put her thumb up and smiled at Tony as he turned round to her. But he didn't smile back. "Good God, Sue, I ought to have had a dozen!" He opened his gun and the cartridge-cases flew out to lie beside the others which were scattered round him. With the toe of his boot he kicked a little cluster apart as he counted them. Seventeen, eighteen, nineteen. The beaters were coming out of the wood, and with them was Daglingworth's keeper, very smart in check breeches and a green trilby with a blue teal's feather and a curly one out of a mallard's tail stuck in the hat ribbon.

"Anything to pick up, Sir?"

"One cock over there."

The keeper contrived to look surprised while remaining deferential. Susan hated him. When he'd gone she said to Tony:

"You're out of practice, that's all."

"It's nothing to do with practice," he said quite sharply. "It's my bloody knee. Worst on this sticky plough of course. It gets me every time I turn."

It had been painful for Susan to watch him because of his twisted stance and the way his whole body seemed to jerk every time he swung to follow a bird. It was all the worse because he used to be such a good shot; next to riding in races, shooting was the thing he enjoyed most. So he'd been almost boyishly excited when the invitation came from Daglingworth. Sandra had rung up Susan: "Bring your wounded soldier to bump off some of Daddy's pheasants . . . I don't think your father shoots much nowadays?"

"He's given it up." Ferdo wouldn't have gone to Dagling-worth's in any case. He'd duly given evidence at the enquiry about the proposed new gravel-pit, and he'd said he believed it would destroy the whole character of Doddington village. Daglingworth's application to open the pit had been turned down. He'd been furious about it, and Susan suspected he was fool enough to believe that Ferdo had acted out of spite, 'getting his own back' for the business of the boundary-hedge. However, he'd been very agreeable to her today, and solic-itous concerning Tony: only of course he'd said the wrong thing at the very beginning:

"Wouldn't you like me to lay on the Land Rover to give you a lift between the drives?"

People were expected to ignore Tony's disability, unless he cared to mention it himself. Although he'd been home for only a fortnight Susan had learned the hard way that there were a great many things which he didn't want to talk about. You mustn't ask him about the prison-camp, its routine, its hardships, its depriva-tions; he didn't want to talk about his fellow-prisoners, and for some reason he became cross when Ferdo, who knew some of the Glosters, began to ask their names. When Susan asked if he'd had her letters, and whether he'd written any to her besides the one she'd had from him, he shrugged his shoulders and said sharply: "What the devil does it matter now I'm home?" On another occasion he said: "I want to forget all about that. It was like being dead. I want to learn how to *live* again." He was obsessed by the idea that he'd 'lost' two years—worse, that he'd been cheated and robbed of them! He knew he couldn't get them back, but he thought he might put things all square if he crammed enough 'life,' whatever he meant by that, into his *next*

two years. Yet for all his impatience and feverish hurry he was
uneasy and unsure. His wound embarrassed him. To be even
partially a cripple seemed to him something despicable, a sort
of shame upon his body; so he tried to cure both his lame knee
and his lame spirit by the absurd expedient of pretending that
there was nothing much the matter with either.

Of course he didn't put into words these attitudes and distresses; but Susan quickly got to know how he was feeling—and
so, somewhat to her surprise, did Ferdo.

"You've got a bit of a job on your hands, young woman," he
said to her one day.

She knew that; and she was glad that at last she had a 'job'—
was even glad that it wasn't an easy one. It both fascinated and
frightened her. She learned that she had to think ahead all the
time, anticipate every turn of the conversation, explain things
without seeming to explain them; it was simply astonishing what
a lot of gaps there were in a person's experience when he'd been
shut away from everything for two or three years! Maybe you
hummed a popular tune and you looked surprised when he asked
what it was; you mentioned a best-seller which he hadn't heard
of; you referred to something which had made headlines in the
newspapers not long ago and he didn't know what you were
talking about, because of course he hadn't seen an English news-
paper during the whole of his captivity. Even Tony's slang was
out of date; and when Susan used an expression that was new to
him he was liable to resent it—because, she suspected, of his odd
feeling that events had outstripped him, he'd been left behind,
he'd never catch up again.

Gradually Susan came to realise how many things had changed
since 1950: sentiments, attitudes, 'the climate of opinion'—some
of her own convictions too. She had scarcely been aware of the
extent of these changes, because they had crept upon her imper-
ceptibly; but to Tony coming out of his imprisonment they
loomed large and bewildering, so that he was at first confused,
then incredulous, and finally resentful,—politicians talked tripe,
the country was getting sloppy, Susan wanted her head looking
at, and so on. Susan, seeing through the bluster, would realise
that each time he came up against these changes his self-confidence was shaken afresh. Whenever she was in his company her

sensibilities had to be at action-stations all the time. Even a little mistake might make an hour uncomfortable or a whole day unhappy.

SHE MADE ONE NOW. She picked up his cartridge-bag and slung it over her shoulder. "Give it me," he said; and almost tugged it out of her hands. They didn't have far to walk, for the guns had been standing in a narrow valley, a mere dingle, between two woods; for the next drive it was more or less a matter of turning round and facing the other way. Tony struggled towards his numbered peg, only about thirty yards off, dragging himself across the lumpy ploughland. When at last they got to his peg Susan could see the sweat glistening on his forehead.

The mixed wood which rose in tiers in front of them wore the full splendour of autumn. The beeches were tawny, the oaks chrome-yellow, the sycamores gold. Tony as he wiped his face with a handkerchief turned to Susan with a grin that momentarily cheered her. "What a sight!" Far away at the other end of the wood the beaters began their tapping on the trees.

Daglingworth and Sandra went by on their way to the next peg to Tony's. Daglingworth's red setter trotted up to Tony, and wagged its tail; he put out his hand and it nuzzled him. Just then Daglingworth gave a sort of dog's growl and the setter flew back to his heels as if it had been attached to him by a piece of elastic. Susan wanted to laugh, the noise which came out of Daglingworth's throat had been so extremely dog-like; and suddenly, briefly, she caught herself missing Stephen. You couldn't share the same kind of jokes with Tony. She glanced at him now, and he said without a smile: "Well-trained bitch. I love those setters. Just the colour of the leaves, isn't she? When I've settled down I think I'll look out for a gun-dog or two——"

"*Two?*" Susan couldn't help saying.

"Well, yes, if I had a setter I'd want a spaniel for rough shooting as well . . ."

The beaters, coming over the brow of the hill now, suddenly began to shout "For-ward! For-ward!"

A single cock flew high over the blazing beech-trees. Having gained enough height, it spread its wings and began to plane down towards the wood on the opposite slope. Susan, knowing it would be a difficult shot, prayed it wouldn't come within range. But it aimed straight for Tony, he fired twice and it majestically glided on. A moment later he missed a hen. Then the beaters in the wood set up a tremendous clamour, they were all yelling at once, and the pheasants began to stream over, high above the valley, cocks with their comets' tails, hens frantically working their shorter wings like sculls to cleave the air and drive them through it. For a few minutes the bangs became a continuous sound as they echoed back from the woods on both sides of the dingle. Susan caught a glimpse of two birds falling together over Daglingworth's head, more black blobs somersaulting against the sky at the top of the valley, the red setter bright as beech-leaves galloping to overtake a runner. There were thuds all round, and there was shotfall sounding like a scud of hail upon the dry leaves at the woodside. The blue sky became speckled as a bird's egg is by dots and spots and blotches; and these were feathers, which hung there long after their owners had met the earth. They drifted overhead very slowly, for there was hardly any wind; and when they got in the way of the sun they became luminescent, tiny drifting pinpoints of light. Most of them were floating down from Daglingworth, who fired with cool efficiency, picking and choosing his birds.

Tony meanwhile had shot the tails out of a couple of hens; he turned to watch one of them as she lurched and wobbled towards the wood.

"I think she's coming down," said Susan.

"She isn't. Oh Sue, for Christ's sake," he burst out suddenly, "go and stand by somebody else! It's not your fault but you put me off."

It was like a blow in the face; and Susan took a step back down the slope, involuntarily. Then another flurry of birds got up and Tony turned back towards the wood. Susan walked away from him, and because there was nowhere else to go—most of the other guns were stationed right at the top of the valley—she went to Sandra, who was standing behind her father. She was wearing a gay little fur cap which she'd bought *pour le sport,* she said.

"Lovers' tiff, love?"

"He's out of practice. He used to be awfully good, you see. He says I put him off."

"If a girl can put a man off his shooting he must be in a hell of a state about her," Sandra said. "*I* think he's madly attractive. You'd better look out, I warn you . . ."

Just then the beaters started yelling *Yi-yi-yi-yi-yi!* as a whole lot of pheasants, running before them, went pattering over the dead leaves in a little clearing. They were within thirty yards of the edge of the wood now, and all the creatures of the woodland, large and small, were on the move in front of them. Jays flew squawking out of the treetops, blackbirds gave their alarums, a grey squirrel scurried between the beech-boles. Another, louder, scream of *Yi-yi-yi!* went up as a fox broke cover away on the right, somebody shouted *Hare forward!*, a cock pheasant came running out of the wood, spotted Daglingworth, and sensibly scuttled back. Unseen by Susan, there were doubtless weasels and stoats and jenny wrens and long-tailed tits and little mice with pattering hearts; and as she thought of the panic of all these creatures engendered by the banging of sticks and the bashing of bushes and the yelping of dogs and the bestial cries of the beaters yelling *Yi-yi-yi!*, Susan despite her country upbringing felt a little ashamed of being human. Sandra at her side was troubled by no such doubts. When the hare broke covert, and her father bowled it over at rather long range, it kicked and cried and whimpered like a child; Sandra shouted to a man who'd gone to pick it up: "Oh, for goodness sake, shut it up quickly!"

Now as the beaters came close to the covert's edge a score of pheasants exploded out of the wood suddenly. With the sun behind them they rose from the blazing bonfire of the trees like those pieces of black charred paper which float upon the heat that goes up from the flames. Daglingworth must have spent a little fortune on his pheasants; certainly there had never been so many at Doublegates before. All the way along the line the guns were firing. Daglingworth had a right and left, then a single bird, then another right and left. That was first-rate shooting. Susan saw a cock thump down behind Tony, a hen fold her wings as she plunged to earth, another cock spread-eagled and spinning in a cloud of feathers: all three stone dead in the air. She'd forgotten all about the terror of the woodland creatures, had forgotten the squealing hare; in her excitement she waved to Tony, and even as she did so saw another cock plummet down behind him.

Then the keeper in the wood was blowing his whistle and

shouting *Out!* The drive was over, and it was the last drive of
the day. Daglingworth broke open his gun, and Susan had
a whiff of the acrid-sweet powder-smell as he turned to her,
pleased with himself, cheerful. "They came pretty well, didn't
they?" One by one the beaters stumbled out of the wood, rag-tag-
and-bobtail and weirdly clad, in ancient jackets which they kept
specially for beating, old battledress trousers, gumboots, bala-
clava helmets. As they shuffled along the covertside they looked,
as beaters always do at the end of the day, like refugees.

''WE'LL GO AND FETCH the Land Rover," Sandra had said.
"Then we'll come back for you and Tony and take you home to
tea. Canoodle meanwhile, lovie!" She and her father went off up
the hill, followed by the keeper with his multi-coloured load of
pheasants, slung upon a stout stick and carried Dick-Whitting-
ton-fashion over his shoulder. (Sycophantic and smarmy,
"You didn't miss many, Sir!" he'd said to his master, as he tied
the birds up two by two, always a cock and a hen coupled in
death together.)

Susan walked down the slope to Tony, and they waited together at the edge of the wood.

The sun sinking behind the trees now began to set the opposite side of the valley aflame. Talk about bonfires, thought Susan
—a whole wood was blazing! Surely she had never seen the
autumn colours so bright. Among the yellow and orange and
tawny of the forest trees there were scarlet splashes of maple-bush
and spindle, there was the wine-red vintage flush of old hawthorn trees, and the warm deep damson colour of the buckthorn.
some reason, as she gazed in wonder at this valedictory magnifi-
cence, Susan's thoughts turned to Stephen, and she was certain
that she knew what he'd have said if he'd been standing beside
her now. He'd have started speculating by what mysterious process the leaves turned from green to gold, what actually happened to the chlorophyll to make it change colour at the time of
the leaf-fall; and he'd have grinned at her in his endearing,
ingenuous way: 'By God, Sukie, if only one had a dozen lives! I'd
like to know all about organic chemistry!'

But Tony, leaning on his shooting-stick, stared at the wood
and said:

"Bloody marvellous!"

Then he turned round to her.

"Sue, I'm sorry for being a so-and-so."

She shook her head. She wanted to say something, but pity and love kept her silent.

"England," he said. "This sort of thing. It hurt like hell to think of it. I used to see you like you are now, always against the woods somehow. You were part of the woods. I can't explain. Then after a bit——"

He broke off and Susan said: "Yes?"

"You faded. Like an old photo."

She was easy suddenly, she could laugh again. "One of those that go yellow?"

He nodded. "Everything was a bit yellow. The soil, the grass, the mountains and the people: not yellow exactly but a sort of pale beige."

Then they fell silent, and Susan listened to the life coming back into the violated wood, as feeling comes back into a numb limb. Mice chirruped, a thrush sang, a cock pheasant vaingloriously boasted that he was still alive.

¶ 2

A COMPASSIONATE WAR OFFICE, still equating Glosters with glory, gave Tony a long Christmas leave before they hi'ed him into hospital to have a check-up and some treatment for his knee. They kept him there for six weeks, until at last the doctors decided to operate. It was another six weeks before he could walk; so that the woodsides were going green, and the pussy-willows were over, by the time he came back to Doddington. After his sick leave he was posted to the Regimental Depôt for 'light duties only'; but his knee wasn't mending as well as the doctors had hoped, and before long he was sent back to hospital once again. Like many people who are aggressively healthy as a rule, he had a morbid mistrust of hospitals and all their mysteries. He had loathed what he called 'that bloody rehabilitation place' in Japan, where specialists of all sorts had poked and prodded and pried to find out what had happened to his body and his mind during thirty months of captivity. This time, however, he was relieved to find that there was no psychiatrist,—'No trick cyclist thank the Lord!' he wrote to Susan, 'only a huge blonde physiotherapist with terrific biceps, of Nordic ancestry I should think. Count Von Masoch would have fallen in love with her. I haven't. I lie upon my back, she hangs weights upon my ankle, heavier every day, and makes me lift them with my bad leg. She said yesterday morning: "We'll have you skipping tomorrow." When I laughed she said "I mean it," and gave me a fiendish grin.'

He added a postscript:

'I did my skipping, and the knee seems to be working after all. Bloody thing's got to work! I've my Medical on Friday. *All depends on it*. Keep your fingers crossed for me then.'

After the Medical Board they let him out of hospital and he came straight to Doddington. He was still there when his friend the Adjutant rang up and told him of the Board's decision. In view of his disability he would be invalided out of the Army.

FOR A TIME HE WAS in utter despair. He'd been a soldier ever since he left school; he had known no other kind of life, and he'd had so much fun out of his soldiering (because he had been very good at it) that he'd come to despise what he thought of as the humdrum routine of civilian existence. He was now quite prepared to despise himself, both for being a civilian and for being a cripple. He had the kind of horror of crippledom that most people have of V.D. His disability, which wasn't very serious in itself, seemed to be associated in his mind with inadequacy, inferiority, a sort of shame.

He was in the mood to give up everything. He turned down Daglingworth's offer of some fishing on the Cotswolds, and when Susan suggested that he ought to try a quiet hack on Trumpeter he said: "What's the fun of a quiet hack if you've been used to riding across country?" He couldn't walk far and he wouldn't read. One day he hobbled along to The Green Man, drank a lot of whisky there and brought a bottle home. He opened it after lunch and when Ferdo refused to drink with him—the only time Susan had ever known him turn down a drink—Tony drank three-quarters of it by himself, then staggered up to bed.

But after this bout, which was a sort of angry protest like that of a man so miserable that he knocks his head against the wall, he began slowly to come to his senses; and Susan, seeing her chance, seized as it were at the very coat-tails of his spirit and dragged him back into the workaday world from which in desperation he sought to flee. He didn't come without a struggle. His moods and his manners changed as quickly as the weather did during that dabbly summer of 1954; changed from tenderness to clumsiness, from melancholy to a disturbing sort of self-mocking gaiety, from arrogance to self-pity. Half the trouble, Susan thought, was his extraordinary lack of confidence. He who had always been so assured was ill-at-ease in almost every way. This to Susan was the most dismaying thing of all. Now and then he had kissed her, very shyly and strangely. Another time—it was in the dromedary corridor, when she was saying goodnight to him on her way to bed—he had been suddenly rough with her, had pulled her clothes about, hurt her, pushed her against the wall. She was bewildered and distressed; but she made neither protest nor response, and as suddenly as he'd started the silly horseplay he stopped it, said "Hell, Sue, what the devil are we doing?" and stumped off to his room. She didn't sleep much that night and was tormented in turn by love and pity and fear. Towards morning she persuaded herself that it was an inescapable part of her 'job' to be hurt by him, and that love was a poor thing if it couldn't put up with a little incident like the one last night. She also recognised the frightening fact that if she wasn't careful she could hurt Tony, in his present state, far worse than he could hurt her. During all that long night she didn't ask herself whether she was in love with him. It was an article of her faith. She assumed it.

OFTEN feel it is LIKE A DREAM [wrote Janet on her wedding anniversary, July the thirty-first] *to see those 2 coming closer and closer and so much in lv. WHO was it said When the ½Gods go the Gods appear? So true of Susan!!! We now see little thnk Gd. of ½ Gd. Le M. tho he still writes to her occ. (odd I think seeing she is more or less Engaged but They are v. thick-skinned always) He even sent her present, record of D. Thomas poems for last Xmas She played it to us I thought incomprehensible and Coarse Do not trust Welsh any more than the other Race understand he is a bit of both But poor Ferdo still misses him*

*Shd. have thought he wd. have had much more in Common
with TONY hunting fshng shtg but apparently No.*

*OUR ANNIE !! Hardly believe it is 27 yrs since I married
my dear F. have never for 1 minute regretted it!!! This mng.
he had funny idea we might see Squirrel if we went same
way again (we saw it on our Annie 4 yrs ago!) so we Hung
About outside Huntsmans with Mrs. F peeking through
window at us as if she thought Wonder what they are after
Then Ben came out into gdn. said Do you want anything? F.
said No thank you He said Oh and went back into cott.
Am told he is Down from Oxford and about to do his Nat.
Service in Royal MARINES !!! wh. perhaps will knock
some of the socialistic Nonsense out of his head !? We did
not see Squirrel never really expected think they are all
Gone but F. will not admit it said Let's walk a little way into
the wood and keep our Eyes Open all the time O how I
wish we hadn't before we had gone 50 yds came upon most
HORRIBLE pitiful DISGUSTING sight shall never forget
it nor I think will F. quite spoiled our Annie . . .*

THE HALF-GROWN RABBIT crouched in the open between
two bracken clumps and did not move as Ferdo and Janet approached it. "There's a little chap that sits tight!" said Ferdo.
Then he walked right up to the rabbit and peered down at it.
There seemed to be something wrong with its head; but he was
short-sighted, though he obstinately refused to wear glasses other
than for reading. He had to bend low to look at the rabbit. Then
he saw that both its eyes, unnaturally extruded, were in the
process of sloughing away. About the suppuration there was a
blackness of flies.

He'd read about myxomatosis, of course, in the *Times*. Since it
came over from France last autumn it had been spreading steadily across England from east to west. But he hadn't met with it
until now, he hadn't known that it had arrived at Doddington.
It made him feel sick. Too late he told Janet not to look; she'd
actually touched the rabbit before she realised what was the
matter. Then Ferdo hit it on the head with his walking-stick and
they hurried on. But shortly they came upon some more dying
rabbits. One seemed to have had its eye pecked out. By a magpie,
perhaps? Janet thought the hideous socket would haunt her in

dreams. This part of the wood seemed to be full of moribund rabbits and unpleasantly dead ones, so they turned back and Ferdo with a shudder said: "We'll have a couple of jolly good gins before lunch and seeing as it's our Annie we'll put all this out of our minds." But when they got to Huntsman's Cottage they noticed two moribund rabbits sitting on the *lawn!* Ferdo said: "Better put 'em out of their misery" and went into the garden with his stick. Then it seemed to occur to him that perhaps you oughtn't even to put things out of their misery on other people's lawns without first asking, so he knocked at the door and Mrs. Fenton opened it. She came out and looked at the rabbits. Though they were blind they still nibbled the grass which they couldn't see, probably couldn't taste, and would certainly never digest, for a sort of deliquescence of their entrails was happening out of their hinder parts: this slime too was a-buzz with flies. Janet who had followed Ferdo into the garden sought to purge her horror with indignation. Some malevolent individual must have brought the germs over from France; wicked farmers were spreading it deliberately across the country; the man who invented myxomatosis ought to die slowly of cancer . . .

"*God* invented it," said Ferdo mildly. "Just as he invented the bugs which give us plague and smallpox and the common cold. Now go on home and I'll be there in a minute . . . *You* won't want to watch, Mrs. Fenton, I'm quite sure . . ."

As it happened Ferdo was very expert at killing rabbits because in the days when he used to be keen on shooting he had been at pains to learn how to despatch wounded things quickly and humanely. It was a matter of seconds to break the necks of these two, which were perhaps scarcely aware of being alive before Ferdo killed them. He carried them out of the garden and threw them into the bracken on the other side of the drive. Then he wiped his hands upon a cool green frond.

W H E N   H E   H A D   G O N E Mrs. Fenton thought about Janet's outburst, and about the rabbits, and in her determinedly honest way about herself.

Her Ladyship, she thought (using the term ironically in her mind) had been quite as hysterical about these rabbits, wishing cancer upon whoever might be responsible for their sufferings, as

Trudy was when she got worked up about fox-hunting and wished cancer upon such people as Lady Seldon herself! Indeed they had much in common, Trudy and her Ladyship, though it would horrify both of them to think so. They displayed the same sort of frantic pity, they both loved animals in the same emotional, irrational way.

Mrs. Fenton looked into her own heart and perceived that by comparison she scarcely loved animals at all. The sick rabbits had distressed her because they were unclean; she hadn't felt very sorry for them, indeed in a way she had hated them as she hated disease and dirt, which were anti-social things.

Proceeding step by step along the path of self-analysis, she realised that she hated everything which seemed to her to be contrary to order and rationality. She agreed with Trudy about hunting, mainly because it was a relic of the old, bad world and had no place in the new, orderly, civilised one. It wasted time and effort that should be better used; it was irrational because it was purposeless; and whatever pleasure the hunters got from it was the wrong kind of pleasure, which probably did harm to them, making them insensitive, fascist-minded and even warlike. It was therefore anti-social, and she disapproved of it for that reason.

But *not* because she loved the fox! She loved foxes (which were anti-social animals anyhow) no more than she had loved those disgusting rabbits. She didn't like dogs or cats or her husband's beady-eyed racing pigeons. She didn't love animals at all. She often thought that she loved those six children of hers so much that she hadn't got more than the merest trickle of love left over, and that had to be shared between her husband and Humanity, which she was committed to loving in an intellectual way.

But she ached with love for Ben and Willum and Gloria and Carolyn and Adam and Eve, and she ached all the more because of that cruel inhibition which somehow debarred her from expressing it. Indeed, she confessed to herself, she was as unreasonably scared of anything 'emotional' as those silly Victorian women had been scared of mice. She drew her mental skirts about her at the least hint of it. So she was always deliberately offhand in her manner with the children, because she was so terrified that she might make a fool of herself, embarrass them, estrange them with any display of love.

Above all she must not breathe a word to them concerning what she most dreaded, their leaving home. She had lived with this fear for years and years; but until now it had seemed remote as death. All at once it was close upon her. Ben was going the day after tomorrow. No doubt he'd come back from time to time; but Mrs. Fenton knew in her heart that it was never the same again after they were fledged. They were welcome visitors, they didn't 'belong' any more.

Next it would be Willum's turn, then Carolyn's; Gloria would get married; and so one by one they would leave her, until the last of them went, and she would turn to Fenton and they would look into each other's eyes and see the truth there: that without the children they might as well have been strangers,—alone together they wouldn't know what to talk about, even her little thin trickle of conventional love would dry up then, and nothing but their long habitude would bind them; for without the children their relationship meant nothing at all.

> . . . *MRS. N who makes it her biz. to know all abt the Fentons says Carolyn plans to go out and teach pickaninnies (?) in Darkest Africa   Can well imagine her earnestly peering at map & encyclopedia in search of mst. backward and Benighted areas   Will be one less Fenton brat anyhow, and B. off today to join R. Marines !!*
>
> *Mrs. N. also says WILLUM (they still call him that) has got to stage of doing his Gynocology (?) How alarming I thought to be Delivered by those Hairy Hands like Esau's and for Baby's first glimpse of the World to be that scowling Vizage enough to turn milk sour !!! . . .*
>
> *Gallant Col D. has strike on his hands Saw him in Elmbury yestdy lkg. v. stern handsome Imperial he will not give an inch tho local paper Bolshie as usual all for the Workers Gloria F. in her column interviewed lorry driver with wife and 4 children got him to say how many hrs. he worked for £10.14.2 wk.   Does not know how lucky he is Mother's grooms WILLINGLY worked many more hrs. for 30 shillings . . .*
>
> *Bad THUNDERSTORM last wk TERRIFIED me as always and now Flood coming up again in cellar and F. as always ½ fascinated ½ frightened by it   Confessed to me he*

*thinks it may make whole house damp and cause DECAY
notice he does not mention DRY ROT just as some people
will say tumour growth etc anything except cancer . . .*

*Myx. (can never spell it) RAGING all over the estate &
upsets F. pr. dear Think nowadays he sees Decay everywhere . . .*

*Just heard Col. D's strike over   He gave all the strikers
24 hours notice they went back like Lambs shows what a
little Determination can do even in these days . . .*

*Mrs. N. says it is definitely decided Carolyn off to
CONGO !!!!   She'll finish up in the Pot says Adam mst.
agreeable amusing child   He and Eve (so pretty) quite unlike other F. brats.   He adores TONY worships him as Hero
trots along just like Spanl. at his heels & this pleases T who is
mst. good to him   He & S. have been teaching the child to
JUMP this wk. in paddock. Tony much better v. nearly his
OLD SELF again Has got himself small pied à terre London
(good for him to get back in SWIM) but spends most of his
time here*

*He & S. v. close I am sure but am slightly puzzled no offi-
cial Engagement nor word of it   Young people v. diff.
AUTRES TEMPS ETC!!!   Think it best not say anything to S.
tho sorely tempted . . .*

*1st cubbing Meet on THURS next 6 am HERE Egbert
says there are 2 BRACE foxes in Jubilee!   Adam F. has
asked if can come on dun pony   How funny Wonder what
Mrs. F. will think of it!!   T. & S. (both on foot) will look
after him and self on Trumpeter will keep an eye . . .*

J U B I L E E W O O D H A D some patches of thick and thorny undergrowth but was crisscrossed by a number of good rides ten or
fifteen yards wide; so while his hounds plunged whimpering and
yelping through the thickets, General Bouverie thundered up
and down these paths, apoplectic and maledictory. At least four
cubs were afoot, there was soon a confusion of fox-scent everywhere, and nearly two hours went by without a kill. The General
set great store upon his 'young entry' tasting blood at the beginning of the season, so he was getting very angry indeed when one
of the cubs ran out into a ride within a few yards of young Adam
on the dun. Wildly excited, Adam yelped rather like a foxhound,
and gave chase. The unwise foxcub with Adam galloping behind
it turned left-handed down one of the cross-rides and ran straight

into the mouths of a dozen hounds which happened to be trotting in the opposite direction. A minute or two later the General
arrived hell-for-leather with oaths and war-cries and toots upon
his horn, and discovered Adam on his pony in the midst of the
milling pack.

Then one of the Whips galloped up, the carcase of the fox was
pulled away from the hounds, the Whip cut off its brush and
handed it to the General, who called to Adam: "Come here, me
boy, I like to see a keen youngster." As if he were a barber with a
shaving-brush, he rubbed the bloody stump all over Adam's
cheeks and chin. Then in the manner of a bluff and a benevolent
uncle giving a handsome tip to a godson he pressed the wet rank
foxtail into Adam's ready hand. "Wish I was your age, me lad,
with a lifetime of sport before me!"

The sun was well up by now and it was getting hot. Half-fit
horses were lathered, and many of the hounds were lame:
"They're as full of your thorns," said the General to Susan
severely, "as if they were bloody pincushions." So he decided to
call it a day.

Adam rode home in triumph, at least as proud as Alexander or
Tamburlaine, carrying his brush and occasionally feeling the
blood on his face, and so transferring some of it to his forehead
and nose.

Back in the stable-yard, Tony said:

"He mustn't wipe it off until next time he goes to church?
That's the rule, isn't it, Sue?"

"No, it jolly well isn't; he's going to clean himself up before he
goes home."

"He doesn't want to. Do you, Adam?" Tony said.

Adam, who was unsaddling the dun, grinned and said:

"No, please, I'll keep it on like you said, till I go to church.
That mightn't be for ages!"

"Give me your handkerchief," said Susan with authority.

"No!"

"Then I'll use mine; *and* spit on it." She seized him and held
him by the scruff on his neck while she wiped his face clean.
"Another thing," she said. "You're not taking that brush home,
not until it's been dealt with."

"He gave it me," Adam protested.

"I'll get it mounted for you, then you can keep it always."

"Promise?"

"Yes, promise. Now rub your pony down, and turn him out in the field."

Between the stable-yard and the Manor Susan said:

"Tony, you *oaf!*"

Her indignation took him by surprise.

"*We* didn't wipe it off, when we were blooded!"

"We're different. What do you imagine his mother's reaction would be?"

"Jolly funny."

"I don't think it's funny to hurt people."

"Oh for God's sake," said Tony, "don't be such a bloody little *prig!*"

She didn't answer; but when they got to the Manor she ran up to her room and threw herself on her bed and wept. She hadn't cried since that time in the green lane with Ferdo, on the day when the news of the Imjin battle came through. Today, with nobody to watch her, she buried her face in the pillow and let herself go. Then she wiped her face with her handkerchief and got up. Looking in the glass, she saw that she'd blooded herself; and she looked such a foolish clown that within a moment or two she was able to laugh at herself again.

As she sat at her dressing-table, putting on a new face, she found herself thinking of Stephen. She hadn't seen him since he had said goodbye to her, casually, easily, in front of her father and mother: "What a bore, Sukie, to have to go back to town on your birthday"—and then a quick glance to tell her: "You and I know this is play-acting but we both know it's the best way." Since then he'd made ingenious excuses on two or three occasions when Ferdo had asked him down to stay; but he hadn't stopped writing to Susan—he was much too good-mannered for that— though he had slightly altered the manner of his letters, to make doubly sure that there was nothing which might embarrass her in them. In all he did he always had a care for her. Susan couldn't forget, she knew she'd never forget, his sensibility and courtesy and care; but she had learned now by the harsh logic of love— had learned with a shock and even with a sense of shame—that you don't fall in love with sensibility, and it isn't courtesy or a man's care for you that makes your whole body cry Yes! at his least look or touch.

Tony with the merest gesture could still do that whenever he wanted to. She knew that when she went downstairs and he said to her, as she was sure he would, "Sorry, Sue, for being such a so-and-so"—and when he grinned in his endearing apologetic way and put his hand on her arm, she would feel her body and her spirit leap together in ready and reckless response to him. Then it would be the same as it had been all these months since his homecoming, she'd be happy when he was happy, and wretched when he was wretched; and because he seemed all the time to be getting easier and more confident and more like his old self, perhaps with a bit of luck she would be happy for most of the time. He was going to stay at Doddington for another whole fortnight; and after that he wouldn't be very far away, because he'd enrolled as a student at the Royal Agricultural College, to learn about Estate Management.

"After all, I can't just loaf about, I've got to do *something*," he said.

Susan's mother had thought it was a wonderful idea . . .

NOT quite sure whether my brilliant notion or T's but PERFECT IDEAL SOLUTION while he is restless and missing the Army—and so v. useful LATER !!! if all goes well as I hope and pray . . .

Have not yet plucked up courage to talk to S. abt T. but LONG TO !   Ask myself what they are WAITING for !!! as T. v. well off in own right & now useful Army pension no need ever look for job   MUST CURB IMPATIENCE!! softly softly catchee monkey !! (F's naval expression).   But F. still v. cagey abt. whole affair   Said to him yestday How sensible of T. to go to RAC don't you think in circs. he shd.take special course in management of WOODLANDS ?? F (v. strange and obstinate) said Why ???   I said Well if you cannot see yr. nose in front of yr. face?!?!   Afraid I was IRRITABLE & X but suffer from hots & colds Ch. of Life cd. nt. explain to poor Ferdo.

His worries grew Apace last night during bad Equinoxial (??) gale one of the Crooked CHIMNEYS crashed terrible noise 2 a.m. thought H-bomb !!   Gt. damage roof tiles mess bricks everywhere now there will be more scaffolding ladders tea in kitchen etc. etc.   1st Consequence I am

*once again GODMOTHER because of this new trouble this
time it is child of nice man who fixes Tiles asked me today
reminds me has been with us Off & On 4 yrs   Builders Bill
came the other day   Went into F's Office as he calls it lkg.
for F cd. not help seeing it still on desk STILL UNOPENED
He is like that now He DARE NOT I find it mst. alarming . . .*

*MYX goes on, on warm muggy days SMELL everywhere
N.B. Order Christening Mug?   spoon?   find out if Gd.
son or Gd. dtr . . .*

T H E   R A B B I T S   R O T T E D   A N D   S T A N K , from Jubilee Wood
to Cuckoo Pen Meadow, from Seven Men's Tump to Elmbury
Back Lane. Because it was a long still autumn, the putrescence
hung upon the air. Ferdo had to give up walking in the woods
because of it. Whenever you went there you walked among the
dying. Once Ferdo stepped on something which squelched under
his foot. He thought it was one of those rabbits and shied away in
horror; but it turned out to be only a patch of evil-looking fungi,
greyish-white, corpse colour. They too stank where he had
bruised them.

This also was the season when the trees that were rotten with
fungus (and in well-conducted woodlands would have been cut
down long ago) glowed very faintly in the dark, like the sheeted
dead.

D E C A Y   A L L   R O U N D   H I M ; corruption in the beloved woods,
and the dear senescent house tumbling down about his ears! So it
seemed to Ferdo, and a growing awareness of invisible maligni-
ties preyed upon his mind, so that he sometimes caught himself
imagining pests which probably did not exist at all. Sitting up
late, muzzy from drink, alone in the silent sitting-room, he would
imagine he could hear the ticking of a death-watch beetle. Then
he would persuade himself that it was only a ticking in his mind,
and he would press his hands to his ears to see if this were so.
The test was inconclusive; and he would be thankful for that,
because he had suddenly realised that a death-watch beetle in the
mind might be worse than one in the furniture.

But surely the sound was due to neither, he would tell himself
then. It was caused by *mice*.

From this conclusion it was but a short step to imagining that there was a plague of mice. There had always been plenty of scuttlings and patterings to be heard after dark in the Manor. Now Ferdo during the midnight silences would hold his breath and listen to the pad of tiny feet, the thutter of a tail.

He told Janet that he was sure there was an infestation of mice, and he went to Elmbury specially to buy some traps for them. He set these in all the likeliest places, but perhaps he set them clumsily, for he had little success, though the traps were often sprung in the morning.

IT WAS RIGHT AT THE CLOSE OF that season of dismal decay, it was at the very back end of the year, that Ferdo learned of a betrayal. Tom Taynton had got planning permission to build fifty houses on Honeysett Farm.

He could hardly believe it at first; because Tom Taynton when he bought the place had sworn that he only wanted to own the farm so that he could improve it, spend money on it, make it more productive; he had solemnly promised that he would not part with one acre of it as long as he lived.

But the report in the *Elmbury Intelligencer* was true, of course; and soon Mrs. Northover, piecing together scraps of village gossip, had the whole story and told it to Janet. It had been Daglingworth who had secretly put up the money for Tom Taynton to buy his farm; now he and Tom Taynton had joined forces with a go-ahead builder in Elmbury and had formed a limited company to 'develop' some of the land. They'd applied for only fifty 'good-class' houses to start with; they talked of trying to get permission for fifty 'superior bungalows' later on. The site was near the north-west corner of the Doddington woodlands, not very far from the field where Daglingworth had wanted to open up a new gravel-pit. Ferdo's objection to the gravel-pit had been that 'it would alter the whole character of Doddington village': but what would fifty or a hundred houses do to Doddington now? Daglingworth could not possibly have taken a neater revenge.

No wonder Tom Taynton could afford to own racehorses! The value of the farm as building land must be ten times as much as he'd paid Ferdo for it. Susan remembered how secret her father had been about the sale; she realised that he had sold it in panic, without even consulting Janet, when he got that enormous estimate for the cost of the repairs. Watching her parents now, in the shocked days just after they learned of the betrayal, Susan noticed one thing particularly. Her mother had not a single word of blame for what Ferdo had done, and she never so much as hinted that she realised the extent of his folly. It occurred to Susan that over big matters or small she had never heard either Janet or Ferdo say or imply 'I told you so,' one to the other. When things went wrong, there were no recriminations between them; they always came closer in misfortune, and it seemed to Susan now that they clung to each other defensively, having no other comfort, and being afraid.

In the week before Christmas, riding Nightshade along Elmbury Back Lane, Susan encountered a huge mechanical digger with upraised neck as long as the neck of a Brontosaurus and since the fool who was driving it wouldn't even slow down, Nightshade whipped round and bolted for fifty yards before Susan could stop her. At last she turned her off the lane into a gateway, and waited there until the great machine had gone by. It was obviously on its way to Honeysett Farm; and next morning, when she rode across the Park to have a look, Susan watched it alternately dipping and raising its giraffe's neck that had a big blunt head at the end of it; now and then the snout would bury itself in the ground and nose its way along there, and then the thing made Susan think of some fearful monster that was grazing upon the very entrails of the earth. Slowly the head was lifted again, and it spewed out a mouthful that might have weighed half a ton.

> *... WITH all these Troubles thank Heaven dear T. coming for Xmas so lkg. fwd. to it   Last yr. it was le M.!!!   T. & S. bless them our 1 HOPE & joy.*
>
> *Fear no chance of help in house over whole hol. time S. says Rmary now wkg. in some Elmbury office permanently cleaner or something & Mrs. F. once again not available while her* JEUNESSE DORÉE *home   Met that Ben now R.M. but in civvies quite the GENT   He was v. polite sure of himself said Pse. remember me to SUSAN !!!   Suppose in*

WORLD TODAY he can call her Susan but made me
ENRAGÉ *!!   Cannot help it—Ch. of L.*
     Must count blessings Life without Mrs. F. at least free
from ARGUMENTS wh. make me lose temper   Composed
in Idle Moment list of HATEFUL things wh. she INFURI-
ATINGLY approves of—
          Psychiatry (??)   wholemeal bread raw carrots   car-
          bolic   kibbutz in Israel (what she reads of them!)
          Bertrand Russell (only Lord she likes!!) Square danc-
          ing   pacifism   Nehru   League Against Cruel Sports
     (Mrs. N. says TRUDY !   coming to Fentons Xmas Look
out for BANNERS   Boxing Day Meet !!!)

¶ 3

CHRISTMAS AT THE MANOR was bedevilled by the flood
coming up in the cellar, and by other things.

The new influx had begun about a fortnight before Christmas
after a longish spell of winter rain. Ferdo with desperate determination announced that he was going to do something about it
this time, and called into consultation the builders, a water-
diviner and an official from the Rural District Council.

The latter arrived first. He thought there might be a leak from
the pipes somewhere, and proceeded to test the mains. But although he listened anxiously with a kind of stethoscope which he
pressed into the ground he could find nothing wrong with the
mains, no burst, no leak, no coronary thrombosis in those surging
arteries of civilisation. In a tone full of foreboding he said: "I
have known *underground rivers* gush up where they have never
been heard of before." Then he went gloomily away.

The builders, delighted to be given the opportunity of playing
with water, came down from the roof where they were still repairing the damage done by the fallen chimney, and dug deep
trenches across the flower-beds where Janet had planted her
favourite bulbs. They poked around with draining rods. Then
they gradually lost their enthusiasm, became wet and cold and
dispirited, and had to be sustained with tea. They went in and
out of the kitchen wearing muddy gumboots, and shook off the
mud onto the floor when they stamped to get their feet warm.

Lastly the water-diviner came with his wand of witch-hazel.

Ferdo's idea was that he might discover the ultimate source of the flood,—an underground spring or a well. He wore an air of abracadabra as he marched round and round the house in narrowing circles. The Y-shaped twig jerked and twitched between his fingers and he said that his arms were aching intolerably by reason of the Vibrations. He also spoke darkly of Magnetic Waves, and Earth Currents passing through his body. At last he came to the back-door, which was within a few yards of the cellar steps; he cast the hazel-twig from him as if it were a poisonous adder and announced that he was in close proximity to a large mass of water. Janet at the end of her tether said she could have told him so.

Meanwhile the flood rose steadily and apparently in defiance of all natural laws, so that by Christmas Eve it had reached the record depth of four feet nine inches. It had practically engulfed the rather primitive central heating arrangements, which occupied an underground space, off the main cellar, and in panic lest it should ruin them for ever Ferdo sent urgently for the Fire Brigade and a pump. The firemen, having set their pump to work, had nothing to do except drink the cases of bottled beer which Ferdo had put at their disposal because it was Christmas Eve. They became slightly drunk, and wandered aimlessly about the back-premises in their shiny black sea-boots, dripping everywhere. Swelling and pulsating hoses like a nest of angry pythons lay about the passages near the kitchen. One of these sprang a leak and sent a spurt of water shooting up to the ceiling, whence it brought down a large lump of plaster. Then the pump went wrong. It would take two or three hours to repair it. A valve would have to be fetched from somewhere far away. The firemen, who had enjoyed themselves, announced that they would come back on Christmas morning. Nor could they be dissuaded. It's all right, your Leddyship, don't you worry, you can rely on us, we won't let you down. Got to be on duty Christmas, see, the kids are always liable to set their Christmas trees on fire. Public servants, us. There'll be somebody in charge at the Station, and he'll ring through to us here if there's an alarm. We won't let a little thing like this spoil your Christmas Day, our Leddyship We'll be back in the morning and we'll have you dry's a bone in no time . . .

CHRISTMAS DAY GOT OFF TO a bad start. Tony had bought himself two dogs, a frenetic red setter and a slobbery spaniel, and Janet because she'd do anything to please Tony had welcomed them as Christmas guests. Of course they started chasing Ophelia, so that Susan had to make a bargain with Tony, that she would shut the Siamese up at certain times of the day if he would keep the dogs confined at others. But after breakfast on Christmas morning Tony forgot about this. He let out the dogs while Ophelia was still free. Ferdo and Susan as it happened had gone down to the cellar to inspect the flood, and had left the door open at the top of the cellar steps. Ophelia with the dogs in hot pursuit tore down the steps for refuge, but knew nothing about the flood, and plunging in would have suffered the fate of her namesake if Susan hadn't leapt in after her. The water was icy-cold and when Susan went up to change she found that it had left a brownish stain, like that of cold tea, all over the skirt of her new dress.

THE FIREMEN CAME BACK at ten o'clock and because it was Christmas Day Ferdo gave them sloe gin, which put them in the right mood to make the maximum mess. The unvanquished water had returned during the night and was already three feet deep, but this did not discourage them. They pumped for half an hour and then the nozzle of the pump became choked with (they thought) small fragments of coke from the heap in the central heating alcove, the top of which now showed like the peak of Mount Ararat above Noah's Flood. The firemen took the nozzle to pieces without hurry, while Ferdo, Janet and Susan went to church. They were still there when the family returned; so they had to be given roast turkey and Christmas pudding in the kitchen and later, when Ferdo had succumbed to the festive spirit, he gave them each a glass of port. Susan and Tony pulled crackers with them. They wore paper hats.

At three o'clock they resumed pumping and, for a short time, while the effects of the drink lasted, used buckets as well. It was clear that they preferred floods to fires; they splashed about in the cellar with the innocent delight of children in a paddling-pool. Soon, however, lethargy overtook them, boredom, and then a sombre despair. The senior fireman, wearing a paper crown, stood at the top of the steps and declared to no one in particular: *Water is a very funny thing.* His second-in-command came up the steps with an overfull bucket, tripped and slopped it all over the passage, and said: "My mate's right, your Leddyship: once it's learned the way in, bricks and martar won't never keep it out." The third fireman, from the bottom of the steps, pointed out that the flood was already rising again. Suddenly and simultaneously they all lost interest in the problem. They took their tips and left.

FOUR O'CLOCK, AS ALWAYS AT CHRISTMAS, was the very nadir of the day.

Ferdo during the last week had been bringing his wine up from the cellar out of the way of the flood; having the bottles handy induced him to drink more; and certainly both he and Tony had drunk too much claret at Christmas dinner. They had now gone up to their rooms, where doubtless they slept and snored. Janet, to punish herself for overeating, had gone out in the rain for 'a good energetic walk' with the two dogs. Susan alone in the sitting-room curled herself up in her favourite window-seat and read *The Collected Poems of W. B. Yeats* which Stephen had sent her. Just the same old Stephen!—but this time he hadn't written any special scrawled message on the flyleaf: only *'Sukie with love from Stephen'*—even the handwriting was sedate! In matters of feeling—in terms of a personal relationship —he had an extraordinary instinct for doing what was exactly right. That was why Susan had always felt so easy and so safe with him. Suddenly she caught herself almost *resenting* him be- cause his civilised and sensitive attitude to life, which stayed in her mind as a standard or yardstick of judgement, seemed so often to imply a criticism of Tony, with whom however much she loved him she knew she would never feel very easy or safe.

She ruthlessly put down the treason in her mind, and read "Byzantium," not for the first time; as ever it set her wits in a glorious whirl, until she was brought back to earth by the two dogs, wet as wet blankets and rank with the peculiar wet-dog smell. Their paws left muddy marks all over her skirt and she went upstairs to change her dress for the second time that day.

Janet taking off her gumboots in the hall called out:

"Are those two men of ours still sleeping? Let's have tea together. I'll poke up the fire—come down quick and make some
toast."

SUSAN WITH HER LONG TOASTING-FORK sat before the
big open fireplace where you could burn logs more than three
feet long. They lay on a bed of soft white wood-ash which from
time to time was collected up in a bucket and handed over to
Fenton to make his tomatoes or his potatoes grow. The fire got so
hot that you could do a slice of toast in less than a minute. It had
already become a custom for Susan to do the toasting at tea.
More and more her parents lived by custom. On Sundays and
special occasions they always had crumpets instead of toast and
argued about whether they were more correctly called pikelets.
It was very extraordinary that Ferdo always forgot that he had
started this argument a dozen times before.

"Been reading?" said Janet, with a nod towards the book on
the window seat. She knew that it was from Stephen and that it
was poetry, and for both reasons disapproved.

"Yes. A poem called 'Byzantium.' "

"Would I like it?"

"No, Mummy, I don't think it would be quite your cup of
tea."

Janet changed the subject.

"How *exciting* that Tony's asked you to go to London on New
Year's Eve! What'll you do, I wonder?"

"Have dinner and go to a show."

"You must ring up Aunt Kitty and beg a bed from her and ask
her to let you have a latchkey."

"Yes, I'll do it tonight. Ow." Susan burned her fingers turning
the toast on the fork. "Did you have a good walk, Mummy?"

" 'M-yes," said Janet doubtfully. "It's a bit depressing in the
woods. Most of the time I had to keep the dogs on their leads
because of the rabbits. Still dying. And the woods look—
unkempt, somehow. We really need a couple of foresters. Egbert
can't do it all. There's a new tree down across the main ride in
Jubilee."

"I know. It's just right for jumping," said Susan.

"And the gate at the top of Jubilee won't open *or* shut, I had to climb it and then go back and lift the dogs over . . . Oh, and I came back by the Otter Pool. There's a bit of the wall down, frost or wind or something."

"Not the wall where the apricots are?"

"Yes. About five yards of it." After a pause Janet went on: "Everything everywhere seems to want doing, all at once. Daddy's awfully worried, pet. He and I often wonder what'll become of Doddington when we're gone."

"Catch, Mummy!" said Susan, and tossed her a piece of toast. "Butter it yourself." She put down the toasting-fork and swung herself round so that she faced her mother. "Yes. I do know. I see it happening. Everything's getting worse and worse. *What are we going to do about it?*"

"Well!" said Janet, smiling at her brightly. "That's rather up to you two, isn't it?"

"Up to——?"

"You and Tony. He's got all Uncle Willie's money. If you and Tony—" said Janet rather breathlessly. She saw Susan's expression: bewildered, questioning, a shade indignant? "If only——" She began again, but Susan was still gazing at her with those steady brown eyes which long, long ago used to surprise Janet by reason of their contrast with the honey-coloured hair. Janet broke off, and muttered something about "Marmite or Gentleman's Relish on the toast?" Susan thoughtfully speared a fresh slice of bread on the toasting-fork and turned once more to the fire. Janet couldn't tell whether she was blushing or whether it was a reflection of the flames.

> *COULD have bitten my TONGUE off !!!!   I shd. never have put it like that   Know she is v. independent obstinate & altho has no truck (I hope & believe) with much modern NONSENSE inclined to QUESTION many things wh. one has always accepted such things as social DEGREES Xtian rules of marriage even the CREED in Ch !!!   Sometimes feel as if I was at INQUISITION when she lks. at me in that way But this must be COMMON EXPERIENCE of mothers One asks Did I really bring into world this beautiful clever but so unlike myself dtr.??!!*

*NEW YRS. EVE in LOND. v. significant ??   T. must
have something UP HIS SLEEVE? will ask her then?   Cannot think otherwise If so wonderful auspicious bgng. to
1955 & end of our worst worries I hope & pray . . .*

¶ 4

THE BOXING DAY MEET always held up the traffic for about
half a mile on each side of Elmbury Cross. In this respect it was a
ritual rather like the two minutes' silence on Armistice Day, only
it went on much longer. Two countrified bobbies by their mere
presence lent tacit authority to the hold-up; and General
Bouverie himself kept at bay any impatient lorry drivers or
thrusting motor-cyclists who might seek to force their way
through the crowd. Urging his horse towards them at the canter,
he would hold up his hand, crying out in a great voice: "Hounds,
gentlemen, hounds!"

If this didn't work he would blast them to blazes with his
weird, unique and fantastical oaths, some of which were simply
terrifying.

Stephen, who had once been at the receiving-end when the
General let fly, used to say that he and others like him represented the streak of madness in our national character; and then
getting on his hobbyhorse he would propound the notion that a
little madness, and a large toleration, were valuable and necessary ingredients in the make-up of a nation,—

"By God, Sukie, look at Sweden. All sanity and suicide!"

Dear Stephen, she thought, and damn him for intruding into
her mind so insistently.

The General was pretty good-humoured this morning. 'An old
bear in a scarlet pelt,' he merely growled when he caught sight of
Trudy bearing her solitary banner on behalf of the League
Against Cruel Sports. He'd threatened to horsewhip anybody of
that persuasion who tried to interfere, as he put it, at his Meets;
but when he made that threat he had imagined that the demon-
strators would be long-haired young men, bearded, arty types, or
pasty-faced pansies like Oscar Wilde,—the sort whom in any case
he would have liked to horsewhip. In the midst of his madness,
however, he retained certain precepts of ancient chivalry, one of

which was that 'A gentleman never hits a woman' and another, 'He should always take his hat off when he encounters a lady even if she isn't a real lady in his sense of the word.' So when Trudy advanced towards him with her banner, and began to address him in terms of pleading and rebuke, he raised his hunting-cap politely, which surprised her so much that she forgot her brief altogether.

"Bellman, Barmaid, Bosphorus!" Embarrassed by Trudy's proximity, he loudly rated some hounds which were fraternising with the spectators. He tootled his horn; and a photographer for the *Elmbury Intelligencer* got a head and shoulders view of him with cheeks blown out and dewlaps distended, immediately above Trudy's banner which said CIVILISED PEOPLE KNOW HUNTING IS SAVAGE SURVIVAL FROM BARBARIC PAST.

Susan saw Gloria standing beside the photographer. No doubt she'd have something to say about the Meet in her gossip column next Saturday. As the hounds moved off down the street Susan waved to her and grinned; she had a sort of half-grin in return, which pleased her, because it suggested that Gloria was getting over her bitterness about whatever happened on Coronation Day.

As she rode past Trudy, Susan said: "Hello!" But Trudy pretended not to hear and turned away.

The dappled pack with thirty tails waving trotted down Elmbury High Street between the two rows of old houses which leaned towards each other as if they were whispering gossips. Old folk waved from windows, shopkeepers came to their doors, children ran along beside the hounds and the horses. Elmbury was all a-buzz—the Boxing Day Meet, the Christmas Cattle Market, the October Mop Fair and now and then a Parliamentary Election were the only occasions which seemed to stir the spirit of the quaint old town.

Hoofs on tarmac clattered loud in the narrow space between the houses. The General took off his cap so often to the ladies who waved to him that he looked from the distance like a clockwork toy, and even if you were close the sound of his *sotto-voce* swearing was a bit like the whirring of internal wheels.

OUT OF THE TOWN and over the beautiful bridge which King John used to ride over when he went a-hunting here seven

hundred and fifty years ago. Through the Council Estate called
New Town, where the kids and the housewives and the still-un-
shaven Boxing Day husbands rushed forth to see the raree-show,
and only a few grumpy or envious ones who could pronounce the
word 'anachronism' muttered their disapproval to neighbours
over garden-gates. And so into the green and open country, and
the first draw, which was a long osier-bed with alders and old,
leaning willows, that filled the space along the river bank between the point where Doddington woods ended and the point
where Elmbury's Council House civilisation began.

It was a mild sou'westerly morning, with a little rain in the
wind. Janet, at Susan's side on Trumpeter, said: "If we find a
good fox today we shall go like hell I think." She always looked
about ten years younger when she was on horseback. "Egbert said
he thought there might be an old dog-fox in one of these
willows . . ."

They reined up and listened to the small dubious whimpering
of hounds that twitched their nostrils at a mixture of smells—
otter and badger maybe, as well as some stale tang of fox?

Susan waved to Tony, who was in the Land Rover with Sandra
and had pulled up at the entrance to the lane. It was silly of her
to be jealous, because this had come about in a perfectly natural
way. Sandra had looked in for a drink on Christmas Eve and had
mentioned that she wouldn't be hunting on Boxing Day because
her horse was lame. Tony had said: "Well, I shan't be riding
because *I'm* lame, so what about us following on four wheels?"
Ferdo didn't want to go, so Tony asked if he could take the Land
Rover; and of course Janet said yes. But this was awkward in a
way, because as a rule on Boxing Day Ferdo had taken Egbert
and Jack Northover along with him, to 'have a look at the
hounds.' It was a day out for them and they looked forward to it.
Yet somehow Susan hadn't liked to explain this to Tony: she
hadn't liked to ask him to take them in the back of the Land
Rover just in case—she knew she was being absurd—just in case
he had looked disappointed, she supposed!

So Egbert and Jack had missed their Boxing Day fun, and now
Susan was feeling a fool, for being jealous of Sandra.

Then, suddenly, the pack was in full cry; that old fox had
probably jumped out of his willow-tree right in front of them:
they were out of the osier-bed and streaking across the fields; and

Susan forgot all about her little jealousy as she settled down to gallop.

They ran hard, as Janet had said they would,—six miles as the fox went, four and a bit as the crows flew, to a furzey waste on the very edge of the General's hunting-country, called Brockeridge. The fox took refuge there in a sort of catacombs of badger-earths; and because it was a rocky place, that had once been a quarry, the General decided not to try to dig him out.

Meanwhile the rain had stopped, the sky had cleared, and the wind which had been backing steadily all morning swung right round and blew hard from the opposite direction; so that a second fox, which they found in some scrub that lay close by the common, ran the opposite way to his predecessor—towards Doddington instead of away from it. He was what the old hunting-journalists would have called a 'straightnecked un,' and he went as hard as he could across the flat river meadows towards the sanctuary of the distant woodland. The meadows were huge, the fences were tall, well-made ones, it was very like riding in a race. Susan as she galloped felt her kinship with those Regency bucks, her ancestors, their wild spirits like a high wind blowing through hers! She told herself exultantly that she'd rather be doing this, at this particular moment, than anything else she could think of in the world; and over a fence that had a wide ditch on the near side of it she made the firm decision, between take-off and landing, that she would enter her lovely Nightshade in the Ladies' Race at the Point to Point next March.

A mile short of Doddington, her mother had to pull up; Trumpeter had burst a little vessel in his nose, not a very serious matter in itself, but of course the blood pumped out of it when he was galloping. It mixed with foam from his mouth and blew over Janet so that when Susan last saw her she looked like the sort of blood-boltered monster which the League Against Cruel Sports doubtless imagined a hunting-woman to be.

The clamorous pack ran on. Over the main road—Susan jumped on to it and off it, and got a wave from a lorry-driver who'd pulled up to let the hounds go by. Into the trees where dusk was falling, full tilt along the leaf-strewn rides, out into the light again and over the Park, and so to Seven Men's Tump, where the elms stood black and gaunt against a sky that faded from primrose to a starling's-egg blue. They killed just short of the Tump, and Susan was one of a dozen or so who saw the stretched-out pack, ghost-hounds in the twilight, close up together suddenly and rearrange themselves into a swirling mêlée on the slope of the hill.

With Nightshade lathered and blown, and the wind still backing into north-east and growing colder every minute, Susan didn't hang around after the kill. She shouted goodnight to the Master—not that he could hear her amid the baying of his hounds—and turned for home. As she trotted down the slope she caught a glimpse of the Land Rover going towards the Tump up the wet and winding lane: Tony and Sandra determined to be in at the kill!

When she got back to the stables, and Jack Northover ran out to meet her, eager to hear every detail of the day, her conscience pricked her and she wished she'd asked Tony to take Jack and Egbert in the back of the Landy—surely he wouldn't have minded, why on earth had she allowed herself to be influenced by that foolish, jealous doubt?

Poor Jack, she felt quite miserable as she told him what a wonderful day they'd had, while he rubbed down Nightshade with a wisp of hay.

But the jealousy came slyly creeping back into her mind when she got to the Manor, because Tony wasn't back yet, although it must be more than an hour since the kill. She went up to change, but instead of lying in the bath and letting the hot water soak her tiredness away she was out in a couple of minutes, had dried herself in another two, and was in such a hurry to get dressed and see if Tony was home that her agitated fingers could hardly do up the hooks and eyes at the back of her bra!

She ran all the way down to the sitting-room where the ash-logs were burning bright, and Ferdo and Janet because it was Boxing Day were having crumpets, and Ferdo was looking for an opportunity to start the old absurd argument,—

"Have a crumpet, Susan: or a pikelet, as your Mother's Mama would always ridiculously say" . . .

"Isn't Tony back yet?" Susan breathlessly said: and then she wished she hadn't, for she heard the front-door creaking and wailing and his footsteps in the hall. Foolish jealousy! Susan was thoroughly ashamed of herself.

"Sorry I'm late, Cousin Janet . . . Sorry, Sue love, but I took Sandra home and had a cup of tea there."

"Have a pikelet all the same." Susan deliberately restarted the argument, just to please her father. She was so happy Tony was back and so contrite about her silly doubts that she wanted to please everybody. She felt like Ophelia, who in the warmth of the ash-logs went round rubbing against everybody's legs in turn.

⁋ 5

TRUDY HAD GOT A HEADACHE and had gone to lie down. Mrs. Fenton knew that it was a psychological headache, due to her getting worked up about the hunt. Ever since she came back from the Meet with her absurd banner she'd been restless and distraught. This afternoon she said she felt shut in, she couldn't breathe, she must go for a walk, fill her lungs with what she called God's fresh air. She had come back in a worse state still, because she'd heard thundering hoofs and the horn blowing and the hounds not far away making a funny noise as if they'd killed something. She took three aspirins and went up to her room.

Mrs. Fenton didn't really like Trudy and she knew why: it was for the despicable reason that she aroused too much of her pity. Long ago they'd been school-teachers at the same Bermondsey school. Trudy had been pitiful because she was always falling in love with the wrong sort of men and looking as if she wanted to eat them which frightened them to death. Mrs. Fenton had been sorry for her, and had taken her to the pictures when she was especially distressed, and Trudy had been so pitifully grateful that Mrs. Fenton began to dislike her, hated herself for disliking her, and felt she had to ask her to tea to make up for it . . . Later on she'd been sorry for her again when what little looks poor Trudy possessed had faded, though she still wanted the young men; and now she was sorry for her because she lived wretchedly in a bedsitting-room in Brixton with no more company than a canary and a gas-fire, and because every few weeks she said she was going to commit suicide but never did. So she had her to stay at holiday seasons, canary and all.

She realised that Trudy has thrown herself into this Anti-

Blood Sports campaign because she wanted to be a martyr. It was her only hope of fleeting happiness, really, if she could suffer some semblance of a martyrdom on behalf of what she thought of as poor defenceless creatures; though surely there was no more defenceless creature in the world than herself. Mrs. Fenton could recognise the symptoms, because in the past she had often felt the urge to martyrdom too.

She was getting over that, thank goodness; but then she had a whole family to love, Trudy had nothing but that one drooping bird.

Pitying her, resenting her, Mrs. Fenton went into the kitchen to make her a good strong cup of tea.

THE CHILDREN, LEFT TO THEMSELVES, huddled among the remains of Christmas in the narrow front-room. Carolyn was filling in forms about yellow fever inoculations and such like; she was off to Africa early in the New Year. Adam and Eve were trying ineffectually to deceive each other with conjuring tricks. Ben looking simply enormous lounged on the floor and read a book. Willum also sat on the floor, with one arm round Gloria's shoulders; he'd always seemed specially fond of her and in a way *protective,* since the occasion when she ran away from home. Very few people knew the truth about her running away; Adam and Eve and even Carolyn believed she'd gone on a hitch-hiking holiday to Ireland. But Ben knew that she'd gone to Birmingham to see Willum, and that she'd gone because she was frightened to death. He still didn't know and he wasn't going to ask whether she'd been frightened of having a baby or having a disease. Whatever it was, Willum had fixed it, and nowadays he and Gloria were closer than any other couple of Fentons, and it was rather nice, Ben thought, to see old Willum like some great gentle grizzly bear with his arm round Gloria as if he'd defend her, come the three corners of the world in arms; while she sat with the Shakespeare he had given her for Christmas open upon her knees.

"'TRUDY SAYS THEY KILLED A FOX. I wish I'd been there," Adam said.

" 'Our pilot,' " declaimed Gloria, " 'led us at a spanking pace from Stick in the Mud Coppice to Bullshit Bog, where he was pulled down in the open by our good bitches, and His Holy Water Sprinkler——' "

"What the *hell* are you talking about?" Willum growled.

"I got it straight out of the old files of the paper. Hunting reports. That's the way they used to write, honest. His Holy Water Sprinkler was his brush, as our sportin' Adam would call it, or as I prefer to say, his bloody tail. Which Adam got smeared all over his face in the course of aping his betters and going cubbin'. At least he *said* that's what was done to him," Gloria grinned wickedly. "We never saw his bloody visage."

"Susan wiped it off," said Adam.

"Susan." For the merest fraction of a second Gloria's eyes turned towards Ben; then quickly back to Adam again. "Susan. That's the terms we're on with them now."

"Otherwise," said Adam, quite unaware of hints and nuances, "I wouldn't have wiped it off until I went to church. And that would have been never."

"O.K.," said Gloria, "we all know why. The Rector likes to give all his choirboys friendly little pats on the bottom now and then. He's ambi-ambidextrous, that man."

"Wherever did you get that word from?" laughed Willum.

"The old reporter on my paper. He's drunk most of the time and his grey moustache is stained yellow with cigarette smoke but he's a bloody good journalist all the same; and he knows more limericks than anybody. Here's a new one." She reached across to Ben and pulled him close to her. He was thinking that for months Gloria had quite lost her sense of fun, hadn't recited any limericks at all. Now she was bubbling with mischief again, whatever her troubles had been they were surely over.

"Not for the kids," she said; but they were busy anyhow with their conjuring tricks. Carolyn seemed more interested in yellow fever. Gloria whispered to Willum and Ben:

> "*There was a young Fellow of Wadham*
> *Who asked for a ticket to Sodom.*
> *Said the clerk: We prefer*
> *Not to issue them, Sir.*
> *He said: Don't call me Sir, call me Modom.*"

Fenton came in, unwieldily ducking to avoid the low beam. He saw the three heads bent close together, and the Shakespeare open on the floor at Gloria's side, and he thought they were talking about booklearning, which he was afraid of though he deeply respected it. He tiptoed out.

Indeed Gloria did pick up her Shakespeare now, and she resumed her reading of *Henry the Fifth*. But not for long. Suddenly the fun bubbled up in her again and she burst out laughing.

"Ben?"

"Yes."

"You in your beastly battledress trousers. Here's Henry threatening the Governor of Harfleur: *'And the flesh'd soldier, rough and hard of heart, . . . With conscience wide as hell'*—that's you—*'mowing like grass Your fresh-fair virgins and your flowering infants.'* Rather gives the show away, doesn't it?"

"What show?"

"Chivalry of war and all that."

"So what?" smiled Ben.

"You let the whole side down when you joined the Royal Marines."

"I had to do my National Service, didn't I?"

"Not if you'd had the guts to tell 'em you were a conscientious objector."

"But I'm not."

"Then you b. well ought to be," said Gloria.

"All decent people are complete pacifists," pronounced Carolyn, looking up briefly from her yellow fever form.

"As for me," said Willum, "I'm quite *ashamed* to tell my friends I've got a brother who's a——"

"Oh are you?" said Ben, and they began to fight, rolling on the floor, as they'd done from time to time ever since they were small boys. It always looked as if Willum would win easily because of his huge shoulders and powerful bear-hugs, but in the end some unexpected wiriness in Ben's long body turned the odds in his favour.

"I haven't been square-bashing for a month for nothing!" he said, as he sat on Willum's chest. Gloria tackled him from behind and tried to pull him off, and Adam joined in on behalf of the

Royal Marines, tugging at Willum's long hair. During this mêlée Trudy came downstairs and wandered into the room. "Oh dear," she said vaguely. With four of them struggling on the floor there wasn't room anywhere for her to put her feet. Suddenly there was a sound—quite loud above the boys' heavy breathing—as if somebody were trying to find the knocker on the front-door: a sort of scrabbling noise. "Oh dear," said Trudy again, "whoever can it be? I'd better go and answer it." Still a bit vague in consequence of her sleep and her aspirins, she made her way out and they heard her open the front-door. But it seemed there wasn't anybody there. They felt the cold wind come in and blow round and round the little stuffy room, stirring the thick air as if it had been a pudding. They heard an owl hoot far away, and the sound of a cat, growing fainter, as it went along the drive. And then they heard Trudy scream.

Ben was the first to get out to her. He jumped off Willum's chest and was out of the room in one bound. Battle training! And he caught Trudy in his arms as she staggered back into the cottage, wildly sobbing. He took her hand, trying to comfort her, felt the stickiness of blood, and for a moment imagined that he was involved in something fantastically horrible, the huge improbability of murder. But Trudy kept crying hysterically:

"*It's on the door, on the door, on the* DOOR!" and he passed her shuddering little body, all bony lumps, on to Willum who now stood in the dorway behind him. So at last he could have a look at the door. It was starlight and he could just see something hanging there. He put his hand up to it and felt the blood; then as he angrily pulled it down he felt the soft ears and the wet open mouth with the little pin-sharp teeth and smelled the foxy smell.

¶ 6

FENTON MUST HAVE TOLD EGBERT; and Egbert bearing firewood on his shoulder so that he looked like Caliban met Janet in the hall just before she went up to change for dinner, laid down his logs and told her about the mask hung up at Huntsman's Cottage. She didn't take it very seriously—it was just a prank on the part of the Hunt Servants most likely; and as for that absurd Trudy, it served her right! Then it went out of Janet's mind altogether, and she didn't mention it to Ferdo until nearly the end of dinner. She only told him then because things weren't going very happily, she didn't know why. Susan was quite unlike herself, withdrawn and what Janet called distrait—Tony seemed put out too, so that she suspected a tiff between them. Ferdo had been drinking gin and French with Tony before dinner, and it was a drink which always had a bad effect upon him. The claret he'd had since made him muzzy and even a bit confused. Janet as always in desperate loyalty had to pretend that she didn't notice.

Out of all this discomposure and disquiet an awkward little silence was born; and Janet suddenly bethought herself of what Egbert had told her . . .

SUSAN HEARD WHAT HER MOTHER was saying but it didn't sink in immediately. She was once again miserable about Tony because he had told her casually, just before dinner, that he had to go up to London the day after tomorrow for a Regimental Dinner or Reunion or something. He hadn't said anything about this when he'd suggested a New Year's Eve party in town, and she had assumed, of course, that he'd be staying at Doddington until then and that they'd be driving up to town together. She'd looked forward to that. But the little disappointment wouldn't have mattered if only she hadn't started asking herself why he hadn't told her about the Regimental Dinner before. She didn't disbelieve him, exactly; but because she didn't understand she felt insecure, and she kept thinking that a Regimental Dinner wasn't the kind of engagement you would forget about and then recollect at the last moment. Then she blamed herself for being mistrustful and disloyal. She swept the doubt out of her mind with brisk indignation as if she were sweeping out an earwig or a cockroach with a broom. And then as soon as her back was turned it came back.

She was in the process of trying to sweep it out again when Janet told Ferdo about the fox's mask and Ferdo who'd been dopey and half-asleep sat up with a jerk and fairly snapped at Janet:

"What?"

Janet had to say it all over again. Then an extraordinary transformation happened to Ferdo. He wasn't just indignant; he was outraged; but instead of losing his temper he was absolutely calm, controlled, incisive. It was the same sort of sea-change which Susan had seen once before, when Janet had threatened to tear down one of Ben's Labour Party posters from a telegraph-pole in the drive and Ferdo had thundered at her "You'll do nothing of the kind." Once again Susan realised that she was getting a glimpse of her father as he'd been when he was in command of a warship, the captain on the bridge, giving orders, immensely formidable. He said:

"If that's true it was ill-mannered and uncouth, and whoever did it we're partly responsible, because we invite the hunt here, we go hunting ourselves, and we stand up for hunting against the Anti's." He looked sternly from Janet to Tony and from Tony to Susan, and exactly as if he were detailing an officer for a boarding-party or some such dangerous job he told Susan:

"You will go down to Huntsman's *straight away* and you will tell them that we don't know who did it but we are disgusted by it. That's an order. Put on an old coat or something. Don't look too dressed-up." And while Susan for a moment seemed to hesitate, simply because all this was so unexpected and she was still collecting her wits, Ferdo in the tone he'd have used to a Sub-Lieutenant said: "Go on, girl. Get on with it. *You'll* know how to handle it: you don't need me to tell you."

Amazed at his authority, she jumped up and hurried out of the room. She gave Tony a quick smile over her shoulder as she went through the door, and was again disconcerted because he didn't smile back. He looked preoccupied and ill at ease. She ran up to her bedroom, put on a coat, and tied a scarf over her head; then out into the cold windy night where all the dry dead oak-leaves were on the march like Lilliputian armies along the drive.

She had been so unhappy about Tony—about not knowing where she stood with him, about the insecurity of her love—that in a way she welcomed this embarrassing errand on which Ferdo had so sternly despatched her. It gave her something other than Tony to think about! But she felt very uncomfortable, and a little frightened too, when she knocked on the door of Huntsman's Cottage and heard the stirring within. She knew exactly

why her father had been so angry: he set great store by good
manners, indeed he often said he didn't care tuppence about
morals, it was manners that mattered. Especially you ought
to be courteous to people who had fewer advantages than
yourself; above all to your tenants and your servants—and
the Fentons were both. It had horrified Ferdo that the family
might in their eyes be associated with the outrage. Susan
wondered who was to blame for it. It might be the Hunt
Servants; it might, alas, be Jack Northover, who had a continuing feud with Fenton—and he could easily have got hold of
the mask, because Susan on her way from the stables had seen the
hound-van parked outside his cottage—the Whip who drove it
was a friend of his and had probably dropped in for tea . . .

THE DOOR OPENED AT LAST: Willum, glowering.
   "Could I have a word with your mother, please?"
   He let her in, and she went in front of him into the sitting
room. She was glad at any rate that Trudy wasn't there. Ben,
Carolyn, Gloria, Mrs. Fenton, Fenton. She remembered coming
here that Christmas Day, when they all seemed to think she was
slumming. But this was much worse. She could sense their hostility: Carolyn and Mrs. Fenton especially. Fenton, who had got up
when she came in, looked formidable only because he was so
ungainly. She knew he'd be on her side, so she addressed herself
to him:
   "We've heard what happened—about the fox's mask on your
door. None of us had anything to do with it, and I don't know
who did. But we think it was a beastly thing to do and my father
sent me over to tell you so."
   Her mouth was dry and her heart was thumping by the time
she'd finished her three sentences; and now there was one of
those awful silences, everybody embarrassed, none of the Fentons
knowing what to say. Still frightened, and extra-aware because
she was frightened, she realised that Fenton was silent simply
because he was tongue-tied, that Carolyn disliked her for ordinary envious reasons, nothing to do with this fox-mask business,
that Gloria was poised half-way between anger and warm-hearted
generosity, and if she jumped her way they could be friends for
ever—but Mrs. Fenton spoke first, and she did exactly what
Susan had known she would do, she responded to Susan's gesture

but spoiled her response with qualifications—and perhaps hated herself for doing so: resentment was built into her personality:

"Thank you for saying that. But we do think it was a horrible thing to do, and it doesn't help us to understand the kind of people who enjoy killing foxes. My friend is a nervous person and she was very upset."

Susan knew that this was well-meant, though as usual all Mrs. Fenton's inhibitions were on show; but she knew also that there was nothing she could usefully say after it, and her only course was to go. But how? She couldn't just turn and flee. What was she to say, then? 'Well, that's that, thank you for letting me say I was sorry, goodnight!' That would be ridiculous. So Susan simply stood where she was and met their eyes: and suddenly she realised that Ben was standing close behind her. As she turned round to him he said in the easiest way imaginable:

"None of us ever thought it was anything to do with you, we'd never think that."

Then he was holding the door open for her—she caught a glimpse of Gloria's grin, warm-hearted at last—she was at the front door, she was out in the cold wind with Ben at her side! It was the second exercise of authority she'd experienced tonight; and because it was so unexpected it seemed more marvellous than her father's: She'd always thought of Ben as diffident and shy. This was quite a new Ben, confidently in charge.

"Ordeal by Fenton family," he laughed. "You were very good. Thank you."

He went down the path with her and opened the gate.

Then he said, surprising her:

"May I walk back with you as far as the Manor?"

"Of course. You'll be frozen though, without a coat."

"I think I'm impervious to anything, after four months in the Marines."

"Do you like it?" she said.

"I didn't; but I'm beginning to."

The wind was a real nor'-easter now, with teeth. It was surging darkly through the wood and crackling a dead branch now and then. It fairly howled across the drive, and the old crab-apple-tree, half-way between Huntsman's and the courtyard gates, creaked and groaned. Susan said:

"You'd think it was about to come down; but I remember

listening to it creaking in the wind when I was about six—and
Egbert saying to me then: 'Tis like they say of a geeut, the more
her creaks the longer her hangs!"

It was an ungainly gibbous tree, that had hunched itself
against hundreds of gales as bad as this one and bent its back to
them in sullen defiance. The wind was shredding the clouds now,
and letting through a gleam or two of moonlight. The crab-tree
was like an old woodcut, stark and black against the pale stormy
sky.

"It rather reminds me of my father," laughed Ben, and Susan
saw what he meant exactly: that crotchety stubbornness!

"I do like your father," she said: and for one awful moment
feared he might think it patronising for her to say that. But she
needn't have worried. As he turned to her in the moonlight she
caught a glimpse of his ready smile.

"He likes you too." It occurred to Susan, How very odd this
conversation would seem to Mummy! and smiled to herself at the
thought. Meanwhile Ben had thoughtfully moved round to the
windward side of her, where he was a substantial bulwark against
the gale. He seemed to have grown both taller and broader since
she last saw him; and his stature matched his new confidence, she
sensed a toughness and strength in his mind as well as in his
body.

"By the way," he said suddenly, "I'm going to lunch with
Stephen next Friday."

"Stephen?" It was so unexpected that she had a moment of
confusion: she had been missing Stephen today. "You mean—in
London?"

"Yes."

"Oh . . . do you see him often?" But he must do, she thought, if
he speaks of him as Stephen.

"Not since I joined the Marines. But when I was at Oxford I
saw him quite a lot. He came down to talk to our Labour Club.
He was awfully good: half of us hadn't known there could be
civilised Tories. Then—you remember—he asked me up to town
to meet Aneurin Bevan."

"What did you think of him?"

"Nye Bevan? Oh, he was all I'd expected, and better, and
bigger. And how he can talk! You ought to have heard him and
Stephen together."

Susan could imagine it. She was suddenly a little forlorn, at the thought of all she was missing through the lack of Stephen's company. She had often felt lately that she'd give a lot to have her arm in his, walking through the woods, while Stephen let loose his ranging mind in pursuit of anything and everything.

"Please give him my love when you see him on Friday . . . Good Lord, that's New Year's Eve, isn't it? Look . . . I've just thought, I've got to go up to town that day; I could give you a lift." She'd thought of going by train, as Tony would be in town already; but she hated cold trains and lonely journeys. She could take the Land Rover and it would be fun to have Ben's company.

"What a bit of luck! . . . Oh, I'll look forward to that!" he said, making no bones about his pleasure, accepting his bit of luck with both hands.

"You'll have to put up with the Landy. The wind comes in everywhere. It'll be like a Commando Course in Norway." She was delighted that she'd thought of asking him; though she wasn't quite sure whether this was because she wanted to see more of him or because she wanted to hear more about Stephen. Perhaps a bit of both, she thought, and for the moment felt spirited and mischievous, though she knew that at the back of her mind there was a darkness of doubt, and she would soon be unhappy again. She had an odd premonition of that. She said:

"In case I don't see you before . . . I'll call for you nine o'clock on Friday. Wear *everything!* Goodnight, Ben."

"Goodnight, Susan."

He put out his hand, not to shake hers, but in a simple and endearing gesture, simply to touch. She recognised this and took it in both her hands. In an extraordinary way she had for a moment a sense of great companionship with him; and because of that imminent darkness of doubt she found this comforting. The part of her mind that concerned itself with wry jokes added Tony to her mother, as people who would be surprised at what was happening; and as a little act of defiance against her forthcoming miseries she said to herself: Serve Tony right. She knew that bravado wouldn't last. But meanwhile there was this comfort and companionship, and she squeezed Ben's hand, then quickly let it go, and as the wind whooshed all around her she ran through the courtyard gates.

❡ 7

SHE DECIDED NOT TO SAY ANYTHING to Tony or her mother; but she did tell Ferdo next day that she wanted to borrow the Land Rover and that she had offered Ben Fenton a lift to town. He said:

"I liked that lad when he came to lunch here. I've always had a hell of a lot of time for the Royal Marines." Then he gave her one of his conspiratorial grins—rare nowadays—from which she deduced that he guessed she hadn't told her mother and that he knew why: that it wasn't for any guilty or sinister reason, but simply to avoid the embarrassment which would be occasioned by her mother's thinking it was 'a bit odd' to be taking one's gardener's son to town. She grinned back at her father: 'Signal received and understood,' and knew that she had his agreement not to risk a silly argument with Janet.

She did feel a bit uncomfortable about not telling Tony; but she had discovered a small unexpected toughness in herself, and this was a private demonstration of her independence: tit-for-tat over the Regimental Dinner! However, she nearly relented, just before he left for town. It was a sparkling morning of frost, and he suggested taking the dogs for a walk before he set off in his car. They went across the top of the park and into Jubilee Wood, where the dogs galloped off after imaginary pheasants which generally turned out to be blackbirds, and Tony sat on a tree-stump to rest his leg.

"D'you know," he said, "I think it's getting a bit better; or I'm getting more used to it. I'm easier in my mind, anyhow. I was an awful mess when I came back from Korea." Watching his face, she saw the beginning of a dubious smile; and such, she knew, always preceded a confession. "I wasn't much good at being a prisoner, Sue."

"I don't suppose anybody is."

"Some were marvellous. I sort of—packed it in. I'm not bad in battles; but when I'm behind the wire I'm a bloody coward. Anyhow—thanks for all you've done to get me back to normal."

He got up and whistled to the dogs, which were scuffling

through drifts of dead leaves a hundred yards away. "What a morning! Good to be alive after all!" He glanced round at the tinselled bushes and the glades of frosted dead leaves glistening in the sun. He suddenly recollected an absurd little rhyme, and recited to her:

> " 'The two divinest things the world has got,
> A lovely woman in a rural spot.' "

Susan giggled:

"Where on earth did you get that from?"

"It's Coleridge, of all people." It always astonished her how much he had read, because she'd hardly ever seen him with a book other than a thriller! He didn't often talk about about books, either; but his reading must have been wide and various, because he knew so much about the by-ways of literature. This pleased her, and she was proud of him because although he did all the tough sporting things there was this other, hidden, surprising side.

And now something else was surprising her: the ready response of her urgent body as Tony on the spur of the moment, matching his actions to the rhyme, took her in his arms and kissed her and pressed her close to him. Apparently her response surprised Tony too. "You little devil!" he said; and then the dogs came galumphing back and jumping up with cold wet paws. Tony let her go and said:

"Goodness, I'd better think about getting to London."

WHEN HE HAD GONE she felt sad and lonely but she forgave him unreservedly about the Regimental Dinner and she told herself that anyhow it was only three days to New Year's Eve. But in no time disillusion overtook her, and it did so in a very ridiculous and treacherous way. She had gone up to do his room; they still had no help other than Mrs. Northover, and she was busy in the kitchen. When Susan had made the bed she happened to glance at the books on the bedside-table: an Agatha Christie, *Best Cricket Stories* and the *Oxford Dictionary of Quotations*. She idly picked it up and without really knowing why opened it at 'Coleridge, S.T. She hadn't expected *that* quotation to be there; but it was; and then it occurred to her to see if she could find the source of another unexpected quotation which Tony had trotted out the other day. She'd teased him about sitting up half the night and drinking too much with her father; and he'd promised he'd be good in future. "All for love!" he'd said, and he had quoted:

> " 'Did ever you hear of Captain Wattle?
> He was all for love and a little for the bottle.' "

She was sure she wouldn't find that one; but she looked up 'bottle' in the Index, and there it was:

a little for the b. 120b

She turned to page 120, and there was the quotation, from Charles Dibdin, 1745–1814.

Reluctantly she let her memory go searching for something else Tony had said. It went free-ranging way back, to the time at the Otter Pool before he went to Korea, and it hit upon something about 'flame-coloured taffeta,' something to do with a red dress she'd been wearing, her first proper evening dress, off-the-shoulder . . . She knew the phrase came from Shakespeare, but she didn't know which play. With horrible disloyalty she hunted for it in the Index, and it was from *Henry the Fourth:* 'A fair hot wench in flame-coloured taffeta.'

Damn! It was only a little thing, but she wished her eyes hadn't happened to light on that *Dictionary,* that she hadn't let herself be so mean and despicable as to go through the Index to see whether Tony really got his quotations from it. Surely if you were truly in love you wouldn't do a thing like that? So a little doubt crept into her mind again, and hard on the heels of that doubt came crowding half a dozen others—doubts about herself, remembering this morning when she'd have readily lain down on her back upon the cold leaves if he'd said 'Go'—hot wench, indeed, she thought ruefully! And doubts about marriage, if Tony ever asked her—she remembered what Janet had said, when they were talking about the ruin of the estate and whether it could be saved:

'That's rather up to you two, isn't it? . . . He's got all Uncle Willie's money. If you and Tony——'

Susan had been horrified. Now she completed the sentence in

her mind: "If you and Tony get married there'll be enough cash to put the Manor to rights and the woods in order. Tony's your father's heir anyhow, although he's only a second cousin; one day he'll be the Baronet and you'll be Lady Seldon, and you'll have a family, and so with luck there'll be Seldons at Doddington still, for ages and ages . . ."

That was the way her mother thought. But you had to be absolutely certain before you got married; you couldn't just sell yourself for the sake of an old house and a lot of old trees!

SUSAN still distrait and hardly spoke at lunch but perh. she is moping for T. Asked her what she wd. be wearing for NYY.E. she almost snapped at me, Mummy I haven't THOUGHT !! Sheer nonsense of course she MUST HAVE thought !!! prob WAS thinking at that v. moment!!! Hope she wears her apricot chiffon she looks so nice in it after all it is v. SPECIAL OCCASION !!! Feel more than ever T must be planning some BIG SURPRISE !!!! . . .

F. says he has great new idea re CELLAR plans install small electric PUMP he rang up Men are coming abt it tomorrow Seems it involves digging deep hole like WELL & some contrivance in hole makes pump pump when water rises?? but not v. clear in my mind abt it never have understood or TRUSTED electric things !!! Hope it does not cost EARTH our exes APPALING Woke up in night lay awake thinking (Do not know WHY !!!) abt Mummy's Will— Wish we had some of her ODD bequests now e.g. she left £1000 to build & maintain HORSE TROUGHS Must be DOZENS all over Warwickshire but now no horses to drink from them Wonder what has happened to them N. B. enquire . . .

This mng. SURVEYOR came re ROAD !! oh it comes nearer now Inevitable you do not think these things will EVER HAPPEN then they do & the shock is just as bad tho you have known they had to yet you somehow refused to believe it Darling F. I expect he mas frightened but he had NEVER OPENED THE LETTERS (County Council ones) S. found them all on his desk & he shd. have done all sorts of things filled in forms etc. made PROTESTS seen LAWYERS etc etc long ago SURVEYOR made me v. angry treating him MY FERDO as if FEEBLE MINDED PERSON I lost temper abt. BUREAUCRACY & we reached IMPASSE but

*then S. took charge and dealt with everything charming
capable CAPTIVATED the man Alas she cannot stop road
tho !! IT WILL COME straight thro woods like JUGGER-
NAUT . . .*

   *S. off tomorrow to town & GREAT Do with T   Will miss
her Always do Little silly things e.g. sitting by fire at teatime
watching her face lit by f. light as she makes toast Then
buttered toast with her & Ferdo it is 1 of those little pleasures
& if it does not happen 1 is put out As we get old we are
more & more concerned with ACCUSTOMED things F says
like animals at Zoo . . .*

   *Tonight S. has her HAIR in ROLLERS lkg. v. absurd
shorn sheep expression but Il faut souffrir pour être belle !!!
Insists on DRIVING up tomorrow cannot think why so
COLD in Landy but starting early will have time recover
Perh. her idea is will drive T. back on N.Y. Day & TELL US
can see it happening & F. opening champagne or am I so
foolish ??? Pictures in the fire ???!!!*

SUSAN SLEPT BADLY ON THE NIGHT before she went to
London, and her brain felt numb with tiredness and cold when
she called for Ben at nine o'clock in the morning. It was a grey
morning with flurries of snow in the wind. She blew the horn of
the Land Rover and caught a glimpse of pale faces like spectres
stirring behind the steamed-up windows. Ben hurried out with
his suitcase—his leave was nearly over, and he was going to catch
the night train back to Plymouth from London. Gloria followed
him, begging a lift into Elmbury. As soon as she'd settled down in
the front seat by Susan she started to chatter merrily. "Isn't it
bloody cold? Believe it or not, I'm wearing *purple* drawers. I kid
myself they're warmer. I found them in that funny old shop by
Elmbury Cross, you know, where they sell old-fashioned undies,
things like spencers and combinations, and corsets like the strait-
jackets they put loonies in . . ."

So she babbled on; and her warm heart warmed up the bitter
morning. When Susan stopped outside the premises of the
Elmbury Intelligencer, Gloria turned to her and whispered:

"I thought you were awfully brave, facing us all the other
night. Who did it, by the way? D'you know yet?"

Susan shook her head.

"No idea."

"Well, not to worry! We've all forgotten all about it," said Gloria, as she jumped out and ran into her office.

UPON THE COTSWOLDS the great fields were streaked with snow. The wind going from slope to slope with giant strides kicked up cascades of white spray. Susan spotted a hare couched right in the middle of a forty-acre piece, among the frosted yellow bents that shivered in the wind. She asked Ben:

"What do you call the fear of open spaces—some Greek word?"

"Agoraphobia."

She pointed to the hare.

"There's one that hasn't got it. But I have, a bit. I think I belong among the trees."

Indeed in her present mood of loneliness and uncertainty she hated these huge lonely hills; she was very glad of Ben's company —though he didn't talk much at first—and she was soon to be still more glad of it. At the point where the road climbed over the loneliest, coldest, windiest hilltop of all she had a puncture. The sigh of the wind found an echo in her spirit; and somehow the place seemed all the more horribly desolate because of the squashed rabbits, white-furred now with an encrustation of snow, which lay about the road. Myxomatosis had come to the Cotswolds later than to Doddington. Here the pandemic was at its height; Susan had noticed dead rabbits all the way for the last ten miles.

"They make you think about the H-bomb," said Ben, as he got out to deal with the puncture, "and what it would be like—a sort of myxomatosis of mankind."

Susan learned quite a lot about Ben while she was helping him change the wheel. Since Ferdo was responsible for the Land Rover, it wasn't surprising that most of the tools were either missing or hidden under piles of odds and ends. Stephen in this situation would have been quite helpless; Tony would have lost his temper and used all the four-letter words; but Ben tackled the job with lively interest and curosity, and every time he came up against some new difficulty, his mouth would twitch at the edges in that very faint smile of his, as if he found it rather fun trying to improvise a wheel-brace or make the jack work with the aid of a couple of flat stones off the wall.

He was lying on his back under the rear axle, pushing the jack into position, when Susan's thoughts, went back to the day when she first met him.

"D'you remember," she said, "letting down Colonel Daglingworth's tyre in our courtyard?"

"Yes, and it worked!" said Ben, as he crawled out and reached for the jack handle. "He stopped just outside our cottage, and tried to change the wheel. We were hidden in the garden, watching him. He couldn't make the jack work so he had to pump up the tyre. He got so puffed we thought he was going to have a seizure. We hoped he would."

"And now comes retribution!"

"If so it was worth it. You ought to have heard him grunt and wheeze!"

He went back to his task of changing the wheel, tackling it methodically with big capable hands. He didn't talk at all while he was doing this; but when the job was finished and they were on their way again he said thoughtfully:

"Yes, that was when I first met you, the day we came to Doddington, when I heard you running across the gravel I tried to hide under the car."

"I saw your feet and said, 'Come out' and you came. You looked very surprised," said Susan.

There was a pause while he seemed to be exploring his memory and examining with interest what he found there.

"I *was* surprised, I don't think I'd ever seen a girl in evening dress before: not close to. It was a red dress and your skirt went swish when you swung round. I was scared of you in a way."

Then he fell silent for a while. It was very different from driving with Stephen, whose thoughts went chasing wildly here and there, jumping obstacles, running in circles and tearing away at a tangent.—That was exciting, but Susan often had a job to keep up. With Ben there was no sense of hurry, and though she liked his talk she also liked his thoughtful silences. She found herself very much at ease with him; and when they stopped at a pub for a drink and a wash after the wheel-changing she made the agreeable discovery that his sense of humour was a good match for hers. She had always thought him to be rather serious, even grave; but she'd never watched him closely before. Now as they sat by the fire in the bar, talking casually of this and that, she had a chance to see what happened when she said something which amused him. It was as if she had set a light to a long slow fuse. First there was that little twitch of a smile; a pause, while he considered; then another flicker, another pause, until suddenly his whole face lit up with delighted merriment.

Susan enjoyed watching this process, especially as she now began to find out that although she and Ben were so different in most ways they seemed to look at the world from the same angle as it were: so that they recognised the same oddities, and sometimes when they glanced at each other quickly it was just like saying *Snap*.

So the rest of the journey went by in no time; and Susan was quite sorry when they got to Western Avenue—London lay just ahead, and so did her problems, her confusions, her doubts. Once again she was frightened—as she had been for most of last night —of this New Year's Eve and what it might bring.

With some help from Ben, who'd been there twice before, she found her way to Stephen's Club; but there was no room to park against the pavement, and she had to edge in as best she could with the rear half of the Land Rover sticking out into the street. Ben as he pulled his suitcase out of the back said with an eagerness which surprised her:

"Can I see you again, next time I come on leave?"

"Of course." She laughed: "I'm always at Doddington. When are you coming?"

"Depends if I have the luck to get an interview for a Commission. I might have a day or two then." A taxi was hooting as if it had never seen a Land Rover before and didn't think such things had any right to be in the West End of London. "Let him hoot," said Ben, with a calm which Susan hadn't expected. "There's room for him to get by. Stay here a minute, I'll try to find Stephen." He picked up his suitcase and dashed into the Club. Susan was uncomfortably aware that she was holding up one line of traffic; the taxi scraped past her, and its driver made faces as he went by.

At last Stephen, followed by Ben, came running out. She'd

hardly had time to feel apprehensive about seeing him again; now for a fraction of a second she was unreasonably afraid. Then, lean as ever, he squeezed himself between two cars parked almost nose to tail, put his head into the Land Rover and kissed her. She knew at once—though she couldn't have explained how she knew—that all was going to be well, that Stephen had come to terms with himself about her, from now on they could be easy together again. Immediately she had a great sense of comfort about this. Three or four taxis were hooting behind her now. She didn't care. "Dear Stephen!" she said. He was just as he'd always been, tense and excited and in a tremendous hurry to say a lot of things at once,—

"What a surprise, unexpected as a ghost orchis—You've never seen it again, I suppose? How's Ferdo . . . Hell, I wish I could ask you in, but it isn't the sort of place, women used to be allowed to sit down and wait for their husbands in the hall but some old Member put a stop to that, he told the Committee *It's the thin end of the wedge.*—Damn those taxis, SHUT UP, I swear I'll never tip a taxi-driver again."

Three or four of them were hooting in unison. Susan, beginning to panic, said: "Look, I'll have to go, I'm holding up everything," and started the engine. Stephen, still looking exactly as she had remembered him grinned and said characteristically:

"Go on then, you can't help it. That's life! It carries you along. Stopping forbidden . . . See you soon!"

"See you soon!" shouted Susan, waving him goodbye, and catching Ben's eye too as she did so. "See you soon!" she cried, to either or to both of them, and drove off into the confusing traffic, once more lonely and afraid.

¶ 8

THE WHITE-HAIRED OLD WAITER, repeating "Coffee for two and brandy for one," didn't need to be told which brandy. He looked at Tony with spaniel devotion and said: "Your usual, of course." Susan had noticed that he never called Tony 'Sir'; he said 'Mr. Tony.' When he'd gone off to fetch the coffee Tony said:

"The first time I ever came here was with my father. We were celebrating my getting a Commission and going into the Regiment. There was a hell of an air-raid and the candles blew sideways every time a bomb dropped close at hand. Funny the things that stick in your mind. The old waiter took no notice of the raid at all. I can remember him bringing my father's brandy. There was a frightful crump, and then the sound of glass breaking. But he just said 'Your usual, Sir.' "

"I suppose it was the same sort as *your* usual?" said Susan percipiently. Tony stretched across the table to light her cigarette. He went on:

"Yes, I'm awfully conservative. I go to my father's tailor and buy my hats from Mr. Locke as he did, and my shirts from where he bought his shirts, and have my hair cut at the same barber's and generally by the same chap who cut his. I like to go where I'm known. So I brought you here. I daresay there are more exciting places."

She shook her head.

"It's been quite perfect. In any case, I don't think I like exciting places, particularly."

"Sure you don't want to go on to a night club, and dance?"

"Not after this." She wasn't in a mood for dancing and smart people and a noisy band. She certainly didn't want anything else to drink; she was still feeling the effect of the cocktails she'd had at the very start of the evening—she'd accepted three big ones, because she was so nervous and on edge. Tony had taken her to the house of some friends of his who were giving a New Year's Eve party. There had been about twenty guests in a fairly small room and they all seemed to be talking about people she didn't know and plays she hadn't seen. She was introduced to a couple of young Guardees with very few manners, and a middle-aged Lord who seemed to be either drunk or dopey, and a couple of bitchy girls who were very well-dressed and made her feel gauche and dowdy. At her Aunt's she had dithered most of the afternoon about what to wear; for she'd been silly enough to bring two dresses, the apricot and a black one. In the end she decided on the apricot, put it on, thought it looked too young, too much like a sort of deb's coming-out dress, and changed into her very plain black one because Tony had once told her he liked it. But now she imagined that the bitchy girls were looking at her with faint amusement; and perhaps after all it wasn't smart enough for New Year's Eve in London. Edging away from them, she came once more into the orbit of the drunken Lord, who asked her if she was going to St. Moritz again this year. She replied that she'd never been to St. Moritz, and he said rather gloomily: "You can't be the person I thought you were then," and relapsed into silence.

She had been separated from Tony early on, and it was the kind of party at which, once you had become separated from a person, you had no earthly hope of rejoining him unless, Susan thought, you had wings and could do a vertical take-off. She began to wish heartily that she was back at Doddington. Then a woman of about forty, with close-cropped greying hair, came up and talked to her. She said: "I love that dress of yours, it's just right, you've got a marvellous figure and it fits you like a glove"; but this didn't give any comfort to Susan who had a preternatural horror of Lesbians and didn't like the way the woman was looking at her at all. Apparently the woman divined this and was hurt; she immediately took a fiendish revenge, adding, "The only thing is you want to be a bit careful that your bra strap doesn't show behind." Having done her worst she went away, and Susan for the rest of the party kept furtively putting a hand behind her back and feeling in the V of her dress to see what was happening there.

Tony, who was talking about racing to his host, who had ridden in two Grand Nationals, seemed in no hurry to leave; and in fact they didn't leave until nearly nine. By then Susan had a bit of a headache and a dry mouth, and a kind of dust-and-ashes feeling pervaded the whole of her spirit. But in the taxi Tony had told her that she looked smashing and that he was glad she was wearing the black dress, which suited her better than anything; and although reason primly reminded her that it was idiotic to let a casual compliment from a man who'd had at least half a dozen cocktails make such an awful lot of difference, she nevertheless sent reason packing, and happiness came welling back into her spirit like a warm and comforting flood, washing all the dust and ashes away.

Everything had gone right since then. It was like unwrapping a whole parcel of pleasant surprises to discover, one by one, the arrangements which Tony had made in order to please her. He'd booked a special table in a candlelit alcove; he'd ordered the meal beforehand, remembering what were her favourite things. One was lobster, another was *crêpes Suzette.* The delicious lobster was done *à l'Américaine,* in a way she'd never had before. When the old waiter and a younger one, bearing their necessary equipment, came to cook the *crêpes,* they wore such an air of serious concentration that they might have been a surgeon and an anaesthetist about to perform a difficult operation; but as soon as the wafer-thin pancakes took shape they at once became relaxed and confidential, the old man glanced at Tony as if to say, 'There you are, look what we've done for you, just the same as in your father's day!' and then he gave Susan a special sort of smile which seemed to assume that she had joined him in a conspiracy of affection for Tony. He said:

"*We* didn't expect to see him back again, did we, Miss, when we heard he'd been caught by those dreadful Chinese!"

''HALF PAST ELEVEN,'' said Tony when they had finished the coffee. If you really don't want a night club what about coming back to my flat and seeing the New Year in with me before I take you back to the Aunt's?"

Susan in her present mood didn't mind where she went so long as she could be alone with Tony. She had been dreading that he'd suggest meeting some of those friends of his whom she didn't like much and whose gossipy smart talk alarmed her; or that he'd want to go and have some more drinks in one of the many clubs he belonged to, where she would have to take a plunge into new company like a cold dive into a pool. So she nodded, "Yes, please!", and through the haze of cigarette-smoke saw Tony's boyish grin of pleasure which always melted her heart.

She was very happy now but with a sort of fragile happiness; she was frightened of breaking it—a little bit reluctant even to get up and leave this table with its close and comforting candle-light. She sat back and watched Tony while he caught the waiter's eye and paid his bill in a tactful, unostentatious way, so that she wouldn't be embarrassed by more than a glimpse of the five-pound note he put on the plate! She saw the young waiter, as he carried off the plate, stop to have a word with the old waiter, who smiled and then seemed to give a nod in her direction—in approval, perhaps, of Mr. Tony's young lady.' It occurred to Susan that she must be a little bit tight, or else very absurdly in love, if she was concerned to have the approbation of a waiter in this affair. She stood up, and for a moment the room swam about her. She'd had a couple of glasses of champagne on top of the cocktails, and she wasn't used to drinking. However, in no time the room became steady again, somebody was helping her on with her coat—"Happy New Year!" from the old waiter, from the young waiter, from the *maître d'hôtel* appearing suddenly from nowhere,—"Happy New Year" from the Commissionaire, who against all odds got Tony a taxi in two minutes though it was within half an hour of midnight on a snowy New Year's Eve. Everything seemed to go smoothly for Tony; though when they arrived outside his flat the taxi-driver was short of change and Tony had to search all through his pockets to try and find the right fare. Susan while she waited felt the light snow tickling her face. Then Tony said, "Never mind, after all it's New Year's Eve," and gave the taxi-driver a pound note.

"Now come in out of the cold!"

Tony took her arm. The taxi-driver called "Happy New Year!" with a particular sort of grin in his voice; she ought to have minded it, at other times she would have minded; but tonight she didn't care what anybody thought.

TONY ASKED HER IF SHE WANTED to go into the bathroom; so she did so, and took off her coat, and had a look at her face in the glass. When she came back into the big bedsitting-room it looked much cosier because Tony had put out all the lights except a desk-lamp, and had lit the electric fire. He was crouching in front of it warming his hands. He said:

"Come here and get warm."

So she joined him by the fire. He looked at her thoughtfully. Then he said:

"I love that glow on your face and arms. When you were out of the room I was thinking of you by the Otter Pool. That day before Korea, when we had a swim."

"I was a little fool," she said: and although it was so long ago it both dismayed her and excited her, to remember that time when she lay beside Tony on the bank of the Otter Pool.

"If so," he said, "I was a clumsy ass. I remember everything. Fetching you the apricot, the feel of the apricot, like touching your skin." He stretched out his hand and ran it gently down her arm. "When I was in that prison-camp I used to conjure up the whole scene and it was like seeing it in colour on the screen at a cinema. Then I had to stop because it hurt too much, it wasn't a good thing, I had to say: *I won't look tonight.* That was when I stopped writing to you."

"But in the end I faded?"

"Everything faded. Now it's all coming back. While you were in the bathroom I've been seeing those brown irises and that great rhubarb thing with a name like a nasty disease, and the grass so green and you so bright lying on it; and the lily pads and the pink water-lilies——"

"D'you remember, I asked about pink champagne!"

"Yes, and that reminds me!" He jumped up. "Three minutes to midnight." He went to a cupboard in the corner and brought out a bottle and two glasses. Did he always keep champagne in his flat, or had he got it specially, knowing she'd come here? The thought was just a ripple on her mind and it died away as all the other questions and confusions had died away this evening. She watched him opening the bottle, efficiently, not spilling any—he did everything well! He glanced at the clock on the mantelpiece as he handed her the glass.

"A minute to go. A minute for me to ask you a question. Tell me, Sue, when are we going to be married?"

Not shall we, but when; yet the way he put it, it did not sound like a arrogant assumption at all, it was like a grateful acceptance of something inevitable, like grass growing and trees fruiting. It had to be, because of Doddington and the woods and their love which had begun so long ago.

Susan wasn't sure whether she ever answered his question: whether she ever said when, or yes, or anything; she thought she just nodded, with her lips pressed very close together because she was afraid she was going to cry. Then Tony took her in his arms, and she opened her lips, and what he had said about marriage soon became unimportant and remote from the urgent present; it was blown clean out of her mind, with all the future problems and the past dubieties, upon a gale of sheer desire. It was quite irrelevant to what was happening to her now—irrelevant as her

black dress, lying upon the floor, which faintly surprised her
when she happened to notice it, as if she were a butterfly looking
down at its chrysalis, or a snake which has cast off its skin.

> . . . . *EXACTLY as I had hoped it might happen   Incred-*
> *ible! Marvellous !!   like dream coming true !!!   Both re-*
> *turned lunch time in Landy told us at once GT. JOY !!!*
> *CELEBRATION !! F went down to cellar to get champagne*
> *(even FLOOD has subsided in deference to occasion!) Mean-*
> *while T goes out to Landy brings in MORE champagne wh.*
> *he'd brought down specially dear boy   F. faced with em-*
> *baras de richesse Asks in Mrs. N   She has 2 glasses Weeps*
> *then goes off INCOHERENT to cook lunch expected dis-*
> *aster but it was MOST recherché !! F says Give her champ.*
> *every day !!!   S v. quiet and reserved but only to be ex-*
> *pected getting engaged is a GT. OCCASION in a girl's life*
> *after all . . .*

PART SEVEN

Make a Fire of Elder-tree

¶ 1

THE ENGAGEMENT LASTED TWO MONTHS to the very day but when it was over Susan felt older by much more than two years.

Of course there was no room or time for doubt during the first week or two. So many things were happening: making of plans, parties (Sandra gave an enormous one), invitations, congratulations. Everybody seemed to be so pleased and *affectionate* that Susan, who always responded to affection, basked happily in the warmth of their pleasure. Soon she began to receive letters of congratulation from old Seldon relatives whom she'd scarcely heard of. Many of them had a common theme, though she didn't at first notice it. What I'm specially happy about, said one of the aunts, is that Tony will be able to *save the estate.* Susan realised that her mother was frequently saying the same thing, especially when she talked about the engagement on the telephone to her old friends. The phone was in the sitting-room so Susan couldn't help overhearing now and then. Soon the often-repeated phrase began to make her frightened, and that was the beginning of the doubts coming back again.

VERY SOON IT BECAME A WAR of attrition between her love and these doubts; she had to call up reinforcements of love to deal with them, and so made the discovery that her love wasn't limitless after all. One day a cold light of understanding shone in her mind and she was able to see exactly how she had deceived herself. When Tony first came home from Korea he had been sick and broken and she had set herself, in love and foolishness, the task of trying to make him well. It had been *giving* all the time then; and when you give love you generate more love, so that you get the impression there is an inexhaustible store.

Well, she had done what she set out to do. She'd helped him to banish his self-reproaches and his bitterness. She'd given him back his confidence and his assurance. He was once more 'the old Tony'—everybody said so. But alas, she no longer looked at that Tony through the eyes of a schoolgirl in love. She was four years older now; and she knew that she had won Tony back to being himself again, only to recognise that state for what it was: a kind of healthy barbarism.

She thought the fault was in herself, to start with. She would catch herself *seeing through Tony,* just as she had done over the *Dictionary of Quotations.* She would watch him with his dogs and see what satisfaction he got from what he called their 'faithfulness.' When one day the red setter refused to go for a walk with her he was clearly delighted. "Good bitch, she won't leave master!" Susan had a glimpse then of all the waiters and the commissionaires and the club hall porters and the sergeants and the corporals wagging their tails at Tony. She hated herself for this, and blamed Stephen for it: Stephen who talked of dogmen. She was so angry with Stephen that she even put off answering his letter of congratulation, "there's nobody in the whole world whose happiness I wish for more . . ."

THE NEXT DISILLUSION was about Tony's friends. Bit by bit she made the discovery that it wasn't an accidental thing, her not liking the people he proudly introduced her to: the kind of people he liked weren't her kind of people at all. Sometimes she hated them. Tony had become the leader as it were of a rather rich crowd of students at the R.A.C. He was older than they were of course, and she could see why they admired him. He was experienced, knowledgeable, charming, he had plenty of money; the world's wheels were well-oiled for him. He would take Susan sometimes to meet a party of these young men at a pub up on the

Cotswolds called The Highwayman. It had a pleasant bar with a big log fire; just the place for a winter evening. In such a bar, among congenial company, Tony was in his natural environment. The young students, recognising Susan as his property, took to her greatly and treated her as one of themselves. This was a compliment in a way but it was an embarrassment too. They talked freely about the girls they took out in their sports cars. The usual question was 'Does she or doesn't she?' Apparently most of them did. The ones who wouldn't weren't very popular. One young man, a bit tight, spoke across Susan to his complaining friend: "If I'd been you I'd have let the little bitch walk home."

Well they were men, and young men were tough and insensitive, she knew. They weren't very sure of themselves either, and half of what they said was probably just talk. If she was to be treated as one of them she'd better not be a prig. O.K., she said to herself, trying to be tough: I'm learning.

And then Tony, stopping his car in Cranham Woods, insisted on making love to her on the way home!

He showed an enormous tactlessness in the way he used her body. Susan knew only too well that in part it was her fault; she'd asked for it. That night in London, and two or three times since, she'd behaved like a little bitch on heat. That was the expression she used to herself. She simply hadn't realised that she had it in her so much to want and to need to be made love to. But because of her eagerness, Tony took her for granted, he seemed to assume she was 'his' and he could have her whenever he wanted her. So sometimes he would take her when she was unready, and would seem to be unaware of what was happening to her when they made love.

THEN THERE WERE THE LITTLE THINGS; and Susan learned that little things can be more destructive of love than the big differences. For instance, there was Tony's assumption that any picture or poem he didn't understand was necessarily 'bogus' or 'phoney.' This sometimes drove her to defend what she herself didn't fully understand, out of obstinacy. Then there was his heartiness, which she'd never really noticed before he went to Korea; it was as if he were pretending to be extra-tough because, perhaps, he had discovered that he was not so tough as he had believed. He was always saying that Britain was getting soft, and grumbling about sissies.

Another thing which jarred was his air of owning Doddington. Susan knew that she was unjust to him about this, because he was probably trying to save Ferdo trouble by dealing with various matters on his behalf. But she once heard him giving orders to Egbert; and that was absurd, you might as well give orders to the foxes or badgers or issue commands to the birds of the air. In any case it was Egbert's immemorial custom to 'take a look around and see what wanted a-doin'.' If you wanted him to do something very specially you had to bring the conversation round to it and ingeniously persuade him that it had been his idea from the start: that he'd thought it was a job that wanted a-doin'. The only result of Tony giving him orders was that he went off to the woods in dudgeon. For three days after that the shoes weren't cleaned, the kindling wood wasn't cut up, and the logs weren't brought into the hall. On the fourth day Susan went to his cottage and in a roundabout and complicated way which her forefathers and his forefathers would have understood she succeeded in making the peace.

But what upset her most about Tony was his attitude to her father. She had no doubt whatever that he was fond of Ferdo; and as Stephen had done he liked to sit up late with him and drink a good deal of port. But Stephen, whose mind she well knew was twice as good as Tony's, had looked on Ferdo as an equal, and argued with him as an equal, drunk or sober, whatever the subject might be. Tony infuriated Susan by treating him as if he were an old fool, dilapidated and done for, who must be humoured and cosseted and agreed with, because, poor old boy, he really didn't know what he was talking about. Once again she was touched by her father's good manners, for he never showed that he resented being patronised by Tony, or even that he noticed it.

F. v. strange and EVASIVE today when I tried to nail him down abt. getting Architect re Alterations IDEAL AR-RANGEMENT I said if WE cd. live in 1 wing and let the Young Ones have rest of Manor but F. insisted Don't lets go mucking abt. with things till occ. arises.   I said Must get it fixed BEFORE they are married F said Yes but how do we know when they will be Have they told you ?? (Wish I CD. get def. date T says Jul–Aug ?? as he will have finished at RAC then but when I tackled S. she said Oh Mummy leave that to US !!! Love her so much but sometimes wonder how much I understand her . . .

Think F. fears ARCHITECT will discover DRY ROT more widespread He will not face it Speaks of the TROUBLE in the roof as if it was some SECRET HORROR concealed there e.g. Rochester's wife !!!!

CELLAR now bone dry but this due to PUMP wh. switches itself on at intervals horrid startling WHIRR heard in sitting room like infernal machine going to BLOW UP then chokes gulps makes noises like someone being SICK then BANSHEE howl then having "PUMPED OUT SUMP" (F. says—do not understand it) switches off with nasty DEATH RATTLE whee-ee-ee-gog-gog . . .

Wish T. & S. LOOKED more like engaged couple but young people v. UNDEMONSTRATIVE today !! Cannot get anything out of S. & she spends every WAKING MO- MENT when not seeing T. on Nightshade getting her fit for Pt. to Pt. who I wish she wd. not ride in v. dangerous Don't I know ??? Collar bone 3 times disloc. shoulder 2 ribs say nothing NOSE 2 teeth !!! I DO think she shd. not do it in view forthcoming marriage Wish T. wd. persuade her Pt to Pt is on Mar 4 she is v. good horsewoman better than me but Nightshade tho v. fast NOT RIGHT for a 1st ride goes too fast at fences I do not trust her sometimes have odd SINISTER feeling abt. her but that is her NAME ??!!

I shall not be able to LOOK . . .

Another go to tie them down to def. date !!! Asked Rector tea didn't tell S so caught her unawares He asked her CASUALLY v. tactful after all he will do it but S. lkd. hard at me & him said something abt Must discuss it be- tween themselves flushed left room . . .

IT WAS A SATURDAY AFTERNOON when the Rector came to tea. Susan watched him eating crumpets—she thought she would always associate him with crumpets—and afterwards wip- ing his soft white fleshy fingers on a handkerchief. His hands gave her the creeps always, and it now occurred to her that her mar- riage was going to be blessed by them.

Tony came for the weekend as he almost always did and on

that Sunday morning, the last day of February, he and Susan
went with Janet and Ferdo to church. An unexpected thing
about Tony was his being rather a stickler for church-going; he
seemed to look upon it as a drill or a parade which you ought to
attend, even if you didn't listen to the sermon and spent most of
the time, as he admitted he did, trying to work out in his mind
the form of racehorses. Sitting beside him while the Rector
read the Lesson from Leviticus, Susan wondered what sort of God
Tony believed in. An extension into deity of some severe but
respected Headmaster or Colonel, perhaps? For her part she
knew now that she hadn't really believed in a personal God for
years—not since her Confirmation had she taken seriously the
kind of God to whom people whined their prayers and bleated
We beseech thee to hear us O Lord. Oh no. If she believed in
anything Almighty perhaps it was Stephen's unknowable divinity
which manifested itself in all things bright and beautiful, all
creatures great and small. She had no time whatever for this
tribal Jehovah whose strange edicts were being proclaimed by the
Rector in his rich baritone, which could make almost anything
sound impressive: Thou shalt not let thy cattle gender with a
diverse kind . . . neither shall a garment mingled of linen and
woollen come upon thee.

JANET HAD PROMISED TO GO TO TEA with some horsey
friends up on the Cotswolds, and somehow or other she had
managed to persuade Ferdo to go with her. "You two can have
the house to yourselves, pretend it's yours!" she said.

During the afternoon Susan rode Nightshade. She'd stopped
hunting her just after Christmas, in order to concentrate on
training her for the Point to Point. She'd never ridden in a race
before; Nightshade had never run in one; so they had a lot to
learn between them. Susan got Egbert, despite his grumbles, to
build four black fences in the Park, well-made of birch from the
woods, with furze off the common at the bottom of them. She
rode Nightshade for two hours every day, practising over these
fences, with long trots to keep her in hard condition and gallops
gradually lengthening until she was going really fast for one and
a half miles.

As things began to go ill between Susan and Tony she looked

forward to these gallops as an escape from her thoughts. She found that most of her troubles blew away on the wind when she was crouching over the mare's neck at about thirty-five miles an hour. But, like Nightshade's flies in summer, they always caught up with her again when the gallop was over.

Tony who had been drinking port with Ferdo after lunch said he wanted to walk it off, so with his dutiful dogs at heel he came out into the Park to watch her gallop. Nightshade by now was racing fit, eating twelve pounds of oats a day, lean, lithe, edgy and beautiful; and before a gallop had taken the steam out of her she was as wicked as sin. This afternoon she did half a mile flat out with her head held high and her mane flying. Susan rode her up to Tony afterwards, and he said:

"Goodness, Sue, she's hardly puffing at all. And doesn't she look a picture?"

He was specially pleased because after all it had been his horseman's eye that had spotted Nightshade when she was all ribs and rakishness at Stow Fair. He had helped with advice and suggestions over her training, and he enjoyed watching her gallops and seeing how she improved. Perhaps, Susan thought, it might make up to him a little for the fact that he'd never again be able to ride a race himself? As he walked away up the slope of the Park, his limp as always reawakened her pity and her love.

Jack Northover didn't work on Sunday afternoon, so she had to see to Nightshade and give her a feed. When she finished she ran from the stables to the Manor through a fleeting snow scud which had arrived on the back of a high wind: March was coming in like a lion. The tickle of the snow was still on her cheeks when she went into the sitting-room, and Tony's two dogs cavorted up to her with wet paws. Tony had only just got in. He was crouching in front of the fire, warming his hands.

PERHAPS IT WAS THE TICKLE of the snow that put New Year's Eve into her mind; but surely it was Tony's attitude—that gesture with his outspread hands—which conjured there suddenly a picture of his flat in town, the champagne on the table, the divan bed, the furniture, the curtains, the photographs on the mantelpiece (one of his father, one of her) above the yellow glow of the electric fire. She was somewhat taken aback by the clarity of her recollection; for she'd been reluctant to look too closely at that evening, and her thoughts about it were frequently confused—though she vividly remembered certain odd and trivial things, such as her surprise at seeing her dress lying on the floor. She was aware, of course, that she had been a little drunk; she realised too that Tony had probably set out to make her so. She supposed she should have felt angry with him about this, but she was more sad than angry, sad that he had supposed he needed to do it: on that night of all nights when she was his for the asking.

In any case Susan didn't like to think that making love was something you plotted and planned for. She thought it should happen naturally and inevitably when the time and the circumstances were just right for it. Certainly it shouldn't be visualised and contemplated beforehand—there was something distasteful about that—nor too closely looked back on when it was over and past. So she had been distressed lately by the reflection that Tony had perhaps planned the whole of the New Year's Eve procedure step by step. His attitude by the fire reminded her now that the very last of all the careful preparations was his warming his hands, while she was in the bathroom, because he was about to touch her and he knew she didn't like cold hands. She always squeaked. In fact, Tony had been doing no more or less than her old family doctor used to do, when he held his hands (and the stethoscope!) in front of the fire before he laid them on her chest. It had been awfully clinical, she thought; and immediately she became strangely uncomfortable about it. She didn't of course suppose that Tony had the same purpose now; but when she went up to the fire, and in a quite ordinary affectionate way he stretched out an arm round her shoulders to draw her closer to it, she stiffened involuntarily because of what had been in her thoughts. Tony felt her go tense and was puzzled:

"What's up?"

"Nothing."

"Well, be matey." So he pulled her to him and kissed her, and when she wouldn't kiss him back he seemed to take it as a challenge. Tony was always like that, he had to win. He began to unbutton her coat.

"How awfully *unaphrodisiac* riding clothes are!" The silly phrase added to her resentment. The whole thing was absurd,

because she knew it wouldn't have happened if she hadn't reacted against his arm round her shoulder, because of that
memory which had curiously shocked her.

"Look, Sue," he said, "we've got the whole house to ourselves.
Let's go up to your room."

"No!"

"Why on earth not?"

"No!" She had never let him make love to her in her bedroom,
among her personal things. She wasn't going to let him do it
now. She clung to this last little privacy absurdly, as if it were a
bit of her virginity remaining.

"What the devil's the matter?" Tony said; and she made the
fatal admission:

"Everything's the matter—can't you see it?—between you and
me!"

"No I can't. Except you've become a little prig or puritan
suddenly."

(Perhaps I am, she thought, in some ways: why, you could be a
wanton and a puritan almost at the same time! Stephen would
enjoy arguing the rights and wrongs of that.—Go *away*, Stephen,
let me deal with this on my own.)

Tony went on, sounding resentful:

"Anyhow, you're always disapproving of things."

"What things?"

There was a short silence while Tony seemed to be searching
through his mind for a stick to beat her with. Susan waited,
angry and defiant; but when the accusation came, it was so unexpected and silly that she nearly laughed.

"All right, I'll give you one example," said Tony. "What
about the fox's mask on the Fentons' door?"

"Well, what about it?"

He didn't answer at once, and she repeated:

"Whatever has that got to do with *us?*"

"Old Ferdo got in a kefuffle and you were filled with righteous
indignation. You dashed across to apologise, you went on about
it afterwards. 'Bad manners' and all that."

He paused, and Susan had such a strong sense of impending
disaster that she actually put up her hand to his mouth, she was
trying to stop him even as he spoke:

"It was only a bit of fun, after all."

"You mean *you* did it?"

And now it was as if their love had a death-wish, which led them both on. Tony said: "We could never understand what all the blinking fuss was about," and Susan, seizing upon that 'we,' said swiftly:

"You and Sandra?" The two of them in the Land Rover, after that Boxing Day hunt! Their complicity hurt her, suggested other complicities. *"You two did it?"*

Then suddenly came the smile, that touching boyish repentent smile, the ready apology:

"I'm sorry, Sue," he said. "Truly I'm sorry. I've been a clot."

There was a pause, and Susan had another of her premonitions. A quotation was coming. It did.

" 'Of all men's clotted clay the dingiest clot!' "

She happened to know it, too, because she'd read "The Hound of Heaven": it was one of the poems Stephen had made her read. That one would hardly be Tony's cup of tea. She knew that if she looked up 'Francis Thompson' in the *Oxford Dictionary of Quotations* she'd find that quotation there!

Tony said, almost smugly:

"Well that's that, I've confessed, I'm bloody sorry, kiss me, Sue, and make it up!"

Even in her anger, she could still be touched by his smile! He drew her close to him and began to kiss her. She tried to say "No, not now" but it was no good, he had undone her shirt and his hand was on her breast. "We'll see," he laughed, and she was infuriated by his assumption that he was bound to get his way. She struggled, and as Tony, enjoying the fight, pressed hard against her she knew only too well there'd come a point of no return soon when she'd dispute with him no longer. So it was rage against herself as well as against Tony that made her do what she did. She ducked under his arm, stood back and slapped him hard across the mouth with her open hand.

She ran out of the room; and the two dogs, eager for a game, went galumphing after her.

MAR. 1st.   S. came and told me this mng. v. tense quiet no tears simply she cd. not marry him SHOCKED DEVAS-

*TATED Cd. not at 1st. believe it Lovers quarrel ???   I said
You'll make it up   She looked at me the way she does those
brown eyes No Mummy pse. I want you to know NOW there
is NO poss.   I will be friends with him but I wd. not marry
him for   STOPPED   I think she wd. have said Doddington
I said have you told yr. father ??   but anyhow I knew she
had   Was v. hurt tho—I said Why didn't you come to ME ?!?
She said Mummy I was afraid to tell you because I knew you
wd. mind so much   So I went to F. said You know more abt.
it than me You must try to do something   He said Why?   I
said WHY !!!   You say WHY !!!!   and he said J.   Do have
a drink or something calm yourself it may all be for the best
in the end   I said But what abt Doddington ???   F said
DAMN DODDINGTON   So I went upstairs and cried then
NOT UNDERSTANDINNG anything Either of them
Loving them too So v. lonely & Feel it is the End of the
World . . .*

¶ 2

BREAST PLATE. NUMBER CLOTH. Racing saddle. Surcingle.
Jack Northover looking as well-groomed as Nightshade in his
bowler hat and treble-polished boots saddled her up while Susan
stood by her head. The mare danced a little while the girths were
tightened, but otherwise she seemed pretty calm. Over the years
Susan had gradually won her confidence by being specially gentle
and quiet. Last night, just before she went to bed, she had gone
over to the stables as usual to make sure that all was well and
had found her lying down in her box like a heraldic beast
couchant, knees to nose. Susan knew that only a very trusting
horse would remain in that engaging attitude while somebody
else came into the stable with a lantern at night. She patted
Nightshade's head as if she were a big dog, and the mare lifting
up her head nuzzled Susan's thigh. Suddenly Susan was absurdly
touched (after all, Tony had given her Nightshade) and she who
had been dry-eyed ever since the bust-up on Sunday incontinently burst into tears. The lantern swung, Nightshade's ears
were like a gigantic rabbit's twitching upon the stable wall.
Susan put down the lantern and buried her face in her hands.

She'd known that this was bound to happen, ever since her visit to Sandra early in the evening. With nobody to see her, nobody to hear her, she told herself: Cry now and get it over; and then forget.

SHE HAD WANTED TO TELL somebody it was all over and then not have to talk about it any more. She had thought that Sandra would be the easiest person to tell, and that once she'd told her the news would be all round the district in no time. So she had gone along to Doublegates at about six o'clock. When she'd said her say Sandra concocted an enormously powerful cocktail, martini or something, and said: "Drink that first and talk afterwards . . . D'you remember me coming along to *you*, with much the same tale?"

"Yes, and Daddy opened a bottle of champagne!"

"This'll act quicker."

A little later, Sandra said:

"You know, love, it would never have worked, with you and Tony. He's too tough and you're not tough enough."

Susan finished the last of her drink. She was always susceptible to cocktails, and this mixture of Sandra's was already beginning to affect her. If she had been completely sober she would never have done what she did. She'd had her doubts about Tony and Sandra ever since the Boxing Day Meet. When Tony had gone off to London, saying he'd remembered a Regimental Dinner suddenly, Susan had done something she was later ashamed of. She had rung up Sandra's house and asked to speak to her. The usual very superior manservant had said:

"Miss Sandra's away for a few days."

Well, there was nothing very significant about that, Sandra was always going away; and Susan, despising herself for her mistrust, had determinedly put the whole thing out of her mind. She'd scarcely given it another thought until Tony had told her that it was he and Sandra who had nailed the fox's mask on the Fentons' door. Somehow that confession had brought all her suspicions back; and now, suddenly, she decided that she wanted to know the truth, however much it might hurt her. She wanted to tidy up the whole wretched business of Tony in her mind. So she played a trick upon Sandra. Inspired by the gin, or whatever it was in that most puissant cocktail, she innocently remarked:

"Er—Tony had a bit of a go with you, didn't he?"

The trick worked perfectly. Sandra at the moment was pouring out a second drink; so she didn't have to look at Susan, she spoke over her shoulder.

"In London after Christmas? He did."

"Yes," said Susan steadily, as if she had known all about it.

Sandra said:

"He wasn't engaged to you then, and I didn't know he was going to be, until afterwards. Then he was good enough to tell me he was having a last fling!"

Susan was so surprised by her frankness that she felt almost sorry for her own deceit. She needn't have pretended at all! Sandra now turned round, with the two drinks in her hands, and looked straight at her with those wide beautiful eyes which Tony and his R.A.C. pals called bedroom eyes—she knew that because one of the R.A.C. boys had told her so. She'd never really known what they meant by that—what quality in your eyes earned them such a description. A sort of mistiness, perhaps? At any rate there was no doubt that Sandra's eyes were the right sort, and all the men knew it. Now *why*, wondered Susan, were men so often specially attracted to girls because they knew they had slept with other men? They were: even decent men; Stephen had once admitted it.

Anyhow, there it was. Tony had slept with Sandra just three days before he'd made love to her, Susan, on the self-same bed. She'd asked for that knowledge and she'd got it. Oddly enough she didn't feel angry with Sandra at all. She felt ashamed of herself, which she hadn't done until now. Knowing what she knew made the whole thing beastly.

Sandra handed her the second drink, and in sheer devil-may-care she drank it down. Then she knew she was getting tight. She said so, and Sandra laughed:

"You, love, you'd get drunk on the smell of a cork!"

Then she came and put her arm round Susan and said:

"Please don't be hurt with me about this. I do mad things which I'm sorry for. Remember what I said about feeling bedraggled?"

Susan nodded.

"Well, this was one of the times when I felt bed-raggled after-wards . . . Didn't you even guess I was going to meet Tony in town?"

"Of course I didn't. You were a Regimental Dinner," Susan said.

"Was I?" The corners of Sandra's mouth twitched in a moment of self-mockery. "I was also a Last Fling. Perhaps it's going to be my fate just to be somebody's Last Fling, always."

She drew Susan to her and Susan, half-laughing, half-crying, laid her head on Sandra's shoulder. The two girls stayed so, for a minute or more, each moved by an affection she didn't under-stand, and each in her different fashion drawing some sort of comfort from the other's embrace.

TEARS, SHE THOUGHT, they wash away memories; they clean up your spirit sometimes. And today was a good day for for-getting, with a cold, strong wind to blow away the cobwebs of the past and the woolly flocks hurrying across the sky, their fleeces very white and shiny against the blue.

She felt strange in her crash helmet, which she'd never worn before, and she thought she must look strange in it too. She'd tucked her hair into a hairnet—there was too much of it to go under the helmet. She began to feel a little afraid. Jack North-over said: "It's just like old times, Miss, when I used to saddle up for your mother." Then the steward's bell rang, very loud and insistent, making Susan's heart beat faster. Jack said:

"That means mount."

She got up and Nightshade gave three very small bucks, which she'd expected. When they were over she eased her left leg for-ward and Jack tightened the girths. He said: "Don't let anyone else touch 'em now. I've heard of *ill-disposed persons* doing 'em too tight, to spoil your chances!" Susan couldn't imagine that anybody would rate her chances so high. "Good luck, Miss," said Jack, and looking down at his little nutty face and honest eyes she realised that she loved him even though she deplored him, about Rosemary and lots of things. She was reminded that she loved Sandra too, though she deplored *her*. Love was nothing to do with approval; and Susan felt she had an awful lot of love in her heart today—perhaps it was something that went with being afraid. She thought of Tony and how he'd longed to ride in a National—what he'd give even to ride in a little Point to Point; and with a reawakening of her pity she was aware of a brief distressing reawakening of love. She thought of Daddy and Mummy—poor Mummy, not understanding about Tony, *never* understanding, she couldn't ever be told. It was brave of her to come today: because people would ask her when the wedding was going to be, she'd have to tell them . . . Susan knew Janet was frightened about the race too; she'd be sitting tight-lipped in the yellow wagon on the top of the hill where all the nobs always sat, not talking to anybody, her eyes on Susan's flame-coloured jumper all the time . . . As for Ferdo, he'd be drinking sloe gin to keep out the cold. He always said he couldn't survive a Point to Point without a flask full of sloe gin in his pocket. He'd told Susan that when Mummy was riding he used to drink eight nips of sloe gin during the eight minutes the race lasted. Perhaps he'd do the same thing today.

Susan as she rode round the paddock could see the yellow wagon, but it was too far off to give them a wave. Looking in that direction, she caught a glimpse of Gloria, and was suddenly reminded that only yesterday she'd received a letter in an unfamiliar handwriting: it was from Ben. He told her that he'd been recommended for a Commission and was up in London for his interview. He'd contrived to get an extra twenty-four hours' leave out of it, and was going to spend a day at Doddington on his way back to Plymouth. He'd love to see her if she was at home.

She ought to have done something about his letter; but after she'd been to Sandra's she'd forgotten about everything else. Anyhow, she thought, if he's home he'll probably come to the Point to Point. She'd keep an eye open for him afterwards. She liked him so much, it would be fun to see him again . . .

NOW THERE TROTTED PAST HER, as she started to parade round on her tense, controlled, explosive Nightshade, the girl whom she'd already designated as her chief enemy and rival in her mind. Her horse was called Romany Rascal and it belonged to Tom Taynton of Honeysett Farm. People said that this girl, who'd been winning Point to Points for the last five or six years, was Tom Taynton's current mistress, and supposing that was true Susan would have felt sorry for her if she hadn't been such a bitch. But even Susan's superabundance of love couldn't spare any for Fanny Finnegan this afternoon. Her father was a dentist from Ireland who'd made a lot of money in Elmbury during the war, and who'd perhaps done the best he could for his daughter, thought Susan with astonishment, when in the Ladies' Dressing Room Fanny took out her plate with about five front teeth on it and hunted round for somewhere to leave her teeth. This wasn't very easy, because there was one canvas washbasin of the Army Disposal kind, some soap, a towel, but no glasses. Somebody discovered a cup which was filled with water, and Miss Finnegan's teeth found a resting place there until the race was over.

Miss Finnegan gave Susan a gap-toothed grin as she trotted by. She said:

"This is your first race, isn't it?"

"Yes."

"O.K. Take it easy, dear, and don't break your bloody neck." She pulled Tom Taynton's big horse into line just in front of Nightshade's nose; and Nightshade gave a little sideways jump in alarm at seeing the chestnut's hindquarters so close. Miss Finnegan shouted over her shoulder:

"Maybe you'll win one day: but not on that animal. Life is sweet, sister."

At this Susan's fear promptly vanished; and as a First Whip from the local Hunt cantered up saying: "Follow me. ladies—I'll lead you down to the start," she looked hard at Miss Finnegan's sizeable bottom and for the first time had a faint unbelievable extraordinary ambition that she might actually win this race, just to teach that hard-faced bitch a lesson. She patted Nightshade's shoulder; and felt her delightfully lengthen her stride as they all cantered along at the heels of the red-coated Hunt Servant.

AT THE END OF the previous race, Ben had drawn some unexpected winnings from a fine fat bookie with a philanthropic air, and had made his way to the beer-tent, which was crowded with agricultural students who seemed half-tight (but most of the time they behaved as if they were half-tight even if they weren't). Ben hated them. When at last he got through to the bar he ordered a double whisky for the first time in his life. He did so partly because he had just drawn seven pounds ten shillings from the bookie, so that a lesser drink would have seemed inappropriate; and partly because he was extremely unhappy. His sister Gloria had just told him, casually and in the course of conversation, that Susan Seldon was engaged to be married.

"Who to?" he asked, so sharply that she looked surprised.

"Oh, you know, that relation of hers. R.A.C. chap, the one she's always going about with. Back in January, they announced it. It was all in the *Intelligencer*. Hadn't you heard?"

Why the devil should he have heard? He'd been down in Devon ever since the New Year, and the only member of the Fenton family who ever wrote to him was his mother; she sent him a short, tidy, inhibited letter in her prim meticulous handwriting, generally wrapped up in some darned socks, regularly every week. It wouldn't have occurred to her that he'd be the least bit interested in the engagement of Susan Seldon. It wouldn't have occurred to Gloria for that matter. Carolyn was the only Fenton who had ever guessed about his secret, foolish, romantic feeling for Susan. She had guessed because she was incurably inquisitive, she watched everybody through her thick glasses and noticed things about them which others didn't see. She'd noticed—ages ago, while Ben was still at Grammar School —that he recognised the sound of the Land Rover's engine when it was going along the drive. Once, when he was still about seventeen, she'd caught him hurrying to the window to catch a glimpse of Susan as she went by. She had never let him forget that. He used to blush in those days, and Carolyn had enjoyed making him blush. She would say: "I saw Susan Seldon in Elmbury this morning," and would watch Ben's face with her pale blue eyes which looked expressionless because the glasses hid them. Then perhaps she'd add: "She goes about with a man old enough to be her father." That was Stephen, of course. Carolyn didn't love anybody much,—at least, she didn't love *individuals*. She had what seemed to Ben an inordinate amount of love for people collectively, for 'humanity' as a whole, for undernourished children so long as they were counted by the million, for black masses, yellow masses, any masses anywhere. And true to this strange love she'd gone off to Africa and had learned a little nursing so that she might work in a leper colony, where she would love the lepers in a collective way and perhaps would even die for them; but individually she would hate them as she looked at their poor scars through the glasses that concealed her thoughts . . .

Ben drank his whisky, which seemed enormous but did nothing whatever to cheer him up. So he ordered another, and nearly lost it when one of the R.A.C. chaps clumsily barged into him. He barged back. He wished that at any rate Susan wasn't going to marry one of that lot, which at the moment seemed to stand for all the attitudes he most disliked and despised in England. But after all, What the hell's it got to do with me? he asked, as he embarked upon his second whisky. The answer was Nothing at all—except that he'd been in love with her ever since he was about seventeen. In love? Why not? There were all sorts of love. When he crawled out from under Colonel Daglingworth's Bentley motor car Ben had fallen in love with a flame-coloured dress, a whiff of scent, slight bare shoulders that rippled under narrow shoulder-straps, a voice, a smile, a kindliness real or imagined. And although in general he was realistic and self-critical, fairly tough and not a fool, he'd cherished and clung to this—this *thing* about Susan, for years. There had been other girls, of course. In particular there had been one at Oxford, very dark-haired and white-browed and wan-faced, like Shakespeare's girl, 'with two pitch balls stuck in her face for eyes,' who had competently seen to the non-academic part of his education. But always in the background Susan remained. He had met her sometimes, walking in the woods at weekends or during vacations. There had been that time when he found her in The Green Man with Stephen, and she'd asked him to lunch afterwards. He'd learned then that her kindliness was real and not imagined. And later perhaps he had come to think that he knew her better than he did because Stephen, whom he liked and admired so much, had been apt to talk so much about her. He guessed that Stephen had been, perhaps still was, in love with her; but he'd never felt jealous of Stephen. He felt bitterly jealous of this second cousin, ex-soldier, heir to the Baronetcy, this R.A.C. chap, Tony.

To hell with it all, thought Ben, taking a last swig at his whisky. They stick to their own kind.

On his way out of the tent he had to push past half a dozen of the R.A.C. lot who were standing by the exit, telling each other stories and neighing like horses at each other's jokes. Ben had changed into civvies when he got home, otherwise he'd have enjoyed using his hefty Royal Marine boots on somebody's toes. All R.A.C. toes represented Tony's toes at the moment! He wondered where Tony was—sitting in that yellow wagon with all the swells, looking through binoculars towards the paddock where the horses were parading now, on the chance of getting a good view of Susan . . . Then Ben, looking up the hill towards the paddock, caught a glimpse of the riders and immediately recognised Susan—*he* didn't need binoculars, he'd have recognised her anywhere, a quarter of a mile away. He couldn't have explained *how*, any more than he could explain how he knew that a particular tree on the skyline was an elm, or that a bird in the air was a jackdaw and not a rook.

She was wearing a red jumper, and by a queer chance it was almost exactly the same colour as her dress had been when she'd caught him letting down the car tyre. He opened his race-card:

Third Race   3-30 p.m.   The Elmbury Hunt–Adjacent Hunts'
                          Ladies' Race

and looking down the list he read:

		NIGHTSHADE			Flame
No. 5	*Miss Susan Seldon*	*bl. m.*		*Owner*	*Green Cap*

The bookies were cawing like a convocation of rooks in the elms at nesting-time, and the one who cawed loudest was the portly avuncular bookie who only a few minutes ago had paid Ben his seven pounds ten shillings, counting the notes into his palm with the air of a rich uncle handing out largesses. Ben's big win had come about in this fashion. When he first arrived on the racecourse, he had bought a card and had noticed that a horse running in the first race was called Royal Marine. This had seemed a favourable omen, and he was on the lookout for omens at that time (he hadn't yet heard from Gloria that Susan had got herself engaged). So he put ten shillings, which was half the money he had in his pocket, on Royal Marine at 3 to 1: it came in first, and the benevolent uncle pressed two pound notes into his hand.

He did so, Ben had thought, with some surprise. From their first encounter he seemed to have recognised that Ben was a stranger to the racing world, not a betting gentleman, not a sporting type, he'd have said. So when Ben, having taken his unexpected winnings, actually returned to hazard the whole of them again, upon an outsider in the second race, the bookie had looked at him with wary curiosity, as he might regard, Ben thought, a Methodist minister on the loose. He'd said: "You really mean it, Sir?" when Ben, still looking for omens, and remembering he was going to Plymouth tomorrow, sought to put his thirty shillings on a horse called Plymouth Rock at 11 to 1. It was a great grey horse, and the least backed of all the horses in that race because it was reputed to be seventeen years old and slightly decrepit. It may well have been; but most of the other horses fell while it remained up on its four languishing legs; and it won in a canter.

Now Ben walked once more along the line of bookies and looked at the odds chalked up on their boards. Evens, Romany Rascal; 2 to 1, Melody; 4 to 1, Tarzan II, Girton Girl and Master Harry; 7 to 1, Gay Golliwog and Nightshade . . .

"Four to one bar two, bar two, bar two," chanted Ben's fat bookie, as if it were some sort of heathen incantation. Ben halted a few yards away from him and counted out his seven pound notes. Then he marched up to the bookie and offered him the lot.

"Seven pounds on Nightshade." Then it occurred to him that he'd kept ten shillings of his previous winnings back, and this was a small meanness, something niggardly, it ill-accorded with his reckless, prodigal, to-hell-with-everything mood. Hazard it all! So he quickly amended: "Seven pounds *ten* on Nightshade"

The bookie raised his eyebrows so that he looked like George Robey.

"Gent's having a flutter, seven-pun-ten to fifty-two pun ten Nightshade . . . And good *luck* to you, Sir!" Holding the notes delicately between his fat fingers, he dropped them into his open bag from a great height, as if to emphasize his belief that it was money down the drain.

THE SEVEN RIDERS ranged themselves in line, ready for the start. Miss Finnegan on Romany Rascal had contrived to get the inside position—she would—and next to her came three bay horses, Tarzan II, Master Harry and Girton Girl, all ridden by local farmers' daughters whom Susan knew.

The girls were good rough riders but their horses were a bit rough too; if the race were run at anything like Nightshade's best pace it would be too fast for them. Next in line—on Susan's left—was Gay Golliwog, a smart horse wearing bandages on its forelegs and a sheepskin noseband. Susan didn't know it— according to the race-card it came from the Warwickshire. It was playing up and fly-jumping so that Susan had to get out of the way. The pretty girl on its back, in Cambridge blue colours, looked as if she could ride. She grinned at Susan over her shoulder and said "Sorry!" The seventh horse—on Nightshade's right —was a very dark chestnut which shone with the glossiness of a chestnut that's just come out of its shiny shell. It belonged to Babs FitzAlan, whom Susan had met at Hunt Balls. She hunted with the Duke of Beaufort and therefore seemed to believe that in other parts of England everything was inferior—the hounds, the fences, the horses, the young men and even the foxes—to those one found in the Beaufort country. But Susan knew she was a fine horsewoman, and her well-bred Melody looked as if it could gallop. However, she didn't know the course and she'd confessed to Susan, when they trotted up together to have a look at the first jump, that she had arrived too late to walk round it. Susan had walked round yesterday afternoon. It had seemed an awfully long way—a mile and three-quarters with nine jumps; and now they had to race round it twice before they got to the finishing post.

The starter shouted:

"Now ladies, do try to get into line . . . I shall give you one, two, *go*."

This was the moment then; and you couldn't pretend, even to yourself, thought Susan, that you weren't a bit scared. They always said that in a Ladies' Race the first fence was the dangerous one, because very few girls were strong enough to hold their horses in the first rush. So you all reached the first fence together and took it split-arse . . .

"One, two, *go!*"

There was a white flag glimpsed in the corner of her eye and there was a hell of a thundering sound of hoofs, much louder than you ever heard out hunting because all the horses were galloping so close together. Not a chance of holding Nightshade, with that noise in her ears! But it didn't matter, because being so fast she got to the take-off just a head in front of the rest, she rose—oh like a pheasant before the beaters!—and fairly flew that first fence, gaining another foot on Melody in the air. Susan had always realised that what was a fault on Nightshade's part in the hunting-field—her tendency to make the fences too fast—would be a big advantage in a race; so long as she didn't happen to hit the top of one and somersault.

But in between the fences, Susan wanted if possible to slow her down. She knew that Nightshade would run best if she could see she had something to beat; if she went right ahead of the field now she might wonder what was happening, finding herself alone,—she might even shorten her stride and if she did that she'd never gallop so well afterwards. So when she was safely over this second jump—there wasn't an earthly chance of holding her before—Susan collected her and was able to shorten rein. Nightshade slowed just enough to let three of the other horses come up alongside her—Tarzan, who looked as if he was running away, Gay Golliwog and Melody. Melody was so close that Susan and Babs were riding knee to knee. There wasn't as much as the tip of a nose between their horses at the next jump. Susan when she safely landed took a quick look over her shoulder and saw Fanny Finnegan exactly where she'd expected to see her, about a dozen yards behind. She saw something else: coming up on her left, and quickly gaining on her, a loose horse, one of the bays, either Master Harry or Girton Girl.

The Tarzan animal, which was certainly out of control, ran slap into the next fence, and Susan as she jumped got a glimpse of its owner clinging on with her arms round its neck and her mouth wide open making a comical O. So now there were three of them bunched together, Melody, Nightshade and Gay Golliwog; there was the loose horse coming up on the left; and there was Romany Rascal still lying just twelve yards from Susan's heels. Very purposeful and professional, Miss Finnegan contrived to keep just this distance behind. She bided her time.

In between fences, Susan caught herself thinking about Fanny Finnegan and Tom Taynton, whom she disliked equally. She'd heard he paid six hundred guineas for Romany Rascal, egged on of course by Miss F. She wondered wickedly if the woman took her teeth out or kept them in when she went to bed with him. People said Tom Taynton was letting the Tithe Barn fall down deliberately—was even hastening its decay, so that perhaps the authorities who looked after Ancient Buildings would decide it had gone too far and he would no longer be compelled to keep it in repair. Yet he'd made more than ten thousand pounds out of the sale of the housing plots. Upon a slope far ahead Susan could see the first three or four houses now, and the geometrical scars on the green turf where dozens more would rise up shortly.

Turning her head just a little further to the left, she caught sight of the yellow wagon—she hadn't realised it was so far away, it was just a splash of yellow on the top of the hill, with an ant-like stir going on about it She thought: To Mummy sitting there on a straw-bale I'm just a red speck in the distance now, no bigger than a ladybird. When and if I'm over the next fence Mummy with her head turned away will be saying to Daddy: "Is she still there?"

SHE STILL WAS. And as the riders came back towards the hill, first time round, Ben watched the red speck growing bigger, watched the four horses galloping neck and neck into the straight opposite the paddock: the one with the woolly noseband, the riderless one, the dark chestnut, and Nightshade, shining black with matt patches where the sweat was spreading over her.

He saw the loose horse turn sideways at the jump nearest to the paddock, so that the other three horses had to take off crabwise to avoid a collision. They all hit the fence, there was a crackle and a spatter of mud, one large black divot spun through the air. For a terrifying moment Ben had the impression that all three horses were coming down; the dark chestnut seemed right on her haunches, but the girl in blue stayed on her back, the chestnut recovered itself and somehow got going again. Ben leaning on the rails had a glimpse amid the confusion of bright hair on Susan's shoulders, as the hoofs thundered, the mud flew, and the three horses galloped away.

OUT IN THE COUNTRY AGAIN, as the pace slowed a little, it was more like a hunting-run, no crowd-noises, no busyness of the ants on the hillside, no bookies' cries like raucous birds half-heard and dying away. Susan had got her breath back and could think calmly again. If she and Babs and the girl on Golliwog hadn't all three thought equally fast, they'd have collided in mid-air and come down in a heap. As it was she'd touched Melody's side with her right knee as the horses rose together at the jump. Poor Babs: she'd had a near shave but she'd made up the lost ground, and was now in the lead and going well, three or four lengths ahead of Susan. The Golliwog seemed to be galloping well an equal distance behind her.

Meanwhile Fanny Finnegan began to move up inexorably. Susan realised that this was in accordance with her carefully laid plan. She came on and on until her horse's head was level with Nightshade's near quarter; and there she stayed, relentless and menacing. 'There's a porpoise close behind us and he's treading on my tail.' Perhaps, thought Susan, she means to panic me; she's trying to persuade me to ask Nightshade for a last effort now, when it's much too soon. Steady, girl, keep going like this, just like this for three more fences, *then* . . .

However, whatever sinister plan had been in Miss Finnegan's mind, she suddenly changed her tactics. Perhaps she'd come to the conclusion that Babs, who was well out in front, was really her chief rival; for the course swung sharply left-handed here, and as they approached the next jump Susan saw Babs very sensibly ride for the inside of the bend—saw Fanny Finnegan overtake Nightshade, slash her horse hard and go like mad for the inside too—and heard her shout as she did so at the top of her voice:

"Move over, you bloody fool!"

Doubtless that sort of thing didn't happen in the Beaufort country. Anyhow, Babs was taken by surprise and indeed intimidated; she moved over. Fanny Finnegan got the inside, Melody muffed her take-off, and Babs not only lost the advantage of her position but two or three lengths as well.

All right, Miss F., thought Susan: I know what I'm up against. I think I'd rather have you in front of me than behind me. I'm going to keep an eye on you every inch of the way.

She began to realise for the first time now that she had a real chance of winning. Nightshade was galloping beautifully, with a long loping stride; and she still had some reserves of speed which Susan had husbanded carefully. Melody was tiring; and at the next fence Golliwog fell. Susan saw exactly how it happened. The nice-looking girl who was riding her had decided, apparently, that it was time for her to challenge the leaders. So the sheepskin noseband came up level with Susan and drew steadily ahead. Approaching the next jump, and going very fast, Gay Golliwog went up on Miss Finnegan's left; and as she did so Miss Finnegan quickly changed her whip from the right hand to the left. The whip was right in front of Gay Golliwog's nose when he came to his take-off. He hesitated for only a fraction of a second, but that was enough. He took off too late, hit the solid middle of the jump pretty hard, and toppled over on to his nose. Susan as she landed saw the girl in blue sprawled on the grass,—then glanced back a moment later and saw her getting up, with both hands pressed to her head.

You bitch, Miss F., thought Susan, I wonder how many more little tricks you have in your repertory? For the rest of this race I shall give you a jolly wide berth. The rest of the race—three fences, or was it four? That was something she ought to know, and Susan panicked suddenly, and realised for the first time how tired she was. She ached all over. Keep *calm,* she said to herself aloud. She looked well ahead, over the sunlit patchwork fields with the cloud-shadows flying across them; they were going as fast as Nightshade was. Beyond the glint of the river Elmbury Abbey Tower, in a small pool of sunlight, glowed among the surrounding shadows. It was a golden landmark on the horizon, like the steeple they used to ride for in the first steeplechases, Susan thought. Ride straight for it fast enough and we win! There were three fences to go, not four; and now, crackle and spatter, there were only two. Fanny Finnegan was ahead by six lengths or so; then came Babs, three lengths in front of Nightshade. How long dare I leave it? Susan asked herself—not much longer!—before I ask Nightshade for that burst of speed. Six lengths takes a lot of making up. *Decide quickly,* or there won't be time before the next jump . . . NO. *Not yet.* Wait. Wait until there's just one jump between us and the finish.

But she overtook Babs without trying to. Melody was tiring, and as she went by her Babs with face all mud-speckled gave her a look which said: Go on, it's up to you, we've had it. She saw her drop the reins, lean forward, pat Melody's shoulder. Good girl, good horsewoman, full marks to the Beaufort: she'd had the sense to pull up.

The last fence but one seemed to come at Susan much sooner than she expected. It caught her unawares, and Nightshade, un-collected, jumped it 'all anyhow,' landed badly—she must have lost a length over that jump, and it was a length Susan could ill afford. Fanny Finnegan had her whip out and was going hard for the finish. But Nightshade had recovered well from her bad land-ing and had picked up her stride again. Surely now was the moment to ask her for that last effort? But still Susan wasn't sure. If only she'd had a bit more experience, if only she'd ridden just one race before! She tried to judge the distance to the next and final fence, and she thought that if she waited any longer it might be too late. Now or never then! *Now*, Nightshade, now get after her! Susan summoned the last of her strength and her will, and used her legs to ask Nightshade for a final burst of speed. She wouldn't hit her, even if the race depended on it she wouldn't do that. There might be horses you had to hit, but Nightshade wasn't one of them. She was responding already to the extra pressure of Susan's legs. Her shoulders seemed to heave her faster forward; her stride lengthened; her ears were still pricked. And now suddenly—taking Susan altogether by surprise—the chest-nut's hindquarters loomed up ahead, Nightshade seemed almost to be *running into them* as she'd seemed to run into the last fence. Susan could hardly believe it when Nightshade drew up to the chestnut, a length behind, half a length . . . Fanny Finnegan could hardly believe it either. She glanced round and Susan rec-ognised her astonishment, mouth half open, showing the gap where her front teeth used to be.

How far to the last fence now? If only I had *judgement,* thought Susan again. The width of our lawn, the length of a cricket pitch . . . Perhaps it didn't matter much anyhow. Janet had told Susan about the last fence at a Point to Point,—she'd said: You've got to go slap bang flat out for it as fast as you bloody well can! She'd said: Most of the race you must think, but if it's going to be a close finish the last bit is just instinct and risking your neck; don't think about *anything* except the finishing post! Susan did think about just one thing; she remembered to ride wide of Fanny Finnegan over the last jump, which they cleared neck and neck, not six inches between them. Fanny was perhaps a shade ahead when they landed, and Susan could see her whip going, she was really belting into her Romany Rascal and Susan hating her for it discovered that hate, even as love, could call up for you unexpected resources. She had hardly any breath left and her thumping heart seemed to be right up in her throat and choking her; but with the very last of her will she asked Nightshade once again, asked with her legs and her hands and her body and the whole of her spirit, and immediately a marvellous thing happened, she had the impression of a sudden huge surge forward, heave of Nightshade's deep shoulders, heave of Nightshade's strong hindquarters, tremendous power carrying her along! One moment she was nosetip to nosetip, the next she was well ahead of Romany Rascal and drawing away. It was extraordinary, it was like surf-riding when you catch a wave just right and it bears you irresistibly along! And now this splendid surge carried her past the flags at the winning post, carried her on and on, so that she began to feel a fool because she couldn't pull up—she was weak as a kitten suddenly; and laughing at herself, laughing at Nightshade, she stopped the mare at last, and turned her round towards the ant-people on the hillside and the shouting and the cheers.

¶ 3

SUSAN HAD TO WAIT UNTIL the last race was over so that she could be presented officially with her Cup and her winnings. Then Babs FitzAlan got a bottle of champagne from somewhere and everybody had to have a sip out of the cup. Meanwhile Ferdo and Janet had already gone home with some old friends whom they'd asked to tea, and Jack Northover had walked Nightshade back across the fields—it was only about a mile, across country by an old bridle path. So at last Susan drove back home in the twilight. She was in that delightful second stage of tiredness

when the substantial world begins to slip away from you and you
feel as if you are living in a dream. The owl which appeared in
her headlights as she turned into the drive, and went before her
for fifty yards or more on slow luminescent wings, seemed to
belong to the unreality. So did the figure in khaki battledress,
walking towards her; she'd never seen Ben in uniform before,
and she was right up to him before she recognised him and
stopped. Even then the dreamlike feeling persisted because of a
confusion between them when he congratulated her, rather formally she thought, and she assumed it was about the race
whereas apparently he was talking about her engagement.

"Gloria told me you were going to be married."

"I was but now I'm not."

There was quite a long pause after that. At last she said:

"It was nice of you to write. I hoped I'd see you at the Point
to Point. Were you there?"

"Yes," he said, "and I won a terrible lot of money on you."

"A terrible lot?"

"More than fifty pounds," he said at last.

"Fifty *pounds?*" She'd imagined Ben was the sort of fellow who
would bet in half crowns, if he bet at all.

"I'd had two wins earlier, and I put all my winnings on you, so
it mounted up." He sounded almost apologetic about it. "I'd
explain, but look, I've got to get into Elmbury to catch a bus."

"Well, that's easy!" said Susan. "Jump in." She turned the
Land Rover at the next convenient place and as they went down
the drive between the oaks the owl appeared once more—she
thought he was Ferdinando's Owl, who always hunted to and fro
on this particular beat at twilight—and he seemed to lead them
all the way to the drive-gates before he banked and glided away
into the blackness under the trees.

"What time's your bus?" asked Susan.

"Oh, not for an hour; but it would have taken me that to walk
to Elmbury."

"I should think so." She laughed. "Even a Royal Marine
would take an hour. And the bus is to where?"

"Cheltenham. Then I catch a train to Plymouth. But that's
not till tennish."

"I could take you to Cheltenham," said Susan. "Save you waiting for the bus."

"You've nothing else on?"

"Nothing."

"Well, look," said Ben. "I've got this awful lot of money I won on you——" He hesitated for a moment, and Susan glanced sideways towards him but the dashlight wasn't working—there was always something wrong with the Land Rover—and she couldn't see his face. She smiled to herself in the secret dark, leaned back in her seat and let life carry her along on its inexorable stream.

"Couldn't we"—Ben was saying—"couldn't we have dinner together in Cheltenham or somewhere on the strength of it?"

"It'll be a drop in the ocean to fifty pounds," laughed Susan. "But let's."

THERE WAS A PUB called The Hobnails on the way to Cheltenham, where they went in for enormous mixed grills designed presumably for hefty great farmers' sons who'd been looking to the sheep up on the hills ever since daybreak: a thick steak and a chop with some lamb's liver and a kidney and fried bread and mushrooms and tomatoes and a slice of gammon and a couple of sausages for luck plus a mountain of chips, which they served country-fashion in the same room as the bar. It was just what Susan felt like at the moment. "I could almost eat Nightshade," she said. While Ben went out into the bar to order some drinks she found the telephone and rang up home. Janet answered and said: "Where on earth are you?" Susan hated lying, but she had a wary instinct not to tell her mother about Ben: not now, at any rate, while Janet was still unhappy about the broken engagement. So she said she'd met some friends after the races, and they'd asked her to go to Cheltenham to a party. "Anybody I know?" said Janet, and Susan inventing quickly said: "Oh, just some chaps from the R.A.C."

That sounded plausible and satisfied Janet, but when Susan joined Ben in the bar it was like a a judgement on her, for there indeed was a whole crowd of young men from the R.A.C., some of whom she recognised. They were on their way back from the Point to Point, and so were full of beer. Half a dozen of them in the far corner of the bar were singing "Three Old Ladies Locked in the Lavatory," and Ben was looking across at them as if he didn't like them at all.

So for a few minutes there was a constraint. Susan asked if he'd
got his Commission and he said he thought he had. He ordered
the mixed grills and at the same time paid for the drinks with a
pound note taken from his thick bundle. He saw that Susan had
noticed the bundle, and he smiled rather shyly as he stuffed it
back into his pocket.

"I've never won any money before. I've got an absurdly guilty
feeling about it. I think perhaps I must be a bit of a puritan."

"I think you'll have to spend it quickly," said Susan seriously,
—her own private puritanism responding to and understanding
his. *"Recklessly!* That's the only cure."

Meanwhile the untuneful singers were roaring away:

> " 'The next to go there was old Mrs. Harwich,
> And she went there to contemplate marriage.' "

Ben shook his head, in disapproval or annoyance. There was
another little silence.

"What *are* you going to spend it on?"

"Gliding," said Ben without a moment's hesitation.

"Gliding?" And all at once his whole face lit up with the
eagerness of delight. He told Susan that he'd learned to fly a
sailplane when he was at Oxford, and that he was sure it was the
most exciting thing he'd ever done in his life. There must be a
club somewhere near Dartmoor, he thought; and he could do an
awful lot of gliding for fifty pounds. "It's just like being a bird,"
he said, "a buzzard riding on the air-currents!" The last little
constraint between them vanished as Ben swept Susan along on
the tide of his own eagerness for adventure. He told her how he
had once got into a powerful thermal current which bore him up
and up into the turbulence under a great thunder cloud: how it
had frightened him, and how he had come to understand that it
was a fine and spirit-purging thing to be frightened now and
then.

"—I was scared stiff this afternoon!" put in Susan; and she
knew she was the better, the wiser, the sounder somehow, for that
purge of fear.

Then Ben tried to explain to her how it caught his imagination when he sailed up into the whiteness and the silent shine
and circled about the vaporous castles in the air,—'the cloud-

capp'd towers, the gorgeous palaces'—and suddenly without any sense of transition they were talking about *The Tempest,* and Ben was saying that despite their names Stephano and Trinculo were as English as a couple of drunken Royal Marines, treating their talking monster with the same sort of humourous compassion as they'd have for the natives of the outlandish place. Susan was arguing that although Caliban was meant to be a monster he was the most human character in the play, whereas she thought old Prospero was a prig and a bit of a bore, as well as being a very petty and mean-spirited magician, to torment poor Caliban with stings and pinches. Ben took Prospero's part, and quoted him— so that when two of the young men from the R.A.C., who knew Susan, came up to her either for the purpose of being polite or with the idea of roping her into their party, they found a private of the Royal Marines reciting Shakespeare to her; marvelling at such a phenomenon, they hurriedly retreated.

Then the mixed grills arrived, and while Ben and Susan both with huge and healthy appetites demolished their assorted platefuls, they went on talking at random about Shakespeare—then somehow switched from Shakespeare to space-travel, and thanked their lucky stars that they were young enough, given reasonable luck, to have a chance of hearing in their old age the travellers' tales of the first men who went to Mars.

They'd almost forgotton the R.A.C. chaps, who were still indefatigably singing:

> " 'If I were a marrying girl,
> Which thank the Lord I'm not, Sir,
> The kind of man that I would wed
> Would be a wing threequarter . . .' "

"D'you mind?" said Ben, looking a bit apprehensive.

"I'm used to them," she smiled. "They're not so bad as they seem. Stephen once said it was chaps just like them who won the Battle of Britain in the Spits and Hurricanes."

"If only *our* lot had had the same chance!" said Ben, combative suddenly, ready for an argument. She'd noticed it before, this toughness in him which showed itself only now and then, and generally over social things. About anything he really believed he would argue with her blow for blow, no holds barred, not over-gently; and Susan found that she approved of this toughness in much the same way as she approved of battledress, a rough, tough soldierly sort of rig.

But now in his thoughtful way he was reconsidering his views about the agricultural students.

"But of course there's nothing sillier than to dislike people collectively. When I first joined the Marines I hated sergeants. But as soon as you get to know an individual, it makes nonsense of the whole thing. You couldn't *hate* anybody, could you, if you really knew them, knew what made them tick?"

Susan shook her head.

"Fanny Finnegan," she said.

"Who?"

"That girl who nearly beat me in the Ladies' Race. For various reasons I was hating her like mad all the way round the course. But back in the dressing-tent afterwards she burst into tears and I realised what a lot it meant to her, to win or lose, so I found myself patting her on the shoulder! . . . I say, look," said Susan suddenly. "The clock! It's twenty to ten, I can't believe it."

They talked hard all the way into Cheltenham, and yet when they got to the station there was still a sizeable queue in Susan's mind of things which she wanted to talk about, ideas which had pleased her or tickled her fancy or awakened her wonder; but it was too late. When they bundled out of the Land Rover, the train was already puffing alongside the platform. Fullfed and tired out and talked out—happier than she had been for months and months—Susan still had the light and airy feeling of being in a dream. There were very bright stars in a brittle cold sky; the March wind caught puffs of steam from the engine and whisked them away. Perhaps if the train hadn't been snorting so urgently, Susan would have had time to say goodnight to Ben more formally and to thank him for taking her out to dinner. As it was, she caught hold of his hand, he quickly said "May I?" and without more ado bent down and kissed her; and all at once as if she were infected by the train's urgency she was clinging hard to his harsh battledress and kissing him back—and then she was sternly reminding herself: You were kissing Tony like this only a fortnight ago, what the devil's happening to you, where are you *going?* So she stopped; and it was like pulling up Nightshade.

She was quite appalled, and perhaps Ben himself was surprised—
at any rate he sounded surprised, as he said a bit breathlessly:

"May I write to you?"

"Of course!"

The Guard was waving his green flag, and Ben slinging his
kitbag, running fast, cried over his shoulder: "Next week?" Susan
in happy bewilderment cried out her answer:

"Yes, as soon as you like!"

¶ 4

APRIL BROUGHT TO THE WOODLAND its anemones, to
Susan its heart searchings, to Janet and Ferdo its sharp remind-
ers of the years flying by, and to old Jakey at the Ferry his last
summons across the river.

Nobody knew for sure who sounded the ancient rusty bell; but
the postman heard it as he bicycled along the Elmbury Back
Lane, and he reckoned that the person who was banging away on
it must be somebody strange to the neighbourhood, for the Ferry
hadn't been in operation since the punt sank, with Squire Seldon
aboard, four years ago. The milkman heard it, as he was on his
way to Ferry Cottage, and he said to himself: They can beat the
bell till they're blue in the face, 'tis sartin sure they won't fetch
old Jakey across the river! And indeed that was certain; when the
milkman called at Ferry Cottage, and got no answer to his knocking, he pushed open the door, and found Jakey lying just inside
it, stone dead at the bottom of the rickety stairs.

Everybody knew that his wits had been wandering of late, and
it was supposed he might have been half-asleep, and that hearing
the loud bell he had harked back into the past as old men will;
forgetting that his long black punt was a skeleton on the bank by
the landing stage, he'd hurried downstairs to answer the summons, tripped up and broken his neck in the course of his fall.

In fact, Jakey's death was due to heart-failure. The doctor who
gave evidence at the Inquest was definite about that. But the
Coroner, who took himself seriously and perhaps was not averse
to getting in the news, had personally inspected the cottage and
was displeased with what he found there. "The stairs were so

rotten I could kick a hole in them with the toe of my shoe." He
asked the doctor:

"Might not this old man, perhaps not very steady on his legs,
have tripped and fallen on his way down those difficult stairs?"

"He might," said the doctor with dry precision, "but his death
was due to cardiac failure occasioned by insufficiency of the
coronary artery."

Nevertheless the damage was done. The *Elmbury Intelligencer*
printed a full account under the headlines:

'YOU COULD KICK HOLES IN STAIRS'
CORONER'S COMMENTS AT DEATH COTTAGE INQUEST

Janet was furious, of course. She was sure there was nothing
wrong with the cottage which a carpenter couldn't put right in a
couple of days; so Ferdo went down there with the builders, who
shook their heads gravely and said it would cost nearly as much
to put the place in order as it would to build anew; and who'd
want to live by the river anyhow, and have the flood in through
the front-door two winters out of seven, when there was no
longer a ferry there or any call for one?

THE BUILDERS HAD ENOUGH TO DO   at the Manor,
without trying to patch up a dilapidated waterside cottage that
nobody would want to occupy unless, said the foreman-builder
genially, "they was web-footed like a frog." The winter gales as
usual had torn a lot of tiles off the Manor roof; a day's heavy
rain in April found the weak spots, so that Janet had to place a
bucket on the landing to catch the drips that fell at regular intervals and sounded just like a big clock ticking. Ferdo, sitting
up late and muzzy with port, heard this faraway plopping and
confused it with the sound of the death-watch beetle which ticked
in the furniture—or in his mind. In the silences between the plops
he listened for, and sometimes heard, the tiny patter of the feet of
the mice. He told himself that he had mice on the brain. He had
taken to dreaming about them. In his dream he had cut himself
shaving—it was a frequent accident with Ferdo—and he had
stanched the flow of blood with cotton-wool. For some reason he
had dropped the scrap of scarlet cotton-wool on the floor, while
he resumed his unfinished shave; but he was continually dis-

tracted by the pitter-patter of mice, which he glimpsed now and
then through the corner of his eye. When he'd finished shaving
he looked for the mice but they had vanished. So had the blood-
soaked cotton-wool; and in his dream its disappearance seemed
ominous and terrible. "They're *vampire* mice!" he cried; and his
heart was still pounding when he woke up. His dreams did not
often last long into the daylight; but this one stayed in his mind
unaccountably, and every time he heard the pitter-pat behind
the wainscotting he was uncomfortably reminded of it. Rats and
mice and such small deer, he said to himself; and the line from
King Lear led him straight to another, which brought his wandering thoughts to an abrupt full-stop. 'O that way madness lies;
let me shun that . . .'

Ferdo decided that what he needed was fresh air and more
exercise; so next day he forced himself out of the tumbledown
house into the tumbledown woodlands, and found precious little
comfort there. The newness of the spring showed up the ruin and
the decay; he came upon two fallen trees sprawled upon the
bluebells and the primroses. He could see from the broken
stumps that they were rotten with fungus; and it seemed to him
that everywhere he went he came upon the agents of uncleanli-
ness and corruption! On his way back across the Park he noticed
that one of the great solitary oaks, one of the Elizabethans, was
beginning to 'die back.' Its boughs would show green this summer, and next summer, and the summer after that; but each
season there would be a little less green, more bare black
branches in springtime as the sap ceased in this limb or in that
one.

That very evening, by a grim chance, when Ferdo switched on
the wireless for the Six O'clock News, he learned that Sir Winston Churchill himself like a mighty oak had been stricken; and
it was hinted that he would shortly offer his resignation to the
Queen.

> *DARE not THINK   what will become of the country no
> longer having HIM to lead us !!!   For a while he made us
> GREAT again !!!   F. says it will now be A. Eden—Nicelook-
> ing but???   F says also there will be Gen. Elect. soon with
> all its nastiness spite doubts confusions   Can never under-*

*stand why in PRESENT STATE OF WORLD cannot have
sensible COALITION GOVT. of Tories + those Libs and
(v. few alas !!!) Labs who are Decent and believe in sound
fundamental principles even tho perh. misguided   But no
hope of this F. says.*

Gather its BY NO MEANS CERTAIN   *S le M. will get in Has
not made himself v. pop. and def. not PERSONA GRATA
in some qutrs.   e.g. wrote quite rude letter to W.I. when
they sent him Resolution asking to bring back flogging for
VIOLENCE and birching for YOUNG THUGS   Also he is
up against Elmbury Town Council TOWN SCOUNDRELS
as they (rightly) call them !!!   They want to TREBLE pop.
of town in 10 yrs more INDUSTRY 100s of houses new
SHOPPING CENTRE etc. but S. Le M.   (I agree with him
abt. this) says No it would alter whole CHARACTER of
town and be bad planning some places shd be preserved
some developed & Elmbury is unique etc etc.   So he will
lose votes in Elmbury and there is new go-ahead Lab. Candidate only 27 with University degree (They are the ones
I cannot understand (like Ben Fenton !!!   We never see
him now perh. Royal Marines will CURE him !!!))   Another thing telling against Le M. is that Col. Daglingworth
his own Chairman is by way of being tied up with Elmbury
Development Company (Wheels within Wheels!!!) & on same
side as the SCOUNDRELS (for his own ends !!)   so he goes
abt. saying his own Cons. candidate is no good   Even rum-
oured he may stand himself as IND. CONSERVATIVE so
splitting vote and perh. letting in Labour   A terrible thing
if this Constituency had Labour Member   It wd be like
Red REVOLUTION !!!!*

*But F. is going to a mtg. abt. it next wk.   S le M. coming
down for it   Hope they will come to some compromise!!?
(Think I was wrong abt. Col. D.   Did once admire him but
now think him Too big for BOOTS & cannot CARRY HIS
CORN . . .*

*F's pump in cellar is mkg. v. strange noises like INFER-
NAL MACHINE + occ. CHOKING & GULPING + shrill
banshee HOWL now and then   F. v. proud of it says cellar
dry as bone but am sure all is not well with it   In any case
it has not got rid of water only kept it at bay   Something
sinister to my mind in that underground river or whatever
it is biding its time UNDER OUR FEET ready to RUSH*

IN as soon as pump goes wrong wh. it will I think it is rattling itself to Pieces.

But if Pump pleases poor F ! . . . He is v. strange quiet silent & (I know) desperately worried NEVER speaks abt. Jakey Only I know how much he took it to heart and the things they put in the local paper More bolshie now than ever before.

For 1st time in our lives CASH actually short F. did not like to write cheque until DIVS came in of course he cd. raise large sums at any moment on land & timber but neither of us wd. do such a thing—DIE first !!!! . .

IF ONLY S. and T. had married !!! Have not heard from him since he threw up Ag. Coll. and went to stay with cousin in Kenya. Do not understand NEVER shall what happened between them but convinced decision was HERS indeed poor Tony nearly said as much when he wrote to me— so nicely—afterwards But WHY ?? WHY ??? Cannot bring myself to ask her Absurd but am shy of her in a way my own daughter !!! Fear there is gt. GAP between us Yet in most ways she is so responsible capable sensible & wise much older than her yrs Look at the way he rode her 1st Pt to Pt extraordinary coolness judgment skill !! Am not sure if even in my best days I cd. have done better Also she is DEEPER than one thinks—so often find her curled up in window seat reading Shakes. (must know it by heart!!!) and poetry She does not get it from ME !!! but F. knows so much tho' does not often show it he read a lot I daresay when he was at sea . . .

Sometimes (e.g. this mng. when she came back from riding Nightshade) she is QUITE LOVELY even in those awful jeans (but they do show her long legs !) & with her hair quite straight long untidy as usual I told her like Old English Sheepdog because it comes over her eyes !! Perh. SOMEBODY ELSE will come along There was that nice Freddie she met at Hunt Ball no money now but heir to PLENTY and he will be a Lord too He rang her up 3 or 4 times but I do not know if she was Interested Have to try hard not to seem too inquisitive but wish she wd. tell me more of her own accord e.g. there have been several letters lately in nice CIVILISED sort of hand but she does not talk abt. them and am too embarassed (?) to ask her . . .

BEN WHO HAD GOT his Commission and was doing his Commando Course scribbled vivid tough concise letters that had something of the urgency of despatches and well accorded with his battledress in Susan's mind. 'All today I who thought I was a civilised man have been learning how to kill other men with a tommy gun, with a knife, with my bare hands; and God help me I have enjoyed it.' Another time he told her: 'We were cliff-climbing all last week. Terrifying but good for me. I kid myself I'm quite a chap when I've got to the top and look down.'

And once he wrote 'from the top of a Tor in a hell of a mist,' and said that he and his section had deliberately lost themselves on the Moor 'to find out what it felt like' and to see how long it took them to get home. 'If all else fails you follow a little stream; and in the end you come to a river; and if you walk for long enough beside the river you're bound to come to a bridge and a road!'

It was something quite new to Susan, and she found it exciting and extraordinary, this business of getting to know a man and to like him more and more through his letters. She began to look forward to getting them, was even a little disappointed if a whole week went by without her receiving one. Each letter told her a bit more about him, and showed her some unexpected aspect of his thought. 'There are stone circles and rows, huge stones put up by the Bronze Age people . . . In the mist they look like men, very tall, giants. I laid my hand on one great stone,—awe-inspiring to think I was touching what had been touched by the hands of those men 4000 years ago of whose language we haven't one syllable . . . My Section wondered what the hell I was doing.'

There seemed to be mists most of the time on Dartmoor. 'Princetown Prison in a soft grey mist—terrifying. Over the main gate, which you enter I suppose when you're first sent there, you see a precept in Latin: PARCERE SUBJECTIS.—Susan's Latin wasn't very good, but she could make a guess at that one: "Spare the overthrown"?—'I wonder,' Ben went on, 'how many of the poor so-and-sos who are marched in through that gate know what PARCERE SUBJECTIS means and realise how ironic it is to have stuck it up *there* of all places . . .

'I saw something awful yesterday. You must believe this, it is true, though seeing it I could hardly believe it. Tourist coaches,

you know, stop outside the prison; it is one of the Sights. If they
catch sight of a working party of prisoners they get a kick out of
it. You see hiking girls in short shorts standing outside the gates
—must be rotten for the chaps inside. Well, yesterday there was a
woman, middle-aged, with a Peke on a lead, standing on tiptoe
looking over the wall to see if she could get a glimpse of the
prisoners in their uniform, I suppose she got a sort of kick, she
being outside and virtuous, they being wicked and very rightly
shut in! When she'd feasted her eyes on whatever it was she saw,
she *picked up the Peke* and held it up so that it too could look
over the wall, Mummy's had a good look now it's little Chu-Chin-
Chow's turn to see the nasty convicts . . . I was nearly sick and I
hated her like hell. But I mustn't. If I knew all about her I'd be
sorry for her, as you were sorry for Fanny Finnegan. More and
more I get to know hate's no good, love's the only thing in the
world, yet here I am cheerfully and happily learning how to
kill . . .'

Janet nearly saw that letter. Susan had picked up the post
before breakfast, and she was reading it when Janet came into
the room. She had to be very calm and casual, and she went on
reading, then when Janet was pouring out the coffee she managed to tuck the letter away. She wasn't ashamed of getting letters from Ben; but it would have been difficult and complicated
to explain to her mother about them. Over the coffee pot Janet
said:

"Pet, I was thinking about that nice Freddie what's-it, he's in
the City, isn't he? We ought to ask him down for the Whitsun
weekend . . ."

Then Susan realised that she imagined the letter had come
from that Freddie fellow, who was wet and stupid, and that in a
way Mummy was clutching at straws, she was still hoping against
hope that she, Susan, would fall in love with some rich young
man who would 'save the estate,' as Tony could have done. But
Susan herself was at last getting a little tough about this. She was
beginning to realise how much it had frightened her, the gradual, growing assumption that she would marry Tony. She wasn't
going to have anything of that sort again; and in her mind she
put that thought into words which would have shocked her
mother profoundly if she'd spoken them aloud. She wasn't going

to swap her body for the preservation of Doddington; because she'd hate the woods and the old house for ever if she did. When she looked back upon the business of Tony she was often terrified —it had been so near a thing, and but for a trivial accident or two she would have convinced herself that she loved him, and married him, and heaven only knew what would have happened to her if she'd been fool enough to do that.

She was still bewildered, but heart-free: not committed to any-one, even in her mind. Stephen in this context was an affection-ate memory. Tony she was determined to forget. Ben was some-where in the offing, for his letters talked to her most agreeably and told her enough about him to persuade her that she would like to know more. When she sat down to write him one back, she remembered suddenly how she had kissed him at the station; and with a little surprise but no sense of guilt at all she admitted to herself that she'd probably do the same thing again should her mood and the occasion make it seem proper. She wrote to him deliberately:

'Please tell me well ahead when you are coming back on leave. Then I can get tickets for Stratford and we can go and see a play. I've been reading *Coriolanus*. Politicians and voters don't alter much, do they? There was a private meeting of the high-ups in the Elmbury Conservative Association and Stephen came down to it. Daglingworth had been working hard to set them all (ex-cept Daddy of course) against Stephen, and when Stephen sensed the majority was against him he said he wouldn't contest the coming election so they've announced he's giving up because of ill-health and Daglingworth is going to be the Candidate in-stead . . .'

GAILY AND (as he did everything else) with an air, Stephen had given up politics for good. On the night after the meeting he stayed at Doddington, and Susan asked him what he was going to do next. He said with a grin that he was going to learn about rhododendrons. Then he explained that just before the war, when he'd been on the short list for an Everest expedition, he'd spent a whole summer climbing in the Himalayas. He had prom-ised himself then that he'd go back just once before he was too old, before his breath began to come short at twelve thousand feet! But he wasn't going to climb much this time; he wanted to see the flowers.

"I've always been mad on rhododendrons." Then with the old absurd schoolboyish enthusiasm he exclaimed as he'd often done before: "If only there was time for *everything!* I love primulas too. And I'm told there are patches of Meconopsis poppy as blue as the sky. How much more agreeable than the faces of the Honourable Gentlemen opposite, which I've been looking at for years!"

Next morning he and Susan walked in the woods and hunted for flowers in humbler fashion. Stephen betted her that he'd find fifty sorts in a couple of hours, and won his bet with half an hour to spare. He had special preferences among the flowers, favourites which he loved far above all the others. One was the greater stitchwort,—'stiff little white prim puritan flower'; another was the heartsease with its surprised face, like a girl's—"I suppose that's why they used to call it Kiss-me-Quick!" he said.

They played another game. One would find a plant with a distinctive scent, the other, with eyes shut, had to identify it and say what memory if any the scent brought with it. Stephen scrab-bled up some leaves of herb Robert with their rather unpleas-ant, musty-old-cupboard, mousy smell. Susan recognised it im-mediately and it took her straight back to a springtime when she was about six, and to the green lane that went along the side of Cuckoo Pen, where she must have got it on her hands when she was looking for birds' nests with Tony. But she didn't want to talk about Tony now, so she kept to herself the latter part of that memory.

They crossed the Park, and went to their favourite, flowery clearing. "Just like old times!" Stephen said, but she knew and was secretly glad that it wasn't quite like that. Their companion-ship was easier, and in a sense it was even closer, now that the idea of anything more than companionship had been cleared right out of the way. Susan with delighted surprise rediscovered her great pleasure in his company, and not for the first time realised how much she had missed him, during the past eighteen months or so.

Beyond the clearing, towards the main road, they saw some men with striped poles, surveying the route of the motorway; in one place the trees which were to come down had already been blazed with the axe, and daubed with a blob of white paint upon the scar. They stood in their spring green, above a carpet of bluebells: each one bearing the mark of its doom. Stephen remembered some old Morality Play in which Death, he said, ran to and fro among the multitude, and marked this man and that one as ripe to be cut down.

Susan had not realised how wide a swathe the motorway would reap through the woodlands, nor what a slice it would take out of the Park itself. Because of the way the contours ran, it wouldn't in fact be visible from Doddington Manor; but it was bound to involve the destruction of some of the great oaks—perhaps even Ferdinando's, which stood close beside its projected route, if not actually upon it.

"Your father asked me to see what I could do about it," Stephen said. "So I wrote to the Minister and said it was a famous landmark that ought to be saved. But I haven't heard from him, and now I'm afraid I'm not going to be much use any more."

"Old Daglingworth wouldn't care tuppence about a tree," Susan said. "In his eyes the Oak would be just a piece of timber —not very sound! . . . How horrible to think he's likely to be our Member. Stephen, *why* did you chuck it up without a fight?"

"I'll tell you about the meeting," he said. Daglingworth, very bluff and Honest-John, 'calling a spade a spade' and all that, had declared his belief in full-blooded Conservatism; Stephen's was 'so watered down you could hardly tell it from the Socialist stuff.' So Daglingworth had hinted that he might stand as an Independent with the backing of some 'good old-fashioned Tories who felt the same.' If he'd done so it would have split the Conservative vote in two; most of the dyed-in-the-wool kind would have voted for him, so would all those flagellant Conservative women, so would most of the Elmbury tradesmen and Councillors who were already displeased with Stephen for opposing the 'development' of the old town. The divided vote might have let in the Labour Candidate, who was an able young man, though Stephen didn't much take to him—"He's one of those glib economists who scare the pants off me." It would have been difficult to conduct a good political argument with him, Stephen thought, while at the same time he was 'being bashed and bludgeoned from behind by the very blunt instruments wielded by his own side.' In any case the split would have got a lot of bad publicity.

"That sort of dogfight," he said, "would have done no good to the party, nor to democracy which in the face of everything I still obstinately believe in, nor to me."

Then Susan teased him, as she used to do, for the fun of starting an argument. She said she saw no great virtue in either of the parties, and all politics were beginning to look a bit like a dogfight to her. As always he rose to her fly as readily as a trout in Mayfly-time. "I know your kind!" he laughed. "You're looking for a Cause. You want a ready-made Crusade laid on for you. Well, you take care. Dictators depend upon your sort. Nine times out of ten they're put into power by starry-eyed romantic idealists like you who are fed up with politicians and who say they're looking for a Cause! There's a lot to be said for dull democracy, with all its faults."

Susan remarked that she couldn't see how it would serve democracy to let Daglingworth into the House of Commons. "Never mind him," said Stephen. "Democracy can look after itself. It works in a mysterious way,—somehow or other the spirit of England expresses itself in the end—you know, the Waters Under the Earth, like your old flood!" Ferdo's precious pump, after making the most extraordinary noises, had packed up at last. He was waiting anxiously for the men who were coming to repair it. Meanwhile the flood, seizing its chance, had burst into the cellar with the fury of a caged animal that suddenly finds itself free. It had risen two feet in the night, and was still coming up at the rate of two inches an hour. Egbert, gloomily prophetic, was shaking his head and saying "There's no telling where it will get to"—as if indeed it might prove a match for Noah's Flood itself, engulfing the Manor, Doddington Woods, Elmbury Abbey Tower and all!

" 'Tis sartin proof," he said to Ferdo, "thee carsn't hold water down. 'Tis a strong and furious thing, as I told 'ee. It bides its time; but it allus has its way in the end."

And so, Stephen argued, in full flood himself as they walked back across the Park, did those mysterious forces which added up to what he romantically called the Spirit of England, so did they bide their time and lie low, only to burst forth in moments of crisis and great decision to determine the course of our history! Powerful, ubiquitous, secret, they were omnipresent beneath the façade of our politics and society, just as the hidden waters lay deep down beneath the roots of the oaks. King or Cromwell or any other strong force might hold them down for a while; but in the fullness of time they would burst out of confinement and have their way . . .

It was indeed like old times, with Stephen's talk going at about one hundred and fifty words to the minute and ranging to and fro from the Barons' Wars to the Industrial Revolution, from Cromwell to Cobbett, from 1066 to Dunkirk! But Susan nevertheless managed to get a word in now and then; and after one of her interpolations his quick mind suddenly pounced on something she'd said—upon some turn of a phrase or some slant of an opinion—and he cried suddenly: "Sukie, you've been talking to Ben, I know it!" Taken unawares—for she didn't even know what she had said that given herself away—she found herself actually blushing and quickly turned her face from him. It was ridiculous, she hadn't blushed for years; and now she was behaving like a schoolgirl when she had absolutely no reason to! Stephen caught her by the shoulders, and laughing, turned her back so that she was face to face with him and couldn't conceal her foolishness any more.

"You've been talking to Ben—or he's been writing to you," said Stephen percipiently. "Now come on, Sukie; confess!"

⸿ 5

DAGLINGWORTH GOT IN, of course. As it turned out he had a slightly bigger majority than Stephen's. Of the Seldons, only Janet gave him her vote. She deplored him in some ways, and over such matters as the housing-estate on Honeysett she realised he was a foe; nevertheless she still saw him as a defender of the established things against the disruption and disorder which menaced them. At least, she said (forgetting that her mother had once said it of Hitler), he was anti-Red!

Susan was in two minds, her political loyalties cast into confusion. She even went to one Labour meeting to hear what the candidate had got to say; but she who had so often heard Stephen expounding politics in terms of poetry could hardly expect to find the Cause she was looking for in an argument about economics. Moreover the Candidate was one of those socially uncomfortable ones who display their chips on both shoulders for the whole world to see; and hating and fearing greatness, he even dared to cock a snook at the stricken Churchill. Susan shouted her protest at that, to the delight of some Conservative hecklers. But she didn't much like the look of them either, and she slipped out before the end of the meeting lest they should join up with her at the exit and she should appear to be one of their company.

As for Ferdo, he contemplated the photographs in the Election issue of the *Intelligencer,* of the beaky bespectacled Labour Candidate and of the jowly and false-jolly Daglingworth shown side by side; and at last he produced a quotation from Dr. Johnson which Stephen would have appreciated. 'Sir, there is no settling the point of precedency between a flea and a louse.' Thereafter, fortified in his old opinion that almost all politicians were cads, blackguards or bounders, he chose to ignore the Election altogether. Indeed on Election Day, when Janet drove into Elmbury 'to see what was going on,' he chose instead to go for a walk in the woods alone. In the course of it he had an unpleasant adventure.

He noticed a gang of youths who seemed to be playing some sort of a game in Jubilee Wood. They were dressed in Teddy fashion, which aroused his curiosity. He hadn't until now seen Teddy-boys at Doddington. It was out of interest therefore, rather than through any sort of resentment at their using his woods for their games, that Ferdo approached them now. They didn't notice him until he was within a matter of twenty yards; in his grey-green tweeds he must have merged, as he always did, into the background of the broad and weathered tree-trunks. So before they were aware of his presence he was able to see at close quarters what the Teddy-boys were doing. One of them had found a blackbird's nest or a thrush's, and had pulled it down from the hazel-bush; and they were throwing the naked nestlings at each other, in some kind of moronic horseplay.

Ferdo had a bird-table outside his sitting-room window, which at all seasons gave him joy. He had got to know many of the birds that regularly visited it—among them many thrushes, and a whole family of parti-coloured blackbirds, some with white tail-coverts, some with white collars, which were easy to differentiate because of their distinctive markings. The featherless nestlings which the youths were using as foolish missiles, might well have been the offspring of those special, cherished birds. So in a furious rage old Ferdo pitched into the Teddy-boys, taking them by surprise and so intimidating them by an access of authority that the most miserable runt of them all, looking into the eyes of a man who'd captained the King's ships in battle, fell a-snivelling and admitted his true name and address. Ferdo wrote it down in his diary, put out of their pain a couple of cold, skinny and twitching objects not unlike mediaeval manikins, strode home and rang up the police.

F. v. upset shocked angry but ½ sorry he's started Prosecution wh. local Press (always agin us!!!) will be bound to PUBLICIZE and get wrong   For me whole thing typical of undisciplined disorderly world break up of everything . . .

. . . Lost temper with Mrs F today she tried EXCUSE these Teddies lack of education Blames US !!!!   (Answer to that children were BETTER behaved when they left school at 14!!) But did not argue as Mrs. F. v. fratchy over Gen. Elect.   Realize F's have special reason dislike Col. D. he sacked them ! (wish F. had!!!)   Fenton & J. Northover will never get on they quarrel over politics & everything across wall between stables and gdn !!!   Great row today something to do with big elder wh. grew against gdn. wall Fenton chopped it down said it shaded pt. of veg. gdn. where he grows Marrows wh. he is always proud of Enormous but inedible Jack N. v. old-fashioned does not like anything chopped down so they had gt. argument Egbert joined in used to pick the berries to make E-berry Wine (Makes wine out of anything Nettles Mangelwurzels Dandelion drinks it all the time   suspect it rots his Brain) E said to Fenton who'd cut up tree and burned it "Make a fire of eldertree Death within the house shall be !!!" (Mrs. Northover heard him, said it gave her a Turn !!!   Egbert is ½ or ¾ mad and full of old foolish tales He is queer uncomfortable HOBGOB-LIN little man . . .

> *Case abt. Teddies comes on tomorrow RSPCA wd. not
> Prosecute They are only interested if its to do with digging
> out foxes or height of Gd. National fences So Prosecution
> is under Wild Birds' Protection Act   Am sure WE shall
> come out of it badly in any case !!*
>
> *But think of those Teddies INVADING our Dodding-
> ton !!? All our life seems to be falling into RUIN like Manor
> & woods I sometimes ask Why do we stay ??   We cd. sell for
> 1000s and 1000s and go ANYWHERE and not be poor any
> more but we cd. not bring ourselves to do it UNTHINK-
> ABLE live anywhere we do not belong !!!   Feel sometimes
> we must be like rabbits fascinated by ferret that sit still and
> let it get them   We do nothing DECISIVE just sit here
> helpless wtg. for something to happen But what ??? . . .   S.
> had another letter this mng. same handwriting   Must try
> not to be curious but hope it is that nice Freddie she met at
> Hunt Ball . . .*

FERDO, OF COURSE, had to give evidence against the
Teddy-boys. Janet, who hated the whole business and felt sure
that no good would come of it, didn't want to go; so Susan went
to court to keep her father company. That was the morning
when she had the letter from Ben. He said that when he finished
his course at the end of the week he'd get a few days' leave before he was posted to a Commando serving abroad. Because
they'd talked so much about Shakespeare the last time they met—
and written quite a lot about Shakespeare in their letters—she
had set her heart on seeing a play with him at Stratford. Ferdo
wanted to do some shopping before the case came up; so she
slipped away and rang up the Box Office to find out what was
on. She booked two seats for *Twelfth Night,* and because she'd
told neither her father nor her mother, and was by no means sure
if she intended to, the simple transaction made her feel rather
wicked, secret, excited and conspiratorial.

She'd arranged to meet Ferdo at the Town Hall, where the
Court was held. There were a few of the Teddies hanging about
outside—among them Goff, with whom Susan had had her latest
encounter only a month ago, when Rosemary had rung up in
distress to say that she'd finally left him and to ask for help
urgently; she'd departed in such a hurry, owing to his drunken
threats, that she'd left her cat Duffy behind. She dared not go

back alone to fetch it; so Susan, who had no fear of Goff and indeed thought she would relish the chance of telling him what she thought of him, drove to the backstreet cottage, found him at home and demanded Duffy. He grunted that she could have him if she could catch him: and under the smelly sofa with its stuffing coming out she found the cat hiding and managed to drag him out. Then she saw that he had an injured leg: and although she had no proof that Goff had kicked it she assumed that he'd done so and called him everything she could think of as he stood, sullen, shifty, and silent, beside the open door.

Then she took Duffy to a vet, but his leg wasn't broken, luckily, and Susan restored him to Rosemary, who was off to Birmingham, of all places, where she'd got a new job. She wasn't very specific about it, but she said Colonel Daglingworth had fixed it up for her, because she was frightened of Goff and didn't want to stay in Elmbury. Susan thought it best not to ask questions. Rosemary had never talked to her about Daglingworth, save once when with a mischievous smile she'd said: "He can't keep his hands off you," adding cryptically: "but I like a man who is a man, all the same." It occurred to Susan that Col. D. was perhaps clearing the decks before he became a Member of Parliament; it might seem more prudent to have his mistress fifty miles away! On the other hand there might be nothing much in it—any pretty girl who worked for him was liable to get patted and pawed! Rosemary, who'd be loyal to anyone who treated her fairly, wasn't giving anything away. Holding Duffy in her arms and cuddling him, she smiled up at Susan. "Glad I'm going," she said, and shrugged her shoulders. Pretty as ever, perhaps a bit tougher, she took the world as she found it, never arguing or grumbling, accepting whatever fortune life might have in store for her with her curiously rueful little smile.

THREE OF THE TEDDIES were fined fifteen shillings each by a Bench whose Chairman obviously believed that boys would be boys and that Ferdo was a bit of an old Blimp for trying to stop them. On her way out of the Town Hall Susan successfully outstared Goff, but when she and Ferdo had gone by he joined up with a little gang of Teddies who though none of them had much self-confidence managed a rather feeble boo. Susan's ears, which were much sharper than Ferdo's, heard something else. "We'll be seeing you at Doddington!" called one of the Teddies, bolder than the rest. Susan had a moment's apprehension, glanced at her father, but obviously he hadn't heard; and she forgot the silly threat in half an hour.

But next Sunday evening the Teddies came. About a dozen of them rode out on motor-bikes and drank themselves silly in The Green Man. Long before closing time the landlord decided they'd had enough and refused to sell them any more. This annoyed them, and they rode down the drive to the Manor, left their motor-bikes by the stables, and perhaps with some childish notion of revenge rampaged across the bottom of the garden doing damage which was as pointless and futile as all their actions were. They broke down the cypress hedge, tore off the scarlet creeper that climbed up it, splashed about in the Otter Pool, smashed the windows of the summerhouse and then fell upon the little bronze statue of the boy. Its nakedness provoked the worst of their folly. They kicked it between the legs, knocked it sideways and then pulled off one of its arms. They found a brick from somewhere and hit it full in the face, flattening its nose. So they left it, which had been so beautiful, emasculated, battered and askew; and Ferdo wept when he saw it next morning.

It seemed that after they left the Otter Pool they went into the paddock. It must have been dark by then. Eventually Jack Northover heard their shouting, called Egbert and drove them away. They got on their motor-bikes, opened the throttles and went roaring down the drive. It wasn't until next morning that Jack realised what they'd been doing in the paddock. Some of them must have had catapults or air-guns. The others had contented themselves simply with chasing the two horses. Trumpeter had a small wound in his flank, which might have been caused by a pellet or a sharp stone, had cut his forelegs on some wire and was dead lame. He'd obviously had a rough time—his head drooped, and he looked 'hanghorse,' as Sandra would have put it. Nightshade was unmarked, but was still in a state of panic,—she sweated in terror when Susan went up to her, just as she'd done long ago at Stow Fair. To make sure she wasn't lame, Susan got on her back and rode her gently round the Park. She

was sound enough, but riding her was like sitting on a powder
barrel with a fuse sizzling.

Bringing her home, still dancing and distraught, Susan happened to remember an expression of her mother's. Janet must
have got it from *her* mother; it was a ridiculously upper-class
Edwardian thing. Whenever Janet wished to imply *fais ce que
vous voudrez*, behave as you like, she would put it in this affect-
edly old-fashioned, curiously snobbish way: and now the quaint
phrase had come home to roost with a vengeance:

"It doesn't matter *what* you do so long as you don't frighten
the horses!"

❡ 6

IT OCCURRED TO SUSAN, as she set off next day to meet Ben
at the station, that she was doing exactly that. One could do what
one liked, and get away with it, within the framework of the Establishment as Janet conceived it: for instance, although she'd
have disapproved, wouldn't have been really shocked, if she'd
known Susan had gone to bed with Tony—or if Susan now
took it into her head to spend a weekend with that Freddie who
was going to be a Lord. But to go off *à deux,* (as Janet would
have put it) to see a play with one's gardener's son (Shakespeare
too!) and what was more to do so clandestinely—that was frightening the horses indeed! Susan herself, with some alarm, surprise
and a little secret smile into her looking-glass, recognised the
oddity of what she was doing. As she came downstairs Mrs.
Fenton on hands and knees was scrubbing away in the hall. A
shaft of sunlight coming through the window made a halo of her
red hair. She didn't look up as Susan went by; when she was
scrubbing she never looked up, and she always appeared stern
and preoccupied, as if in her mind she were scrubbing away
the blemishes from an unjust society. She would probably
have been as horrified as Janet would have been, to learn that
Susan was on her way to meet Ben in secret.

However, this awareness that she was engaged in an adventure
utterly incongruous to her background and upbringing didn't
make any difference to Susan at all. Thinking about Ben this

morning, re-reading his last letter, she found herself looking forward to the meeting with an intense curiosity and excitement,
which she supposed was something well on the way to being in
love. If that was unreasonable, then love was unreasonable. Yet it
was less than six months since she'd been sighing her sighs about
Tony! Perhaps, she said to herself, I am at heart as much of a
wanton as Rosemary—it runs in the Ferdinando blood! Worse
than a wanton, I am a cheat as well, considering the appalling
lies I told to Mummy. But having admitted all this to herself,
Susan couldn't, to tell the truth, bring herself to feel ashamed.

This was her deceitful little plan. She had asked Ben what
time his train arrived at Cheltenham, and had arranged to meet
him there. They would then drive to Stratford, and would have
the whole afternoon and evening together. After the play she'd
bring him home to Huntsman's. As it happened, she hadn't
needed to invent an elaborate story for her parents' benefit.
She'd simply said that she was going to meet some people in
Stratford who were making up a party to see *Twelfth Night*.
She had been prepared for Janet, at any rate, to cross-examine
her about this; but much to her surprise her mother asked no
questions at all. Both she and Ferdo had been preoccupied and
unhappy yesterday; Ferdo was brokenhearted about the damage
to the little statue, Janet was more concerned about the horses
and whether there was any risk of the Teddies coming back
again.

"Trumpeter's lame as a cat," she'd said to Susan after breakfast. "Perhaps later on—in the cool of the evening—I could borrow Nightshade and have a bit of a gallop? I'm feeling down in
the dumps; I want to blow the cobwebs away."

"You'd better sit tight, Mummy," said Susan. "Take care you
don't blow away too!"

SUCH DECEIT as Susan had practised deserved, she suspected,
at least punctures and thunderstorms, if not indeed the final dis-
integration of the Land Rover's big-ends, which had been making ominous noises for weeks. In fact, everything went right for
her. Ben's train was dead on time. The hour-long journey from
Cheltenham to Stratford seemed, in Susan's mind, to occupy some
dozen or so minutes. At Stratford they walked beside the river

along a path which, they kidded themselves, Shakespeare's feet
had trod, and leaning over Clopton Bridge they laid their elbows
upon the well-worn parapet where perhaps he'd laid his elbows
some time when he leaned there with chin cupped in his hands.

The sun shone for them. Flotillas of white swans sailed upon
the Avon for their delight. Lest the unbroken blue of the sky
might suggest a suspicion of ennui, some charming small puffs of
snow-white cloud appeared in it and sailed by serenely as the
swans. Tawny-finn'd fishes, dim-seen in the deeps, moved among
the lily-stalks. Dragonflies hovered there, shining slim bodies
borne by invisible wings. It was these dragonflies, and the flat
green lily-pads, that reminded Susan of the Otter Pool; how often
and how persistently her mind went back to that! She remembered that one one of the lily-pads, when she swam among them,
a solitary beetle had crawled; and she had said to Tony that it
was a Robinson Crusoe beetle. Just a little while after that, lying
on the bank by the boy's statue, she had made a marvellous little
fool of herself, and it had seemed like the end of the world. Well,
you had to serve an apprenticeship to love, she knew that now;
love needed learning, and perhaps you went on learning all the
time. Ben as he leaned over the bridge at her side was preoccupied with the dim shadowy fishes. Susan took a quick glance
sideways at him, intent grey eyes under the untidy hazelnut-
coloured hair, and she felt certain that the curiosity and excitement with which she'd looked forward to this meeting had its
source in something genuine and real. It wasn't just a piece of
foolishness dreamed up in her mind. Then where the devil are
you going, girl? she asked herself severely; what do you imagine
you're up to, and where is it going to end?

There were no sensible answers; but her spirit felt wild and
bold and carefree, and she didn't care a damn.

THEN IT WAS TIME to go to the theatre.

For them, and it seemed for them alone, Sir Toby and Sir
Andrew clowned; Maria bubbled laughter like a freshet in
springtime; Olivia wept, Orlando longed, Viola masqueraded,
Malvolio minced, and Feste made his immortal affirmation that
ginger shall be hot i' the mouth too. It was only the savage
baiting of Malvolio at the end which seemed to flaw for Susan
the prettiest comedy that any man ever wrote; but it rather sur-

prised her to find that Ben, despite what she thought of as his battledress toughness, felt exactly the same. "I always hate that bit," he said as they walked out into the mothy dark afterwards. "But of course it isn't fair criticism to hate it. The audience Shakespeare wrote for had probably all watched at least one traitor hanged, drawn and quartered, at least one heretic burned alive. And remember, the Queen herself had been two years old when her mother's head was chopped off in public by order of her father!"

The theatre was floodlit, and threw a great reflection in red and gold which lay across the Avon, rippled now and then by the wakes of ghostly swans. Susan and Ben walking beside the river talked about those Elizabethans who had dared so much with their bodies and their minds. They both had a sharpened sense of adventure as they did so, were aware of a continuity and closeness, caught a glimpse across three and a half centuries of the blaze and the brightness, seemed to rekindle a little of that brightness in themselves.

Ben was emboldened to tell Susan something he'd obviously been longing to confide in her. There was a chance that he might be invited to put himself forward for a Constituency up north which was already held by Labour. The sitting Member was an oldish man who would probably decide to retire before the next General Election. He hadn't yet made up his mind. The seat was a marginal one—the majority last time had been less than a thousand. The party wanted a young man to fight it, and somebody had suggested Ben. He thought Aneurin Bevan might have had something to do with that—perhaps he'd pulled a few strings. Ben's National Service would be finished in a year's time, so if he were lucky enough to be chosen as the Labour candidate he would have to get a temporary job of some kind while he was waiting for the Election. "But that mightn't be for two or three years!" Not soon enough for Ben! When Susan said he'd be only twenty-seven he was almost impatient with her, told her that Pitt had been Prime Minister at twenty-five. He had a great self-confidence, though he wasn't conceited at all. "Willum's the really bright one of our lot," he said. "He's going to be a hell of a good surgeon one day. See if I'm right!" For himself, he was simply in a hurry to play his part in putting the world to rights; and for a start, arguing excitedly in the Land Rover on the way home, he and Susan together began to build a new Britain. Ben cheerfully demolished the existing Establishment stone by stone; Susan picked up a piece now and then which seemed to her to be valuable and spoke up for its virtues; Ben with that twitch of a smile which she sensed though she couldn't see it in the darkness seriously considered her argument, sometimes disputed, sometimes agreed. In this fashion the journey went by as swiftly as had the drive to Stratford from Cheltenham. They felt easy enough now to laugh at each other and to tease each other while they argued; and thus they got rid of all pretences, because neither would allow the other to maintain any pretence for long. And of course while their minds sparred, wary at first, inquisitive, probing, then tussling and contending as they warmed to the game and came to closer quarters, they were by no means unconscious of their physical closeness too. But they kept that provocation secret, though each knew well that the other experienced it likewise.

DODDINGTON MIGHT HAVE BEEN a hundred miles away; but suddenly they were there, they were turning into the drive between the overhanging oak-trees, the dark enclosing branches were all about them, and the problems inseparable from Doddington were pressing close upon Susan too. Like an omen—good or ill?—the indefatigable Ferdinando's Owl appeared in the headlamps. He went ahead of the Land Rover for thirty yards or so, his feathers fringed with light. Then they were at Huntsman's Cottage. By a strange mutual understanding they were now in a hurry to part; both aware of embarrassments and incongruities which had scarcely troubled their minds from the time they met this morning until they turned into the drive a minute ago. Susan didn't switch off the engine and Ben didn't offer to kiss her goodnight—she didn't expect him to and she knew it was right that he shouldn't. But as he pulled his suitcase out of the back seat he said very quietly:

"Can I see you again before I go?" He had told her that he was being posted to Malta, and that he'd probably be away for six months or more. It seemed desperately important to Susan that she should see something of him before he left.

"Of course we must meet. Oh yes! Tomorrow?"

"Where, when?"

They still had this sense of hurry to be parted. The unanswerable questions would catch up with them if they delayed a second longer! Susan said the first thing that came into her mind:

"Ferdinando's Oak. Tomorrow. Noon!"

HER THOUGHTS IN A TURMOIL, excited as well as frightened by the difficulties, dangers and obstacles which now loomed ahead, Susan drove into the courtyard and through the narrow gate into the stables, where the Land Rover was garaged. There were a lot of lights on in the Manor; she'd hoped that Janet and Ferdo would have both gone to bed. Then, to her surprise she noticed lights in Northover's cottage too; and now as she came out of the garage Jack Northover appeared hurrying towards her, a torch in his hand.

"What's up, Jack?" she called, before he was close to hear.

Then he came up, almost running.

"Miss Susan. I waited up for you. Nobody knew where you were. We couldn't get in touch——"

"What's the matter?" She knew from his voice it was something bad.

"Nightshade—" he began.

"Nightshade? She's hurt?"

"There was an accident. The mare bolted. Oh, Miss Susan, it's her Ladyship. I wanted to tell you before you——" And long before he'd finished the sentence Susan understood that her mother was dead.

PART EIGHT

The Waters Under the Earth

¶ 1

SCREAMING scent marvellous terrific cry wake anyone from dead !!! Gen. B. galloping past me shouted Ain't it BLOODY beautiful ? tears pouring down his cheeks cd. have been cold wind but I think emotion My dear old Trumpeter ears pricked cd. not understand why I held him back But cannot go like I used to It isn't the same TOUT PASSE TOUT CASSE TOUT LASSE??? *Real reason prob. concern about F.—To go like hell you must not care DAMN abt anything but thinking abt F. I care DEEPLY He NEEDS me . . .*

Susan had noticed the diary lying on the desk in what used to be her mother's study. It struck her that if Ferdo came in here (though she didn't think he ever would) he might begin to read the diary and that would upset him. So she picked it up to take it to her room. Then on an impulse she opened it at random and began to read it herself. It was rather eerie—like hearing her mother's voice again after all these months. Janet still seemed very close in this room, which had been shut up ever since the day she was killed. The loony hares, the blah otters, the smart-aleck foxes peered down from the walls. They'd have to be dusted—or destroyed. Susan hated them, but they'd been Janet's, so she thought they'd have to remain. Mrs. Northover would come in here, tearful, with the Hoover. She had told Susan yesterday:

"We ought to think about spring-cleaning. Her Ladyship never let it go later than March. The spring sunshine showed things up, she used to say."

It was showing them up today. The cold pale light coming through the window that needed cleaning threw a freckled pattern upon the opposite wall. Dust danced in it and was agitated by the draughts which seemed to blow everywhere in Doddington Manor, though you could only feel them in the winter; because of the dust-flurries you could *see* them now, like a microcosm of the world's winds; here a mistral, there a levanter, at ankle-level upon the landing a steadily-blowing trade!

The two spivvy foxes over the fireplace beadily gazed at Susan as she tried to decipher the abbreviations and the hieroglyphs. There were foxes, she discovered, in the diary too. On hunting days Janet, who went in greatly for doodles, had never failed to draw a small, neat, formalized fox. It had two pricked ears, a sharp muzzle, and a long straight brush. Within the outline were certain letters: 'H,' 'NC,' or 'E,' according to whether Janet had gone out with the Heythrop, the North Cotswold or the Elmbury. There was a little 'k' if they had killed, '2k' if they'd killed a brace.

On the day at which Susan had opened the diary they hadn't killed at all.

Ran into mkt. gdns WIRE everywhere one horse hurt then over main road SCORES cars hounds nearly run down exhaust fumes scent vanished then got going again good open country but STRAIGHT on to land of that OKKARD farmer (as if fox knew it !!)   who last time threatened shoot ? fox ?? hounds ??? US so Gen. B. swearing worst I ever heard apoplectic lkg. (it is so bad for him!) WHIPPED OFF Riding home wondered What wd. Mummy have Thought??!! In her day whole Warwickshire country was ORGANIZED for hntg.   I was too young but did get a GLIMPSE thro' her eyes of those times likened in a book I read to 'LONG GDN. PTY'   How true !!!   Book said it was as if SHOWER OF HAIL finished it (?? 1st World War?)   Never been the same since however hard we try to pretend   Lkg back on it I see lovely smooth green LAWNS tennis parties where nobody was v. good nobody tried to win Sometimes politer to lose No worries abt. staff   good relations with

everybody who worked for you   Trim little black and white
parlourmaids like Rmary once was (POOR CHILD !!!)
Manners Courtesy No Teddyboys then except of course
King E.7   great UNIQUE Teddyboy ?! but nobody
minded !! & Nobody minded us having more than them be-
cause we looked after them too BELLE EPOQUE !!!   Gone
forever will never come back now different outlook every-
body out for themselves equality etc. etc all v. well but think
(unfashionable nowadays!) much money in hands of a few
made for GRACIOUS LIVING preserved much Beauty Ele-
gance Decency Proprieties etc. now all Gone w. the wind . . .

AND I WONDER WHAT BEN would have to say to *that*
argument! thought Susan with a rare smile, her spirit leaping at
the reminder that she'd be seeing him again in three weeks' time.
Only this morning she'd had his letter from Malta telling her
that he was coming home. It would be nearly nine months since
she'd seen him. Their last brief meetings had been during the
distressful days after her mother's death, and Susan's recollection
of them was fragmentary and muddled because all had been in
confusion then. The house was in a kind of jungle darkness,
because Mrs. Northover in her old-fashioned way had insisted on
drawing all the blinds. They were mostly green, and the sunshine
seeped greenly through them. The unearthly light lent a ghostly
strangeness to the figures that moved about in it: broken Ferdo,
going without point or purpose to and fro from room to room;
the District Nurse, a-tiptoe; the undertaker from Elmbury who
was obviously a native of nightmare and much at home there:
whenever Susan encountered him his head was slightly bowed
and he was carrying his top hat in his hand. Into these Stygian
shades, at some time or another, stepped Ben with Gloria, and
Gloria was in distress also because, it seemed, she had chanced to
write that week in her Gossip Column some sharp quip or
lampoon about Hunting Women in general and about Janet in
particular. Too late she had tried to prevent it coming out in the
paper; it was in print already and the paper would be on sale
tomorrow. In fact Susan never read it or looked for it; but when
the *Intelligencer* came that Friday she put it on the fire to keep it
from Ferdo. So she never knew what mocking valediction her
mother had from Gloria's pen. Understanding Gloria's wretchedness, she'd put her arms round her, in front of Ben, and had

hugged her tight: and while she and Gloria in this odd way were sharing their distresses the telephone had started ringing, and Gloria sensing Susan's reluctance had said: "All right, I'll answer it." While she did so Ben said hesitantly: "Gloria might be useful, if you'd like to let her try. Being on the paper, she knows about things." Then Gloria had taken charge and dealt with various funeral matters, and with the sinister tophatted man who had crepe soles upon his boots and moved about the Manor in a dreadful silence, not even the dry-rot creaked beneath his tread.

Next day Susan had said goodbye to Ben, and he had said with the first smile she'd seen for days: "I'm leaving you in the charge of Gloria. Write to me about everything and I'll answer airmail by return." Then they shook hands; no kiss or touch of anything because it was the day of the funeral. The dim green forest of the house was inhabited by relations, some of whom Susan until now had heard of but never seen. Then the hearse, the flowers, the man in the top hat who reminded Susan somehow of an illustration in *Struwwelpeter,* and the rich brown butterscotch voice of Mr. Goodbody intoning (according to how you looked at it) the holy or the blasphemous words: "We give three hearty thanks, for that it hath pleased thee to deliver this our sister out of the miseries of this sinful world . . ."

BECAUSE HER FATHER at the graveside had looked as if he were going into battle upon the bridge of his ship, and because she'd had no experience until now of the numbing effect of grief, Susan had taken about a week to arrive at the realisation that it was she, not her father, who was now in command. When the numbness wore off and the pain returned he started drinking again, sometimes desperately, seeking to use drink as an anaesthetic. But of course it didn't act in this way; because it sharpened memories before it dulled them, it caused more pain than it was able to assuage. So he tried to stop drinking, and sometimes he kept off it for weeks on end. Even then there were days when a cloud would settle upon his mind, and Susan could make no contact with him while he brooded alone in his dreadful darkness. This frightened her because it couldn't be dismissed and explained away with the usual excuse of too much claret.

Yet there were other times when his mind seemed as clear as

the morning, when he was a whole man again instead of a broken one, and because of the contrast with his bad days he appeared to Susan to be just as she remembered him years and years ago. Then love and pity for him would tear at her heart, and she understood why Cordelia had loved *her* father and how much *her* love must have hurt. She saw now that as you went through life you learned more and more about love in all its aspects all the time. One lesson she learned concerned her mother. Some of Janet's attitudes had been so out-of-date and silly that Susan hadn't realised how much love lay hidden behind them, nor how much Ferdo had relied upon her over almost every trivial thing. She must have known long ago that Ferdo's mind was beginning to fail; yet Susan remembered an occasion when her mother had almost lost her temper with her because she had suggested that all was not well with him. "Rubbish! Your father may be forgetful but his mind's as good as yours or mine." Janet had fairly snapped at her; and Susan had thought: Doesn't she *notice,* why doesn't she use her *eyes?* Little fool! She ought to have guessed that Janet was short with her because she had seen only too clearly what was happening; had fearfully watched that cloud creeping across Ferdo's mind; had perhaps tried hard to persuade herself that it was nothing—and so was shocked and upset because Susan had noticed it too.

> *He NEEDS me* [Susan read on]. *"Too much port etc. etc I know (only too well!) but there is SOMETHING ELSE and am sure his old wound is at the root of it His stammer a little bit worse every year and bad headaches sometimes give him BLACKOUT wh. he hasn't had for yrs. Have tried & tried to get him see Dr. but he is obstinate & I know why !! afraid of facing truth in case it may be bad just as he is abt the dry rot will not admit it yet is afraid of it (will not GO into some parts of house because of it !!) and it is all part of his strange OBSESSION idée fixe almost!! abt decay fungi mice all sorts of pests etc Met him on the landing yestday carrying MOUSETRAP in his hand he had set it looked at me ODDLY didn't want me to see it it went off & caught his finger One cd laugh but oh GOD nothing funny really knowing him so well I get INSIGHT how his mind works and am frightened He sees pests decay etc everywhere . . .*

SUSAN SAW HOW HIS MIND WORKED TOO. Through all the nightmare autumn and winter she had watched him, had sought to cheer and to comfort and distract him, had tried to understand his fears and his fantasies in order that she might be able to help him keep them at bay. One night over his port he had told her about the vampire mice in his dream and had made a joke of the whole thing. "Have you ever heard of such a ridiculous dream in your life?" But he was always cutting himself when he shaved nowadays, and Susan was always finding little bits of bloody cotton-wool in his waste-paper-basket or on his bathroom floor. Once she saw a mousetrap there too. Then, in dismay, she began to wonder whether perhaps there was not for Ferdo some undefined frontier between his dream and reality, a twilit borderland in which those vampire mice scuttled even by day . . .

As for the dry-rot, she'd disobeyed his orders and had started to do something about it. She'd taken the builders to the places where the queer sweet smell was worst. They had pulled up some of the floorboards, and now they were finding dry-rot everywhere. There was one whole floor which was actually unsafe, where they said the joists were so rotten that 'they'd flake away when you scratched 'em like dry powdery cheese.' One consequence of the builders' pulling up some of the floorboards was that there were more draughts in the Manor than ever before. In the stillness of the night you could hear the ghostly stirring of a curtain as its hem just brushed the floor. Windows rattled, floors creaked, the wind whined in the crooked chimneys, mice—real ones!—scuttled and squeaked. Mrs. Northover discovered 'a nasty smell' in the pantry, and said she was certain that there were cockroaches there. And indeed one day she caught one, which had only just hatched and so like a horse-chestnut just out of its shell) was cream-coloured instead of brown. She put it in a matchbox and carried it to Susan: "a white blackbeetle," she said. It seemed to Susan even more disgusting than the ordinary kind.

Susan sometimes wondered if she was catching the obsession from her father, if she was herself becoming infected with his haunting awareness of decay. Certainly if you looked for it, both inside and outside the Manor, decay was manifest everywhere. One night a most disagreeable thing happened. Susan had been

out to dinner with Sandra—Sandra with frantic generosity had
lately been trying to cheer her up, to 'take her out of herself,' to
make up to Susan perhaps for that lapse from loyalty, when she'd
let Tony make love to her in town! It was fairly late when Susan
got home, and she found her father sitting in the dark beside the
last faint embers of the fire. He'd put out the reading-lamp by his
chair and presumably had fallen asleep; otherwise he'd have seen
to the fire. But he wasn't asleep now. He said to Susan urgently,
as she opened the door:

"Don't put the light on. Come here. I want to show you something."

She went quickly across to him in the dark. He was sitting up
tensely in his chair, his hands tightly clutching the arms.

"Look over there. *Can't you see it too?*"

Then she saw it in the log-box, a very faint, greenish phos-
phorescent glow. She went over to the log-box, and then she realised what it was. Egbert, she knew, had been cutting up some of
the dead and dying trees. This must be a piece of one of the
fungus-infected ones which she'd seen in Jubilee Wood glowing
dimly in the dark. She picked up the log and showed it to Ferdo.
He shuddered:

"Burn it, burn it, get it out of the way."

She poked up the fire, and when there was a good blaze going
she threw on to it the log which didn't look any different
from any other log, now that she'd switched the lights on. She
wondered how long Ferdo had been sitting there in the dark,
awake or half-awake, staring at it.

IN HER LETTERS ONCE A WEEK she told Ben everything:
about the luminous log and the vampire mice, about the road
marching inexorably through the woods and all the problems it
brought with it, about her interviews with the Bank Manager and
the lawyers and her efforts to make some sort of order out of the
general chaos of Doddington. She had the whole responsibility
on her shoulders and no one but Ben to confide in. Stephen was
six thousand miles away, botanizing in a Sikkim valley from
which on a clear day he could lift up his eyes to the shining
splendour of Kanchenjunga. Letters took weeks; she hadn't had
one since Christmas, when he told her he was camping at the

edge of a whole forest of rhododendrons, and he enclosed some pressed petals of a special rhododendron which, however, the mail had not been kind to: when they fell out of the envelope they were no more exciting than half a teaspoonful of rather powdery tea.

Even if Ben hadn't answered her letters, she thought she would have written to him all the same. It helped a lot to set her problems down on paper, and the questions she asked him were the questions she was asking herself, and to which very often she didn't know the answers. But Ben, as he'd promised, answered always by return; seriously, sensibly, intimately—and sometimes through the seriousness she was aware of his slow smile. As they had done before, they came very close through their letters; but now it mattered to her very much more. She was always listening for the postman on the mornings when they usually came.

His answers really helped her; she acted on them as a rule. But there was one thing which he couldn't understand and which she knew they would have to argue about when he came home. It seemed crazy to him—and obviously in the light of the Seldon finances it was utterly crazy—to stay on in the tumbledown house which they couldn't afford even to keep in repair. The remedy seemed so simple. Ferdo should sell some of his land and with the money he got for it build a smallish house, in the woods if he liked the woods, and as for Doddington Manor, he should sell it or pull it down. Of course this made sense; but Susan knew in her heart that come what may they had to stay on at the Manor, though when she tried to explain why it was as difficult, and as fruitless, as trying to explain an obscure poem. She only knew that as long as her father lived he'd have to remain at Dodding-ton even if the very roof collapsed over his head; and for as long as he lived she had to stay there too and look after him. Com-monsense didn't come into this business at all. It simply wasn't arguable; and Susan accepted the situation without question or complaint—though it did occur to her as funny that she used to feel guilty about living idly at home and not doing a job,—as if she had belonged to her mother's generation! Well, she'd got her job now, with a vengeance.

SHE CLOSED HER MOTHER'S DIARY and went to the speckledy window and looked out. Beyond the stables there was a row of tall elms. She noticed their warm colour, almost purple in the sun, and the golliwog rooks sitting in them among the blobs of their nests against the blue sky. She was aware of the quickening of the spring, and felt her spirit quickening with it; she hadn't *noticed* such things as rooks or trees or skies for months. Against the wall of the stables the forsythia was in full flower, exactly the colour of scrambled egg. And right underneath the window, in the little bulb-border her mother used to look after, crocus candles were burning out of the dark soil. Across the courtyard flew the Fenton washing, looking quite gay; the fresh wind was playing about with some dashing pants of Gloria's—but they wouldn't be seen at Doddington much longer, because Gloria had been offered an exciting job as reporter on a London daily, and next week she was off to town. Doddington couldn't hold the young Fentons; only Adam and Eve were left now, and in a few years' time they too would be spreading their wings. Looking down from her window over the courtyard wall upon the back-garden of Huntsman's Cottage, Susan caught a glimpse of the angular figure of Fenton himself, curiously foreshortened, as he manipulated the washing-line, lowering it so that Mrs. Fenton could stretch up and reach Gloria's dancing pants.

Susan's thoughts went straight back to Ben.

She'd told her father about him: at least she'd said that she was writing him letters, and getting his letters, and she liked him very much. Ferdo had simply said, as he'd done once before: "I've got a lot of time for the Royal Marines." But then—it was one of his good days—he'd leaned back in his chair and had given her an odd look, quizzical and confidential. She wondered what conclusions he'd drawn from those weekly letters. Whatever it was, it didn't seem to trouble him. He grinned and said: "You know what Kipling wrote—'A kind of a giddy Harum-frodite'—that was his term for a Royal Marine!"

He'd been much better lately. He wasn't drinking too much, and during the winter weather he'd renewed his interest in the bird-table rigged up outside the sitting-room window. On some days he was content to sit and watch it for hours. Susan had left him there after breakfast this morning. The argy-bargy starlings entertained him, and he was probably sitting there still. She collected up all the diaries she could find on her mother's desk, to hide them in her room and keep them safe from Ferdo. Then she would go down and tell him that Ben was coming home from Malta.

EGBERT HAD MADE THE BIRD-TABLE, which fitted close against the sitting-room window. It had a pole with a sort of yard-arm arrangement, designed by Ferdo, from which was hung the lump of suet for the tits. Like everything carpentered by Egbert it had been made to last for a hundred years. He had grumbled, of course, all the time he worked on it. He thought it would encourage the spadgers and other pestses. And so it did; but it afforded Ferdo the greatest pleasure as he watched the starlings which played up like low comedians, and the acrobatic tits which he got to know individually and for which he invented names. A regular attendant was Whisky, one of the black-and-white blackbirds whose nestlings, Ferdo thought, had been destroyed by the Teddy-boys. In the coldest weather there had been rarer, more exciting visitors. One day a nuthatch came, but it found nothing to its liking, and after a quick look round it flew away. Two or three times during January a greater spotted woodpecker, splendidly incarnadined, had alighted upon the lump of fat and pecked away at it for twenty minutes or so. It made a happy morning for Ferdo, when the woodpecker came.

Sometimes he would doze in his chair, and the birds coming to the table would seem to fly in and out of his dreams. This morning, after one of these catnaps, he opened his eyes to see a grey squirrel, bold as brass, rippling towards him across the lawn. Another of those little bastards, another of those pests! He still blamed the grey squirrels for usurping the red ones; they didn't belong to Doddington and they had no right here. They were pests of the woodlands, as mice were pests of the Manor. This one now stopped in the middle of the lawn and cautiously looked around. Ferdo leaned forward and quickly pushed open the window. Then he went to the gunroom and fetched his 12. bore. He slipped in a couple of cartridges, sat himself comfortably in his chair and took aim.

Just as he was about to pull the trigger, however, the squirrel
sitting up on its hind legs began to clean its whiskers with its
paws. This was so endearing an action that Ferdo could not
bring himself to shoot. After a minute or two he laid down the
gun. The grey squirrel hopped a bit nearer. Now that he could
see it better, Ferdo was amused by its pert and intelligent air. It
was less than a dozen yards away, and he could have blown it to
smithereens, but he decided not to. Perhaps it intended to rob
the bird-table. That would be fun—a squirrel on the window-
sill! He remembered that somebody had told him grey squirrels
could be tempted by chocolate, so he pottered off and found the
remains of a box of Suchard which Susan had given him for
Christmas, because it was his favourite kind.

When he came back the squirrel was within a few yards of the
bird-table; but it caught sight of him and scurried away. It did
not go far, however. It stopped at the edge of the lawn. Ferdo
broke up one of the pieces of plain chocolate and put some of it
on the bird-table, some on the window-sill. He settled down to
wait; and before long he went to sleep again. Soon he thought he
was dreaming, because he saw the grey squirrel sitting on the
bird-table. Perhaps it had made some little sound when it landed
there, and this was what had woken him up. He sat very still in
his chair, and at last the little beast picked up a morsel of chocolate in its front paws, examined it suspiciously and began to
nibble it. When it had finished it moved an inch or two nearer to
the window, and took another piece.

Ferdo was delighted by all this. He had never seen a grey
squirrel at such close quarters before. It even came close enough
to seize one of the pieces of chocolate which he'd laid on the sill;
but just then it must have noticed some slight movement on his
part, and it jumped back on to the edge of the bird-table. From
that point of vantage, sitting up on his hind legs, ready at any
moment to flee if need be, it peered into the room. Its whiskers
twitched. The lips drawn back in excitement or curiosity
showed the little teeth and gave to its expression the semblance
of a smile.

You cheeky little upstart, thought Ferdo, ousting your betters,
those beautiful bright red squirrels, from my Doddington woods!
They've lived here since long before Domesday Book. Nobody
in these parts had *heard* of your kind twenty years ago . . .

Your betters, I said. But who's to decide what's better or worse in your world of squirrels? Maybe the better squirrel is the one who knows best how to survive in the rough tough world as it is today; the one that's got the most enterprise and the most guts!

Good luck to you, little upstart, thought Ferdo, as the squirrel made up its mind to go home and poured itself almost like a snake over the edge of the bird-table. Come back and see me another day! Then Ferdo dozed, and dreamed and half woke, saw the bird-table was deserted, dozed and dreamed again.

He was woken up by Susan's voice, speaking urgently.

"Daddy!"

He shook himself into consciousness.

"Daddy, are you all *right?*"

"Yes, of course. Why?" Then he saw her looking at the gun on his lap. She'd sounded frightened.

"It was a g-g-grey squirrel," he said. "It came over the lawn."

"You didn't get a shot?"

"No, it jumped up on the bird-table and I gave it some chocolate instead."

"It's ages," she said, still a bit doubtfully, "since I last saw you with a gun." She picked it up off his lap, and broke it open and took out the two cartridges. "Do grey squirrels really eat chocolate?" He knew she was still wondering if he'd dreamed it.

"This one did . . . What's that letter you've got in your hand?" he asked her.

"I was going to show you. It's from Ben. He's coming home from Malta. In three weeks' time. You know I like him, Daddy."

"Your giddy Harumfrodite?" He grinned at her. "Yes, I know you like him. Lucky chap."

❡ 2

THOSE HALF DOZEN DAYS AFTER BEN came home were the greenest April days Susan had ever known. And down by Cuckoo Pen when she took him walking there she heard the cheerfullest cuckoos and the most welcome chiffchaffs, smelt the sweetest violets, saw the mauvest ladysmocks, the laciest white umbels, the longest lambikin-tails on the hazels, the yellowest yellowhammer (he was so gorgeous he looked like some tropical bird!), the most highly-polished celandines and the most richly-enamelled kingcups with the busiest attendant bumbles buzzing about them.

In the paddock behind the stables the grass was lusher than ever before and the horses were shinier. They lay down in the deep grass as horses do only in the pleasantest spring weather; they allowed Susan and Ben to walk up to them and to play with their soft ears. The dun pony which young Adam rode was so fat that its body would have fitted perfectly into a hoop! Nightshade was as glossy as a berry once again; even old Trumpeter's light chestnut coat looked as right as a lion's pelt in the sun which shone so bright for Susan because her winter had been so dark. On the third day of Ben's leave she decided that she must teach him to ride; he must become a Horse Marine. So she put him in the saddle upon sobersides Trumpeter, while she rode Nightshade a-dance beside him along the lane.

She was teaching him too about the things which for her were part and parcel of Doddington: about its flowers, which she'd learned from Stephen, its birds and trees, which she'd learned from her father, its lore and legend which she'd learned from Egbert. It surprised Ben and greatly amused him that she could so easily slip into the Gloucestershire speech to tell a story or repeat a country saying. Ferdo could do it too, of course; he'd told her once that the Seldons were always bilingual. In her case she'd learned those broad vowels from an Old Nanny who had been born at Doddington—the daughter of great-grandfather Seldon's cook—getting on for a hundred years ago. The garrulous old dame had talked very much like Juliet's Nurse, chuckling to herself and clucking her tongue and saying her little jokes three times over. 'Thou wilt fall backwards when thou hast more wit' would by no means have come amiss from her!

Ben had been quick to realise that the inhabitants of Susan's England, whether bird or beast or flower or human, were much the same kind as those which Shakespeare had grown up among, thirty miles and four hundred years away. Again and again, in these woods which might have been Arden, Susan would show him something or tell him something which would remind them both of this; and they would share a quick awareness of the blessed continuity of English things.

But in other respects, of course, Ben's England was much wider than hers. It included his Cockney childhood, for one thing. Then he had spent whole vacations, when he was up at Oxford, looking at factories, docks and mines; he'd explored the industrial Midlands and the North,—he thought it was just as important to do this as to go abroad. So his view of England took in the shipyards of Tyneside and the slums of the Black Country, comprised Lancashire mill-girls and car-body bashers of Coventry, Derbyshire miners and Hull trawlermen and Liverpool dockers, the backstreets of Birmingham and the dark satanic mills sprawling across the West Riding from Huddersfield to Leeds.

All these things were a far cry from the cuckoo-buds of yellow hue, and the lark that tirra-lirra sings, and a hey and a ho and a hey nonino, he told Susan.

BUT THE NEW ROAD smashing its way through the woods brought such things every day a little bit closer. Only forty minutes from Doddington to Birmingham when the motorway was done! In the bluebell-glade now the doomed oaks had been cut down and carried away. Where last spring the blue carpet had stretched between the trees was an ant-heap activity of machines and men, going on against a background of mounds and craters which might have been a landscape of the moon. During the winter muddy lakes had formed there among the huge heaps of ochre-coloured clay. The water in the lakes had become yellow, matching the yellow bulldozers and diggers which bunted and delved and splashed and wallowed among them. The men with shovels and wheelbarrows wore shiny shapeless yellow weatherproof clothes; they looked like spacemen who had just landed on the moon. It was the most depressing spectacle that Susan had ever seen.

But now at last the lineaments of the road were beginning to show through the chaos. Susan took Ben down there upon a morning of fitful sunshine and brief, glistening showers; and they stood at the edge of the busy ant-hill beneath a stark and broken oak from which the ubiquitous olive bird gabbled against the rattle of machinery: *Chiffchaff–chiffchaff–chiff*—seeming to leave an uncomfortable question-mark when with its statement unfinished it abruptly ceased its song.

The chiffchaff repeated itself against a chorus of concrete-mixers. At the other side of the ant-hill a flyover was taking shape, by which the giant road would stride across Elmbury Back Lane. At this point, for the information of all who passed by, a large yellow noticeboard had been erected. Its awe-inspiring legend ran:

EARTH MOVING BY DICK HAMPTON

Ben took a good look at it and said at last:
"Earth moving! How grand. Like a boast of the gods!"
"Or the worms," said Susan, and was rewarded by his slow appreciative smile. Their minds matched well and went along together. Susan had never been so close to anybody in her thoughts before.

FERDO HAD SUGGESTED TO SUSAN that she should bring him home to lunch. This was his last day at Doddington, although it wasn't quite the end of his leave; he'd been asked to go up to his prospective Constituency for an interview with the Selection Committee before he went back to Devon to rejoin his Commando. Susan was going to drive him to the station in the afternoon.

It was one of Ferdo's good days. He'd had a small triumph this morning in his wooing of the grey squirrel: he'd persuaded it to come in through the window and take a piece of chocolate out of his hand. He was very proud of this: "I had to hold my breath and stay dead still. In spite of all the booze my hand can't be shaking *too* badly!" During the whole of lunch he was his old self again. He liked Ben, and he admired the Royal Marines, cheerful Jacks-of-all-trades who could turn their hands to almost anything on land or sea: *Per mare, per terram* for their motto, and the Globe and Laurel for their badge! He'd served with them, he said, all over the world from the West Indies to the Yangtze Kiang. He was a very good storyteller and today for Ben's benefit he told some excellent tales, about his service during a couple of wars and during the precarious peace in between.

It happened to be Mrs. Northover's day off, so Susan cleared away and did the washing up, while Ferdo took Ben on a tour of the family portraits.

"Would you like to start at the beginning or the end?" he asked; and he approved of Ben's reply.

"I think the best way to look at history is from where we stand now. Let's begin at this end."

So they started with the Orpen picture of Ferdo himself, looking very much like a young pirate, as a Lieutenant-Commander in the early Nineteen-twenties, and finished with the likeness of the first Ferdinando, done to the life as an old pirate, in 1580 or thereabouts. There were a dozen footnotes to English history in the form of period portraits in between. Ben had paused before the last but one, which was of the first Ferdinando's daughter, the girl Benedicta who'd eloped with a wool-stapler from the Cotswolds when she was sixteen. Ben had said:

"She's a bit like Susan, Sir, isn't she?"

"Hm," said Ferdo judicially. "I daresay. There's certainly a look in the eyes; and the mouth. She was the bad girl of the family—ran away with a chap they didn't approve of." Ben looked so alarmed at this that Ferdo had a job to keep a straight face when he added charitably: "Don't altogether blame her: she looks as if she knew her own mind."

Then he took Ben into the sitting-room and gave him a glass of port.

"So you're hoping to stand for Parliament. Good luck to you. The country and the world, they both look a hell of a muddle to me."

"To me too," Ben smiled.

"And of course you want to put it to rights . . . I expect," said Ferdo, "those Seldons I've been showing you, and whatever they represent, all seem a bit irrelevant."

Ben pleased him a second time when he answered honestly:

"No, Sir. Nothing's irrelevant. I mean we inherit the lot, all that's gone before us, good and bad and splendid and silly, and it's up to us to make the best we can of it."

Ferdo then remembered Stephen talking about Ben: it was after he'd been to Oxford to speak to the Labour Club or whatever it was. He had said he was in favour of rebels, but he wished they could all be classical scholars like Ben, so that they'd have an eye to the past as well as to the future. He'd surprised Ferdo by saying: "If Ben Fenton does go into politics, there's no one

I'd sooner put my money on than him." Ferdo, whose career had given him a bias in favour of simple solutions, still mistrusted politicians of every colour impartially: but he'd altogether taken to this young man whom Susan was obviously fond of. He wasn't such an old fool that he couldn't see that! He had seen it coming on, all those letters,—he'd watched her going broody, as Janet would have put it in the case of anybody's daughter but her own. *What in the world* would Janet have thought about the present situation: about Susan and this young scholar and officer and gentleman—gentleman by any sensible standards, though not by hers? Ferdo in sudden panic bundled Janet out of his mind because he was frightened of thinking about her, scared stiff of calling her up into his memory at all. He poured himself out another glass of port, and quickly drank it, and before long though Ben was sitting on the sofa opposite him he felt himself beginning to doze. He gave Ben an apologetic grin, and the young man grinned back.

When he woke up Ben was still sitting there, reading the paper. Ferdo was able to observe him carefully, while Ben thought he was still asleep. The more he looked at him the more he liked him. He judged by a simple Naval yardstick. In an action, if things were a bit sticky, would I give him the difficult, the dangerous, perhaps the sacrificial job? Deciding that he would do so, Ferdo half-dozed again. The next time he opened his eyes was when Susan came back from her washing up. She too assumed he was fast asleep. She glanced at him briefly, then looked towards Ben with at first a dubious smile, her April expression as Ferdo thought of it, like a cloudy morning with the sun just about to break through. It broke through, delightedly. She gave a little toss of her head, and ran up to Ben sitting on the sofa, and settled beside him like a settling bird.

¶ 3

THE NEXT TIME BEN CAME HOME it was late summer and the weather had broken suddenly. A petulant wind tugged at the laden boughs of the oaks and the acorns came showering down. They rattled on the bonnet of the Land Rover when Susan drove

between the trees in Elmbury Back Lane, on her way to pick up
Ben from the station. She had a sharp sense of the summer ending as she glanced up at the branches tossing against the grey sky.
Two or three evenings ago, in the garden after dinner, Ferdo had
pointed out to her that the swifts had departed; and she'd listened to the silence, suddenly surprised by it,—she'd become so
used to them screaming low over the lawn. Her father was always
the first to notice when in turn the swifts and the martins and
the swallows took their departure. He was sad when they left;
he said it made his tummy turn over to think of those small
things setting out on the hazardous journey across the sea. Also of
course their going was a reminder of another summer gone.

He'd been restless and unhappy for a couple of days; and
Susan knew he had another cause for disquiet than the passing of
a season. He couldn't settle down to anything. He even alarmed
his grey squirrel by his impatience, so that instead of coming
through the window for its chocolate it took fright and scurried
away. About a dozen times a day he switched on the radio (generally on the wrong station!) to listen to the news. He told Susan
he didn't like the way things were going in Egypt. The old
warhorse sniffed war.

On the 26th of July Nasser had dramatically announced his
seizure of the Suez Canal. There had been urgent comings and
goings of statesmen ever since. The Prime Minister had been
seeing the Chiefs of the Services. The French said they were
ready to use force if necessary. John Foster Dulles flew hither and
thither soft-soaping everybody. But more warships were going
out to the Med.

Even near at home, ominous things were happening. The big
depôt for Army vehicles just outside Elmbury became a hive of
activity suddenly. Military policemen appeared at the entrances;
motorists were told not to loiter, photographs were forbidden.
Yet the secret operation which was going on at the depôt was
plain for the whole world to see. Hordes of workmen with tons of
paint were changing the colour of hundreds of lorries, tanks,
scout cars, DUKWs and ambulances from olive-green to pale
beige. And even the stick-in-the-muds of Elmbury realised that
pale beige was the colour of sand.

Two of these sand-coloured DUKWs, labelled ON TEST in big

letters, had been driven down the Ferry Lane and into the river, to make sure that they would float; and to the surprise of the members of the Elmbury Popular Angling Society, which upon that day was holding its annual Contest, they failed to float. Their crews, providently wearing Mae Wests, managed to swim ashore.

"Bugger the Suez Canal!" said Ferdo. "The world would have been a damn sight better off without it. The blessed Canal lost us India for one thing."

This was a pet theory of his, that relations between the British and the Indians had been excellent until the cutting of the Canal shortened the voyage to India, so that it was convenient for wives to visit their husbands there. Previously, said Ferdo, there had been the usual class distinctions but no distinction on the grounds of colour. Your General or Administrator would feel himself infinitely superior to a sweeper; but he would regard himself as the social equal of, say, the local Rajah's sons or brothers. It was the British women, in Ferdo's opinion, who had introduced colour prejudice and the damn-silly notion of white superiority into our Government of India; and who, of course, had propagated the idea that it was unthinkable to marry a 'native' and wicked to sleep with one. "What could be more insulting," asked Ferdo, "to any people whom you set out to govern than the attitude that it's wrong to make love to them?" Before long this attitude had so permeated our society that the inferiority of 'natives' everywhere became an article of our faith. We inculcated it into tens of thousands of public schoolboys and sent them all over the world to govern various 'natives' whom they'd been taught to despise. As a further demonstration of their contempt they segregated themselves in social clubs and bridge clubs and tennis clubs and golf clubs from which the natives were excluded, and contrived to reproduce as nearly as possible, whether in Sarawak or the Sudan, in Colombo or in Cairo, the nearest possible approximation to life as it went along in middle-class suburban England.

"So it doesn't altogether surprise me, Susan," said Ferdo with a grin, "when Colonel Nasser or anybody else like him, demonstrates that he doesn't exactly love us. I've been all over the world and it's broken my heart to see what a cock we've made of

our marvellous Empire But by seizing the Canal I reckon the
Colonel's gone a bit too far. I've got a feeling that before long
something's going to blow up with a rather loud international
bang."

BEN SAID THERE WAS certainly a flap on; he'd got only
forty-eight hours' leave because of the flap. The Suez affair had
presented him with a personal problem too. His period of National Service was due to finish at the end of the month; but the
Marines had asked him to stay on as long as the crisis lasted.
Simultaneously, he'd had a letter from the Chairman of the
Constituency Selection Committee telling him that his name was
now on a short list of three. They wanted him to go up for
another interview; there was a great hurry because the sitting
Member had had a mild coronary, which had frightened him
considerably, and he was anxious to retire soon instead of waiting for the Dissolution. There might be a by-election in a matter
of months; so the Party had to make up its mind about a Candidate immediately . . .

"But of course you had to say no," said Susan.

He shrugged his shoulders. "I'm a Royal Marine," the shrug
seemed to say. All the same, damn the Marines and damn Suez!
But for the crisis he might have been an M.P. by Christmas.

"But I really believe there is going to be a showdown," he said.
"The Marines think so, anyway. The funny thing is that I'm
dead against trying a military solution. I don't think that's the
way. But if you're in the Services you have to abdicate your
judgement. You've got to shut your mind, and you know how I
hate doing that——"

He smiled at Susan, and she knew very well that was what
mattered most to him. Ben wouldn't be afraid of bombs and
bullets. What he dreaded was the sacrifice of his citizen's privilege of making up his mind about what was right or wrong.

"But if I'd opted to get out, and there was a landing and my
Commando was there—you can see how I'd feel."

He was a Royal Marine: so there had been no choice really.

HE TOLD ALL THIS to Susan on the way back from Cheltenham station; and now it was sinking in, now she was beginning to
understand that this might be the last time she would see him

before the battle or the war or whatever it was going to be. All her delight in meeting Ben again was swallowed up in this sudden fear. Forty-eight hours' leave—he'd have to catch a train tomorrow evening. She felt the minutes flying away,—and here they were already in the drive, bouncing among the potholes, fetching up with a bump and a splash in the biggest pothole of all, which was immediately in front of Huntsman's Cottage.

"The one Colonel Daglingworth stuck in," Susan said, "when you let the wind out of his tyre!"

Ben smiled.

"I often think of that; I suppose because that was the day when I first met you. There I was in your courtyard, with the gravel hurting my knees, and you so close. Your scent and your shoulders—funny what sticks in one's mind! You've never told me why you were on our side against Daglingworth?"

"He pawed me. It was as simple as that."

"He would," said Ben. He added, meaning it: "How right I was to hate him."

"Well, you mustn't any more," said Susan. "Now he's got everything he wants, money and power and Parliament and a knighthood in the offing, he's got lung cancer too. Sandra told me yesterday. He knows. But he's pretending to everybody, including Mrs. D. and Sandra, that he doesn't. Sandra cried because he was being so brave. He means to die like a——"

"In the high Roman fashion," said Ben. She'd been about to say 'like a Roman emperor,' because she'd always seen him like that: nightingale's tongue, a purple toga, lust and vulgarity and greed and pride and a sort of arrogant vainglorious courage.

It pleased her as always to see how well her thoughts went along with Ben's. It was an intimacy which, until now, had taken precedence over their physical closeness. They'd been moving towards that more slowly, more hesitantly; not always assuredly, handicapped by their separations, set back by partings. As Ben got out of the Land Rover and reached into the back seat for his suitcase he leaned against her by accident or on purpose, and straightway her thoughts went back to that frantic, hurried parting—as if they had been afraid of what was happening to them—after they'd been to see *Twelfth Night:* The day her mother was killed. Ben had been humming the tune of "O Mistress Mine," in embarrassment, probably. Now as Susan in her head matched the words to that tune: 'Present mirth hath present laughter, What's to come is still unsure,' she knew she was frightened of what was to come, and with that fear came a physical urgency, a sense of hurry, a drumbeat in her body and in her mind.

FERDO HAD SAID: "Bring him in to dinner, upon my soul, I take to your Royal Marine"; but Susan hadn't liked to invite him when she learned that he was home for only one night. It wouldn't be fair to his mother and father. Heaven knew what *they* thought about this business! It was something Susan would have to face up to one of these days; tonight she funked it, and put it right out of her mind. She must contrive to see Ben somehow, it was the hours not the minutes which were flying away now, he'd be on his way to Devon this time tomorrow evening! In the end she told him that Ferdo would like to see him before he went back, and suggested that he might come round after dinner. He had said he would come about nine.

And now she was glad she hadn't asked him earlier. Ferdo was in poor form, he had a bad headache, it was one of those occasions when he looked old and ill. He'd had some gin and French before dinner; then he'd opened a bottle of claret. Susan drank a couple of glasses, out of sheer nervousness really, because she was waiting for Ben. They acted on her quickly, as drink always did; Ferdo pressed her to have another, and after that she felt as heedless and headstrong as Benedicta looked in her portrait, smiling confidentially down at her as Susan passed by on her way out of the dining-room.

Then at last she heard the front-door bell.

Ferdo had taken the port with him into the sitting-room. He poured out a glass for Ben, and asked him what he thought about the crisis. It was fun, as always for Susan, to watch Ben's disciplined mind getting on terms with a problem, questing and questioning, accepting nothing before he'd carefully examined it. She thought how exciting it would be to hear him debating in the House of Commons. Perhaps she would one day!

Then Ferdo said:

"But you'll forget all the arguments when the guns start!"

"I hope I shall, Sir."

Susan was suddenly frightened again. Ferdo put down his wine-

glass and leaned back in his chair; soon she saw his eyelids drooping. He'd doze now for half an hour or so. Then he'd wake up
and pour himself another glass of port! She signalled to Ben,
conspiratorially, and on tiptoe she led him out.

When they were through the door she whispered:

"I'm sorry, Ben. He's not himself tonight. It's one of his bad
days."

"Yes," he said. "I could see that."

"I couldn't leave him," she said. "I've got to look after him,
you realise that?"

This was something they'd never talked about before, but
there was no need for long explanations between them now. Ben
looked at her and nodded in quick understanding.

Susan said:

"We couldn't go on sitting there, with Daddy snoring! Let me
show you the house. You've never explored it before."

She took him up the wide shallow staircase with the carved oak
balusters, on to the first floor landing where the grandfather
clock ticked so loudly that Ben said: "If that was in our cottage
we wouldn't hear ourselves speak." In the silences between the
ticks two pairs of long curtains sighed softly as the mysterious
draught stirred their hems and brushed them over the floor. The
curtains hadn't been drawn and there was a wild moon outside.
Susan switched out the light and let the moon play its theatrical
tricks with the shadows. The two long narrow windows threw
down their latticed oblongs of light. The landing had never
looked so dramatic as it did now, with more moonlight spilling
along the corridors which ran off from it, showing up the arches
with their huge and rough-hewn beams.

Susan breathed: "This way; but duck your head when we
come to the cross-beams." There was no reason to be quiet, no
one to hear them save the mice! But somehow you couldn't help
whispering here, standing in the fuzzy dim grey no man's land
between pitch darkness and the moonlight.

She led him down the dromedary corridor.

"Mind the hump."

The loose boards squeaked.

"This is my room," she said. The drums in her mind and her
body were beating very fast: frightening her, reminding her
'What's to come is still unsure'! She took Ben's hand, she opened

the bedroom door and drew him inside. This was something she had never given to Tony; indeed it had strangely shocked her when he had wanted to come up to her bedroom and make love. She was thankful that she hadn't let him do so because it was as if this was something left of her virginity which she could offer now to Ben and to Ben alone. She had realised tonight that for the first time in her life she was wholly and utterly and unreservedly committed to another person. She wanted to give him everything she had. So she drew him into her room with its moonlight and its darkness and its friendliness and its privacy and its secrets and everything that was hers; and in the darkness it was she, not Ben, who slipped the dress off her shoulders.

¶ 4

THE SWALLOWS HAD GONE, and the house martins, and the little sand martins which had nested in holes in the red sandstone banks along the river. The sky seemed still and empty without them. The leaves dropped off the trees in such a quietness you could hear each one fall.

As the countryside fell quiet, so did the town. Elmbury was strangely silent after the bustle of the last few weeks. In long convoys the sand-coloured lorries, the ambulances, the DUKWs, the tank transporters had left when the swallows left—and in the same direction. Old men remembering old wars had stood along the pavements to watch them go.

And Ben had sailed away from Plymouth. The last of half a dozen letters which Susan had read so many times that they had come apart at the folds, and it would have been difficult to read them if she had not already known them by heart—the last one had told her that within an hour or two he'd be on the sea.

The whole world seemed to be waiting for what would befall.

ON THE AFTERNOON OF the 28th of October, Ferdo felt restless and disquieted by the quiet. He couldn't find Susan, and he thought she must have gone up to her room, where she read and brooded,—she'd been tense, preoccupied and secret for weeks.

Ferdo had an uncomfortable feeling that there was 'something in the air,' both here at home and in the wide world beyond. The news bulletins said that Washington was warning American tourists to get out of Israel. *Something was going to happen.* Ferdo had a premonition that it would be bad. He was troubled about that boy, Ben, because Susan was so fond of him. He went a walk in the woods and saw a single magpie, flying across his path. Coming back by the stables he saw the Northovers' white cat. He was only too well aware of the silliness of these superstitions. They were part and parcel of some slow occlusion of his reason, which he was aware of too. Both they and their foolishness equally frightened him.

With the notion of distracting himself, he went up the garden and lit the bonfire which he and Fenton had been building for weeks. The smoke, like a signal, attracted Fenton, who joined him, carrying a pitchfork. Suddenly a wind got up. It was extraordinary: half an hour ago all seemed still as the grave. Now the clouds were hurrying across the sky and Ferdo could feel the wind's buffets on his check. Comets' tails of brown leaves began to stream away from the oaks. Sparks flew from the bonfire. A mutual excitement affected both Fenton and Ferdo as this sudden blow, bred in the Atlantic, grew up into a full gale. They remembered they were sailors. They thought and talked about war. Over this Suez business they were both on the same side. Neither felt very sure about the rights and wrongs of the original argument; both blamed it on to the politicians, who they were agreed were billymugginses always. (The expression was Egbert's, from whom they'd acquired it.) But Nasser, said Ferdo, in seizing an international waterway had certainly overstepped the mark; and Fenton concurred: "It's time he copped it, time we called a halt. We've sin enough of them fucking dictators, you and me." He and Ferdo agreed about many things nowadays. They still shared their bacon pigs, and had recently bought a breeding sow. They had both been elected to the Parish Council in April, and because the Doddington vote was such a small one certain mathematicians in The Green Man claimed to have worked it out that they must have voted for each other. Neither denied this. There was one thing they had never yet spoken of:

the matter of Susan and Ben. Even now, in this hour of crisis,
they steered clear of it.

"That lad of yours," said Ferdo. "If anything does happen, I
suppose he'll be in the thick of things."

"Ar," said Fenton. "He could o' got out if he'd wanted; but
when the blokes who's supposed to be running things makes a
blooming muck up of it, I daresay we've got to have a go. I'd have
thought less of him if he'd got hisself out to go into Parliament.
The missus," he added after a pause, "thinks different."

When the bonfire had burned itself out, which it did rather
quickly because of the high wind, Ferdo went back into the
house. There was still no sign of Susan. He dozed in his chair for
a little while, thinking about war, remembering those Halifax
convoys, and that poor little arse-end Charley, the *Welsh Primrose,* which he'd sent back because she couldn't steam fast
enough. And her skipper, what was he called, Ianto something or
other, who'd gone down the plughole with her. He'd wanted to
be home by Christmas because his wife was expecting her sixth.
It had been bloody bad luck on Captain Ianto; but you couldn't
look for justice in war, which after all was like a huge cloud of
injustice, blotting out everybody's rights and wrongs.

Ferdo remembered the beginning of what he called The Last
Time: the balloons over London looking like pregnant elephants
floating in a surrealist nightmare, the trenches and sandbags in
the Parks, people carrying their civilian gas-masks in oblong
cardboard boxes slung absurdly over their shoulders on bits of
string; the baby's gas-mask in its pram with its dolls; and the way
people would glance a bit furtively up into the sky, wondering
what was going to come out of it.

But of course this Suez thing, if it happened, would be only a
local affair? Well . . . Ferdo supposed so; but then it must have
seemed pretty local when they bumped off that Archduke at
Sarajevo.

It grew dusky outside, and Mrs. Fenton, doing duty for Mrs.
Northover, came in and switched on the lights. She asked him,
severely, if he was ready for tea. "Would you like anything to eat
with it?" she said. Ferdo suddenly had an inordinate desire for
some buttered toast, with Gentleman's Relish spread on it. But
somehow one couldn't ask Mrs. Fenton for Gentleman's Relish.

It would have sounded awful. On the other hand to ask for Patum Peperium would have been intolerably pompous; and Mrs. Fenton wouldn't have known what he meant, anyhow. So Ferdo murmured non-committally, and she said quickly: "Just a pot of tea, then?" and went out to make it.

THAT UNCOMFORTABLE SENSE OF 'something about to happen' was troubling Susan also. She had been for a walk after lunch, across the Park to Ferdinando's Oak, to bid farewell to it. One thing that was going to happen, during the next two or three days, was the felling of Ferdinando's Oak. It lay right in the path of the motorway; even though Stephen had written to the Minister, Ferdo's fight to save it had failed.

She stood for quite a long time by the tree and listened to the wind getting up as the leaves stirred, and now and then a little rout of tawny ones blew away. There were some wild-looking mares-tails streaming across the sky; it was going to blow hard tonight, and this would be the last gale that would ever go blustering through the oak's great branches. She wondered how many gales it had stood up against, during its four hundred years.

She looked up into its branches that towered so high and spread so wide. She thought of all the summers and winters, the storms and the sunshine, that went to the making of such a tree; yet it would take the men with their mechanical saws no more than a couple of hours to cut it down. After that, they had told her, they would have to blow the butt to pieces with a charge of dynamite. The roots went so deep into the clay, there wouldn't be a hope of grubbing up the stump with their bulldozers.

Susan remembered how she'd told her secrets to Ferdinando's Oak when she was a small girl. She remembered the games she used to play there with Rosemary; and Rosemary coming out of the winter fog to meet her under the tree: 'Miss Susan, you must help me, please——'

Goodbye, Ferdinando's Oak. Ferdinando's Owl, you'll have to find another hiding-place . . .

Across the Park she could hear the roar and rattle of the bull dozers as they routed like monstrous mechanical pigs in the green turf.

WHEN SHE GOT HOME she went up to her room and yet once more she read Ben's letters, which he'd written in pencil during the last few days of exercising before his Commando went abroad. There was a thick mist on the moor,—and in his mind, he said, a bewilderment of love. One of the letters had been written while he sat on a granite boulder in a place called Wistman's Wood. The Dartmoor men said it was haunted; certainly Wistman's Wood was a haunted-sounding name. It was a queer place altogether, because although the trees were oaks they had been dwarfed by the weather, or perhaps by some unkindness in the soil. They looked as old as Druids; yet when you stood up you were taller than they were. They had thick gnarled trunks and yet they were all twisted and elbowed, and their branches crawled about among the boulders like snakes . . .

But they bore acorns like any other oaks. Ben had just picked one up, and he'd been looking at it and thinking about Doddington. The neatness and beauty of its little chalice, the perfect fit, like an egg into an egg cup, fascinated and pleased him. Ever since his forty-eight hours' leave—ever since that time with Susan —he'd found himself looking at familiar things with new wonder. Nothing would ever seem the same again; it was a new world, perpetually surprising. The whole of love, he said, was wonder and surprise.

His last, short letter had been written in Plymouth just before he embarked. He couldn't, of course, say where he was bound for: Malta or Cyprus, Ferdo had thought it would be. Those were the likeliest jumping-off places for any invasion of the Canal Zone. 'From now on I'm not going to think about the rights and wrongs any more. I'm a Royal Marine, not what your father would call a bloody politician! I'm sure he was right when he said I'd forget all about the arguments when the guns started . . .'

Susan folded the letters carefully, opened the drawer in her dressing-table to put them back, and saw the little pile of Janet's diaries, which she'd hidden there. She picked up the most recent one, and rather reluctantly—she didn't want to do so but she was under an odd compulsion to have another look—she opened it once again at the final entry. She heartily wished she had never seen that last half-page of her mother's handwriting; it had puzzled and troubled her ever since she had first read it, weeks ago.

> *Could not sleep all night thinking of those Teddyboys and poor old Trumpeter (his forelegs have come up like BAL-LOONS !!) & all my other Worries too About dear F. and my beloved S.* [The 'S' was underlined three times.] *"The Whole world now quite BEYOND ME. Je suis en desespoir ! As F. was saying Nothing has ever gone right since the red squirrels vanished !!! Remember so well when he and I saw last one It was our ANNIE July 31st 1950 I think of it as the day when all the bad things began for us . . .*

That had been written on the morning when Susan went off to meet Ben at Cheltenham and take him to Stratford to the play. Could her mother possibly have guessed?—might she perhaps have gone into Susan's bedroom and happened to see Ben's letter lying open on her dressing-table? She would never have pried deliberately, Susan knew; but if she'd just glanced at it and read something by accident——?

And that had been the morning when she had said she wanted to blow the cobwebs away, and could she borrow Nightshade?

And she hadn't asked any questions about what Susan's plans were nor whom she was going to meet . . .

Susan had tortured herself for days after she read that entry, wondering and wondering whether her mother could have known that she was planning a secret meeting with Ben—an *assignation,* Janet would have called it in her mind. Susan would never find out now; and she had tried hard to put it out of her thoughts for ever. After all, her mother was frequently feeling *'en desespoir'* about things—about the state of the world especially. There was probably nothing in Susan's uncomfortable suspicion after all. She read through the entry once again, slowly and thoughtfully, all the way through to the very last words her mother ever penned:

> *. . . July 31st 1950 I think of it as the day when all the bad things began for us . . .'*

Upon an impulse Susan routed among the heap of diaries in her drawer until she came to the one for 1950. Turning over its pages gave her a rather uneasy feeling, as if she were turning over the pages of her life.

> *S. went back to school Her last Term! Amazing to think*
> *she'll no longer be a schoolgirl !!! N.B. Must soon think abt*
> *her clothes a suitable dress for evg etc.*

That had been the flame-coloured one. Susan picked her way
among the exclamation marks which exploded everywhere, and
the peculiar doodles, and the private memoranda which Janet
thought embarrassing unless they were written in French, until
at last she reached July the 31st:

> *TONY to stay see his bed aired the Upper Wells (!) to*
> *dine . . . FENTON (new gdner) and FAMILY (!!) arrive*
> *(feel we're taking a risk) . . . Korea news still bad T. says*
> *might be serious   Mysterious FLOOD in cellar . . . FEN-*
> *TONS installed brats all ages . . .*

Janet had subsequently underlined the words 'FLOOD' and
'FENTONS' in red. It was an odd habit of hers to hark back
through her diary recollecting things, and underlining with a red
pencil those which had acquired a special significance. Obviously
the flood and the Fentons, though in no way related, had been
associated in her mind: she thought of both as sinister, both had
made their appearance on the same day!
The whole of that date, July the 31st, was ringed thickly in
red, as if to emphasize its import.

> *Saw red squirrel Rare as dodo now !!!   Good omen on*
> *our Annie ??   Hope so !*

Susan turned over a few more pages of her past.

> *STOW FAIR !!! . . . T. bought S. a blk. mare WILDLY*
> *GENEROUS of him !! . . . T had sudden recall from leave*
> *by tgram Fear it is for Korea . . . S. seems v. distrait—Missing*
> *him?   In a year or twos time IF ONLY those 2 ??!!*

Susan flipped over a month or two together. Then she came
to:

> *FILTHY FOG all day !!   Ophelia howling mad for Toms*
> *Vet says best to fix her . . . 6 p.m. Ophelia got out!   Too*
> *late to fix her now !!! . . . S. came to my study to talk to me*
> *abt Rmary (so WISE of her!)   The poor child has got*
> *INTO TROUBLE !!!   Northovers v. cut up naturally &*
> *angry with her   Mrs. N. says Jack has even SHUT HER*

*UP in her bedroom will not let her out to see her young
man well if that isn't shutting the stable door after the milk
is spilt ?!!!*

Susan recognised the mixed metaphor. It came from her Old
Nanny and had for long been a joke among the family. (Sometimes old Nanny would vary it, saying "After the eggs are
broken"!) So with Janet's voice close at her elbow as it were,
Susan sat at her dressing-table turning over page after page of the
close scribble interspersed with doodles and the hieroglyphs, the
complicated brackets within brackets, the strange abbreviations,
the personal phenomena recorded so modestly in French, *Com-
mence ... finis ...*

Susan raised her eyebrows at herself in the looking-glass. It was
when she had started to read her mother's diary, three or four
weeks ago, that she'd first begun to suspect what she now knew to
be true. No use shutting the stable door after the milk was spilt
indeed! At first the suspicion hadn't troubled her very much,
she'd made the usual excuses to herself and half-believed them.
But now she couldn't make the excuses any longer; she knew
for sure that she was going to have a baby.

She was much less frightened than she would have expected to
have been. Indeed there had been some devil-may-care moments
when she'd felt almost glad, because what had happened to her
seemed to tie her even more closely to Ben. But she was desperately lonely, having no one to confide in. She'd toyed with the
idea of going to tell Sandra, but she was reluctant to go to
Doublegates because Colonel Daglingworth was slowly and defi-
antly dying there. Also Sandra was much preoccupied with a
new young man—a very rich one, who was on the Stock Exchange. Susan had once predicted in fun that she would end up
by marrying a rich stockbroker.

She suddenly decided that she would screw up her courage and
tell her father now. So she ran down the stairs and into the
sitting-room where he was sitting with his pot of tea in front of
the fire. She said:

"Daddy, what on earth have you been doing? Your face is all
black with smuts."

"F-F-Fenton and I have been having a bonfire."

She was all keyed up to tell him now; but he started fiddling
maddeningly with the portable radio beside his chair. It was

badly tuned as usual, and a variety of excruciating noises came out of it.

"I've been trying to get the Home Service," he said. "It's nearly time for another news. There was a special bulletin a half an hour ago. The Israelis have launched an attack across Sinai——"

Susan's heart sank and she knew she wouldn't bring herself to tell him now.

"Britain and France have issued an ultimatum. I didn't hear the terms exactly; but I don't think there's any doubt about it. We're going in."

¶ 5

THAT NIGHT THE WIND BLEW as if it would blow the crooked chimneys off the roof of the Manor: as if it would blow down Ferdinando's Oak and save it from the cruel saw!

But in twenty-four hours it blew itself out; once more there fell a calm. The world was holding its breath again. It was during this hush that Susan plucked up her courage and decided to do something which she knew would be painful and embarrassing and difficult, and which she ought to have done before. She must go along to Huntsman's and see the Fentons, and in whatever terms were most fitting she must tell them, somehow or other, of her feelings for Ben. She hadn't the faintest idea how she would do it; she only knew it would be dishonest and dreadful if, on what might be the very eve of battle for Ben, she didn't say something to them now. But when she found Mrs. Fenton alone in the cottage she knew the whole idea was mistaken, that she would do more harm than good. It was too late to retreat now. In utter embarrassment she began:

"Mrs. Fenton: I felt I ought to say something to you. About Ben and me——"

"I know," said Mrs. Fenton shortly. "He told me about it before he left. I—I don't know how it will turn out, for either of you."

Then there was a long silence. If only Fenton had been there it would have been easier.

Susan said:

"I had to come specially because of Suez——"

"He was against it!" cried Mrs. Fenton, flushing suddenly. "All Labour's against it—you've read the papers. He had a chance to get out. I believe he *would* have got out, if it hadn't been for you and what you stand for——"

She suddenly started crying: the short dry difficult sobs of one who didn't cry easily. Susan put her arm round Mrs. Fenton's shoulders and felt her whole body stiffen, the shoulder blades hard and thin and bony against her hand.

Neither of them said any more. There was nothing useful that they could say.

THAT WAS THE DAY the bombing started. It was announced on the Six O'clock News that "Bombers of the Royal Air Force had begun an offensive against Egyptian airfields and other military installations." Next day the news was much the same. It was explained that we were aiming to knock out the Egyptian Air Force. Susan had been expecting to hear of an immediate invasion, and the news of repeated bombing raids troubled her. It wasn't what she'd expected from 'our side.' Ferdo had to explain that it would take five days to mount an amphibious operation from our nearest bases in Cyprus.

"But I know exactly how you feel," he said. "I think it's a national characteristic: we always feel slightly unhappy about taking part in any war which we are not in imminent danger of losing!"

A lot of people were feeling that way, apparently. The papers reported fierce arguments and protests in Parliament and in the country. The letters in *The Times* filled more than two columns every day. Suddenly the whole of Britain was in a ferment; and sleepy old Elmbury, as a microcosm of Britain, fairly sizzled with passion too. Susan one morning had to take Ferdo into town to see his lawyers. Afterwards, in The Swan bar, they met Mr. Tremlett, the retired tailor, who confessed that he'd just had such a row about Suez with Councillor Walker, whose suits he'd made for forty years, that they were never going to speak to each other again. The Swan bar was like a disturbed ant-heap, all a-buzz. Four different arguments were going on in four different corners; and everybody was drinking more and arguing more simply because they *felt* more strongly.

That evening there was a Protest Meeting in Elmbury, organised by the local Labour Party. *The Intelligencer* had a full report of it, with photographs of a scuffle outside the Seldon Memorial Hall. Apparently some young men from the R.A.C. had got to hear of the meeting; and they'd thought it their duty to go and break it up. They'd expressed their patriotic point of view mainly by blowing hunting horns.

It had seemed monstrous to Susan, an appalling betrayal, that anyone should 'let the country down' by making his pacifist protests at the very moment when, perhaps, our men were about to make a landing under fire. She felt more passionately partisan than she'd ever been over anything. Forgetting for the moment that Labour was Ben's party, she actually hated Labour. But she realised too that the young asses from the R.A.C. didn't do much good for what she saw as the patriotic cause. She remembered Ben or Stephen saying—it might have been either of them—"In politics it's generally your own side that lets you down."

BEING SO RESTLESS and angry and troubled and apprehensive, she would set out for a walk in the Park, would then remember that it was nearly news time and hurry back to listen to the wireless; then because she dreaded sitting still she would go out into the Park again. It was during one of these walks that she heard Ferdinando's Oak come down. She'd got so used to the shrill scream of the saw that she scarcely noticed it; so she wasn't expecting the sudden much louder shriek of timber tearing apart —a sound like the mandrake was supposed to utter when its roots were ripped out of the earth! It was brief and terrible, and it was followed by the long thunder and crackle of the huge tree breaking up as it hit the ground.

LATER, WHEN SHE WAS HAVING tea with Ferdo, came the bang. It rattled the windows, and startled them both— shocked Susan a little because she'd been thinking about the bombing.

"What the devil was that?" Ferdo said.

There was no point in keeping it from him; he'd be bound to

know tomorrow that Ferdinando's Oak was down and done for.

"They've cut it down at last," she said. "They told me they would have to blow the stump up with dynamite."

Ferdo said nothing. His chin sank forward on to his chest, so that she could see the long livid scar of his head-wound.

After a little while, to change the subject, she said:

"Daddy, when do you think they will land?"

"Tomorrow at dawn by my calculations."

"Tomorrow?"

"Yes. It happens to be Guy Fawkes Day."

Then there was another silence, and because her loneliness had become intolerable she gathered up all her courage and told Ferdo about her pregnancy.

She didn't want to watch his face while she was telling him; so she had gone across to the window and had looked out at the sunset, blazing red and golden behind the trees. Then she'd spoken to him over her shoulder. Now she dared turn round to look; and Ferdo was on his feet already, he was coming across the room to her with quick strides, he'd caught her by the shoulders and was holding her tight. The change in him was extraordinary. A few moments ago she'd been almost pitying him, he'd seemed so broken and old and helpless. Now all at once he wore his authority again.

"Look here," he said. "Look, young woman: Don't worry! *Pro bono publico. No bloody panico.* Remember my motto? I'm on your side, and everything's going to be all right."

It was astonishing. Ferdo was the captain on the bridge again; and she looked to him for assurance like a frightened sailor going into action for the first time.

¶ 6

FERDO HAD KNOWN what he was talking about. Next morning the news on the wireless reported that Anglo-French forces in an amphibious operation had gone ashore at Port Said.

Susan listened to all the subsequent bulletins, but none of them told her much more about the invasion. Mainly they reported the rows in Parliament and the disapproval of the Americans and the threats of the Russians and the howling indignation of the Afro-Asians; to say nothing of all the arguments going on among the politicians and the papers and all the people all over the country who believed they were qualified to sit in judgement over any question of foreign affairs, military strategy or international morals.

On the following day the news bulletins were a bit more informative. They said that the Marine Commandos with their supporting armour had gained control of Port Said after heavy fighting. The advance along the Canal was continuing.

At mid-day one of the tree-fellers came to the back door of the Manor and asked to see the Squire. He brought with him a piece of wood from Ferdinando's Oak—a few square feet split off from the smooth side, upon which the soldiers had carved their initials during the last war. It had caught his eye, he said, because some chaps belonging to the Sherwood Foresters had scratched their names there, and he happened to have had a brother in the Sherwoods: he was killed in France. He thought Squire might like to have the piece of wood as a memento; he'd been real sorry to see that tree come down, but there it was, you couldn't stop Progress, could you?

Susan asked him in, and Ferdo gave him a bottle of beer, and they sat side by side on the sofa in the sitting-room, with the sliver of wood resting upon their knees, deciphering the scratches on it, talking about the war. The tree-feller had served in the Tanks. He'd fought at Alamein, all the way across the desert to Tripoli, then up through Italy, as far as Monte Cassino, where he'd been wounded.

"Funny how when we was demobbed we thought we'd done with wars for the rest of *our* lifetime."

Ferdo switched on the wireless to hear the news; but there was nothing fresh. Heavy fighting . . . no information yet released concerning casualties . . . advance continues . . .

In the afternoon when Susan felt she could bear the suspense no longer, she took it into her head to slip out of the house and go for a ride on Nightshade. She didn't tell her father what she was doing, because of what had happened to Janet, and because she hadn't liked to mention Nightshade to him since the day Janet was killed.

So she crept out quietly while he was trying to tempt his grey squirrel with a walnut to come in through the sitting-room window, and went across to the stables. She'd brought Nightshade in a month ago, and Jack Northover had clipped her, on the chance that she would be able to get an occasional day's hunting; though lately she hadn't felt that she could leave her father for long. Old Trumpeter, looking very shaggy, was still out at grass in the paddock. He came trotting down to the gate, and Susan gave him a bowl of oats. She remembered that Ben was the last person who'd ridden Trumpeter. On that last morning—the morning after they'd made love—she'd saddled the two horses and taken him for a ride. Ben would never make a horseman, she was sure. Even Trumpeter had seemed surprised by his long-legged awkwardness, and had amused Ben by turning his head reproachfully as if to look at his rider.

"Like Xanthos," Ben had said.

But Susan had forgotten, if she had ever known, about Xanthos.

"He was another chestnut," laughed Ben. "The wonderful horse of Achilles. He could talk, among other accomplishments. One day when his master had annoyed him he turned his head round and prophecied to Achilles about the nasty things that were going to happen to him."

Susan now thought she must be as superstitious as her father; for she had caught herself wishing she hadn't remembered that.

THE ELMS WERE AN ORIFLAMME on Seven Men's Tump, for the golden leaves clung late this season. Trafalgar Wood on her left, Waterloo on her right, spoke to her of battles long ago. Just across the river lay a field known as The Bloody Meadow, because of the great slaughter done there in a fight between Lancaster and York. The beaten Lancastrians had fled for sanctuary into the Abbey; some of the slain Knights had been buried there, under the huge square tower which had been built in the days of William the Conqueror.

There had been oaks at Doddington as long ago as that. The

wood which Susan now rode into had been mentioned in Domesday Book; Ferdo had told her that it had been a *sylva de 30
porcis* then,—there was room for thirty pigs to run among the
trees and guzzle the acorns at the season when the acorns fell.
You rode through history wherever you went at Doddington.
The trees in this wood weren't as old as the oaks in the Park; but
Ferdo reckoned they were about three and a half centuries old.
So they'd have been very small saplings when Queen Elizabeth
died; tidy young trees with a few withered leaves clinging to
them on that winter day when we cut off the head of Charles the
First; bearing acorns in time for Oak-apple Day when we were
celebrating the restoration of Charles the Second . . .

Susan rode through a great glade which reminded her of Elmbury Abbey, either because of some quality of the light, or because of the hush, or because of the grandeur; out of the dying
bracken mottled green and yellow and brown the great grey
trunks rose up like pillars in an aisle. When she looked up
through the bright tawny leaves she could glimpse the mighty
boughs making curious Gothic patterns, black against the brightness.

Without caring or even much noticing where she was going she
went through the woods which lay nearest to the river until she
came to the place where long ago she had found the ghost orchis.
It was only a little distance from the route of the motorway, and
the ground had been churned up by the tracks of the caterpillars.
There would probably never be another ghost orchis in flower
there. Stephen had nearly wept when he saw the place all cut up
and devastated. She had brought him down here when he'd spent
a couple of days at the Manor, just after his return from India,
three weeks ago. The mess which the road was making of Doddington woods had shocked him. He said he hated motorways
anyhow. He'd driven on the M.1. and it had terrified him.

"It's beautiful in a way, it has a kind of grandeur but it isn't
like an ordinary road which draws its life from the countryside it
runs through. You know what I mean, Sukie: your ordinary road
has tributaries, by-roads and farm lanes, and out of them come
village postmen and bakers' vans, straying beasts, kids on ponies,
packs of hounds, lightless bicycles, courting couples, tractors,
women pushing prams, combine harvesters and jolly farmers
going to market. The country traffic mingles with the motor

traffic. But the singleminded motorway exists in another dimension from the scene it runs through. Tearing along in your car you're like someone in a good seat at a Cinerama show. But you don't *belong* to the loveliness you look at; you're not part of it because you can't stop! In a way the traffic is like an electric current flowing along an insulated cable."

Nature, he said, couldn't exist on a motorway. If it ventured there it was obliterated. He'd seen what was left of a most foolish hedgehog that had thought it had business beyond the wire fence and had trespassed upon the M.1. Its profile, worn paper-thin by the tyres of the lorries, was printed on the road like a fossil in a rock-face.

Think of those frail butterflies, Stephen said, your wood-whites which flutter about in May! Can't you imagine them caught in the slipstreams, tossed in the fearful turbulence, whirled along in horizontal spirals into the bonnets of the hundred-mile-an-hour cars? 'How with this rage can Beauty hold a plea?'

"Oh Sukie," cried Stephen, leaning against a beautiful beech-tree trunk, mottled lime-green and elephant-grey in the sunshine, near the place were the ghost orchis had grown,—"I know we've got to have these things. I suppose it's progress of a sort. But do you remember the Manley Hopkins poem?" And out of that marvellous ragbag memory he'd quoted to her:

> " 'What would the world be, once bereft
> Of wet and of wildness? Let them be left,
> O let them be left, wildness and wet;
> Long live the weeds and the wilderness yet!' "

SHE HAD TOLD STEPHEN about Ben. Not about her pregnancy of course—she hadn't then been quite certain of that—but she'd told him that she and Ben were lovers. He was the only person she could have told. She had been sure he would understand; and he had. He'd promptly put his arm round her and kissed her to wish her luck, "It's *right,* it has a splendid poetic rightness which I don't think even you yourself could understand. There's something specially and curiously apt about it. The most beautiful Cavalier I know; and the wisest Round-head!"

Before he left to go back to town he said again:

"My God, Sukie, I hope and pray it goes well for you. I know there are awful complications and risks and difficulties. I'm frightened for you sometimes."

"Why?"

"I don't know. I've got a feeling that you—attract the lightning, my dear."

Then he asked her if she had read the collection of W. B. Yeats's poems which he'd given her just before he went to India; and if she had noticed the one he had specially marked for her called "A Prayer for My Daughter." She hadn't; but he told her to look it up because it expressed most of the wishes he wished for her.

After he had gone she did look it up, and she read the verses which he'd marked with a thin pencil-line in the book's margin:

> May she become a flourishing hidden tree
> That all her thoughts may like the linnet be,
> And have no business but dispensing round
> Their magnanimities of sound,
> Nor but in merriment begin a chase,
> Nor but in merriment a quarrel.
> O may she live like a green laurel.
> Rooted in one dear perpetual place.

HE HAD TALKED A LOT about Suez. Much to Susan's surprise he agreed with Ben, about the unwisdom of seeking a military solution. But he could see the other point of view very clearly. Cavalier and Roundhead, he said—wasn't I *right* about the Waters Under the Earth? Can't you *feel* them bubbling and sizzling away under your very feet now?

You wait. In a matter of days and weeks they'll be bursting forth like the flood in Ferdo's cellar!

And so they had. Now that the fighting had begun it seemed as if England were divided almost exactly in two concerning Suez; and the division cut clean across party and class. For the Northovers, who equated England with Doddington just as the Seldons had always done when England was at war, it was simply a case of Us versus Nasser: never a shadow of doubt to trouble their innocent minds! Rosemary too—she wouldn't have known anything about it, but Susan was sure that she'd be by instinct a Cavalier. Egbert? She'd tried out of curiosity to find out how he felt but he was cagey and non-committal. ('We are the people of

England that have never spoken yet!') Fenton, mistrusting and despising foreigners, was all for having a go. Mrs. Fenton, a quintessential puritan, was naturally against it; but she wouldn't have been much at ease with some of her allies—with the Reverend Pigling Bland, for instance, who had dared to say to Susan, when she met him yesterday in the village "Another old crisis— Really what a *bore!*"—or with Sandra's rich stockbroker, whom Susan had met for the first time yesterday. Although he was a dyed-in-the-wool Conservative, he disapproved of the whole business. Susan thought that this was probably because he was so rich. Tom Taynton, who'd been arguing with the locals in The Green Man, had been dead against it too: but he'd ingenuously declared his interest: "If there's a *big* schemozzle I've got too bloody much to lose." Susan hated him for that as much as she hated him for letting the Tithe Barn fall down. She had been thinking of the men who had their lives to lose.

FROM THE BOTTOM OF Jubilee Wood, close against the river, Susan looked up towards the Manor high up on the slope of the hill. Fenton's racing pigeons, which he'd let out for exercise, circled above it against a brilliant evening sky. The sun was sinking into wind-torn sunset clouds; and in the dying light the brick walls of the Manor glowed a warm orange red, the timbers were black as old Jakey's tar. Senescence graced the house and lent a kind of dignity even to its defects, the crooked chimneys and the licheny weathered tiles, most of them cracked, which the gale the other night had once more played havoc with. The dear perpetual place! Then Susan saw the telegraph-boy on his 2-stroke motor-bicycle chugging along the drive. Even though he was so far away, she could recognise him by his bike. But Nightshade was playing up, bucking three bucks at a time because Susan wouldn't allow her to gallop on the way home; so she didn't think any more about the telegraph-boy until she reached the gate at the top of Jubilee Wood, when she noticed him once again in the drive on his way back to Elmbury, weaving from side to side to avoid the awful potholes. Then suddenly she realised that the only two places he could have been to with his telegram were the Manor or—or Huntsman's Cottage. Then she panicked completely for the first time in her life. She kicked Nightshade's sides really hard, the mare gave a tremendous bound, and set off hell-for-leather across the top of the Park. She galloped faster than when she was winning the Point to Point. They came to a little grip that ran across the Park and Nightshade lengthening her pace took it in one huge bound. Susan was hardly conscious of sitting on her back. She had made up her mind that the telegram was about Ben, and she was aware already of a vast and interminable loneliness.

She clattered into the courtyard—there was no one about there; but Jack Northover hearing the sound of the hoofs rushed out in alarm from the stables and caught hold of the bridle.

"Miss Susan!" he cried. "When I heard the mare galloping—it was like the day when her Ladyship . . . Did she run away?"

"Yes," lied Susan, to save time and explanations. "I started a gallop and I couldn't hold her . . . Have you seen Fenton anywhere? Or my father? There's something I must——"

"Funny you should ask, Miss Susan. I saw Fenton running across to the Manor, I think he must have wanted to see your father about something. He came out a few minutes ago. Maybe he's gone back to the cottage."

But Susan dared not go to Huntsman's. She ran across the courtyard and into the house; and there was Ferdo and she rushed up to him and clung to him, not looking at his face:

"Fenton's been here. I saw the telegraph-boy. It's Ben?"

"Listen, my dear." Ferdo held her close to him, and this was another of the occasions when he was in command of things, he'd gone back twenty years to being the captain on the bridge. "Ben's wounded. His father came across to me. 'Wounded in action, letter follows.' That's all we know. But the telegram doesn't say 'severely,' so I don't think it's too bad. I do know a bit about these things. *It's going to be all right.* Now cry and get it done with!"

But already Susan was pulling herself together.

"I must go and see the Fentons," she said.

"Yes." Ferdo thought for a moment. "Yes, I think you ought to do that."

"I'll do something to my face first." And Susan ran upstairs.

FERDO WENT BACK into the sitting-room and settled himself in his chair by the bird-table. A few minutes later he watched

Susan going across to Huntsman's, taking the short cut across the lawn. The bright sunset lit her, and he could see that she'd made up her face again; there were no tears. She held her head high and proud and she walked with a swing. Whatever her distresses, she had never looked so lovely to Ferdo as she did now. He could see a bit of Benedicta in her, and a lot of those pretty girls with April faces in his favourite family portrait, the daughters of the hot-blooded old squire.

All the generations came to flower in her, he thought.

She went out of sight behind the courtyard wall. The last of the tattered sunset blazed splendid behind the trees. Their shadows crept out and out over the lawn. The wind had fallen light with the evening. In the still house Ferdo heard the pump whining down in the cellar. After two or three minutes it gave its choking cough and ceased. Ferdo thought of Stephen and his talk about the Waters Under the Earth. He was right enough, you might keep them at bay, but it was no more possible to command or suppress them than it was for anyone to command or suppress the living spirit of England. As the Kings and the politicians had learned from time to time, to their cost.

Ferdo looking out across the lawn could see the drive with its dark oaks and that ancient, gnarled crab-tree which stood beyond Huntsman's. It was black and bent and formidable against the stormy sky. He watched Egbert walking along the drive; he paused by the crab-tree and seemed to ponder,—looking around to see what wanted a-doin' upon this estate where he knew every ditch and field-drain? He stood there for a few moments and scratted his yud, as he'd have put it; Ferdo could imagine his thoughts ramifying as they always did back into the past.

Then along the drive on his bicycle came Adam Fenton back from school in Elmbury. He wore his school-cap on the back of his head, and had his usual air of lively cheek and enterprise. *His* thoughts, whatever they were, would be thrusting forward into the future. Hadn't Ben said something about Adam getting a scholarship or being likely to get one—he'd be going up to University too? What was it he was supposed to be so good at? Engineering? Physics? Ferdo couldn't remember. He was tired again, his headache throbbed, he closed his eyes as the shadows crept out across the lawn.

Half in a doze, he heard the sound of a tree falling. He wasn't sure at first if he had dreamed he heard it. The sharp dry crackle of branches breaking, which followed the crash and the roar, was like the sound of flagging musketry slowly dying away when an outpost is overrun in a battle.

Then his ears caught the murmur of machinery, the ripping sound of a saw, and he knew that he couldn't have been dreaming. The road was still marching forward across his Park.

The tree shadows had advanced so far over the lawn that they had left only a small contracting enclave between the darkness and his window: diminishing, threatened, soon to be overwhelmed, like Doddington, like the England Ferdo knew and loved and identified with Doddington, the Seldons' and the red squirrels' England.

But England didn't end. There was going down and there was rising up. You only had to know a little of her history to know that. The new England would belong to the kind of people who designed and built the motorway; to young Adam pushing his way into the future; to Ben and to Susan and the child already growing in her womb. A new England but an old one too; for its roots would ramify like Egbert's thoughts, would go down into the past and draw some sustenance from it as the roots of the oak-trees did. Nothing's irrelevant, Ben had said, we inherit the lot, it's up to us to make the best we can of it . . .

There was only one small pool of light left on the lawn now; and suddenly as Ferdo watched, waiting for it to vanish, his grey squirrel came hopping out of the darkness and perkily appeared there. Taking a good look round, it sat up on its hind legs, surveyed its world. It had none of the agoraphobia which affects most squirrels; this one wasn't frightened of the open spaces or of anything else. Ferdo whistled to it. He'd taught it to come to his whistle. It flicked its tail and came hopping towards him now, jumped up on to the bird-table and then, as cheeky and curious as Adam, it contemplated Ferdo from the window-sill.

Kemerton
March 1961–January 1965